THE LOST ROAD TO HOPE

By

RONALD J. ROSSMANN, JR.

THE LOST ROAD TO HOPE

By

RONALD J. ROSSMANN, JR.

Cover design by Carly McCracken

Published by

Crimson Cloak Publishing

©2025

ISBN 10: 978-1-68160-798-6

ISBN 13: 1-68160-798-0

Edited by Denna Holm, Carly McCracken and Kate McCracken

Publisher's Publication in Data

Lost Road to Hope, The

1. Fiction 2. Science Fiction 3. Fantasy 4. Horror 5. Thriller

I dedicate this first novel to my mother, Rosemarie, who inspired me to do great things, and my loving wife, Tammy, who gave me the strength to accomplish them.

CHAPTER 1

The Long Road

(Alex)

This has to be the longest drive and yet the distance is the same. The hum of traffic seems so lonely today and the overcast sky only adds to that. It's one of those days that no matter what song plays on my satellite radio, it irritates me.

How did it come to this?

The thought bolts through my mind before I can catch it. I'm going to be strong, just like always. This is not going to drown me! I survived Afghanistan. There's no way this is going to destroy my resolve.

I glance over to my right at the letter lying face down in the passenger's seat, knowing its contents all too well. I had just received it from the clinic: dates, times, procedures, what to eat before, what to expect after. It was all so mechanical, like reading the instructions for installing a Blu-Ray player. No humanity to it, so cold and inorganic, summing up my existence into simple bullet points and prescriptions. It was nobody's fault. It's just the way things were, the simple reality of the matter. Everything I'd worked for and achieved was suddenly void and my future reduced to one sheet of paper.

On top of the ominous letter is a picture of my wife and daughter. Gracie just turned six this year. They still don't know. My wife has been through so much already: my tour of duty, the academy, all the long nights worrying whether or not I would come home. She's been the real hero in all of this.

I often ask myself why she stayed, a question I can never bring myself to ask her. I had the courage to face every enemy, knowing in a second it could be lights out. Bullets flying by me like mad hornets on a tear in Afghanistan. Blood, flame, and the horrors of combat had surrounded me before, sometimes on a daily basis, but with all that, I never winced or hesitated, not for a second. But to lose her, that's the only thing I ever truly feared.

When Gracie was born, it felt like every broken piece of my life suddenly fit together. She became the end-all, be-all, of my existence, with everything else dropping down to the bottom of the list of my life. She was the very breath in my lungs. Everything in life that didn't make sense before made sense now in the beauty of her delicate smile. I'd been blessed far more than I ever deserved, and I got that.

I had promised Sara this would be it. A couple more years on the force and then I'd find some senseless desk job, work security at the mall, sell cars, whatever, just to give her some peace. A night where she could finally sleep, not fearing what news the next day would bring. It was all about Sara and Gracie now, and they had earned that level of importance a thousand times over.

With all that said, now this happens. As if it's some tragic cosmic punch line to a universally bad joke. The pain started just a few short months ago. I figured I'd just pulled something, a symptom of getting older and forgetting my limits. Stress maybe, an old sports injury rearing its ugly head before the dawn of a mid-life crisis. Through two tours and constant fire fights, I never saw a scratch, not even a hangnail.

They called me the Ghost!

Bullets never could seem to find me. The enemy never saw me coming. I could navigate through kill houses so quickly it was as if I moved through the walls, not around them. I saw friends of mine lose limbs, eyes, worse, and yet I was the one who always made it out alive, always able to escape the physical price of combat. But never the scars of seeing others you would die for fall.

With all that said, here I am.

It figures. One stone took Goliath down and he never saw that coming, either. The pain got worse, so I finally went to the VA and got checked out. That prompted more tests and more visits.

I didn't tell Sara. I always used excuses, some new training detail, an advanced class in forensics, anything that I could sell her that she might believe. I just couldn't bring myself to put her through something else. I'm supposed to be her strength, her provider, not a constant source of bad news.

When the final barrage of tests finally did come back, it was definitive: prostate cancer. You know what the funniest part of it was? It wasn't because of chemicals from my time in the service, or what independently self-prescribed pharmaceuticals I'd introduced to my body during my infamous college years, the wrong diet, or even hereditary. I was just lucky enough to pull the "one in whatever many chances card." There was no rhyme or reason to it. It just was.

And now we get to this final letter. Here's how my treatment begins. At least a year of chemo and radiation, special diet, possible surgery, loss of my ability to be intimate with my wife, no more kids, and with all of that, I might live long enough to be in enough pain and depression that I wish I'd never started it all to begin with.

I mean, what the hell!

Now my wife will have to take care of me. Now she'll lose all the time and attention she's been so patiently waiting for to care for a husband who probably won't see his daughter turn eight, maybe even seven.

Who makes the rules here?

I did my time, served my country, truly loved my wife. While the other guys were out dicking around, fucking anything that had a pulse, I stayed back at the barracks, trying to keep up with the life I'd left a thousand or more miles away. Now, as a detective, an honest cop, a dying breed naively trying to uphold the law, serve the idea of justice, I've tried to be a good man, not the best, but nowhere near the worst.

I've buried so many friends, lost so much time, and now you tell me it's up. No break, no honeymoon, just, "Thanks for your service and sacrifice, son. Now we have to punch your ticket." To be robbed of even the chance to go out like a hero, with a bang, a selflessly brave act, or triumphant charge to victory. No, instead I leave this world with a whimper, decaying in front of everyone I love. I'll become a shell of a man while my wife and daughter are left to helplessly watch and pick up the pieces. Forced to miss out on all the good stuff, Gracie's first years of school, her graduation, prom, and a dance with her father at her wedding. To have my wife struggle to survive, having missed out on the life she could have had, had she not hitched her wagon to my sorry cart.

What have I done? I ruined their futures, tainted their happiness, and will forever darken their memories.

I suddenly realize I'm going about ninety on the interstate, so I pull off at the next exit into a gas station to try to settle down. I'm literally shaking. I've never had the shakes in my life. Turning off the ignition, I sit there and try to recoup, falling deeper and deeper into my own isolated debate.

As I look around, everyone seems to be moving in slow motion. I already feel like I'm the odd man out, like a needless vapor. Now, I truly am a ghost!

This is the crossroads, the point before the "go" in combat. I either let this thing eat away at my soul or I fight like hell, like I've done all throughout my life. I may not be able to look this enemy in the eye, but I still plan on staring and beating it down. The hell with the odds. If the odds were right, I'd already be a statistic. The odds were created by men who never *do*, who don't have the courage to act.

My courage suddenly rushes back in like a tsunami. I bow up, as if I have strength, but it's short-lived as my wife and daughter's faces appear before me again and the mighty wave of confidence quickly dissipates. I can beat this, but do I want her to have to nurse the wounds of my battle, to again suffer through sleepless nights, afraid of what the next day holds?

I run my hands through my hair and vigorously rub my face. I can't have my wife go through this! This has to be my battle and mine alone. I'll figure out how to protect her from it. I have no choice.

It begins to lightly rain. The sound of drops hitting the windshield wakes me from my futile contemplation. I glance around again. The clouds are gray, benign. They shield the sun and the new day. It's the epitome of dreary, as if the day is being defined by my own state of mind. I look at my smart phone, only fifteen minutes until my appointment.

I turn the ignition and the car comes to life. I sit still for a second as the questions continue to pile up in the silence, just like the raindrops on the glass. I grip the wheel tightly, wringing my hands around it, as if to strangle it, then gradually pull out of the lot and head back on my journey.

Before I know it, I'm back on the interstate, finally proceeding at a legal speed. The clinic is five minutes away, and so is the beginning of this undeniable process. The rain continues, as does my rapid-fire thought process. I just can't stop it! There's no training for this, no preparedness or battle plan. This is a foreign soil that no map can guide me through.

My heart pounds as I pull into the parking lot. No matter how I plead or what inventory I take, it's here, it's real, and there's no turning back.

A knock on my window draws my attention to a tall man wearing a raincoat. He knocks again, and I roll my window down.

"You're in a handicap spot," he bellows.

"What?"

"You're parked in a handicap spot," he scolds and points to the obvious sign.

I nod, and the man throws his hands up, dismissing my ignorance as he walks away. I pull out and find a new spot to park. As I exit the car, I grab at a picture of Sara and Gracie, which had slipped through my fingers and fallen to the floorboard. How tragically ironic!

I pick it up and place it face-down on the dash. Stretching, I glance at the digital display from the built-in clock in my dash. Already five minutes late for my appointment, I gather myself and look in the rearview mirror. Tears were visible. I quickly wipe my eyes and face and regain my composure. Leaving the picture, I grab my cell phone off the console. I don't even want to expose their image to all this.

The clinic stands before me, as does my future, or what little there is left to it. Not the one I would have chosen, but one that's unfortunately chosen me. I crinkle the letter in my fist and squeeze tight. Before I know it, I'm standing at the door. I stare at it with a sense of doom, taking a deep breath before I turn the knob.

The silver-haired nurse at the front desk smiles and says, "May I help you?"

"I'm late for my ten thirty appointment," I reply, grimacing.

"That's fine, honey. Have a seat and the doctor will see you shortly," she replies pleasantly, handing me a clipboard. "Just fill this out while you're waiting."

I accept the clipboard and reluctantly take a seat. The lobby is spacious and well lit—earth tones, I guess, to create a relaxing ambiance.

Does that ever work?

I place the clipboard in my lap and begin filling out the information with the pen attached to it. Here I am at a crux in my life and I feel like I'm reapplying for my driver's license at the DMV. As I continue to halfheartedly answer the questions on the form, I find myself glaring at my surroundings and those seated within it.

A young mother sits nervously two seats to my left, blonde, very attractive, but deeply fatigued, clutching a brown leather

Gucci bag crammed in her lap. To my right, hugging the wall, is a living suit, head in his lap, rocking ever so gently back and forth. An attaché case is clenched tightly between his feet as if it were going to run away. He must have got some good news too!

Why does he look familiar?

On the other side of the L-shaped lobby is a young girl. She's dressed in a pink sweatsuit with a matching pink bandana wrapped around her head. She's pale with tired eyes, reading a year-old copy of Vogue and deeply engaged in it. Finally, there's a man in a green polo and worn blue jeans; he's on a cell phone. He immediately notices me, smiles and winks. He's in good spirits, definitely looks out of place. Must be a sales representative of some kind. I smirk at him with an expression that translates simply, *"Eat crap and die!"* Yet, he still smiles back at me.

Clueless moron!

My wife used to hate when I did that, size up a room. It's instinctual, I guess. I've always had the gift of observation, sizing up people, my environment, no matter where we were. It's what made me such a great soldier, and then as a detective. Still, it went unappreciated by her. She always believed you could never judge a book by its cover. There was always something deeper. I firmly believe perception is ninth tenths the law. Still, if she had used that ideology with me … Well…

Everyone else saw a misguided teen, a potential criminal, then later a soldier, the hard-boiled cop. As an adult, I was the man who was always solid as a rock, with skin to match, but she saw through all that crap, to the soul who was simply looking for reason and meaning to life, a cause and purpose to exist.

I finish the forms and bring the clipboard back to the desk. The overly polite, silver-haired nurse takes it from me and smiles again.

"Thank you, darling. We're almost ready for you." Even though she says it so very sweetly, it's the most ominous statement I've ever heard.

I return to my seat and slump down. By this time, sweatsuit chick is checking me out. I give her my signature glare, but it doesn't faze her a bit. She returns her stare with the same disdain. Now she's sizing me up.

I sit up and really give her the evil eye. Surprisingly, she's taken aback by it and retreats to her pretend reading. I know that because the magazine is actually upside down. I regress back into my chair and smugly and silently celebrate putting her in her place.

Am I that guy now?

With a mix of guilt and shame, I realize what I've done. Nice one, dickweed!

I'm still too proud to offer an apology. I'll just let it go for now. What does she care, anyway? I'm just some angry stranger that she'll never see again, right? She'll get over it. I grab a two-year-old copy of Sports Illustrated and begin my own disconnected reading. Right now, the waiting seems to be the worst part. I'm sure I'll be proven wrong as we progress.

CHAPTER 2
Pretty in Pink
(Kayla)

What a douche!

I act like I'm reading but I want to get up and smack the shit out of him.

What a fucking jerk!

Like his life is any worse than mine. I slam the magazine on the chair, fold my arms, and glance up at the TV. Great, all they show here is FOX News, like they need to add insult to injury. The closed captioning scrolls across the bottom of the screen.

"In other news, another suspicious suicide in a small, rural Mexican town. Details when we return."

They muted the volume again. I guess they don't want to disturb us sickly freaks as we wallow in our misery. They could at least pony up and get some new magazines. Lord knows they make enough here nursing us sick freaks.

I look up at the clock on the wall. They're not coming again. Why would they after I unloaded on them like I did? She just had to nitpick again, trying too hard to be the mother she never will be. She's still upset that she got stuck with the cancer kid, a little more than she bargained for.

What a bitch!

I know it's the new, big, hip thing to show how wonderfully selfless you are by taking in troubled kids. But heaven forbid, not one who is terminal. God, I hate her, with her perfectly poofed, dyed blonde hair. She thinks she's a real fashionista. I wonder what her desperate housewife friends would think about all her trips to Wally World.

Just another fucking wannabe!

And don't get me started about her robotic, ball-less husband. I bet she keeps them in her imitation Gucci purse.

I look back at the TV as the captions continue to scroll.

"The seventh alleged suicide occurred in a small rural village deep in Mexico. Another individual was discovered this time, the result of a single gunshot wound to the head."

What's this trash about? The words continue to spew across the screen.

"Authorities believe the deaths may be related. Neighbors and family of the deceased report the same strange behavior prior to the suicide that was eerily similar to that exhibited by the other victims. In this most recent death, the male victim, whose name has still not been released, told anyone who would listen about seeing strange creatures at night that tried to attack him on several occasions, appearing out of nowhere and then disappearing just as quickly.

"The prior victims also allegedly conveyed similar comments. Some accounts told in even greater detail, providing illustrations of the alleged creatures."

Enough of this shit! I pick up another magazine. Nah! I fumble around in my pockets. Where the hell is my iPhone? Not in there. Instead, I find an old brush. Won't be needing that anymore! I fling it at the trash can. It misses and ricochets off the wall.

Whatever! Where the hell is my phone?

I continue to search. My foster mother had to pick a fight right as I woke up today! She knows how I get every time I catch a glimpse of myself in the mirror first thing in the morning. I get to start every day with this thing I've become staring back at me.

What the hell is wrong with her? Is she that clueless?

It's not here!

Damn, I forgot it again. I hate this stupid sweatsuit. I hate pink. I look like a big bottle of Pepto. But this is all she could find in my size, or so she says.

Such bullshit!

Why in the world would I trust her fashion sense? I see the disaster that it is on her every day. "You look so pretty, baby," she told me before we left.

Yeah, and you must be stoned, bitch!

When you drink as much as she does, your judgment is a bit impaired. But if I was married to ball-less, I would drink constantly too. If I woke up every morning being her, I'd hit something harder.

I realize my body language is not as private as I thought. Everyone in the lobby is staring at me. Oh well! My face must be red as a baboon's ass. Maybe it'll distract everyone from this fucking stupid flamingo suit.

He's glaring at me again, that jackass.

You guys want to stare at me! You want something to really look at? I rip off my bandana so my melon can shine brightly under the fluorescents.

Take a look, freaks! Behold the bald, pink, princess of cancer kingdom and go straight to hell!

"Ms. Young." The nurse sighs as she stands before me.

Damn, she's getting quicker!

"Now let's stop that and settle down. The doctor is almost ready to see you," she ever so gently corrects. What a patronizing bitch!

She smiles at me, making the desire to slap her almost unbearable.

"Yes, ma'am," I concede as I flash her my infamous plastic smile. "Sorry about that. Must be a mix of the pain killers and anti-depressants acting up again."

She can easily sense my thick, relentless sarcasm and insincerity, but she doesn't miss a beat. "Well, dear, that may be true, but we can't have you disturbing the other guests," she says sternly but patiently.

Who is she, fucking Mary Poppins! These people are not guests. We're fucking patients. No, make that dead men walking. You fucking plastic android!

That's what I want to say, but what came out was something like, "Yes, ma'am, I apologize," or "Okay, thank you," or some shit like that. What's the use of standing up anymore for anything? Who would care, or remember? She walks away.

The others have stopped staring and returned to their own wallowing. Maybe they think if they act like I'm invisible, I'll just go away.

Yeah, good luck with that, idiots! I'm as real as it gets, beauty slowly transforming into a decaying beast.

I don't know what hurts more, the pain or the anger. There's that stupid guy again, and he's still staring. As much as I want to kick him in the crotch until he can taste his testes, I have to respect him. At least he has the courage not to look away. Maybe he actually gets it, or maybe he's just a mega freak.

I still remember the day it all started. I'd been in and out of foster care for years. Typical story, mom was a crack head, dad could be … well, anybody. At age three, she left me in a parked car in front of a convenience store while she was—let's just say—servicing one of her many customers in the restroom. Guy beat her up and left her unconscious.

While she lay there in layers of urine and whatever the hell else was stuck to the tile floor, I sweated it out in the car. Finally, a patrol car swung by and saw me. I was there for hours. If it had been in the summer, I'd have been dead. She went to the hospital and then jail, and I went into the system.

I was always sick. At first, nobody could figure out why, and Lord knows my foster parents weren't going to put up the cash to find out. They were too busy hoarding the government checks for their own dope. It's truly amazing what you can do with food stamps. It was a happy childhood that bloomed into some of the most marvelous teenage years. I used to call myself "Lady U-Haul, moved around so much and treated about the same as luggage.

Then there was the litany of my so-called caregivers. There was the ultra-religious family who said I was sick because of the sins of my mom. I think I saw the inside of a church more than my own bedroom. When all the hours of prayers didn't work, they felt God was moving them in another direction, which meant I was moving out.

Then there was Mr. and Mrs. Hippy. I got removed from them when I called 911 because of the huge clouds of smoke bellowing out of the bathroom. When the fire truck finally arrived, the two of them were so blitzed they were stone cold passed out on the floor. That seems to be a running theme in my life. The firefighters and cops said they got a contact high just entering the house. The greenhouse full of pot plants was the biggest bust they had made in the metro area in the last five years.

The rest were a rainbow of freaks who just wanted to be put on the government's glorious payroll, and it seems I got to sample every one of them. I did one year in juvie for almost removing the manhood of a foster "uncle" who thought I was too young to seriously defend myself. Guess he learned that lesson the hard way. Trust me; it wouldn't have been that big of a loss for him if I'd succeeded.

Fast forward to now and here I am. Enter the newest parenting losers, the rich lawyer and his trophy wife. She did the whole foster care thing because a friend told her she needed to build up some positive karma, not to mention the esteem of her brain-dead peers. She actually told me that the first day she brought me to her home. Right then I knew this was going to be a blast. Only this time, when I got really sick, they actually had the money to have me fully checked out. Trying to score brownie points with the cosmos, I guess.

Next thing I knew, I was in the hospital, and after what seemed like never-ending tests, they told me I had advanced ovarian cancer. I sat in my hospital bed and realized my life was about to drip away like the rain on the windows of my sanitized hospital room. Then came the weeks of chemo and radiation, the puking, crapping myself, sleeping for days. Food tasted like hell no matter what it was. And then the final blow, losing all my hair.

They try to put on brave faces, but I know they've been trying like hell to find a way out. This time the system really stuck it to them.

Careful what you wish for. Karma's a bigger bitch than me.

So this morning we fought again. I can tell they're done with me, just going through the motions. I'm alone again, facing the end. I know how much more time I have left. We'll keep doing the chemo thing, but it's only prolonging the inevitable. My reign as the putrid pink princess of cancer is coming to an end. And you know why I'm so pissed about it? Because I'm the only one who believes I deserve better than this even if no one else does. To them I'll be just another statistic.

Dammit, I'm a person. I'm worth more than that, even if I am alone in that belief. The hell with everybody!

I realize the tears are falling fast all over my pink sweatpants. I wipe my eyes but the tears quickly replenish.

I can't stop!

I glance around the room again. This time they all ignore me. Why not? I would.

But not him. He looks right at me, not staring this time. Is he actually tearing up too?

Why? Who the hell am I to him?

Or maybe it's not even about me. Maybe I'm simply a reflection of his own fate, one that he can't handle.

The scroll rolls on as my attention inexplicably returns to the TV. Maybe it's because I just can't look at him any longer. Too intense, and I don't have time for any connections right now.

"Despite the strangeness of the details of the incidents, the police are taking these deaths very seriously. There have been tales of strange beasts in this area before, tales of the chupacabra, UFO sightings, and random paranormal activity. These tales were recently featured on the newest worldwide internet sensation, The Shadows of Presence website, which alleges it is the only website with credible and factual evidence regarding a barrage of worldwide conspiracy theories."

I've seen that site. What a bunch of trash!

"This site exploded into the mainstream just three short months ago with its exposure of the recent, now infamous, UFO sighting over Canada."

I saw that too. What a farce!

"The footage of a large object that seems to be floating over Vancouver has spread like wildfire over the internet in the last few months, and expert after expert has not been able to identify or debunk it. This image has been described as more organic than mechanical, with a myriad of conclusions ranging from an elaborate hoax to a possible new species of animal."

The image darts onto the screen. Wow! What the hell is that? I'm locked into the broadcast.

"Whatever it may be, it has the social and scientific communities buzzing and baffled."

No shit!

"It is now being reported that a team from that website that has been investigating the suicides in the region has allegedly disappeared."

Another picture appears on the screen of a woman and two men. They're young, dressed like tourists. Bad idea from the start. Probably asked directions in the wrong part of town and the cartels got them. Drugs, yeah, it can't possibly be that!

"Police are asking everyone, even Stateside, if you have any information on the location of these three individuals, to contact the following number or the website directly."

"Ms. Young," the nurse interrupts. "It's time." She stands over me with her hand outstretched. Her voice is extremely gentle, as if I'm so fragile I may spontaneously break apart at any moment.

"Huh, okay." I stand up. That guy's looking out the window now. I wonder who he is.

What's his story?

Wait, what the hell is up with me? Who cares what his story is.

It really must be the meds. I follow the nurse through the door. The door closes. Wow, I never noticed that sound before. How lonely it is.

CHAPTER 3

The Last Dawn

(Alex)

That chick has more issues than *Time* magazine. Thank God she finally left. I mean, who does that?

Even Mr. Sunshine across from me was affected. Now he just keeps staring at the door. At least he's finally off his cell. I know she must be going through some serious shit, but c'mon, kid, get a grip. We're all here for the same reason. Once you allow it to get to you, it's over. As if I'm one to talk.

Maybe she's just as conflicted and tortured as I am. I mean, you can't escape this. It's not like you can move away from it. It's always there, part of you. Last time I checked, you can't take a vacation from yourself. Boy, wouldn't that be a blessing.

Poor girl, so young, it's a fucking crime. I guess she's just putting it out there the way we all wish we had the balls to do rather than simmer in silence. Now I'm envious. She did what we all should be doing; be brave enough to face it out loud.

Kudos, Pinky Tuscadero!

Shame on me for being such a bastard.

I hope she makes it. Very few people have that much spirit. Maybe she'll beat the odds.

I'm tired of reading this outdated magazine and watching TV so I look out the window. It's still overcast, dreary, a perfect day for all this. I couldn't have designed it better.

Huh, that's interesting...

There's some kind of blue hue out there. I mean, I've seen a greenish hue before, especially before or after a storm, but never blue. I wonder where it's coming from.

"Mr. Trevor." The nurse taps my shoulder. "Dr. Foster is running a little late, about ten more minutes. Will that be okay?"

Like I have a choice. Where am I going to go? "No problem," I quickly but gently retort.

She walks away. I rub my eyes. They're wet. I clean out the tears quickly.

What is happening to me? I used to be made of stone.

I look back out the window. It's actually bluer now, if that's a word. And the clouds are gone. I glance back around at the lobby, as if to say something. But what would I say, and who would I say it to?

Nobody would care.

I turn around again, thinking about my wife walking down to the altar in that small country church. God, she was so beautiful. When she finally arrived everything else just washed away. Suddenly it was just her and me. I was lost in her. She smiled and my whole life made sense. My past was past, and now, all that mattered was a lifetime with her. It was a tiny crowd stuffed into small wooden pews, about twenty, maybe twenty-five people. There was some family but mostly friends.

We didn't care; after all, it was all about us. We were finally breaking free from the chains of bad history and family drama. We were boldly moving forward to a new life, with the only limitations being the ones we set for ourselves. We were drunk in the fascination and wonder of each other. As she read to me the vows she had written herself, her voice sounded again like an angel engulfing me in peace and hope. I struggled through my vows when it was my turn, fighting back my emotions but failing miserably.

My dad sat in the back row with his typical look of disgust. He was disappointed as usual, this time that I had made something of myself and didn't end up the loser he expected me to be. He'd repeated that fact to me without ceasing throughout my entire life. My mom sat there silently, always so complacent. She was such a strong and wise woman, but he had so effectively beaten her down emotionally that she had forgotten who she was.

I lost my mom to cancer two years ago. Dad started dating right away, maybe a couple of months after the funeral. They'd been married for forty years. He always talked about how much he loved her, even threw himself on the casket at her service. He should have been an actor, would have won a fucking Oscar for that one. He defined the idea of a son of a bitch, and I believe the bastard was proud of that fact.

But all of that didn't matter now. I was free. We were free. He'd lost, and I won. And you could see that in his eyes. That was the best wedding present he could have ever given me.

"Mr. Trevor," the nurse calls to me. I turn again from the window. "The doctor's ready to see you now."

I shake my head and begin to get up. Suddenly I feel weak and begin to lose my footing.

"Mr. Trevor, are you okay?" the nurse calls to me.

I can see her moving toward me, but everything is blurry, fading out. I look out the window again. It's bright and blue, almost blinding. Suddenly, I can't hear anything. The silence is painful. The nurse grabs me as my legs buckle. My head is pounding, my entire body burns, I have pins running up and down through my veins. I fall to the floor, grabbing my head on both sides. The pain is beyond comparison.

I'm dying! I have to be!

My body tightens, and I can't open my hands. They've completely recoiled into fists. My toes curl and my knees snap back. My body involuntarily retreats into a fetal position. The burning is unbearable.

I can't see!

I know the nurse is there, but I can't feel her touch. The pain has completely overwhelmed me.

God, what is happening?

I can't cry out; my mouth won't open. My teeth grind together as my jaw feels like it is going to explode.

God, help me, please!

I can feel myself losing consciousness. My memories are scattered as the pain in my head intensifies. My body feels like it's being pressed harder and harder into the ground.

God, if this is it, please take care of my family. Please give them the strength to make it through this. I'm so sorry I wasted so much time.

God, can you hear me?

I'm being crushed and I can taste blood in my mouth and feel it in my nose. Please God, I can't take it anymore! Please let it end! Let me die!

I see Sara, Gracie, my best friend Boone, my dad, Mom, buddies, and friends. All my life is on a speed reel. I can feel my blood boiling.

God?

God!

God!

CHAPTER 4

Awakening
(Kayla)

What am I lying in? It's warm and—oh my God, what is that smell?

I look around, barely able to focus.

What the hell just happened?

I try to pick myself up, exhausted from the battle with pain I just went through. My whole body and face are wet, and my head is pounding. I push myself up, feeling something dripping wet. I look down. Yeah, that's what I thought. It's vomit. A LOT of vomit! I'm lying in my own vomit.

I gag but only dry heave. Based on the lake I was laying in, there must be nothing left. The smell is intense. I make it to my knees and wipe my face. It's gotta be an inch thick, but at least it's not chunky. I guess that liquid diet worked out after all.

I'm still in the examining room. Where the hell is that nurse who was checking my blood pressure? I still can't see straight, and I rub my eyes.

Great, I just got that shit in my eyes. Perfect!

I gotta find a towel or rag or something. I try to stand, but that's not going to work, and I immediately fall back to my knees. Let's try something else, shall we? The examining table is behind me.

I slide through the muck on my knees toward it. God, this feels just awful. It hurts when I grab the table and try to pull up, but I struggle through it until I'm standing upright. Careful now, don't slip. This is so disgusting.

Bracing myself, I look around the room, my head full of sharp rocks. I turn cautiously; it feels like my head's going to snap off at any second.

Where the hell is that nurse?

The floor is covered with vomit, the smell hovering like a thick fog. I gag again. On the counter across from me there's a towel dispenser. I try to carefully make my way to it. It's only a couple of feet away but it might as well be a mile. I take each step one at a time, sloshing through what appears to be a week's worth of contents from my stomach. I finally make it, grab the towels and begin ferociously wiping my face. It takes several towels to properly do the job.

Oh God, it's all up my nose!

I quickly blow, freeing the blockage, and make the mistake of looking at the aftermath.

Gross!

I gag again, my sides feeling like they're going to burst.

"Hello, is anyone there?" My voice is low and raspy but I'm sure it can be heard. "Hello?" I grab more towels and clean my hands and arms. It comes off in layers. Well, this suit has had it. At least there's one silver lining. It's wonderful how the vomit and the velour is bonding, quite the sensation. It's even in my damn underwear.

I'm not going to think about it. I can't.

I wade over toward the door. "Hello, somebody, anybody!"

The door is open, and I slowly make my way to it. I step on something new and look down. It's a nurse's uniform. It's sitting on top of more slime. My sides scream when I bend down to pick it up.

Nasty! Why the hell did I do that? It's covered in what looks like Jell-O from hell. I quickly drop it. This is really turning out to be a banner day.

I continue toward the door. "Hey, somebody fucking answer me," I scream down the hallway. "I need help here. I just barfed out most of my organs. Is anyone there?"

No reply.

What the hell?!

I head out into the hallway. Thank God, carpet. Oh, my sneakers are shot. Damn. They used to be white. I don't know what color they are now, and I don't want to. They slosh when I walk as more vomit sprays out from their sides.

Wonderful!

How am I still alive with that much spewage?

My head and sides agree. I walk down the hallway to the front check-in. I can't see anyone. Then I step into another fucking puddle.

What the hell?

It's another uniform. This time I can see the name badge. A Judy Hobson, RN. The check-in nurse. I've seen her every week for the last four months. She's sweet as hell, like too much syrup on pancakes. You get diabetes just from meeting her.

I step over the pile of clothes and whatever the hell else that they are sitting in. "Hello," I continue calling out as I reach the front.

There's no one at the counter. I look around the lobby. They're all lying on the floor. Are they even moving? I call back behind the check-in counter, "Hello, I need help." I grab the phone on the counter and dial 911.

I'm shaking now, feeling the panic grip me. The phone rings and rings and rings, and rings. "Guys, get up," I call out to them! No one is moving. Are they dead?

It's still ringing.

C'mon, pick up!

"Guys, get up!" I call out again. Still no response! The phone is still ringing.

I look up at the TV and it's still on, but there's just an empty set on the screen. No one is there, just the desks that the anchors were sitting at. No movement behind it either. No one is there. Okay, I'm officially totally freaked out!

I finally hang up. Maybe it's the phone.

I dig in my pockets, looking for my cell. Finally, there it is! How the hell did I miss it? It's covered in shit too! I frantically wipe it off on my sleeve. Not much of an improvement, but I hope it still works. As I dial again, my hands shake so hard I can barely type the numbers.

Please God, someone pick up!

The people are still not moving! The only sound I can hear is the ridiculous Muzak playing overhead.

Tears stream down my face as I listen to the endless ringing, growing more panicked by the second.

Please pick up! Pick up, pick up, pick up!

"Move!" I scream at them.

Fear grips me with all its might. I'm numb and feel cold at the same time. I can't make sense of any of it. "Please, somebody move!" I scream at the top of my lungs! "Oh God, please let somebody move!" I fall to my knees. "I can't do this."

I drop the phone.

"Please, somebody help me," I desperately cry out, my voice strained and raspy. "*Please,* somebody!" My head collapses into my hands. I can still hear the phone ringing as I surrender to the tears, to the loneliness that is suffocating me. All I can do is weep. "Please, God, somebody." I look up, sobbing.

"Shut up, already," a man calls out. "I'm lying right here!"

His lone voice breaks the stranglehold of fear. I jump up and search around frantically with my eyes. Oh my God, it's the weirdo, Mr. Stare. He's alive!

Thank you, God!

"Please, just shut up," he continues to growl. "My head is already killing me!"

He's face-down on the floor but he's moving. His voice is quiet but strong. A giant weight lifts off me and I rush to his side and roll him over. Maybe not the best move but I don't care.

"Wow, you stink," he says as he opens his eyes.

I laugh through my tears. "You're alive, you freak," I reply, relief rushing through me.

"Mostly," he retorts. "Seriously, though, you reek!"

I hold him tight to me.

"Okay, I got it, you're glad to see me, now ease up," he gasps.

He looks up at me, straining to focus. "What the hell just happened?"

I pause and look around again, then look back at him. Our eyes meet and lock. We stare in silence for a few long seconds. He reads my eyes, and I can tell he knows immediately I have no answer.

CHAPTER 5
Aftermath
(Alex)

I struggle to get up. She assists me. I'm so weak that without her, I could never make it to my feet. Slowly, I begin to focus. Okay, we're still in the lobby.

That's a good start.

"What happened?" I ask. God, she reeks. I hope I don't puke too.

"I don't know. I passed out in the examining room back there," she replies. Her voice is shaking, and tears stain her face.

I gently break free from her hold and try to get up and walk. I stagger and stumble toward the front counter, stepping into a large pile of God knows what. I try to avoid stepping in it any further, the puke thing getting closer and closer to happening. The rancid smell in here is unbearable, and it's not just coming from her.

It smells like there was a slow burn. I've experienced it before. All too well! It's the smell of burnt flesh. The memory of my best friend Boone flashed through my mind. He was always the life of the party, so we were two peas in a pod, so tight we could finish each other's sentences. We survived boot camp together; cleaned the insides of more toilets than the Tidy Bowl Man. I still somewhat gag whenever I use a toothbrush. The war was nearly in full swing, and he couldn't wait to get out there and fight. He never was that bright. Then again, neither was I. Again, the whole two peas in a pod thing.

We had been through so much, survived so much, and then there was that damn kid. Boone had always had a soft spot for kids. When he saw the kid take a hit from shrapnel flying all around us, he couldn't leave him. I mean, why was the kid out in the middle of the road during a fucking fire fight to begin with?

The kid went down, and Boone couldn't help himself. He took off like a shot after him. The boy couldn't have been more than eight. He'd been playing in the street while bullets and all manner of chaos were breaking all around him. That's the kind of place it was. He must have been so used to it, used to all the death and destruction, that it just didn't faze him anymore.

Boone grabbed the kid, scooped him over his shoulder, and bolted back, but there was absolutely no cover. The first hit tore through his chest like wet paper. The momentum of the impact pushed Boone forward as he tumbled toward our position. When he dropped, we let go with everything we had. A second shot tore his left leg right out of the socket. We had to get to him before they tore him to pieces.

I got to Boone and dragged him behind cover as the rest of the platoon pressed on, decimating everything in front of them. Because of Boone's sacrifice, our fear was transformed into blind determination. In the simplest of terms, we wanted payback.

When I saw a clear path, I picked Boone up—my body armor drenched in his blood—and carried him to the extraction point. Waiting for that chopper had been the longest minutes of my life.

I carried Boone to the chopper, held him until it landed, watched him take his last breath. You know in the war movies how the two friends always get to say their goodbyes right before the other one dies?

Yeah, that doesn't happen.

I quickly shake off the thought, no time for that now, and move behind the counter. "Hello," I call back to the offices.

The girl is right behind me now, closer than a shadow. I can feel her trembling. I turn to comfort her. As if I can. "Relax, we'll figure this out."

She doesn't look convinced. Neither am I. I head back into the offices to search, scanning each room. I see a half-full cup of coffee, an open romance novel, files strewn along a desk, an iPod with headphones sitting alone amongst some paperwork. She's still with me, closer now.

I look up at the TV. "What the hell?" I blurt out. It's on, but no one is there. Just a news set. I frantically search for the remote. There it is, next to the computer. I grab it and turn off the mute.

Nothing!

I flip through the channels, seeing a few reruns, some cartoons, and a cooking show. I search the numbers and plug in the weather channel. My eyes widen. Again, just an empty set. Watching for a moment, I hope something will change, or someone will pop up.

"I know, nobody's there," she says.

I can tell she's really struggling to keep it together. The look on her face is nearly void.

"Stay with me," I say, then gently grab her arms. "Just breathe."

She stares at me, peering deep into my eyes, as if to grasp for some shred of hope.

"Come on, stay with me," I reassure, and massage her arms. She's barely there. It's consuming her. I take her by the hand. "I'm here. Hang in there with me." I lock my gaze with hers, trying to calm her. "You still here?"

She squeezes my hand and nods. It's a fragile reaction, but for the moment I have her confidence. I flip through more channels. This is pointless!

"We'll call 911," I say, turning back to her.

"Already tried," she weakly responds.

Frowning, I pull out my cell phone and dial without looking away from her. It rings and rings and rings.

"Don't waste your time," she cautions. "They won't answer."

I reach for the phone on the desk.

"Tried that too, same result," she says as the fear begins to veil her face. Her lids grow heavy. I can tell I'm losing her again, and I move her quickly to a chair.

"Sit here, breathe," I instruct as I lead her into a nearby chair. "I'm going to check on everyone else."

She nods, but I wonder how much she actually absorbed. I move away from her to check on the guy in jeans lying on the floor next to us. He's breathing, thank God. I shake him gently. "Sir, can you hear me?"

He slowly acknowledges me. "Is it over?" he grunts. "Are we dead?"

"No, we're still here," I answer, not really knowing whether I'm being truthful with him. He's very woozy, so I help him up.

He rubs his face and neck. "I went down pretty hard, right after you did. You okay?"

"Yeah, considering," I reply. "Hey, please keep an eye on the girl for me over there. She's struggling." I point out Pinky.

He grimaces. "What's she covered in?"

"Don't ask," I retort, and help him up. "You got this. Can you stand?"

"Yeah, I'm good." He struggles to gain balance. "I'm Matt," he says and reaches out to shake my hand.

"Yeah, great."

I'm in no mood for salutations right now. I assure myself he's steady, then move to the suit across the room. Matt sits next to Pinky and puts his arm around her. They are whispering something to each other. I kneel beside the suit and gently shake. "Dude, can you hear me?"

"Yes, the entire time," he scolds.

"Can you get up?"

"If I could, would I be lying here?"

Great, a smart ass. Just what I need! With a little less care than I did the others, I grab his arms and move him to his feet.

"Thanks, good thing I didn't have a neck or spine injury," he quips as he dusts off his jacket and pants. "You think they could sweep this floor once in a while. What the hell happened?"

"I'm working on that," I reply. The irritation in my voice is palpable. "Do you want to stand or sit?"

"I'm good. Let me walk it off."

He begins to walk around the room. I shake my head in disbelief. Some people!

I move to the lady in the far corner. She's face down in the seat on her knees, rocking back and forth.

"What the hell is that?" I hear the suit shout. He'd just stepped in the same pile of nasty goulash I had earlier. A steady stream of profanity follows as he dances around the mass, trying to wipe his shoes off on the floor. All he manages to do is slip and slide around. What a douche.

I quietly chuckle as I kneel beside the lady and massage her shoulders. "Sweetie, can you hear me?" She doesn't answer. She's breathing fast and really shaking hard. "Sweetie?"

I touch her shoulder. She's weeping deeply. I try to pull her toward my chest, but she resists. She's clutching her purse with a death grip.

"C'mon, girl, it's going to be okay."

"Is it?" She quickly looks up at me, her face soaking wet with tears and sweat. She called me on it! It's not okay. But the attempt has to be worth something. "Please leave me alone," she scolds, her voice raspy and injured.

"I'm afraid I can't do that, ma'am. We're in this together, like it or not."

"It's over," she retorts. "What's the use!"

If her eyes were loaded, I'd be dead. "We don't know what happened yet. But we're all still here. Let's get you up." I try to coerce her out of her position, but she resists.

She pulls away from me. "Please, just leave me alone."

In my training, both in the military and in the academy, I learned in crisis situations that everyone acts differently. There are those who rise above with great strength and diligence, but most just collapse like a house of cards. In some cases, there are those who simply shut down in order to mentally reboot. This is the only way to reset and get a handle on what is going on. With that in mind, I decide to let her work this out on her own, at least for now.

"I'm here if you need anything," I assure her as I rise.

She returns her face to the seat of the chair. I'm deeply worried about her, but we're getting nowhere fast and time is no longer a luxury that can be carelessly spent.

"I'm going to check out the examining room. Stay here with them," I call out to Matt.

I don't know this guy from Adam's cat. I don't know if he can manage all this, but for now he's all I've got so he'll have to do.

He's holding Pinky and rocking her back and forth, comforting her. It seems to be working for now; she appears to be calm.

Suit is back in the corner, frantically dialing his phone. He's been at it since I spoke with him. I watch him out of the corner of my eye as he's been nervously punching numbers. Maybe he'll get somewhere with it.

I begin down the hall. There are three examining rooms on each side. Thankfully, the doors are all open. I quickly shift gears from concerned citizen to soldier mode. I sweep each room as if I am moving through a kill house.

Pause … *Ensure I have adequate cover.*

Look … *Absorb the room, take in every detail.*

Then move in … *Slowly, methodically.*

All clear!

Okay, next room.

Rinse and repeat. I slide into the first room to the left. It's empty and clear. I hold my breath with each entry, trying to anticipate every possibility. I'm unarmed and unprepared, but that creates little hesitation. I have no choice. There could be others who need help. All my gear is outside in the car. Who would have thought I'd need it here today?

I enter the second room to the right, sweep, its empty too.

Where the hell is everybody?

So far, I smell Pine Sol instead of that horrific odor in the lobby. All my senses are full on, laser-focus. Third room on the left side. Okay, there goes the refreshing break of smelling cleaner. I discover yet another pile of that weird, nauseating goop in the middle of the floor.

What is this shit?

This time there is a uniform on top of it. I get near it, but not too close. A nametag is visible. It's a doctor's badge and I can see a stethoscope barely sticking out of the horrific pile. I can't read it, and I'm not getting any closer. There's a fine line between bravery and stupidity. Okay, this has moved way beyond bizarre. The smell is the same and I gag a little. It's getting to me now. The rest of the room is clear.

Fourth room to the right, everything is clear until I hear what sounds like a whimper. I immediately pause, searching the room quickly with my eyes, examining every angle, every inch.

Nothing. But the sound is still there. It's weak but apparent. I move slowly, cautiously, into the room, and try to pinpoint the source.

There's an examining bed in the center. I guess that's what they call it. Counters cover the back half of the room, top and bottom. Everything is shut. Same as all the others I'd just searched. But this is a larger room. I can smell medicine. Then I see an IV hanging from its pole next to the bed.

Now where does the line from the IV end up?

I follow it with my eyes. It leads behind the table. The line is moving ever so slightly, as if there is a slight breeze in the room. The paper that lines the examining bed is torn.

A patient was here. Or still is.

I move even more slowly now. The whimpers stop. I pause. My heart skips a beat. I'm stronger than this. I'm supposed to be fearless.

Not today.

I move toward the bed. Every step is silent. I can hear someone breathing now. It sounds labored and unnatural, or like someone is trying to control it to be as quiet as possible. If they are hiding, they're scared.

If I startle them anymore, they could turn violent, like a wild animal backed into a corner. I know I would, especially in this chaos. I would do anything to defend myself.

I don't want to continue to sneak up on them. The IV may still be connected. If they are startled or spooked in any way, they might pull it out. That would create or worsen any injuries.

Do I call out? What choice do I have? "Hello, is anyone in here? It's okay, I'm a police officer."

Silence. No response, but I can still hear the breathing.

"There is nothing to be afraid of. Come on out."

Again, nothing!

I move in, one step at a time. "Please come on out. My name is Alex."

Still nothing!

I'm right next to the bed, almost able to look over it. The IV line is trembling. I take a deep breath. "Don't be afraid. No one is going to hurt you."

I look over the bed to see another gross pile. This time there are footprints in it. Someone tracked through it.

"Okay, I'm coming around the bed now; don't be scared. Everything is going to be okay."

I slide around the table and our eyes meet. Time stops. He can't be more than ten or eleven. He's shaking almost uncontrollably and holding his knees close to his chest. He's wearing a ball cap, Yankees, but I can tell he's bald underneath. Definitely another patient. I remember Dr. Foster telling me his specialty used to be children's oncology. His stare burns right through me. He's waiting for my next move, like a startled cat preparing to jolt away.

"Okay, don't freak, I really am a police officer. I know I don't have my uniform on but here's my badge."

I slowly reach for it and pull it from my front pocket. He retracts. I know he's going to jump. I can feel it. I hold out my open wallet, exposing my badge.

"What's your name, Captain?" I bend down to lay my badge on the floor, gently sliding it to him. "What's your name?"

He doesn't respond, his stare intense and frightened.

"How old are you?" I try to continue the one-sided conversation, hoping it might relax him. I know it's not working on me. He may be in shock. I need to keep him focused on me, so I move a little closer, but he retracts again and begins to slowly slide away from me.

"Wait, kid, c'mon, give me a break. You think you're scared, just think how I feel?" Not a textbook or skillful way of negotiating, but I'm quickly running out of ideas. I run my hands through my hair and then look back up at him. Let's try this. "I mean, I hate the Yankees, and yet I'm still here with you," I nervously joke. "I mean, I really hate the Yankees. We are talking a real hate; a loathing, steaming pile of hate. You get what I am saying."

Okay, I'm desperate now.

Wait a minute, wait, is that a smile forming? Yes! It's a smile! He's smiling!

And then, miracle of miracles, a small giggle. It only lasts a split second, but it's definitely progress. I smile back. "Well, now that we've broken the ice, can I get your name?"

I try to keep the momentum going. He doesn't speak, but he slowly grabs my badge and looks it over.

"I assure you its real, or at least that's what the guy at the toy store told me."

Another small smile.

He slowly gets up and hands the badge back to me. "You look different from your picture," he says.

"Yeah, well, I was a little younger then. Not much though, but a little younger."

Suddenly, we're best friends, like we've known each other for years. That's the resilience of kids for you.

"My name is Jude. Have you seen my mom?"

Damn, I didn't think of that. Of course this kid has a mom. Oh God, what do I do now?

"Is she here, waiting on you?"

"Yes, she was waiting in the lobby."

Oh God, please let her be the weeping willow out there.

"What does she look like?"

"She's blonde and tall."

"Does she have a really fancy purse?"

"Yes." His face lights up.

"She's in the lobby, waiting for you. Do you wanna go see her?" Relief washes over me. A little light in what seems to be a never-ending tunnel of darkness. I take his hand and gently help him to his feet.

He smiles again, and I flash him a smile in return. We head for the door to make our way to the lobby.

And boom, there he is!

We stumble back in shock. Jude screams.

"Stop, it's just me," Dr. Foster says. "Don't be alarmed." His head is bleeding badly.

"Man, what the hell were you thinking?" I scold. "You scared the hell out of us!"

He quickly apologizes. "I'm sorry. I heard your voices from my office."

"What happened to you?"

"I don't know. I blacked out and must have hit the edge of my desk when I fell."

He runs his fingers over the gash on his forehead with shaking hands.

"Well, you're bleeding bad, dude!"

Dr. Foster moves into the room and heads for the cabinets. He scrounges through the middle top cabinet and pulls out some gauze. He begins wiping his wound. There's blood all over his white coat and hands. "You always bleed the most from the head," he calmly explains as he cleans the wound. "I know there's some alcohol up here somewhere."

He searches the cabinet further.

"I hope it's whiskey," I half joke.

Dr. Foster turns and smirks. "Unfortunately, no. That particular kind is located inside my desk." He laughs. "Hey, Jude, how are you doing, kiddo?" Dr. Foster leans on the counter and holds the gauze over his bleeding wound.

"I was okay until you scared the crap out of me, Doc!" Jude says, still recovering from his fright.

I look down at him and smile. "You can say that again."

"Where's your mom?" Dr. Foster asks.

"Don't worry, she's in the lobby. She's shaken but I think she'll be okay," I reply.

"Alex, is everybody else okay?" The concern in his voice is thick.

"Let me reunite Jude with his mom, then we'll talk."

He immediately reads my eyes and nods.

I kneel next to Jude. "Okay, enough surprises. Let's go see Mom."

Jude agrees and we head into the hallway. "Officer Alex?" he nervously asks.

"Yeah, kid?"

"What don't you want me to know?"

I stop dead in my tracks and look down at him. He's a smart one. But he's probably been through hell, so he's had to grow up faster than he should have. "How about this. Let's get you with your mom. I know she's desperate to see you. Then we'll talk."

He pauses and thinks for a moment. "I can handle it, you know." His face is like stone.

I nod in agreement. "I know, kid, but right now, I'm trying to get a handle on it, okay?" The kid deserves honesty; it's the least he deserves.

Jude pauses for a moment and then reluctantly concedes. "Okay."

We begin toward the lobby again. I can see Jude's mom still weeping in the corner. She's cut off from the world, drowning in all her own fear and misery. She's oblivious to us, but Jude sees her immediately and sprints to her.

"Mom! Mom!" he screams.

Wow, he's a fast little booger!

She awakens from her dread and looks up. When she sees him, her face illuminates the room. "Jude!" she cries, her voice hoarse from weeping. Jude grabs her around the neck and squeezes her tight. They begin crying together.

"Oh, my boy, my wonderful boy."

She holds him as if there's no tomorrow. I hope she's not right.

She kisses all over Jude's face, covering him with her lipstick. He's helpless against her loving assault. The first bit of normalcy since I woke up. I can't enjoy their endearing reunion for long; there is still too much going on.

I search the room. They're all here, and they all look totally lost. Reality sets back in. I head back to the room to talk with Dr. Foster, praying he may have some answers, but almost certain he's just as confused and bewildered as the rest of us.

CHAPTER 6

My Freakin' Wonderful Life
(Kayla)

This guy is a total stranger, yet I can't help but find some solace in his arms. Maybe because it's been so long since somebody actually held or cared about me. I realize I have a much deeper hunger for it than I want to recognize. I feel secure with his arms around me.

This is so stupid! I'm surprised he hasn't tried to cop a feel yet. He says his name is Matt and he was a preacher once. A good reason not to trust him, and why this all feels so very strange. I'm not exactly what you'd call a person of faith, except in the worthlessness of people—now that I believe with all my heart.

The guy who brought us together, Mr. Stare, bolted back down the hall after reuniting that kid with his mother. Those two have been in what looks like an eternal hug, but at least Mom finally put her purse down for five minutes.

Matt looks at me deeply. "You hangin' in there?" He's attempting to sound hip.

Fail!

He's tall, has short brown hair, hazel eyes, and a refined look about him. He's either in money or had it at one time. He's wearing a polo shirt and jeans—looks like they were freshly pressed or he just bought them.

Trying to look good for us peons, I guess. The unwashed masses.

"Yeah," I retort, not really knowing anything better to say.

"So, you said your name is Kayla?"

"Yeah, that's right." I feel my strength returning, so his comfort is becoming progressively less necessary.

"Good. Like I said before, my name is Matt," he continues, despite my rapidly increasing cynical tone.

"Hey, Matt, I appreciate the support and all, but how about we try a little more space right now." I quickly pull away, my tears drying along with the whole damsel in distress thing I had going on.

"Oh, okay."

He quickly retreats and takes his arm off my shoulder. "Glad I could be of some service."

I can tell I've embarrassed him with my jaggedness. "Don't get me wrong, I appreciate it." I try to demonstrate some sign of care for his damaged feelings. I don't know why. "But I'm good now."

Matt looks over at the mom and son pair, who'd not broken their incessantly annoying hug. The boy is snuggled in his mom's lap. I never did that, the whole snuggling thing. It's just not me. In fact, normally, when I saw it, it filled me with a strong desire to punch someone's lights out. But the kid looks happy, and so did his mom. So I didn't mentally or verbally shit on it.

Matt looks at me again. "Kayla, anyone here waiting on you?" His voice is slightly shaky, so I can tell he's either insecure in his question or just plain scared to talk to me now.

"Yeah, my boyfriend is sitting outside in his sports car. We're heading to Spago's for brunch after my appointment." I don't know why I'm being such a sarcastic bitch to him. I guess old habits die hard.

He nervously smiles. "Well, you're a little late for brunch, and I've never seen a Spago's in this area, but I haven't been here that long."

Okay, he can be a bit of a smartass himself. How very unpreacherlike.

"*Touché*, preacher man. No, it's just little ole me."

He smiles more securely now. I guess he feels like he's reaching me. I let him believe that for now. What can it hurt? "Do you know who that man is, the one who brought us together?"

He shakes his head no. "I think he may be a police or fireman."

I wonder how he deduced that. He answers before I can even ask the question.

"It's the way he's handling all this, very calm and collected."

"Maybe he just has his shit straight." I can tell my profanity offends him by the look on his well-tanned face. Get used to it, holy man. It's only the beginning if we're going to be friends.

He quickly recovers from my obscenity. "No, it's more than that. I'm going to head down the hall and see what's going on. Will you be okay here?"

Somehow, I can tell his concern is real. Boy, I'm not used to that—people being real, that is. I'll try not to let it go to my head. I give him the sarcastic thumbs up.

Across the room, I can't help but notice the guy in the suit is still burning up his cell dialing numbers, to no avail. What a tool! *Where do I know him from?*

Who gives a shit.

I guess we all have our ways of dealing with stress. His is psycho dialing. Matt gets up and heads down the hall.

God, I stink!

I get up and stretch my legs, the vomit now dry and crusty, starting to flake off. Ain't I the picture of femininity?

The mom is pulling out her cell phone now. Wow, that's a nice one. Must be the latest and greatest. She touches the screen. I can't really see from here but based on her reaction it isn't working. Must be out of juice. She drops it back in her purse in frustration.

Her son doesn't move an inch. He's immersed in the safety of her lap. I can't even begin to know what that's like. The only time my mom ever held me was during a sting. She held me close to conceal the junk she had on her to avoid a search. I don't know how she got away with it. I got the news last month that she was dead. Overdose.

What a fucking surprise, right?

I hadn't heard from her in forever. Yeah, she was the picture of modern motherhood. I found out later that just hours after I was born, while I was laying in ICU with tubes coming out of everywhere, she went out to score. I was born premature, of course, a month early, and apparently strung out on crack. I don't remember much more from those years.

Does anybody?

But in between foster homes, the holders at DSS loved to tell me the stories. They said she was continually strung out, a big ole dried out ho-bag, either out screwing or getting high. Hit the pipe even while she was nursing me. She was the only woman who produced powdered milk from her tits. I don't know how she got away with me living with her even for the three years she had me. They said I just fell through the cracks.

How ironic!

It's weird, but despite all this chaos, I've never felt better in my life. I'm experiencing strength and resolve I've never felt before. Ever since I blacked out, it's like I feel physically reborn. Maybe it's just the adrenaline. Who the hell knows?

Oh, shit, here comes the suit!

"Hey, princess stank," he begins. "Do you have a cell?"

He's definitely the kind of guy you just want to smack right across his weasel-looking face. "Yeah, why?"

"I need it," he snaps.

"Looks like you gotta phone, dick. You've been playing with it forever."

He moves right up in my face. "I need yours!"

Is he seriously trying to intimidate me? I shit bigger than this douchebag!

"Not happening, asshole, so step back," I say, voice strong and hard.

Neither of us move an inch. It's a true standoff.

"Just give me the damn phone!"

I feel his breath in my face. Well, until I slug him.

Wow! Where did that come from?

He falls back and hits the tile floor, hard. I hear the wind leave his body. My hand is throbbing, but that felt so damn good.

The mom across from me screams, "Oh my God, what have you done?" She springs out of her seat like a Lynx speeding to the fallen jackass, while nearly launching her son from his comfortable position in her lap.

"Mom," the kid bellows after he hits the floor.

The suit is out cold. His cell flew and struck the window, shattering it.

Damn, how hard did I hit him?

His lip is bleeding badly. The mom tends to him. She shakes him, trying to wake him up.

"Yeah, lady, I don't think shaking an injured man is a good move."

She glares at me for a moment, then returns to her care of him. "Sir, are you alright, sir?"

He begins to mumble.

Wow, his lip is bleeding badly.

He begins to wake up. "What the hell?" He looks up at the woman and spins around to get up. "What the hell, you bitch!"

I think he just realized what happened. He touches his lip and sees the blood. "All I wanted was your damn phone and you had to go all psycho on me!"

The woman rises as he searches for his phone. "Young lady, what were you thinking?" she says.

Yeah, the whole "young lady" thing? Not happening! "He was in my face, Mary Poppins. What did you expect me to do?"

"Well, not cold cock him!"

She's probably never stood up to anyone in her life. By the way she's dressed, her heels, and high-end purse, she could be a clone of my current foster shrew.

So now I instantly hate her.

"Back up, priss. This doesn't concern you!" I'm so angry, I'm shaking! I can't stop it! It wells up like a volcano and I clench my fists. "Nobody gets in my fucking face!" I turn my attention to the suit. "It's over there, asshole." I point to the shattered remains of his phone by the window.

He ran to it. "Great, it's destroyed."

"Yeah, that's what you get, you freak." It's as if all the years of pent-up hostility finally reach a breaking point. I want to tear him apart.

No, really, I want to destroy this idiot!

"You want anymore?" I scream.

The woman rushes over to me. "Sweetie, calm down!"

I know I'm out of control, but I don't care. This explosion is such a release. Like some amazing drug finally kicked in.

It felt awesome!

"Back up, bitch!" Now I know I'm crossing the line, but I just can't stop.

She steps back, a look of shock on her face.

Matt is back in the room. I didn't even see where he came from. He grabs me, holding me back. I didn't realize I was going for her too.

What's come over me?

I struggle with Matt, feeling invincible, unstoppable. Matt is having a rough time containing me.

"Kayla, stop, stop," he pleads.

I don't care. I feel renewed, anger pumping through my veins. Matt wrestles me to the ground. If I get my hands on him, I'll take him out too.

He holds me down. "Kayla, stop! What are you doing?"

In the struggle, I see suit boy trembling in the corner. He's cowering like the punk I knew he was. The woman just stands there, frozen in shock.

What a wimp!

And then I see her son again.

Oh my God. He's screaming!

In my fury, I hadn't even heard him. He's terrified.

Because of me!

Why am I still fighting? I can't stop! Why can't I stop?

Matt has a solid hold on me. He has me on the floor, hunched over, face on the tile.

"Let me go, you asshole," I scream.

"Alright, knock all this shit off," I hear a voice command from out of nowhere.

It clears the room, loud and strong. My body responds and I freeze. Matt is pulled off me. I'm suddenly and aggressively lifted off the floor and slammed against a window.

"Knock it off!"

I'm face to face with Mr. Stare. I can't match the fierceness of his glare. His hand is on my neck, bracing me against the glass. I could swing, my arms are free, but I chose not to. This guy isn't like the coward. He means business. I realize in that moment that Matt might be right. He looks like a cop.

A pissed off cop!

"Calm down," he commands.

He lets go and we face off. I want to hit him, but I hesitate. I can sense how intense he is. He'll hit back, I know it. He's probably taken down bigger than me. I don't think he cares whether or not I'm a girl. To him, right now, I'm the problem. And cops in this neck of the woods typically have an abrupt way of handling problems.

"Fine, back off," I scold, as I try to catch my breath.

He steps back. They're all staring at me. Can't blame them. I would too.

"This is not solving anything," he scolds. "Everyone just relax."

Matt puts his arm on my shoulder. That's like sticking your hand in a pitbull's cage that hasn't been fed in a week. But I don't strike, no matter how bad I want to. I digress. The anger was subsiding as quickly as it reared up.

Seriously, what was that all about?

"Are you good?" Matt cautiously asks.

"Yeah, I'm fine." Order is temporarily restored.

"What happened?" Matt questions.

The suit speaks up before I can. I think he needs to check his pants. "She destroyed my phone. That's what happened."

I get another sharp glare from the cop.

"It doesn't matter," the suit mutters. "There's no one out there to call."

"What?" the cop shouts.

"I must have called every contact I have. No answers, just voice mails or empty, endless ringing." The suit slouches down into a chair. "They're all gone. Everyone is gone."

How pathetic is this joker!

"You got nobody?" the cop asks.

"What did I just say, man? No, nobody is out there."

The cop looks back at me. "Same deal with 911," he says under his breath.

I hear him and nod in agreement. Everybody is silent. The weight of the possibility comes crashing down on us.

The cop's eyes widen and his face turns pale. "Sara," he whispers. I see fear and anxiety in his eyes. He pulls out his cell and looks down at it, staring for a moment. When he looks up, his gaze is blank, lost in thought. He begins to dial, raising the phone to his ear. We are all still; I don't know why.

I can hear it ringing. He's accidentally left it on speaker. The suit stands up again, everyone poised, as if something big is going to happen. It rings and rings. The cops pale face hardens. We can hear what sounds like a prerecorded message. He listens through it till it ends.

"Sara, pick up," he begins. "Sara, pick up! Sara, *pick up*!"

My heart drops into my chest. I can feel the tension, almost suffocating. It must be his girlfriend or wife.

"Sara, pick up, it's Alex! Please, God, pick up!" He waits patiently. In his other hand is a set of keys. He rubs the keychain with his fingers, his grip so tight that I can see the veins in his hand.

"Sara!"

His voice grows louder, more desperate. There's no response. He stops, disconnects, and then looks back at me, his gaze heavy. I can barely stand it. He dials again. The woman begins to move closer. Matt and the suit stand perfectly still. The kid just sits there. It looks like a bad family photo. The cop holds the phone to his ear again. His eyes are wet but there are no tears. His face is so tight it looks like the skin is going to burst under the stress.

The speaker is off now but I see his eyes lift, as if he hears something, and then a look of disgust. It must be the message again. He waits. "Sara, pick up!"

I can feel his terror, his pain. It surrounds me.

"Sara, please pick up. It's Alex!"

Again, no response. His eyes tell the whole story. Now, the strength so evident before is beginning to melt away. A tear makes its way down his face.

"Sara, please!"

I want to go to him, but I can't move.

Why?

He's nobody, and yet we are the same: lost. He stops, drops the phone to his side and rubs his eyes. The woman moves slowly toward him. He just stands there. She gets close, trying to put her hand on his shaking shoulder, but she never makes it.

He looks straight up. I can tell he wants to scream. I feel it in my throat too. The woman stops dead in her tracks. He tightens his grip on the phone and keys. The phone begins to crack. His other hand begins to bleed from the sharp edges of his keys. He looks straight ahead, right at Matt.

"Alex?" Matt sputters. That's all he says. What else can he say? What else can anyone say?

Alex looks out the window, moving like he's in a trance. He puts the phone back in his pocket. I doubt it works anymore; how could it survive that death grip? He walks toward the exit door with determination. As he passes me, the doctor emerges from the hallway.

"Alex, stop," he calls out.

Alex either ignores him or doesn't hear him because he continues outside. Then he abruptly stops in the middle of the doorway. He turns back to the doctor. "She's out there," he whispers, his eyes on fire. He goes outside, slamming the door. We all jump as the glass shatters.

I have to follow him.

Why? Who the hell knew?

I pursue him out the door, Matt right behind me. He's heading for the cars in the lot. I stop, finding a strange blue hue all around us. Not a cloud in the sky, not a single cloud, but where the hell is the sun?

I can't find it no matter which way I turn. Just blue all around, and a weird smell in the air. I can't make it out, like metal or something.

Matt passes me in pursuit of Alex. There's silence, no sound at all. No traffic, birds, anything. It's all completely still, as if the world is dead. I shiver, as if someone has run a cold, wet finger up my back. I see Matt reach Alex. They're arguing. I rush to them, afraid they'll fight.

I don't know what good I'll be if they do.

CHAPTER 7

The Sky Is Falling

(Alex)

"Alex, what are you doing?" Matt grabs my arm as I fumble for the keys to open my car's trunk.

I jerk away with a growl. "I need to get to them!" I can see Matt is deeply unsettled by my aggressiveness.

"I understand that, but we have no idea what's going on. We need to stick together right now. Safety in numbers and all that."

I hear him, but his words mean very little. All I can think about is my wife and daughter. When I left, everything was okay … normal. It was her rare day off from the office. They were going to have a mother-daughter kinda thing. She'd planned it all week. Breakfast first at the local diner, the same place where she'd first told me she was pregnant. Then clothes shopping in my wife's continued attempt to turn my little girl into a fashionista.

Gracie starts kindergarten this month. Sara is so nervous about it. I'd already hoarded a full pantry of Kleenex, anticipating the level of weeping mess she would devolve into as she sends her off for her first day. That is, after taking about half a million pictures to commemorate the occasion. The poor kid will be posing in front of every shrub, sign, wall, bulletin board … the list goes on and on. No other child, or person for that matter, has ever been documented in pictures like my Gracie. I suspect there were fewer pictures taken of the Kardashians.

After spending what little money we have on her new fall wardrobe, they were going home to have a tea party. It's Gracie's favorite. They'll dress up as suburban socialites or thrift store princesses, drinking sweet tea and eating little cucumber sandwiches. Sara had made them day before. I never eat them when I'm dragged into this gala event. Usually, they become a surprisingly healthy treat for our dog, Max.

Thank God Max'll eat anything!

However, I always dress appropriately, dusting off the ole wedding tuxedo for such a *special* occasion. It meant everything to Gracie, so it does even more for me. I can hear her sweet voice now, "Daddy, come play with me." Who could resist those green doe eyes gently staring up at them?

These are the days when I'm her hero. They pass so quickly and disappear without notice. I take advantage of every moment, especially with the little time I have at home. Every fraction of a second spent with her means more than she'll ever know.

After tea, they nap, Mommy's favorite activity. I don't think my wife has achieved more than three hours of sleep on any given night. She told me yesterday she will try to make it to four after Gracie gets married.

They'll end the day with a Barbie video (probably the one she's already watched a hundred times), a few board games and, finally, dinner as a family, when I come home.

"Alex, please," Matt screams, jarring me from my unplanned stupor.

I realize I've already opened the trunk, strapped my belt and holster on, and am now tightening my vest. Unconsciously, my body is acting on its own, out of instinct, and it doesn't need my brain or its thoughts slowing it down. I retrieve and open my lockbox, extracting my pistol.

Matt just stands there in shock. "Alex, we need to assess the situation. We need to work together." He tries desperately and unsuccessfully not to panic.

I load a magazine into my 9mm, placing the other two in my pocket. After throwing the lockbox back into the trunk and shutting it hard, I move quickly, effortlessly, to the driver's side door. I can no longer see the sun, or a single cloud in the sky, just that damn blue glow all around. Unlocking the car door, I stoop in, placing my vest on the seat to free up my hands to grab the CB to call the station.

Matt follows right behind me, still talking, but I've tuned him out completely.

I get nothing from the radio, so I thrust the key into the ignition, nearly snapping it in two, and rotate it to activate the battery. I turn the radio on, anxiously tuning it to the local talk station. It's a commercial for the local pizza place. I call in again. Still nothing. The commercial ends. Then a station identification spot comes on. Desperation overwhelms me as I hurl the handset onto the dashboard.

The radio spot ends. Silence. I wait. More silence. Turning the knob, I try to access another channel. I finally hear music, just music.

Running through the channels, I try to find the local public station. When I finally arrive at the channel, I'm met with even more frustrating silence. I open the glove compartment, fumble around inside, but can't find it.

I always have it with me. Where can it be?

I extract all the contents from the space, but it's not there.

Dammit! Where the hell is it?

I spin around and check in the back seats, noticing my laptop. It has Wi-Fi. Grabbing the computer, I exit and place it on the roof of the car. Matt remains silent, staring up at the sky, his expression three shades of white. He's mesmerized by something.

I look up to see what he's staring at, seeing nothing at first, but then I notice a plane approaching in the distance. Even from our vantage point, I can tell it's wobbling.

I turn back to Matt, who's frozen in fear. Looking back at the plane, it's clearer now: a Boeing 747. The airport is not too far from the clinic, just a short distance to the east. They just added a runway so there's been a significant increase in air traffic in this area. More low-flying aircrafts than usual.

"Matt, you alright?" He's stiff. I grab his arm. "Matt, snap out of it."

He's trembling. I've seen this kind of fear before. The plane's engines are now audible. Looking up, I can make out every detail. It appears to be heading straight at us, its wings swaying up and down, violently now.

I get it now, I get what he's thinking, and I swing back around. It is almost on top of us!

I grab Matt, abruptly pulling him down. The plane soars right over us, passing just a little more than a couple of hundred feet above. It's as if I could almost touch its belly. The rush of wind and energy knocks us down. We lay there face up as it passes. The plane continues down, barely hovering over the highway and clearing the tree line. I jump to my feet, visually pursuing it.

Oh my God!

It disappears over the tree line. Then the explosion comes. It rocks the ground all around us, nearly stealing my balance. The fireball ascends into the sky, illuminating the area in red and yellow, the only interruption to that incessant blue. Debris from the crash rapidly ascends into the sky, then falls just as quickly.

Matt flips over, shielding his head with his arms.

I hear a second explosion to the south. The building it struck erupts in fire and volcanic-like rubble. The structures all around it burst into flames, exploding into a hellish shower of brick and shrapnel, collapsing like a deck of cards.

It's unreal!

Then another explosion rattles us to the north, farther away, deeper into the city. We have front row seats to the aftermath of one of the skyscrapers taking a hit. What's left of the craft bounces off it, spinning down to the ground, lost among the metal monoliths until it explodes upon impact. Fire is everywhere. More planes fill the sky. Some close, some distant, barely noticeable.

Matt jumps up. "We need to get inside!"

The bleak and suffocating smoke surrounds us, billowing from every angle of my line of sight. It's as if hell belched and vomited up the chaos of its abyss. There's another explosion in the distance, outside the city.

"Alex, we have to get inside now!"

Why? How much safer will we be if one of those things hits the clinic?

After a few more horrific seconds, Matt gives up on me and runs inside.

I watch another plane fall, straight down this time, like an arrow shot at the ground. It's to the northeast, near the lake area. Another is followed by a fireball. The ground has not stopped shaking since the first hit.

I can't move, cemented to the street in a morbid trance. Another plane passes over. It has more altitude than the one earlier but is heading away.

I wonder how many more are up there.

It's a Monday afternoon, a busy flight day and time, a lot of arrivals. The smoke evolves, becoming thicker, desperately trying to steal my breath. My visibility quickly dissipates. I hear another explosion.

I turn back toward the clinic, watching Kayla cower behind what's left of the glass door. She'd been outside earlier. I lost track of her while gathering my gear. I heard her scream when I saw the first plane but was too lost in anarchy to react to it. She made a run for the building once she realized the magnitude of the horror raining down on us.

Smart move, but does it matter?

Despite the duck and cover routine, we are held hostage by the luck of the draw. Disturbingly, unexplainably, I feel safer outside in this chaos rather than trapped in a potential concrete tomb. I can barely breathe in smoke that has completely engulfed me, blind to anything more than an inch from my face now, and the stark reality strikes me again.

Sara! Gracie! Oh, God! What they must be going through! I need to be there! They need me to be there! Please God, let them be okay.

The thoughts that race through my mind are almost unbearable. The weight of their absence is too heavy to deal with. I must get to my family.

I choke as the black clouds of ash strangle me. My eyes burn, my throat on fire. From out of the impenetrable void, a hand reaches me, grabs tightly, violently. Someone is pulling me. Despite their best efforts, I'm embedded like stone, unmovable, paralyzed. A second hand joins the first. Then I hear her voice.

"Cop, c'mon! Please, it's Kayla!" Her hands hold tightly to my arm. "Please!" She penetrates the veil of smoke, putting us face to face, her expression drenched in tears. "Please come with me."

I stare at her soaked face, stare past her panic into an emptiness of my own dismay. She pulls on me with all her might. "I can't do this without you!"

Her tears may be in free fall, but her voice remains strong. I gaze deep into her green eyes. They had seen too much of life, especially the bad side of it.

"Kayla, stop, I have to go!" I attempt to extract her hand, but it's fused to my arm. But where am I going to go? I'm standing in the middle of chaos.

"Cop, we're going to die if we stay out here!"

"And what makes you think we won't die in there?"

But the air is no longer hospitable, completely toxic. If I can barely breathe, Kayla can't either. We'll both die out here if I continue. I force myself to comply, conceding to this futile and asinine tug of war. She sighs in relief as I follow her, stumbling through the dark and dense canopy to find the door to the clinic. She's undaunted by all the horror around us, pushing forward with near demonic determination. We make it to the entranceway, pouring into the building with the smoke in tow. The room rapidly fills with a gray haze.

My lids feel fused shut, the incessant pain providing the weld. I hear coughing and force my eyes open. They burn as they meet the fresh air—well, at least the recycled AC. We both struggle to fill our lungs, choking in accidental unison, a wheezing, hacking chorus.

"What the hell were you thinking?" Her voice is raspy, barely decipherable from the trauma.

I try to right myself, but it's taking too long to regain my composure. Matt is back by my side. He tries to help me straighten out, giving me a quick, awkward hug. I pat him on the back but quickly pull away. The doc assists Kayla.

"Dude," I say. "I hope you don't mistake all of this as a first date." I can barely get the quip out between gasping breaths.

He smiles and chuckles. "Sorry, you're not my type."

I look up at him and return the smile. First one since this whole menacing experience began. It's funny how even in the direst situations you can find that kind of release. I stand up to check on Kayla. "Thanks, kid." I gently rub her back.

"The next time—" she says, struggling, "I'm leaving your sorry ass out there!"

Even with all the smoke, ash, and the relentless odor of continual burning, she still stinks of vomit. Impressive!

We hear the horrific symphony of explosions continue outside as more planes crash all around us. I can tell the doc is waiting for one to come straight for us. In fact, it's strikingly present on the faces of everyone around me.

"Okay folks," I announce in my feeble attempt to muster control. "We need to hold it together despite all of this and find a way through it."

I see in the doc's eyes that he has something to say. I swiftly move toward him.

"Don't say it," he warns.

I've never been one to allow a bad joke to slide, even in this horror show. "What's up, Doc?"

Dr. Foster gave me the equivalent of the finger in his glare. "We need to talk."

I agree. "Okay, troop, here's what we're going to do." After a quick survey of the room, I direct my attention to our overdressed asshole. "Yo, suit, what's your name?"

"Jackson," he replies sharply. "Jackson Mallory."

"Okay, Jackson, I want you to keep trying the phones, loved ones, friends, police, fire, anyone and everyone."

"No!" Jackson snaps back. "I don't know who you think you are—"

"Jackson, let's not do this. We need to work together and try to figure out this insanity."

He's not buying what I'm selling.

"Bullshit! Listen, hero—"

Before I knew it, I'm in his face. "Now is not the time for a pissing contest!"

Jackson, surprisingly, didn't back down. "Listen, supercop, you have as much use here as Charlie Sheen in a 'just-say-no' PSA, so back the fuck off!"

My blood instantly boils. Should have let Kayla finish off this douche bag. "Fine, if you don't want to help, just sit there and do what you do best, act like a pussy."

It's apparent that Jackson's macho bluff was called, and he quickly and meekly backs off. "We're all going to die, so just knock off the rah-rah, gung-ho bullshit. It doesn't serve any purpose," He groans as he slowly begins his retreat.

I laugh off his half-ass bravado without an answer. Moving toward Jude and his mom, I ask, "Ma'am, what's your name?"

"Tara," she softly replies. "Tara Rayne."

"Okay, Tara, can you try the phone thing for me instead?"

"Okay, it'll keep me busy. Lord knows I need that now, and Jude can help."

"Jude, you good with helping Mom?"

"Got it!" he answers with a smile.

What a resilient kid! So is his mom. If I were his age, I'd be freaking out to no end.

His mom seems to be taking it all in, unlike before, keeping it together and using her focus on Jude to block out the ever-present terror. The building shakes periodically as the frequency of the explosions begins to subside. It must have been a heavy flight schedule for the last hour. If those were the incoming flights, that may be all of them. The later flights obviously won't be arriving any time soon. There certainly won't be any more taking off.

"Kayla, you okay now?"

Kayla sits down again, giving me a haphazard thumbs up. She's still having difficulty breathing.

"Matt, can you come with us?"

"I'd rather stay with the group," he replies. "Make sure everyone is okay. It's kinda my thing."

"Okay, whatever."

Just then I notice how dark the room has become. We must be completely enveloped in the never-ending smoke outside. There's no light coming in, not even that crazy blue hue. As expected, the power had gone out. The TV and all the overhead lighting are dark. I walk over to the wall and try the switch to validate what I already know. Nothing.

"Shit, great, now I'm going to miss Judge Mathis," Kayla coughs out.

We all just stare at her. Misplaced humor seems to be the flavor for the moment. It's not a new concept for me. It's the same defense I used before or after combat, a sure-fire distraction. When you're facing possible annihilation, humor seems to be an effective tool to find sanity in absolute chaos. It provides a brief calm in the midst of the storm. A determined and welcomed denial. We need it here. The pressure of everything is reaching critical mass.

We are all playing a part to get through this. Right now, I play the leader. But my agenda, though hidden from those around me, is clear. I will find my way home, return to Sara and Gracie, no matter what!

I'm just waiting, literally, for the smoke to clear. The anticipation is unbearable, and no amount of delusion will dilute it.

I must get home at any and all costs.

CHAPTER 8

Exodus

(Kayla)

I still laugh but it's just a cover. I have to do something to keep from losing my mind. All those poor people on all those planes. The thought is unbearable. I can't dwell on it any longer or I'll completely crash out. The explosions still ring loudly in the air.

Please, let it stop!

The cop is right, as much as I hate to admit it. Are we safe in this place? I mean, one could hit this building at any minute.

That stupid cop. What the hell was he thinking? Was he just going to leave us here?

My throat is on fire. I try not to cough because of the burning but holding it in only makes it worse. Everyone looks so lost. With the smoke outside so thick, the world falls into darkness in an instant. It entombs us. I look to my left. The doc sits there, weary, running his fingers through his hair. The debutante and her son are huddled up again.

Sickening!

The suit—what's his name, Jackson?—is pacing again. That guy's gotta be on meth or something.

Where's Matt? Is he doing … is he doing what I think he's doing? You have got to be kidding me.

He's praying. Matt's kneeling in front of his chair.

Unbelievable! Where's your God now, dude? Not here! Never was!

Alex stares at me. I can't figure out what he's thinking, but whatever it is, it's intense. Like a statue, he's frozen, processing everything. Hope he's doing better than me.

I never liked cops. They're all corrupt. I got busted for boosting so many times I lost count. But there was this onetime I'll never forget. I got nabbed by the manager in a rinky-dink jewelry store, one of those that sold high-end costume crap. The manager pulled me inside the store's storage room and called the police. After an eternity, this overweight jerk-off arrived to question me.

The pig of all pigs!

So he asked me a few basic questions. I was used to the routine. But then he unexpectedly stopped and smiled at me. The creepiest smile I'd ever seen.

"You know, with your record, you'll definitely be going to juvie," he sneers through yellowed teeth.

I ignored him, keeping my head down.

"You're a real pretty little thing for a tough girl."

He had that tone I'd heard from so many loser boyfriends before. I think they call it a bedroom voice, although that's the one place I hadn't heard it in.

"You know, I can make this all go away."

He bent over and began lightly stroking my hair. I had such beautiful long blonde hair once. It was one of my only redeeming qualities. I loved my hair. It would have made Rapunzel envious. This perv touching it made the situation even worse. I looked up at him from the hard plastic student chair and knew right away what was coming next.

"What do you say, princess?" He winked. "You know what I'm talking about?" He flashed his crooked smile again. That must be what the devil looked like when he smiled. He backed up, never losing eye contact with me, and closed the stockroom door.

"It's up to you. We can do this quick and easy, or you take a trip downtown and sit in the tank all night. Got a lot of rough ones in there tonight, much tougher than you. I would be so much gentler."

He moved up to me, unzipping his pants. A toxic mixture of disgust and hate washed over me. I just sat there, unfazed. He slowly extracted what little manhood he possessed.

Don't think for a second I hadn't been schooled in the ways of true collective bargaining. I'd gotten out of many a tight space through the world's oldest profession. The reality of life: guys need one thing and one thing only. They'll forgo food, shelter, just about anything, to get their rocks off. They'll steal, cheat, fight, and even kill for those few fleeting pleasurable moments. For most, that's all it takes, even less for others. Judging by his size and gruesome good looks, I can see why this guy chose to be a cop. He needed a long nightstick to compensate.

He slid in beside me. I hate his face, with that stupid look, like he has all the power. They all think they're in control. They always think they hold all the cards when the truth is I'm running the game. I'm providing something that he needed but couldn't get anywhere else. His poor wife, if he had one, she's probably *shtupping* the mailman right now just to see what a real dick felt like.

He held it to my face. I looked up at him again. When you do it, you just go dead inside. You leave yourself; find a place in your mind where you can hide for a few minutes if it takes that long. It doesn't have to be a happy place, just any other place but here. It's a frame of mind where you can remain numb and sane at the same time. It took a while to find it, but with all the shit I've been through, I got there fast. I don't even taste it anymore. I used to chew a whole pack of gum afterward, but now my tongue is just dead.

I started, in handcuffs and all. I'm sure that got him off even more. I don't look up to see if he is enjoying it or the anger will overtake me. I just went through the motions. Then he made his fatal mistake. They always had to take it one step too far. He grabbed my hair and pulled hard.

"Suck it, you little bitch!"

Now the emotional mixture before had become lethal. The conflict was hard fought, between control and rage, and rage won the battle. I bit down, hard!

Now you're my bitch!

He flew across the room and smacked the wall. Blood spewed. I saw him screaming but there was no sound. I was lost in the moment, everything moving in slow motion. I tasted the blood, could feel it dripping down my chin. He fell on the floor, flailing around. Blood was everywhere, my crimson stained independence sprayed across each wall.

I had never made a stand before, but that was the moment, the moment I'd caught my limit of shit. That's the mark in history where I became a fighter and never stopped. No one was going to take anything else from me again.

Nobody! Ever!

When the manager ran in, he stopped and puked all over himself and the cop. It was brilliant. I spit out the blood, although I did, for a millisecond, think about swallowing.

Guys always ask you to swallow, right?

I laughed uncontrollably, maniacally.

Who's smiling now, fat boy!

By the time the ambulance and his partner got there, it didn't take them long to put two and two together. To avoid any explanations, I was let go. I didn't even clean myself up; it was a badge of honor. I had no idea how he explained his injuries at the hospital, or to his bosses for that matter. But he knew shit would have hit the fan at light speed if they'd brought me in for questioning. If he left me alone, I wouldn't talk, not with my history. I bet the wifey had some questions of her own. That would have been fucking hilarious to see!

In the end, I scored two gold bracelets that were never found. They were worth about fifty bucks, sold for twenty, so the night wasn't a total loss. When you're me, that's the way you had to look at life.

That was the worst one. I've had other "so-called cops" beat, berate, and remind me that I was just another mistake, one that would never escape the system. The cancer changed that. In the end, I broke free from the system. The cosmic joke was that to do it, I had to contract a deadly disease.

Figures!

So, I don't like cops, and this Alex guy is no exception. He was going to leave us. That is until the sky fell all around him.

I watch the doc and him head to the back together. I follow them, but not too closely. They move down the hall into one of the examining rooms. They haven't seen me. I stand quietly outside the door, eavesdropping.

"I didn't want to talk in front of the others. They've already been through so much already," Doc said. "While you were outside, doing whatever you were doing, I searched the entire building. I can't find any of my staff."

I peek in. Alex has his back to me, and the doc faces him. He looks frustrated. I can hear Alex talking but can't see his face.

"Seriously, Rick, you can't find any of them! Please tell me you're fucking kidding. What the hell could've happened to them?"

"We don't really know anything, Alex. I don't want to speculate. That would just cause a panic."

"What's left of your staff are those piles of God knows what out there!"

His insane statement is followed by total silence that seems to go on forever. The doc finally breaks it with a deep and determined breath. "I know. At first I couldn't tell what they were, but then I searched the piles—"

"Are you crazy?"

"Don't worry, I wore gloves."

"Oh, well, I feel so much better now."

"Listen, most of their clothing wasn't visible because it's so deeply covered by what appears to be their remains. If the power was back up, I could verify it. We have a full lab here. But even without that equipment, there's no doubt they are human remains."

"Any ideas on how it happened?"

"No."

I look down the hall at one of the piles and threw up a little in my mouth. If it's true, was it painful? Did it happen quickly? I mean, we all were out for a while. I can't imagine how awful, what they were feeling, seeing? My God, what a nightmare.

"I'm going to take samples. If and when the power comes back on, I'll be able to run detailed tests."

"When the power comes back on? Are you fucking kidding me! Who is going to bring the power back on, Doc? What do you think is happening out there? What happened in this office has happened a million times over out there. And if so, we don't know if any like us escaped it."

Just as soon as he finishes, the color washes from his face. His voice begins to shake. "I have to go!"

"What?"

"My family is out there, in this nightmare. I've got to get to them."

"You're leaving again? Just like that."

"Yes. If it's clear, I'm heading out." After a moment of silence, the cop adds, "You'll be safe here, but I can't stay."

"You have no idea what's going on out there. How are you even going to make it home?"

"It doesn't matter. My family is out there. They're alone, probably scared to death, and I need to get to them."

"This is madness. We have no idea what we're dealing with, or why it even happened! You can't go out there alone."

"I've seen enough shit in my life that nothing scares me anymore. Nothing."

"Well, this situation might just test that theory, Alex."

Alex has his back to the counter, leaning on it. I still can't see all of Doc Foster.

"I'm going, Rick, and nothing you can say or do will stop me."

I'm distracted by something scratching on the wall. It's faint, but constant. I turn but there's nothing there.

"Look, you stay here, try to figure it out," the cop says. "I've got your number in my cell. I'll keep in contact. As long as you stay here, you'll be alright."

"How can you be so sure?"

"Well, you're a hell of a lot safer in here than out there."

"It seems to me you need to heed your own advice, Alex!"

The scratching has stopped as abruptly as it began. Probably a rat in the walls or the ceiling.

"I'm sorry, Rick, I've gotta go."

Alex turns to walk away, but the doc quickly grabs his shoulder. "Please give me just a little more time."

"No, there's no time left." Alex pulls away, heading for the door. I scurry down the corridor and slip into an open office as Alex exits and swiftly moves down the hall. I wait a few seconds. The doc doesn't leave. I follow Alex.

The scratching sound is back. Now it's all around me, muffled, but definitely there. What the hell?

I look all around, but as quickly as it began, it stops. I breeze through the lobby as I continue to pursue Alex. He's not there. Matt's gone too.

Wait a second. Are they both outside?

I look through the doors. The smoke has cleared considerably. I run past Mom, son, and suit boy, heading out the doors to the parking lot. Matt is talking with Alex. Hell, pleading with Alex. I can't make out what they're saying yet. I dart, hunched down, toward the car they are standing next to. About ten feet away, I stop.

"You can't leave, Alex!"

"You're watching me do just that."

"We need you here!"

Alex opens the trunk, pulling out a shotgun and a small box. He hands them both to Matt. "You ever fired a shotgun before?"

"No, never!"

"Better learn fast then! Here's the ammo. Should be enough." Alex closes the trunk and reaches for the laptop he'd left earlier on the roof. "Thank God it's still here. Here, this has a full battery and Wi-Fi." He hands it to Matt, who struggles to hold on to all the items. "Maybe you can get online, find someone, anyone else."

Alex moves to the front of the car. Matt just stands there like a deer in headlights, holding the shotgun and laptop in his arms. Alex opens the driver's side door and begins to furiously search for something. "It's gotta be here!"

He shuffles through the papers, junk food wrappers, and miscellaneous crap in his car.

"Alex, please…"

"We don't need him," I shout. "Let the little piggy run!"

Alex looks up from his search, glaring at me. Matt stands there, clueless.

"Cops aren't good for anything anyway. Never have been! So go, you fucking jerk, and good luck to ya."

The look in Alex's eyes is nearly indefinable, somewhere between anger and sadness. After a few moments, he returns to his search.

"Kayla, you don't mean that," Matt scolds.

"Hell if I don't. Every cop I ever knew was a corrupt piece of shit. They're all bullies with badges. He's no different. Let him go!"

Alex has found something. It's a small, black, velvet-looking box. A look of relief washes over his face. He empties its contents into his pocket and throws the box back onto the seat. Exciting the car, he slams the door and walks up to me, full stride, and then stops dead.

"You should watch your mouth if you want people to think you're a lady. But then again, I don't think you've ever been one."

I look into his eyes. I've seen that kind of anger before. Every day in the mirror.

"Bite me, pig!"

We stand off for what seems like years. He breaks his stare, shakes his head, then turns away from me.

"Bye, Matt, good luck."

"Alex, please!"

Matt's words fall on deaf ears. Alex leaves the parking lot and makes his way down the street. The world is still silent. Not a bird chirping, no wind blowing. It's suffocatingly quiet, and that ever-present blue glow mocks us all. Matt watches as his hero abandons him, just like his God.

Guy's not great at picking role models, is he!

He sighs deeply and begins to walk back to the clinic. I watch Alex become smaller and smaller in the distance, until I can't make him out at all anymore.

Did that just happen? Did he really leave us? Why am I surprised? Every man I've ever known has let me down. Why should this cop be any different?

I gradually head back toward the doors. Matt and Jackson are arguing. The doc is nowhere to be found. The kid looks out the window while his mom psycho-dials the phone. I enter and my face must say it all. Everyone stops. I've never felt the weight of stares like that before and there's never been a shortage of them. I breeze past them all and down the hall. The doc meets me halfway.

"Kayla, are you alright?"

I look up at him, feeling tears streaming down my face. "Never have been, Doc. Never will be. And now it's a little late to care, don't ya think?"

I move past him, and I can feel him watch me as I walk away. I turn into the last office. It's the doc's. There are photos of his kid and wife on the wall, vacation and school pictures, all that kind of crap. I head toward the desk and collapse into his leather chair. His office is wall-to-wall brown, with wood paneling, and a very rustic-looking desk covered in papers and files. He has a small crystal globe in the far-left corner, and some kind of monolithic-like award on the right. In fact, now that I look around, I notice just how many awards he has among the silver frames housing pictures of him with other doctors and politicians and such.

I lean back, noticing a large bookcase behind me which covers the entire wall. Floor to ceiling, it's filled with technical books and knickknacks of all kinds, all with a medical theme. Still, surrounded by all these memories and accolades, it seems like a very lonely place. I wipe the tears from my eyes; they just won't stop. I'm not crying, just leaking.

I start to run my hand over the top of my head. What is that? Do I feel … stubble? I mean, real stubble.

It was smooth as a baby's bottom this morning. I rub it again.

I can't believe it. Yes, it's stubble.

I've been bald for the last six months thanks to the chemo and radiation. I couldn't buy a strand of hair. My curiosity is interrupted by that damn scratching sound again. It's a little louder this time.

Where is that coming from? For a second, it sounds like it's in the walls, then it's above me. They must have one hell of a major rat problem. The doc enters the room.

"Kayla, it's better this way."

"What?"

"Alex leaving. He needs to do what he needs to do. We don't know what's going on or what we might face out there. This is probably the safest place for now."

Doesn't he hear that noise?

Just then, Jackson burst in. "It's a good thing the wacko is gone. An armed loose cannon is never a good thing."

I glare at him. What a douche!

"You saw how he was acting. He's losing it!"

"As opposed to you, the picture of Zen," I mercilessly scoffed.

"What the hell is that supposed to mean?"

"Uhhh, the pacing, panicking, making me have to kick your ass. Don't you recall any of that?"

Does anyone else hear that damn scratching? Is it getting louder now?

"Jackson, calm down," Doc interjects. "This is definitely doing no good. The two of you need to call a truce."

"Whatever," Jackson snaps back. "What do we do now?"

Doc pauses and looks around. "Do you hear that?"

Thank you! Finally! I thought I was really losing it.

"You mean the scratching sound?" I say.

"Yes, what is that? It's getting louder and louder."

He moves to the wall, leaning his ear against it. "It's coming from inside the walls. Not scratching so much, but it sounds almost like—"

Jackson interrupts with, "Rats?"

"No, but definitely like something is moving in there." Doc continues to patiently listen.

I get up and join him.

"Wait, it's moving down the wall."

I lean in. He's right, it's like something is running up and down the wall.

I watch Jackson step out of the office. "I'm going back to the lobby," he says. Then he stops dead. I keep listening, but I can see the idiot out of the corner of my eye. He's not moving. The sound stops. It's almost silent; only the echo of our own breathing.

"That was absolutely bizarre," Doc says. "We've never had rats in this building. Not even a bug problem." He shakes his head.

I move away from the wall. "Did it sound like rats?"

"What else could it be?"

Douche still hasn't moved.

"Hey, dude, what's up with you?"

"Did you see that?" he whispers, voice and body trembling.

"See what, Jackson?" Doc asks.

"That thing on the wall." Jackson raises his finger, pointing out in front of him.

The doc steps out into the hall, searching in the direction where Jackson has indicated. "I don't see anything."

"I saw it," Jackson continues, fear dripping from his voice. "It moved down the wall. And fast!" He turns to the doc.

I've never seen a whiter shade of pale. The doc moves past him and down to the end of the hall.

Is he fucking crazy? I lunge to grab him. "What are you doing?"

"It's fine, Kayla, there's nothing there. With all the chaos, it probably did stir up some vermin, and I bet they're more frightened than us."

"That was no rat," Jackson calls to him. "Not that big, and rats have four legs, not eight!"

Doc freezes. "What did you say?"

"That wasn't a rat. I've lived in the city all my life. I know a rat when I see one, and that wasn't a rat."

Doc looks back down the hall. "What do you think it was?"

"I don't know, but it wasn't a rat."

"Okay, we've established it's not a fucking rat!" I yell in frustration.

Jackson begins to back up. Suddenly, I feel something fall on my head. I look up; it's some of that white stuff from the ceiling tiles. The tiles move and shake ever so slightly.

"Uh, Doc, what the hell is that?"

Like he has any answers at this point.

Doc glances up, but the tiles are now still. The noise returns, this time louder, coming from all around and above us. "Okay, let's everybody head back to the lobby."

"Best idea I've heard all day!" I say.

Jackson backs up, and the doc follows.

As I leave the room, the noise peaks, then stops again. We all freeze, our eyes locked down in the hall.

"You guys hear that?" Jude calls out from the lobby.

None of us speak. A flurry of white dust falls from above as the ceiling tiles again shake erratically.

"Cool," Jude exclaims. "How are you guys doing that?"

"Which way are they moving, toward the lobby or away?" The fear in Jackson's voice is chilling.

The tiles stop moving again.

"Jude, do not move," Doc commands. "Tara, can you hear me?"

"Yes, Doctor Foster, what it is?"

"You and Jude stay in the lobby. We may have a problem."

"Dear God, what now?" I can hear her grab Jude. "Are you alright?"

"Don't know yet. Just stay calm and very quiet."

When the noise doesn't return, we begin to slowly move toward the lobby.

Jackson jumps back. "Did you fucking see that?"

"You almost gave me a heart attack, you jackass!"

"There, on the wall." He points, almost smacking me in the face.

God, I want to knock him on his ass so bad!

"Where?" Doc scrambles to find what Jackson is pointing at.

"There, at the end of the hall!"

I see it now. It looks like a shadow about a foot long, motionless. I can't make out what it is, it's too dark. Then it moves.

Oh shit, it does have eight legs. Jackson was right, definitely not a rat!

Wait … there's another one moving next to it, then another. We get showered with white powder as the tiles above us break apart.

"Oh, the hell with this." Jackson takes off like a bolt, knocking me down and the doc against the wall.

I land hard on my ass and look up. Shit, there they are. Are they spiders? Fucking huge ass spiders?

Doc attempts to pick me up, but he falls in the process. They swarm all over the back wall. The ones above us climb down the walls to the floor. I scream so loud my throat feels like it's going to explode.

They are all over the floor in seconds, moving fast toward us. I see them clearly now. They're horrific. Black, brown and red eight-legged spider-like creatures covered in slimy scales, with a set of crablike claws protruding from the front. There are long, thin worms or wires on the top of their heads that wiggle and squirm constantly, and they have tails that are more like a scorpion's stinger.

Holy shit!

I've never seen anything like them, not even in my nightmares. I try to get up, but I stumble. Just then, I see Jackson run out the doors.

What a pussy!

I hear them coming; what a terrifying sound. Doc grabs my arm and pulls me down the hall, nearly dragging me. "C'mon, Kayla, get up!"

I turn back. The entire hallway is filled with them. The sound of their movement and their claws snapping together rattle my soul. I pull myself up using Doc's arm as we scrambled to the lobby. They're nearly on top of us now, falling from the hallway ceiling as if someone poured them into the building. They begin stinging and attacking one another as they frantically scurry toward us. Then that odor hits us, foul and chemical. It doesn't take long to ambush us in its vile presence. We make it to the lobby, and Jude and his mom are already outside the door.

What if there are more of these things outside? Oh my God, is this how I'm going to die?

I get to my feet. Doc and I hit the doors and keep running. I don't want to look behind me, but I have to. The lobby is drowning in them. They're everywhere. The interior of the building is completely dark, eclipsed by the sheer volume.

But wait, they're not leaving the building. They stop at the door. Instead, the lobby just keeps filling with them. I hear the stress on the glass from the weight of their press. Within seconds, the glass shatters and sprays everywhere. We're at least thirty feet away and the shrapnel just barely misses us. I hear high pitch screeching as they spill outside. It's a shrill, piercing scream that tears at you from the inside. The walls begin to buckle.

How many can there possibly be? I don't want to find out anymore.

I turn and see the group is trembling, Tara weeps so hard she can barely stand up. Jude is in utter shock. Jackson, hunched over, is barely breathing. Doc is completely mesmerized by what's happening in front of him. The outside steps are covered. The creatures begin to convulse and frantically dart back and forth. More and more pour out as the building can't contain them anymore. They attack each other again, ferociously tearing at and mercilessly stinging each other.

A glimpse into what may be in store for us.

They rip each other to pieces. Black goo spews from each gash, tear, and dismemberment. That awful smell intensifies. My nostrils pulse with a searing agony.

"We gotta move." Doc grabs my arm.

I realize I don't see Matt anymore. Where the hell is he? *Oh, God, they must have got him!*

We retreat as the horde grows in front of us, but they aren't pursuing. Instead, the confused, chaotic cannibalistic carnage continues. Suddenly, I hear a blast from the side. It's deafening. I watch as several of the monsters explode in front of me, black goo spraying everywhere.

Thank God, we are just out of reach.

Another blast and more shatter like glass.

It's Matt. He is shooting them. Guess he did learn fast.

He fires again and again. They burst like water balloons filled with tar. Matt has drawn their attention now. They swarm toward him. He reloads, firing again. Gunsmoke fills the air, combining with that foul stench. It must come from them. I can barely breathe without gagging. A loud boom, another hit. But they don't scatter this time. With each blast, they regroup in greater numbers. Matt retreats while firing at them.

How much ammo does he have left? How much can ever be enough?

Unbelievably, they move as one unit now, with each blast from his barrel having less and less of an effect. A second group moves toward us. I back into a car, then realize there's a liquor store right behind me. Doc and Jackson grab Jude and his mom, heading down the street. I run to the store. It's open.

Finally, a break!

I frantically search. There it is. Vodka, the good stuff. This'll do the trick! I carelessly grab some bottles off the shelves. *What about lighters? Are there any lighters?*

Matt's incessant gunshots echo through the air. I finally find the lighters and grab one. Filling a shopping buggy with bottles, I sweep the shelves clean while busting a bunch on the floor.

Now rags! I need rags!

I run behind the counter and slip in a pile of goop.

I don't even want to think about it!

Undeterred, I get up quickly and find some newspaper. This will have to do.

I gather my goodies and head outside. The entire clinic is engulfed now. It pulses with its freakish second skin. The structure looks alive, an abomination my mind refuses to truly comprehend. Popping open the bottles as quickly as my hands will move, I roll the pages of the newspaper and slip them inside, creating makeshift wicks.

That's when I see it, one of the biggest ones yet, poised to strike on a car's roof in front of me. Another crawls right next to it, then another.

Do they see me? They must!

I freeze. Their tails stick straight up. I know they're ready to attack, and I have nowhere to go. Now there are five. The first launches straight up. I scream. There's a loud pop, like a car backfiring. The thing explodes midair, fragmenting all over the place. Then the others, one by one, are picked off like a shooting gallery.

"Alright, kid," Alex shouts. "Are you going to get these Molotov cocktails going or what?" He picks off another one with his 9mm. "I only got so much ammo!"

Unbelievable! A cop when you actually need one! It really must be the end of the world!

After I rapidly finish my prep work, Alex and I sprint down the parking lot. Matt stops firing, making his escape down the street.

"Light 'em up!" Alex stops, taking cover behind a Buick.

I light one and throw it.

Damn, I missed!

"You're going to have to do a hell of a lot better than that!" Alex blasts a few more as they rush us.

I light another and hurl it hard.

"Good arch!" Alex picks off two more.

This time it lands straight in the center of the swarm, gloriously exploding and lighting up the sky, spraying flames all around.

"Good hit, kid!"

I get ready to light another, but before I can there's a huge explosion. The shockwave knocks us back to our asses. The swarm erupts into flames, engulfing them instantaneously.

"What the fuck did you use?" Alex struggles to his feet, helping me as well.

The fire spreads back to the building, and in moments everything is ablaze.

"Let's go. I don't think we'll need the rest."

"Hell no. I'm taking these with me."

He smiles as I wheel the cart away as fast as I can. The smell from the burning horde is putrid, nearly unbearable. We meet Matt halfway.

"Nice job missy, what's in those things?"

"Everything a growing girl needs!" I can't believe it, we almost bought the farm, and here I am making some lame joke.

"Alex, what a surprise," Matt huffs.

"Yeah, thanks."

"Why did you come back? I thought you were a long way gone."

"I was, but I ran into a snag, and then I heard the gun shots."

"What kinda snag?"

We made it to the overpass of the highway, and I see the rest have stopped, just standing there. Alex points down to the highway below.

"That snag."

I look down. The highway is wall to wall with cars, stopped dead, barely any space between them. It stretches as far as the eye can see. There are numerous accidents, some cars still smoking, while other are burnt out entirely. It's an ominous sight.

"Must have been rush hour when it hit." Alex catches his breath, hunched over with hands on his knees. The scene creates an eerie feeling, everything still, like some horrific photograph. He gulps in some air. "I've been down there already. There's no one left."

His words chill my blood. Now, I'm finding it hard to breathe.

"Same thing we found in the clinic is in most of the cars."

Doc is silent, but I know he knows what Alex is talking about. The rest just can't make sense of it. I've never had the feeling of such absolute fear and unrelenting numbness at the same time.

"I'm going to take the back roads." Alex pushes off the rail and begins to walk away.

"Wait, you're leaving again?" I rush in front of him.

"My family is out there, Kayla. I have to get to them."

"Newsflash, they're dead, everybody's dead! What the hell is wrong with you?"

Alex pauses, eyes becoming fierce. "They're alive. I know they are, and I'm going to find them."

"Alex, think about what you're saying. I mean, look at all this." Doc motions back to the highway. "We may be the only ones left."

Matt joins in. "Alex, we need to stay together, now more than ever!"

"Listen, there's no discussion here. I'm going home, that's final." He begins to walk down the off ramp.

"Are you crazy! There's nothing out there, cop!"

Jackson follows him. "I mean, how far is this family of yours anyway?"

"About fifteen miles south, and now I'm wasting time."

"Fifteen miles! Are you serious? Man, you've really lost it!"

Alex stops again. His stare burns right through Jackson. It's an expression of determination and dedication that I'd never witnessed before. "I'm going to find my family."

"So I guess we're on our own then, huh?" Jackson says, stopping.

"We follow Alex," Matt quickly responds. "I don't think we have any other choice."

"He's right," Doc chimes in. "Alex is both a cop and former soldier. He's our best chance for survival."

"That explains a lot!" Jackson mocks.

Alex pauses, aggressively rubbing his eyes. I can see he doesn't want us tagging along.

Jude steps between the doc and Alex. "Please Mr. Alex, don't leave us again."

Alex just stands there. I can feel his conflict. To tell the truth, I would leave us too. He plops down on the curb, rubbing his head as he surveys all of us. "Fine, but if we're going to do this there are a few rules that everybody follows, without deviation. First, I'm not your savior. I'm not your hero. Second, your survival relies on doing exactly what I say when I say it. This is not a democracy. And finally, we stay together; no one roams alone."

I watch Jackson. If he rolls his eyes any harder, they'll fall right out of his head.

Tara pulls her son in close. "No worries about that."

"We head for the local police station. That's about five miles north. We'll see if we can find guns and equipment."

"Okay, Roger Ramjet, or whoever the hell you think you are. What the hell are we going to do with the guns?"

Jackson is tempting fate again. Will the guy never learn!

"To kill anymore pests we may come in contact with and save your sorry little ass."

"Yeah, and what about food, Mr. NRA?"

"There's a gas station about half a mile away. We'll see if we can find food there."

"Sounds like a solid plan," Doc says, then gently places his hand on Jackson's shoulder.

The rest of the group agrees without hesitation. I say nothing. I just stand there hapless, helpless, scratching my head. The stubble is now soft, almost like peach fuzz. I quickly look around, finding a car side mirror on the ground. Picking it up, I examine the top of my head through the reflection. It's covered in what looks like a fine blond moss.

It's hair! I'm growing hair!

The group begins to move, following Alex. Following a man has never worked out for me. I hope to God this time I break my own streak.

Looking back at the highway, I can only think, this is what alone looks like to its utmost degree. I'd always felt hopeless, bitterness, anger, and vengeance, but this is an entirely new sensation, a whole new level of isolation, and I know it isn't going to get any better.

Looking up at the sky, there are still no birds, no sun, just that strange blue glow. I check my watch. It's only ten a.m. It feels later than that.

Shit, the day's just begun. Isn't that ironic!

CHAPTER 9

A Stark New Reality

(Alex)

How did I end up here?

I had made it to the overpass when I heard the shotgun blasts. I just naturally sprang into action. Old habits die hard.

What the hell were those things?

My head throbs from so many thoughts racing through my mind. The pain of trying to make sense of it all is just too intense. I need to get to Sara and Gracie and that relentless need tears my soul apart. Now I have this motley crew in tow. It's too heavy a burden to carry them too. I'm not equipped to be a leader now.

Why did I go back?

They are strangers, nameless faces that, until today, didn't exist. Why would I sacrifice the time I need to find my family, time I don't have, for them? Too many questions and every answer escapes me. With each step, I feel them calling to me. I incessantly hear Gracie's terrified voice. *"Daddy, where are you?"* It haunts me, repeatedly piercing my heart without relief.

I can feel Sara's tears on my face. In my mind's eye, I see her trying to comfort Gracie, praying they'll be alright. I sense her all around me, see her as if she is standing right in front of me. She's present in my every thought, reaching out to me, but just out of touch. The torment is unbearable. The desire to hold them both is barely containable.

We're back on the street. More cars, dead and cold. I don't dare look inside anymore. The sight of the mounds and masses of putrid sludge is like a waking nightmare.

Did they even see it coming? Was there pain in the process of their demise?

Dear God, why? What type of judgment is this? What level of anger was spawned to have it end this way? Why were we spared?

My pace is steady; the group can barely keep up. I know I should slow down but I don't care. This is my journey, not theirs. I didn't ask to be their savior.

The last time I tried that bit, I lost Boone. He never wanted to join the military, more the Peace Corps type. But we were inseparable, same school, jobs, sometimes girlfriends (he never forgave me for that one). We faced it all together. Whether it was broken bones from falling out of the death trap we called a tree house or that suspension for gluing the principal to the toilet seat in elementary school. We survived high school even with the umpteen fights I dragged him into. We lost most, but we never ran away. That was the very reason we shared more nights in the local holding tank than I cared to remember.

He joined the military with me because I had nowhere else to go. He could have done so much more, been so much more, but because I was enlisting, he had too. For him, there was no other choice. I'd dragged him into so much shit, and he never questioned it, always there for me. I took it for granted. He never did.

His death forced me to finally get my shit straight. It should have happened long before that. Maybe he'd still be alive if I had. Boone was the kind of friend you meet once in a lifetime, if you're lucky.

I visit his grave once a week, talk to him about the job, my cases, Sara, Gracie. I made him godfather to Gracie when she was born.

What better godfather than a guardian angel?

They tell you to let the dead go, that it's the only way to move on. But only his body died that day; his memory is stronger than ever. The dead walk with you. You just have to be brave enough to face them. It's a hard thing because they bring with them all the pain and regret of your own life. But if you ignore it, you die, too. It condemns you to a sort of living death as you become a soulless, animated corpse, existing in an eternity of resentment and emotional decay.

Boone keeps me alive. I know he's still got my back, still trying to set me straight.

God, I miss him so!

We are almost there, this half-ass platoon of mine. They're a ragged bunch, been through so much already, but who knows how much more we still have to face? That chick, Kayla, what is she, seventeen, eighteen, nineteen?

What a hard case!

She gets on my nerves, probably because she's a perfect reflection of me at that age. But she seems to have a better head on her shoulders than I did. Of course, that's based on the fifteen minutes I've known her. She's a fighter, and if I'm right, most of her battles come from inside. If she's truly like me, she'll be her own worst enemy. Stubborn, strong-willed, and too eager to prove that she's anything but who you think she is. I see the pain in her eyes. It's unmistakable.

I know that pain!

Matt's a different case. I can tell something happened to him, something drastic, but I don't know what. I can usually read people fairly quickly, gauge what they're about in a short time. I know he's one of those annoying optimists. But he's a preacher, so it goes with the territory. He seems to be truly concerned about this group. I wonder how he feels about God now that everything he believes has been turned upside down and inside out. At least for me it has been.

Jackson is one of those ivy league bastards who believes life owes him something. Spoiled, entitled and angry because deep down inside he probably realizes that he's the asshole everyone already knew he was. He's a lawyer; I could just say that and it would be enough.

The doc is a rock. I know his story and how he survived to become the man he is. It's just short of an absolute miracle. I don't know if I could have come back from that. That's why he's one of the few men on this planet I truly respect. He's tried his best to make this thing as easy as possible for me. It's an impossible task, but you wouldn't know it by the way he's cared for me.

I got to him too late, ignored too many of the symptoms. Although, that's always been the way I handled things. He didn't sugarcoat it, gave me the straight story. Just another reason why I admire the hell out of him. He explained the treatment options and what the results would be.

No good news to be found there.

The longest conversations we had were figuring out how to tell Sara, so that when the time came, she would be taken care of. I have everything set up now: the will, the funeral arrangements, financing, Gracie's college fund, everything. Everything but balls large enough to tell my wife I'm dying.

There's enough money to cover the bills. She doesn't know about my secret stash—how can she, me being the spender of the family? It was originally set up for the honeymoon I owed Sara. We never had one, thanks to me. She's always wanted to go to Scotland, that's where her family's from. I think she may still have some there. I was going to give her the trip of a lifetime: two weeks in Scotland, then to see all of Europe. I had the works set up; five-star hotels, the finest dining, a new travel wardrobe for her. Gracie would stay with Sara's mom. Oh, how she loves her grandma, even if her grandma doesn't love me.

Anyway, the dream vacation was paid for in full. Even with my prognosis, I couldn't bring myself to cancel it.

She deserves it. She'll need it! And even with the money spent on the trip, she'll have enough to survive.

Shit, I'm crying! Did the others see?

I do a quick take to see if the crew has spotted my tears.

Right now, I need to appear strong. Any weakness would deteriorate their already waning resolve. I swiftly wipe my eyes. There's no time for this.

We're almost there. I can see the gas station. It's empty. We've passed building after building, vehicle after vehicle, with no sign of life or movement. The world has gone absolutely silent. The stoplights still work and change as programmed. Somehow that sums up the whole thing for me. We pass a delivery truck; a dolly full of boxes lies on the ground behind it. I see yet another pile, a uniform mixed within it.

I smell exhaust fumes from the cars that are still running, which tells me the drivers knew something was going on.

There were a lot of accidents, some bad—at least ten to twelve cars on fire from the crashes. Two or three were totally consumed. The only contrast to the ever-present blue glow is the black smoke billowing from the highway. No bodies. The only remains are those vulgar piles. I manage to travel a few hundred feet before I can't take it anymore. They have no odor, as if sanitized, only a horrific blend of colors: black, brown, green, gray and red. The images are forever burned into my mind, as if I hadn't already witnessed enough death and tragedy in my life.

There are very few shops left on this stretch, and a lot of empty buildings where people's hopes and dreams once stood. Most of them lost their livelihood during the recession and closed. Any left simply struggled along. There's a cleaner's, a couple of doctor and lawyer's offices, a real estate agency, and a dojo remaining. This town died long before this freakshow happened.

I can't bring myself to investigate the windows as we pass by. I walk by a day care and I don't want to think about what's inside. Doc looks in a building every now and then. I can tell by his expressions he can't digest what he's seeing.

My pace quickens. Too much thinking. I need a break. There it is, the gas station. Five cars sit at the pumps, and more piles line the concrete. They are never-ending reminders of this stark new reality.

We cautiously walk between them. I hear gasps from the group as we pass each one. Their breathing amplifies how terrified they are. I walk on. My stride must not break. To stop for a second means they'll dwell on what they're witnessing.

"Keep 'em moving," I call to the doc.

I turn to see Tara carrying Jude, his face buried deep in her shoulder. I don't know how she finds the strength. I'm already physically and mentally exhausted. Her face has deep tracks from relentless tears. She looks like she's aged at least twenty years.

I think we all have.

Jackson moves past me into a store. His face is pale and expressionless. Kayla walks up to me. I see the level of fear in her eyes. She's barely managing it.

"Go inside," I command.

She nods. She still reeks of vomit and the black goo those spider creatures spewed on her once-pink velour sweatsuit. I can barely stand it. I gotta find her a change of clothes. She heads into the store.

Doc takes Jude from Tara, flashing me a desperate look.

I know, Doc, I know.

As Tara passes me, I gently take her arm. "You alright?"

"Really?" she quickly responds. "How can you ask that?" She pulls free and heads into the store.

I look out at the town. It's a wasteland. Even the air is dead. I take a deep breath and turn to the store.

They're all frozen in place. Shit, I should have thought this out better. I let them walk right into death's menagerie.

I sprint inside, and everywhere you look there's a hellish pile. The store must have been busy today. I need to get them out of here. The shock is too much. They're shutting down.

There's a small restaurant at the back of the station, one of my favorite dives. Good food, lousy service, cheap prices. I knew they opened at one in the afternoon. According to my watch, which, thank God, is still working, it's ten thirty. I grab the doc and tell him to check out the café to see if it's clear. He's the only one not paralyzed by the horror in front of him. He quickly agrees and scouts the area.

I extract Jude, who's back in his mom's arms. "Okay everyone, look up, and don't look down! We knew we would eventually see this."

Doc calls to me, giving the all clear.

"Let's head to the restaurant back here."

"I can't take it," Tara gasps. "It's just too much!"

She's falling apart, and quickly. I hand Jude to Matt. "Take him, and grab Kayla, too!" I make my way to Tara.

She's weeping uncontrollably. "We're in hell, I know it," she sobs. "We've died and gone to hell!"

I quickly but carefully embrace her. "We're not in hell; the décor is just the same. C'mon girl, get it together, for Jude. We'll go to the restaurant, one step at a time. There's nothing in there, I promise."

"Yeah, right! Death is all around us!"

"I know, but not in the café. I promise!"

"What can you promise?" She looks me straight in the eyes.

"That we're going to make it," I reassure her in the most convincing tone I can muster.

"Make it where?" she asks between sobs. "Where are we going to go?"

I hold her tight, her fear beginning to contaminate even me. "Right now, all I can promise you is that the café is clear!"

She attempts to pull away again, but her resolve has almost completely faded. "Please make it stop! Make it all stop. Make it all go away!"

"I can't, honey. All I can do is get you to the café."

With each word we get closer and closer to our goal. She holds me tight now, a full-on bear hug.

"You have to be strong for Jude. Think about Jude."

"That's who I am thinking about. How I can protect him, help him, when I can't understand any of this."

"That's what parenting is all about. We pretend we know what's going on and that we're in control, just so they can feel safe. Even when we're just as confused and scared as they are, we find a way to bring calm to their storm."

Tara takes a deep breath and pauses. Good, I'm getting through. "How many do you have?" she asks.

"One. A girl, six years old."

"Is she ever scared with a dad like you?" She looks up at me, her gaze so deep it's terrifying.

"No, but I am … constantly."

She laughs.

We enter the café. "We're here; you made it! Let's go lie to your son and tell him everything is going to be okay."

She laughs again. "Thank you, Alex. I don't know how we would make it without you."

Her gratitude is unearned, but I reluctantly accept it. She turns to approach Jude. "The problem is … my son is a lot smarter than me."

"So is my daughter, but somehow it still works, because they still believe in us."

She nods in agreement and then rushes to Jude. They embrace as she whispers into his ear. He looks at me, thanking me with his eyes. Jude holds her tight, gently rubbing her back.

"Okay, let's get some food into these people," Doc says. "You up to it?"

I nod as we head back out into the store. I fill several shopping baskets with food and water. Doc gathers first aid supplies. I head behind the counter, finding a cash register drawer open, and money scattered all over the floor. The clerk must've been ringing up a sale when it happened. I collect a radio and some gum. I see a T-shirt rack in the corner and jump the counter, speeding toward it, then quickly forage through them.

Here's one that might be her size.

I grab some soap and shampoo. Matt walks into the store and snatches up the baskets. I follow him back to the café. Entering the café, he quickly doles out the rations.

Kayla accepts the shirt and toiletries I hand her.

"Head to the bathroom and clean yourself up."

She glares at me.

"Hey, if you want to smell like sour milk and ass the rest of the day, by all means…"

She storms off to the ladies' room.

Jackson helps himself to a pack of cigarettes, puffing away, his hands still shaking.

Jude tears into some chips as Tara begins to make bologna sandwiches.

I'm hungry, but every time I think of food, I'm brutally reminded of those damn piles. No lunch for me today.

Doc has built a makeshift medical kit. Smart thinking.

That's when I notice it. He was wearing a lab coat earlier, but now it's balled up on the table, but it doesn't look empty. He calls out to Matt, but I can't hear what they're saying. He hands

Matt my laptop, whispering to him. I approach as Matt rushes with the computer to a nearby table, quickly finding an outlet and powering it up. Doc's lab coat is stained and saturated with a black liquid.

He finally notices me. "Good, I'm glad you're here," he says. "There's an auto shop in back, right?"

"Yeah."

"Well, it's not ideal, but it'll be out of the view of the group. Meet me there in about five minutes, but make sure the rest stay here." Before I can ask any questions, he picks up the rolled-up coat. It reeks of a chemical-like odor, the smell all too familiar. During the melee earlier, we all got sprayed with that black and sticky tar-like shit.

Doc is out the door in the blink of an eye. I step over to Matt, who is furiously typing on the keyboard, a man on a definite mission. I slide into the seat across from him. He doesn't look up or acknowledge my presence.

"Matt, what's up?"

He looks up for only half a moment but then returns to his work. "Doc asked me to look something up."

"Okay, you wanna fill me in?"

"Not sure how to explain it. He thinks he might know what attacked us back there."

"Oh, really, and how is that?"

"He's having me look up some kind of isopod."

"Did you say isopod?"

"Yes," he replies, feverishly typing away.

"What the hell is that?"

"Here it is."
Matt abruptly ends our conversation by picking up the laptop and travelling toward the mechanics area, leaving me behind, totally confused.

I get up and snag Smokey the Bear by the arm. "You need to keep everyone in here, okay? Don't let anyone come back to the mechanics area." Not until after I learn what's going on.

"Why?"

"Not the time, Jackson, just do it!"

He stares at me scornfully. "Fine!"

"No one in the mechanics area, got it! You guard it like a pit-bull!"

"I said OKAY!"

I see Jude enjoying his sandwich as I proceed toward the garage. Tara flashes me a half smile. "Stay here," I say. "I'll be right back."

"Where are you going?"

"Just give me a minute. Jackson's on watch."

"Are you trying to make me feel better or worse?"

I grin and head into the garage. I enter to see the doc hovering over a steel table. Matt is at his hip, showing him the screen.

"Okay, are you two going to let me in on what's going on?"

I approach them both and freeze. It's abundantly clear what the doc has on the table. Lying on top of his now open lab coat is one of those dead creatures covered in black goo.

"An autopsy of sorts," Doc explains, after noticing my abrupt shock. "And I'll need your assistance."

Matt places the laptop on the table next to the carcass.

"Matt, would you see if you can find any kind of cutting tools?"

"Absolutely!" Matt begins his search with the ghoulish delight of Igor following the commands of Dr. Frankenstein.

"What are you doing, Doc?"

"We need to know what we're up against."

"Are you fucking crazy? You don't even know if it's safe to touch that thing!"

"Don't be silly. I'm wearing gloves."

Matt brings back a hacksaw and a large box knife.

"This is all I could find. The rest of the toolboxes are locked."

"This should work." Doc spreads out the footlong creature and begins to remove each leg. "Rigor mortis has set in, so I have to do it this way to get to the abdomen and thorax." He examines the creature and then stares back at the screen. "It does look close to this, but these appendages aren't right."

Black goo oozes out of each freshly removed limb, the smell nauseating.

"Hand me those dust masks from that counter over there." He motions to Matt. "We better put them on, just to be safe."

Yeah, that'll keep us safe! No problem, but I put one on quickly when Matt divvies them out. It only mildly stifles the scent.

"What is that?" I point to the screen.

"That's an isopod. It's as close a match as I can find to this creature. They do get this big but the way the legs are configured doesn't match. It seems to be more like an arachnid than a crustacean."

"Don't those live in the water, Doc?"

"Obviously not this one." Doc severs the remaining legs. "The appendages seem to match that of a mutated or enlarged Camel Spider. Simply amazing!"

I don't share his enthusiasm, but Matt is completely enthralled by it all.

"It's definitely a hybrid of some kind. The legs measure at least six to seven inches each. They have sharp pincer-like protrusions at the ends that must help them grab, as well as provide propulsion."

With all the legs removed, he begins to cut into the creature. "This first incision is tough, definitely a crustacean-like exoskeleton," he dictates, as if we're his students and he's the professor dispensing his wisdom.

The smell nearly knocks me off my feet. "How do you know that?"

"My son and I used to love to scuba dive. In Aruba and the Caribbean, we liked investigating the coral reefs and document the different species. You know, he always wanted to be a marine biologist. We had a huge aquarium at the house. I spent more money on it than I care to admit."

Doc scratches his temple. "These claws up front don't match either. They're more like pistol shrimp, very large and powerful. Anyway, it would be a bad day to be on the business end of these."

I'm a bit taken aback by his absolute casualness in all this. It's as if he's at some science symposium, literally enjoying the experience.

"Cutting the abdomen and thorax now. Shell is very tough and segmented like a crustacean."

Matt also appears enthralled by the procedure. I'm somewhere between disgusted and totally creeped out. Goo continues to pour out of each incision. The smell fills the garage, assaulting my every sense. My eyes are so dry it hurts to blink, and my nasal cavity burns, as though I've stuffed ghost peppers up each nostril.

"Matt, open that tab right there." Doc points to the screen and Matt complies. "The physiology is wrong. I can't make heads or tails of it. Pardon the pun."

I roll my eyes, thinking, *Really, jokes at a time like this?*

"The organs are somewhat recognizable but foreign in placement. This makes them hard to identify." He looks back at the head. "Look at this. No eyes, none at all. These antennas are wrong too." He moves them around with his fingers. "They're more fibrous than rigid, and there are so many of them. I don't believe this creature can see but rather senses its environment."

He flips it on its side. Goo drips down the table onto the floor. "Its mouth is hidden by this soft flap." He lifts it to expose a horrific round opening with layers and layers of tiny sharp teeth imbedded in its circumference. "This thing doesn't bite, it grinds. It must use its claws to tear prey apart and then inhale the pieces like some nightmarish garbage disposal. Imagine thousands of sharp teeth cutting at rapid speed, like a shredder, reducing its food to particles the size of sand. Very effective."

Okay, I'm officially disturbed.

"What a horrendous way to die, shredded alive by hundreds, thousands of these things swarming all over you. No, these creatures don't behave like isopods or arachnids at all. They attack in numbers, like swarming bees or ants. I believe once they detect a food source, they use their scent to attract the others, like a chemical trail."

"Is that why they stink so bad?" I ask.

I'm ignored.

"There's nothing like this in the natural world. There can't be. And look at this tail." He points to the scorpion-like stinger attached to the back of this mini beast. "This is completely illogical. I don't know if it produces poison. It may be used to trap or tear prey rather than paralyze it."

He moves on to the viscous black liquid. "This black goo is evidently its life force, but it doesn't behave like blood or any bodily fluid I've ever seen. The odor it produces is phosphorus. Apparently, the creature's blood is saturated with it. That explains why the entire horde burst into flames when they came in contact with Kayla's Molotov cocktail. With Matt and you blasting them, spraying their internal fluids all over the horde, they became instantly flammable, like pouring gas on dried kindling. I recognized the odor right away but didn't want to speculate because it just doesn't make sense. Any amount of phosphorus that comes in direct contact with exposed skin should have caused an immediate and dangerous reaction. It's extremely toxic, resulting in nausea, cramping, and drowsiness. It does permanent damage to the heart, liver, and kidneys. Yet none of us have demonstrated the slightest response to its exposure. Not even any sign of the slightest irritation. I know I got sprayed with small amounts of the gunk myself."

Confused, Matt and I just stare.

Doc notices our bewilderment and explains. "Although white phosphorus occurs in nature, and phosphates exist as a crucial energy distributing part of DNA, they do not occur to this extent in any living organism. It would be lethal, yet in this creature, it appears to be a predominant element of its makeup. I can't discern how much exists, but based on the strong odor, it's quite dominant. I can't glean any more information in this setting without the proper equipment. This is one deadly predator. It can't be consumed because it would be toxic. It attacks in unrelenting numbers and has an arsenal of weaponry at its disposal. The black fluid is thick and heavily viscous, indicating to me that there's very little water in its system. For a crustacean, that's entirely implausible. This is an impossible hybrid. It has to be an entirely new species."

Tara bursts into the room. "Doc, you have got to come see this!"

Matt and I shield the creature from her eyes with our bodies.

"I'll be right there," Doc replies. "Let me wash up first."

Tara appears visibly shaken, more so than before.

Doc rips off his gloves and then scrubs his hands vigorously in the sink. As he washes, he completes his dissertation. "We have to consider that whatever attacked us may be a mutation generated by the same occurrence that has killed so many people, although for the mutation to occur that quickly is nothing short of miraculous. And if that is so, what else could be out there?"

Now that's a chilling thought!

He proceeds into the café with Matt and me in tow. Tara stands over Jude, who is happily munching away at his bologna sandwich.

"What is it, Tara?" Doc asks.

"Look." She points to her son.

Jude flashes a smile, bread and meat bits sprawled across his teeth.

"And?" Doc is trying hard to stifle his mild annoyance.

"Look again!"

We all three gave each other a puzzled look.

"That's his third sandwich!"

Doc and I stand there, confused. "And?" we respond in unison.

"He hasn't eaten an entire sandwich in three months. Most of the time food just makes him sick. He also ate four candy bars and an entire bag of chips."

"Don't forget the can of dip and two Pepsis, Mom," Jude mischievously chimes in.

Tara glares at Jude.

Kayla finally exits the bathroom. "I can't get this stupid black crap out of my pants!" She vigorously rubs at a spot with a rag. "Nothing works!" She looks up, catching us all staring at her. "What!" she bellows. "I changed. I can't still stink as bad as I did."

I can't take my eyes off her.

"What already? What are you people starring at?"

"Hair." Matt breaks our collective silence. "Blonde hair!"

He's right. I don't know how it happened, but her hair is growing back, and fast. It's short, but thick. Kayla freezes and then runs back into the ladies' room. "The mirror in here is busted, dammit!"

She runs into the men's room. "Here's one! Oh my God! Hair! My beautiful hair!" She begins to sob and laugh at the same time. "It's back!"

Doc enters, offering comfort to her.

"So what," Jude blurts out after swallowing the remainder of his sandwich. "I have some too."

"What!" Tara swings back around.

Jude removes the hat he was wearing to reveal fine brown stubble on the top of his head.

Tara screams.

"Can I have another sandwich, Mom?"

Doc comes out of the bathroom as Tara feverishly checks Jude's new 'do.

Jude pushes his mom's hand off his head. "C'mon, Mom, I'm still hungry."

Obviously overjoyed, she gets busy making him another sandwich.

I notice Jackson staring out of the window, his face drained of all color.

Oh, shit, what now?

I move quickly to him. "Jackson, what is it?"

"People." His voice is hollow, eyes glazed over.

"What?"

He shakes himself awake. "There are people out there. Look!"

Oh my God, he's right. A group of people were stumbling around outside, some in hospital gowns. "Doc, you better come see this. Looks like we have company," I say as the doc joins us.

"Dear God," Matt says, then sprints out the door.

"Stay here," I instruct Jude and Tara.

"No problem!" Tara's still overwhelmed by her son's unexplained progress.

I dash outside, with Jackson close behind.

CHAPTER 10
Death From Above
(Kayla)

air! I can't believe it! I have hair!

It's short, but oh-so lush and blonde, thick and soft. It tickles my fingers as I run them through it. My tears fall like rain, effortlessly, uncontrollably.

Thank you, God!

It seems like such a simple thing, but I haven't seen or touched normal in a long time. A flood of peace washes over me, even in all this chaos and horror. Then, as quickly as it starts, it ends, and the familiar haunt of loneliness visits me again. This wondrous moment is voided by the hell that surrounds us, engulfing us, and getting worse with every passing second. Looking around, I realize I'm alone. Well, except for Tara and her kid, who are staring out the window.

Wait, didn't Matt say something about others … others outside?

I run to the window. Oh my God! There they are! People! But how?

I sprint outside to join the others. They're all frozen, watching, speechless. Moving past Jackson and Matt, I cautiously approach Alex and the doc. I've never been so happy to see complete strangers.

There are two men and three women, and they look lost and weary. I stand next to Alex, the air stale and still, and whisper, "Who are they?"

He doesn't answer. Like he would know. He's as clueless as the rest of us.

Alex calls out to them, "Hello, are you folks okay?"

The group turns in unison, as if they are connected at the hip.

I feel Matt slide in beside us.

One of the men waves at Alex.

"I'm a cop. We have food and provisions," Alex says.

The man nods, motioning to the others. They acknowledge and follow. It all reminds me of a scene from one of those late-night monster movies I watched as a kid. The group seems completely mindless, just going through the motions, mechanical, like zombies.

Oh, God, I hope that's not the case!

Alex leaves us to meet up with them. The remainder of our little troop stays behind. I run to follow and quickly catch up with Alex. What appears to be their leader meets him halfway.

"What's your name?" Alex questions, reaching out to shake his hand.

"My name's Bob," he quietly replies, shaking Alex's hand. "Bob Regent." He seems friendly enough though utterly confused.

"Where you folks coming from?"

"The hospital, about a mile or so down that way." He points south.

"City Memorial?"

"Yeah. Do you know what the hell is going on here?"

"No, not a clue. In fact, you guys are the first signs of life we've seen all day."

"Same here."

"Really, nobody else?"

Bob shakes his head. The rest of his group finally joins him. "This is Tim, Kat, Cindy, and Marge."

"C'mon, let's head to the café and get you folks something to eat."

The group agrees and begins to head back with Alex. I follow alongside, catching a glimpse of Matt. He's locked on Bob, white as a sheet.

Stopping, I grab Matt's arm. "What's wrong?"

Matt turns to me but says nothing.

"Hey, dude, you're scaring me."

"That man," Matt answers, half dazed. "I know him."

"Okay, and…?"

"I visited with his family yesterday at Memorial," he shakily continues. "They called me to pray with them. The doctors said he wouldn't live through the night."

A shadow flies over me.

What the hell?

"How can that be?" Matt rambles, unfazed. "I saw him. they told me the machines were keeping him alive."

I look up to see what just buzzed me. Nothing, the sky is empty.

The group is almost at the door of the restaurant.

Something swoops down, buzzing the group.

What the hell is that? "Get down!" I scream at them.

Reacting to my shrill call, the thing abruptly ascends into the sky and disappears. But how? There isn't even a damn cloud up there.

Everyone hit the ground. Alex pulls his gun. "What is it, Kayla?"

"How the hell should I know?!"

Before I can say another word, something hits me, sending me to the street … hard. I pull Matt down with me. Whatever it was had smacked right in the back of my skull. I look up again. Nothing.

"Did you see it?" I call to Alex.

"No, it's too fast."

"Well, shit!"

"Run back here. I've got you covered."

Matt pulls me to my feet, but we get slammed again. Matt lands face down this time, and I'm straight on my back, knocking the wind out of me. I still can't see it!

"Alex, did you see it?" Matt cries out.

"No!"

I gather what little breath I can. "Nice cover, dude!"

A high-pitch screech echoes through the air, tearing at my ears and rattling my bones. Then another and another, getting louder each time. The sky is filled with strange, fast-moving shapes. *What are they?* They screech and circle, moving so fast I can't count them.

They're not birds—definitely not birds.

Wait, I've seen something like them before. But that's not possible.

It was at the local aquarium, on a field trip, one of the few class trips I was healthy enough to take. In a large, circular tank, there were dozens of them. Black, gray, brown … I even got to touch one. But those things live in the water. They look like… Could they be?

Yes, yes, they look like stingrays. Oh my God, yes! They look like black stingrays.

One swoops down again, right by my face. God, it stinks too! Smells like something dead and rotten. They're the size of small dogs, circling us. With each revolution they drop lower and lower, like vultures. Suddenly, I hear some loud pops, like random firecrackers. It's Alex!

Great, now he covers us!

But he can't hit them; they're moving too fast. Another descends upon us. I can see underneath it now. It opens to expose eight long spiderlike legs, resembling the bottom of a horseshoe crab. I saw a few of those too, same trip.

It hovers above us. How can it just hover like that? Floating, as if it's lighter than air.

"Don't move," Matt quietly demands.

I can't anyway, frozen in absolute terror. It moves so gently, so effortlessly, just small gusts every time it flaps its wings up and down. Well, I guess they're wings. The stench is unbearable, making me gag.

It drops closer, only inches from my face, its legs spread, exposing a horrific mouth with serrated teeth within its abdomen. But it can't bite me. It can't reach me.

Unless ... oh my God! It's trying to land on me!

A long thin tail unwinds from its back. Where the hell did that come from? Unable to even scream at this point, I close my eyes. I won't watch. Then I hear another loud bang and liquid pours all over my face and neck. It's warm, the odor putrid. The creature falls onto my chest, flapping frantically. I refuse to open my eyes. Matt yells something, but I can't make it out. The creature slides off my chest to my side. I can still feel it wriggling, hearing those terrifying legs clicking open and closed, followed by a whipping sound.

Gun shots continue to ring out as Alex bellows, "Move!"

Matt jerks me up, my eyes still closed. He drags me away, but my legs refuse to move. I'm utterly paralyzed by fear. More gunshots and screams. I feel the speed of our escape increase. Nauseous, on the verge of puking, I'm propelled through the air. I land hard, slide across a cold tile floor, then over something gooey, and finally crash into a wall.

I hear Matt call the others, but I can't understand him. More gunshots echo.

I must be inside. As I slowly open my eyes, something wet drizzles into them. My vision is blurred, assaulted by a crimson haze. I don't dare breathe in or open my mouth. What I can decipher is more hellish screeching, now mixed with human screams. One of my arm's is trapped under me but I'm able to extract it, drenched in something sticky.

Don't think about it, Kayla!

My eyes burn and I rub them on my arm, making it worse. I try to get up, but I'm stuck on the floor. Searching behind me for something to brace against, I push up on a shelf but slip right back down. The screams are louder now, and so is the screeching. I try again to get up, using all my strength, finally making it to my knees. I try to wipe the gunk off my face, but my hands are soaked, so I pull my shirt off and use it. At least I can see now.

Oh God, they're attacking the group!

One of them lands on a woman's head. Its tail instantly wraps around her neck. Seconds later, the creature's body engulfs her face with a horrific crunch. Then its tail impales her neck, blood spewing everywhere. She collapses as it devours what's left of her head.

Is that how they feed? What a horrific way to die.

My fear and disgust are indescribable. There's another body lying headless on the ground, surrounded by blood. Matt tries to pull Jackson inside, but he has a death grip on someone's leg. A screaming girl is suddenly muffled, followed by that horrific crunching.

Jackson screams. Matt wraps his arms around his chest and hoists him in, like a pro wrestler, smashing the asshole against the floor. Wow, that dude is stronger than I would've guessed.

Alex reloads. I try again to get to my feet but slide in the goop. Oh God, I know what this is!

"Tim," Alex screams. "Get down!" He fires again.

Tim is one of the new people. He tries to run to Alex, but it's a futile escape. Two of those things drop on him. One entangles its tail around his legs while the other attaches to his head. He struggles, screaming.

Alex fires again.

The creatures pull Tim back into the street. Several more swarm him. Alex fires one last time, and then click, click, click.

Matt grabs Alex by the arm. "There isn't' anything more you can do." He struggles to pull him inside, but Alex fights him with every step. "It's over. Do you want to die, too?" Matt finally wrestles him into the store.

Oh my God, where is Doc? I search the room frantically with my eyes. No sign of him. Please God, no!

The screams are cut off and I know Tim is gone. The screeching intensified as the flying nightmares begin to slam against the windows of the store.

"Where's the doc?" I scream. "Did they get him too?" My tears mix with the slime on my face, and it burns. "No!" I scream, the sound echoing through the building.

Alex runs into the café as the creatures continue to strike the glass, harder and harder each time. Matt collapses in front of the store counter, bloodied and bruised, trying to catch his breath. Jackson weeps on the floor, face down.

"Kayla, you, okay?" Matt asks, gasping for breath.

"No, where's Doc?"

He coughs. "I don't know."

"He's dead," Jackson sobs. "Dead like the rest!"

"He's in here," Tara calls out. "He's okay. He came in the side door."

Oh, thank you, God!

I finally find my footing and stand up, struggling to keep my balance. I try not to slip again in the goop below me. I stink even worse than before, covered completely in sticky and gross shit. Everything hurts as I head back to the café, even my teeth. I make it through the sludge, past Jackson.

More and more of those things bombard the windows. Hungry bastards. Haven't you had enough yet?

Entering the café, I see Jude cowering under one of the tables, his face soaking wet. Tara is in front of someone sitting at another table. I can't make out who it is.

Alex blows past me, almost knocking me down, bolting to the back of the store. When Tara turns to me, I can see it's the doc leaning forward in his chair, head in hands. He's breathing heavily. A wave of relief crashes over me and I almost fall to my knees.

My eyes are like waterslides as I sprint over to him, hugging his neck tightly. He's cold, motionless. "Doc, you okay?" I ask, barely able to speak between sobs.

No reply. I hug him tighter. Behind me is a sudden loud thud, followed by the ricochet of broken glass.

Tara gasps. "They're breaking in!" Jude is trembling so vigorously that the table shakes.

The danger sharpens my senses and I gather myself quickly. "Doc, get up!"

Still no response, just mumbling, quiet mumbling.

Another thud and the glass fractures even more, creating large spiderweb patterns that sprawl across the window.

"It's not going to take much more," Tara cries out. "What are we going to do now?"

Since the doc is comatose, I sprint back into the store. "Where's Alex?" I call out. I quickly take in the whole room but don't see him.

Jackson's finally on his feet, the window next to him badly splintered. "He's behind the counter," he mutters. He takes a step back, slipping in a puddle. "Shit!"

Matt has his back to me, leaning over the counter. I hear furious movement back there.

"Please God, let there be one," Alex says, flinging open cabinet after cabinet, expelling their contents onto the floor.

"What are you looking for?" I ask.

He ignores me, continuing his relentless search. Matt looks over at me as the whole building shakes.

"They're going to get in and kill us, aren't they?" I scream.

Matt's eyes say it all, void of all hope.

"Got it!" Alex jumps up, holding a large revolver in his hand. He flicks open the chamber and spins it. "It's loaded too! This place has been held up about five times this year alone. I knew the owner would finally break down and buy a gun. Even with this, if they break through, I won't be able to hold them off for long. I only have six shots."

"Maybe the sheer noise will scare them off," Matt replies.

"Hasn't worked so far," Alex retorts.

I hear a chair slide across the floor. "What the hell is that?" I scream.

The three of us run to the café with Jackson in tow. Tara meets us at the entrance.

The door to the mechanics area swings wildly back and forth. Alex and Matt pursue, glass shattering in the front as the sound of screeching fills the building. We quickly shut the large double doors that lead from the café to the store.

"We need to brace it shut," Jackson shouts, leaning all his weight against the doors.

Tara and I grab a table, but it's bolted to the floor. We rapidly switch gears and grab a bunch of chairs, piling them on top of each other, creating a makeshift barricade. We can hear the destructive sounds coming from inside the store. They must be tearing the place apart.

"I gotta find Alex!" I say, then head back to the garage.

Tara and Jackson continue to stack chairs. Another window shatters as the horde rushes in. The doors and chairs begin to shake, and the barricade shifts.

"Shit! Alex!" I bellow as I enter the garage. I bust in on a conversation already in progress.

"You're absolutely bonkers," Alex scolds the doc.

"I think it's their natural defense," Doc frantically explains. "It keeps them from being eaten. I know it sounds crazy, but I think it'll work."

Matt shakes his head in disbelief.

"They attacked Kayla, so your theory can't be right," Alex argues.

"Kayla cleaned herself, that's why," Doc retorts. "We still have the stuff all over us."

I'm totally confused.

"Oh, he's got my vote; let's give it a shot," Matt says. "But how do we do it?"

"Fine!" Alex lunges at the table in front of him and uncovers the creature from the clinic.

Oh my God, they kept one! Who would do that?

Alex grabs the thing, snapping it in half. Black goo sprays all over the table and him. That's the grossest thing I've ever seen, which says a lot considering what I've been through recently. He sprints through the garage to a receiving door that leads back into the store.

"Alex, wait! It's only a theory!" Doc yells.

Alex throws the gun to Matt. "If I don't come back, if this doesn't work, you'll need that." He spreads more of the black goop all over his face and shirt.

"Wait, we can use the Molotov cocktails. We have a cart full," Doc pleads.

"They're outside. You wanna get them, go for it," Alex calls back without missing a step.

He's not coming back! I can feel it! "Alex," I call to him, but it's too late. He's already inside the store. I hear fierce screeching and the movement intensifies. We just stand there.

"They stopped hitting the doors," Tara yells back to us.

Of course they did. They have live bait now. He won't last a second. What a stupid cop, trying to be a hero. Now he's a fucking martyr.

The sounds of chaos rock the store as the walls shake. I hear shelves spill over in the aisles. It's a feeding frenzy.

"If he dies, I'll never forgive you," I scold Doc.

"Neither will I."

The tears come again. There's no use trying to prevent them. The noise is intense, unrelenting. Their screeching penetrates your soul, tearing you apart from the inside out.

"I've gotta go in!" Matt makes a run for the door, but Doc quickly stops him.

"There's nothing you can do but get yourself killed too."

The riot inside the store gradually begins to dissipate.

"I think they're leaving," Jackson says.

"They are," Tara agrees. "And in droves."

I run to the window. They're right! They are bolting. Shooting up into the sky! Is it a retreat?

Doc and Matt are still in the garage. I sprint back. "Where's Matt?" I ask.

"He went in," Doc gasps, frozen in utter disbelief.

"What?!"

There are no sounds of gunfire, and any remaining noise subsides. I can hear movement, but it's slight.

Jackson returns to the garage. "It looks like they all left," he announces. "Wait, where's Matt?"

I point to the receiving doors.

"Are you fucking kidding me?"

We slowly move together toward the doors. The building falls silent except for the sound of our breathing and footsteps. We're only a few feet away. Jackson takes the lead, reaching for the handle. He opens the door and one of the creatures spills into the room. I think I peed myself.

Doc kicks the creature. "It's definitely dead."

Jackson enters the room. I'm right at his shoulder. We peek in, finding the place in utter shambles, as if something exploded inside it. Suddenly, a creature falls on us. Jackson screams, and I jump about ten feet. Now I know I pissed myself, and maybe more. I'm pretty sure Jackson did too.

Jackson grabs his chest. "Shit! Enough already!"

I scrape myself off the wall. "Matt, Alex," I call out. There's no response. I can't see them anywhere. Moving farther into the room, we step over groceries, boxes, and debris. "Do you see them?" I call back to Jackson.

"No, but if one more thing falls on me…"

I walk a few more steps to find the front windows all smashed, shards of glass periodically dropping to the floor.

Jackson snorts. "Damn, these things stink."

I can't disagree with him there.

Then I hit something with my foot, something hard. I look down. Oh shit; it's a foot! Someone's foot!

A small gondola covers the body. I bent down to feel. It's still attached. I tug on it, but there's no movement. "Jackson, I found something."

"What is it, more of those things? I don't want to see it."

"No, I think it's Matt," I snap. "I recognize the shoes. I need your help. There's a shelving unit on top of him and he's not moving."

Jackson made his way to me, stumbling through the mess. He stops above me. "Oh God, no," he gasps.

"Help me lift it!" I grab one end.

Jackson maneuvers around me to the other end, finding a grip. He sighs. "I know this is not going to be pretty."

"Just lift." I prepare myself for the worst.

"On three," Jackson says. "One … two … three!"

We lift it straight up and drop it about a foot away. Matt is buried in boxes and packages of bread and snacks and such. We dig him out slowly, carefully. Jackson gasps as he pulls his hand out, covered in blood.

"Is that yours?"

"No," Jackson replies as he turns three shades of green. "It came from the boxes." He can barely speak. "I can't do this!" He springs up and tries to leave but trips and stumbles, falling to the floor. He catches himself halfway down and then vomits.

Great. One more smell to complete the ambiance of the room.

He gags incessantly, painfully.

I can feel it well up in me too, but I resist, moving to where Matt is to help clear off the boxes. I feel blood. Everything is stained with it. The taste of those bologna sandwiches fills my throat. *Not as good now as they were going down.*

I close my eyes and lift. Matt's head comes up, covered in blood. I don't know if I can hold on.

"You're not going to puke on me, are you?" Matt coughs.

I freeze.

"Please don't. I've had my share of fluids for the day." He turns his head and spits.

I scream with glee and begin to laugh and cry at the same time. "You're all right!"

"I guess," he replies, then spits again. "Oh man, it's in my mouth!" He coughs as he sits up.

"Are you hurt?" I ask as I continue to dig him out.

He shakes himself free of the mess and tries to stand. I give him a hand.

"My ego is. I ran in and slipped on this junk, fell over the gondola and it flipped on top of me."

I try not to laugh.

"You can laugh," he adds with a smile.

"What about all the blood? It's all over the floor."

He sighs, shrugging as he wipes himself off.

"Where's Alex?" I ask, trying not to panic.

"I have no idea. I had my little accident before I even saw him. It's just a good thing the gun didn't go off and shoot myself."

Jackson finally finishes throwing up. "Hey, Matt."

"Jackson, you look like you're doing well." Matt surveys the ruins. "So, they're gone, those creatures?"

"For now, I guess, but where's Alex?"

"I'm right here," Alex calls out, emerging from a small hallway in the corner. "I was in the bathroom, cleaning off my face."

My heart literally leaps in my chest. "What the hell, cowboy. What were you thinking," I scold.

"I wasn't," Alex retorts. "But it worked."

"That's a hell of a chance you took," Jackson replies as he stands, wiping the vomit off the front of his shirt and flicking it away.

"Doc was wrong, though," Alex explains. "The goop from these things doesn't just repel." He holds up what's left of the carcass of the first creature. "If they come in contact with it, it drives them to their deaths! And that ain't a pretty sight."

"What happens to them?" Matt asks, continuing to steady himself. "Mr. Clutz here missed all the action."

"When I ran in the room, I started whipping this thing around." Alex shakes the freakish remains. "When the goop hits them, it burns them at first. Then within a few seconds they started freaking out and slamming against the walls, floors, ceiling, each other, sheer pandemonium."

Matt looks around the room. "That explains all the blood."

"Yeah, when these things hit hard enough, they explode," Alex said.

"Why didn't they explode when they were hitting the windows," I ask.

"That's true, they didn't," Matt adds.

"Who cares," Jackson says, tripping over debris as he moves to the receiving doors. "Let's get out of this room."

"Can you please put that thing down?" I say, pointing at the creature's remains. "I think it's empty."

Alex holds it up and stares at it. "I guess so." He throws it down.

Matt half laughs as he says, "Is it a bad thing that I don't smell it anymore?"

"Don't worry, Kayla makes up for it."

I glare at Alex, but he's right. I reek worse than before.

Jackson is already out of the room. Alex signals for us to follow. We make our way out, trying to avoid twisting and spraining our ankles on all the junk around us. The walls are decorated with winged beasts. What I assume are their innards are now very much sprayed all around, creating eerie green and red Rorschach patterns.

Nasty!

I can't stop staring at Alex as he leaves the room. That idiot risked everything to save us. I mean, he literally ran blindly into that hell without hesitation. Who does that? I mean, if he's so hell bent on finding his family, if he really believes they're still alive, why would he take that kind of risk? What good would he be to them dead? It didn't make sense. Maybe he finally realized they were gone and he wanted to die too.

I leave the room and head through the garage. Doc, Matt, Jackson, and Alex are in a small huddle, arguing.

"So, it didn't just chase them off. It caused their deaths?" Doc asks.

"Just like I said, when they came in contact with it, they went nuts."

"It's possible the toxins in the first creature's fluids could have had an effect on their nervous system," Doc speculates. "But if those fluids are heavily saturated in phosphorus, as I suspect, it shouldn't have had a reaction like that. It doesn't make sense. Of course, neither one of these creatures make sense. They should not exist in this environment. Nothing about them fits into the natural and physical laws that we understand."

"You got that right," Jackson quips.

"If contact with this black goop drives these things insane," Matt says, "then why hasn't it had any effect on us?"

"Who said it hasn't?" Doc replies.

Matt's eyes widen and his mouth drops open, totally taken back by the doc's comment. "What do you mean?" The anxiety in Matt's voice is palatable.

"We have no idea if, or when, it will affect us. This is way beyond any of my understanding. However, I recommend no one else smear it all over their bodies." He turns to Alex, who is still wiping the gunk off his face with paper towels.

Alex smirks. "It worked, didn't it!"

"I don't know if that qualifies you as extremely brave or just mad," Doc says.

"Flip a coin." Alex continues his rigorous wiping. "Listen, Doc, the only thing that scares these things off and wipes them out is this crap. And I don't think we've seen the last of them. I can't protect any of you like this." He throws the saturated towel down, frustration building behind his eyes.

I can relate.

"You guys need to be able to protect yourselves if you're going to come with me. The police station is only about three miles south. It has weapons and provisions. If you're going to survive, I need to arm each of you. They built a kill house behind the station. It's in an open field where the S.W.A.T team does drills. They store their extra gear in our weapon's locker: rifles, body armor, night vision goggles, and such. We'll gather the weapons and ammunition and try to suit everyone in the armor. It's our only choice. We can make it to the station if we use that creatures' fluids to repel those winged bastards. We'll use the Molotov cocktails in the cart if that doesn't work."

"The cart will make too much noise," I say. "Every step will let them know where we are."

"There are backpacks in the store," Doc replies. "I saw a rack of them. Each of us can carry the cocktails in the backpacks."

"Everyone but Jude," Jackson says.

"Jude wears one too, and he'll learn to fire a gun," Alex growls.

His answer shocks us all.

"He's just a kid, you moron," Jackson snaps.

"If he wants to survive, he's gonna have to know what it takes to survive!"

"You're a psycho," Jackson snaps. "I knew you were from the first moment I met you. Arm a kid, so he can shoot himself or one of us, that's freakin' brilliant. I know you're loving this, soldier boy, no rules of engagement, just the Wild West!"

Alex's face turns to stone as he walks up to Jackson, who, once suddenly emboldened, is now cowered in Alex's shadow. "These things don't care if he's a child, and they don't care if you're an asshole. All they want is to kill and eat us. If we don't arm ourselves, protect ourselves, we're all going to die."

I can't believe he hasn't just hauled off and slugged that jerk by now. I know I would have.

They square off. Jackson looks like he's going to hurl again.

"Do you get me, Counselor? If you think you can negotiate with these things, by all means, go for it. Don't let the door hit you in the ass on the way out."

Counselor … I knew it! That guy had lawyer written all over his face. Normally I could smell them from a mile away. Just weasels in suits, looking for the next ambulance to chase. That explained his whole dick complex.

Oh, shit, now it looks like Alex is going to slug him.

Doc steps in. "This is not helping, gentlemen. Everybody take a deep breath. Jackson, under normal circumstances, I would agree with you. To arm Jude is a radical idea, but these are not normal circumstances, and Alex knows what he's doing."

"I never asked any of you to come with me," Alex says, interrupting. "You chose to come. If you want to stay alive, you do exactly what I say, just like I explained before we set out on this little field trip."

"Like we have any choice," Jackson scoffs. "Either follow the psycho or deal with carnivorous shrimp and flying death bats. I think we lose either way."

"Then stay here. If you do, I'm rooting for the carnivorous shrimp and flying death bats." Alex walks away.

Jackson lets out a big sigh of relief. He'll probably need to check his pants too. If those things don't kill him, Alex will. It'll be justifiable, as far as I'm concerned. Jackson remains behind as Alex heads back into the café. His first smart move of the day.

Doc follows Alex, and Matt approaches me. "You alright?" he whispers.

I want to be pissed off at him for asking me. In my experience that whole question reeks of falseness, but with Matt I can tell he's truly concerned about me.

Why? What am I to him?

"Fine," I quickly reply, then pursue the doc out of the room. I leave Matt and enter the café, finding Tara consoling Jude. Poor kid went from one hell to Hell 2.0. Doc and Alex duck into a corner. I quietly approach, staying hidden, getting close enough to hear their conversation.

"That was absolute madness, Alex," Doc whispers. "Why?"

"Because I'm the only one who would or could," Alex replies, speaking through his teeth.

Doc grabs his arm. "You could have died, then what would have become of us? You're not only our best chance of survival, but our only chance."

Alex removes the doc's hand but doesn't release it. "Again, I didn't ask or want you to come. You chose to, and now you want to question the methods I use to protect you."

Doc grimaces under the pressure of Alex's grip. "Have you lost your mind?" He tries to pull free.

"No, but I won't lose my family either." Alex finally releases him. "If you want to follow me, then help me keep these people alive. Stop fighting me. These people trust you more than me. If they see you working against me, we're doomed."

Doc rubs his arm, as Alex shakes his head and turns away. He pauses for what seems like an eternity. "We head for the station. Do you agree?" Alex says.

"Yes," Doc nervously replies.

"Sorry about your arm." He walks away without hesitation.

Matt touches my shoulder, scaring me half to death. I recoil. "What?! Don't do that!"

"Sorry. What's going on?" he whispers.

"The cop is crazy, that's what is going on."

"Have faith in him, Kayla. He's stronger than you think, and so are you."

"I hope so, or this is going to be one short trip."

Doc collapses in a chair, lowering his head into his hands. Matt moves past me to go over to him.

I sit at one of the tables next to them. I'm not ready to die yet!

For the first time in a long time the desire to live is stronger than all the pain, disappointment, and hate. When finally faced with the end of who we are, one realizes how desperately we wish we had more time. Even when life is as much of a fucking Greek tragedy as mine.

CHAPTER 11
Confessions Without a
Chance of Redemption
(Alex)

Where is all this anger coming from?

I would've asked the same questions, had the same concerns as the doc. I'd witnessed the desperation and fear in his eyes. All he needed was reassurance from me, even if it was just a small amount. And I couldn't give him that.

I need to get to my family. They're so far away, all alone, and I have so little time, if any. But what do I do with this group? Whether I like it or not, they are under my care now, my protection. I can't forsake them. I feel like I'm going to implode. Never have I experienced this level of pressure, not even in combat or on the force. It's utterly overwhelming!

I'm a fighter, never flinched in the face of death, not once. I've seen blood fall like rain, fire fill the sky, lighting it up as if it was the dawn of a new day. Heard the screams of my fallen brothers while I watched them succumb to their injuries. I fought through pain and exhaustion just to make it through the next second of combat. Marched on legs made of lead and fire. Pressed on when every bit of strength and resolve had vanished, and sheer will alone drove me forward. Death and failure were never an option. I was the ghost who haunted the battlefield with vengeance. Used fear and fierceness to my advantage as I ransacked the courage of those who stood in my way.

Now, that unrelenting, unyielding soldier was faced with a battle where there could be no victor. A war that would not only take his life but slowly and methodically reduced him to a shadow of his former self.

So I began to pray.

I laid it all out before God, how I desperately needed His intervention. I begged for forgiveness for all my bad decisions. I apologized for every person that I'd hurt in my past, too focused on my own selfish desires and endeavors. I prayed for my precious Gracie. What good could come out of all this? She would grow up without a father. He wouldn't be able to walk her down the aisle on her wedding day. I prayed for Sara. She'd given up so much for me. Now she would be alone. How fair was that?

God has been silent all this time, offering not even a small dose of peace or assurance. Maybe He thought I'd strayed too far, got lost in the ravines and abysses of my own design. I think we build a little personal portion of hell every day, eventually creating the architecture of our own damnation. God is silent, and now, so is the world.

All the doc wanted was a little hope in a hopeless situation. Just as I did. Turning back, I walk toward him. Matt continues his conversation with the doc as I slowly walk over to them. I can barely hear their intense discussion, but their expressions speak volumes. I stop just out of their line of sight and listen.

Matt places his hand on the doc's shoulder. "You alright?" he whispers, the compassion in his voice deep and penetrating.

Doc's only motion is to rub his eyes. Our conversation really took a toll on him. "I hope so," he begins, his voice trembling. "I hope we're all going to be alright." He releases a loud sigh. "I need to know something, more so than ever before."

Matt leans in as the doc looks up at him, his eyes damp and wide. "What is it?"

"Do you still believe in God?"

I put my hand over the left side of my chest, his question piercing my heart.

Matt pauses without losing eye contact. Time seems to stop as we both await his answer. "Yes, without a moment's doubt."

I see the absolute sincerity of his answer and in every nuance on his face.

Doc pauses. Time feels unmoved. "Good ... because right now, I don't know where I am." Tears begin to fall. "Matt, you were there during my darkest hour, when I felt like I didn't have the strength to take one more breath. You were an angel who gave me the comfort and friendship I so desperately needed."

Matt shakes his head.

"I know you're too humble to ever admit it, but you're one of the few people I know who I can attach that trait to and mean it. Doc's voice trembles more and more with each sentence. "You helped me find my faith when I thought I had lost it through all my grief and confusion. I don't know how, but you did. I thank God for that every day, but now I'm more lost than ever."

Matt grabs his shoulders. "I know, Rick, I know. Listen, I don't know why this is all happening, or to what end, but my faith remains unchanged."

Lifting his head, Doc wipes his eyes. "How? Do you really think this is what God intended?" he sobs. "Is this how it's all supposed to end?"

"I don't know?"

"If all this defies everything you've been taught or know, then how can you still have faith?"

Matt pauses again and then cautiously, gently, answers. "Faith, for me, has never been about the outcome or the product. It's always been about how I held onto God in the process. How I handled myself in the journey."

Doc looks as confused as I feel.

"The whole purpose of faith is to trust in God when everything around you tells you not to. To believe when it makes more sense to walk away. What good is faith if I abandon it every time I find myself unable to understand it? My faith is solidified by the love and trust in God no matter what may happen. And although it can be shaken or stretched, it will never be broken."

Doc stands up and attempts to regain his composure. "That makes absolutely no sense at all … and yet, at the same time, is the most comforting idea I've ever heard." He wipes away more tears. "For a moment, when I realized what had happened to all those people, I was angry. Not for why you might think. I realized I'd had the chance to finally be with them and I missed out."

"That's not how you want to leave this earth to be with them," Matt says softly.

"Oh yes, Matt, some days I'm willing to go by whatever means possible, as long as I get the opportunity to be with them again. If it wasn't for my practice, patients, and friends like you, that desire would overtake me. I struggle with it daily, yet it's that faith, the faith you remind me of, that keeps me here. I hope it's all worth it, that I have some purpose far greater than my pain. But no level of spiritual strength or insight could have prepared anyone for what's happened in these last few hours."

He starts to walk away, then turns back to Matt. "And yet, in all this chaos, your faith seems unmoved."

"Oh, no, it's been moved, put through a meat grinder, but I will not, cannot, give up on it. These few hours, and the many more to come, will require me to unconditionally rely on it without faltering."

Doc smiles. "And that's how God used you to find the dawn in my darkness."

Matt stands there, speechless for a moment. "As long as you live by it, so shall I." There's a renewed boldness in his voice and manner.

"We will survive!" Doc concludes, lifting his hand in a wave as he walks back into the café.

Matt sits motionless.

I turn away as memories begin to overwhelm me.

Gracie had been going through her "terrible twos," so my wife had been chasing her around the house all morning. Needless to say, she wasn't in the best of moods. The thought of hours upon hours of pouring through tedious reports hadn't put me in the best of moods either.

I kissed my exasperated wife and wished her the best, knowing I would pay for that later.

A call came in around eleven a.m. It was a light shift day and very few officers were in the building, so Malloy and I were quick to take the assignment.

Malloy had been my partner for three years. He came down from narcotics, where he'd had a slight issue with some of the very drugs he was attempting to get off streets. He'd been clean the entire time we were together, and we built a pretty solid friendship. He was about ten years older than me and working on his fifth marriage, which had also been headed to divorce court.

Malloy had a foul mouth, an impressive gut, and told the worst jokes, yet despite all these eccentricities, he was an excellent detective. He had a real gift for putting the pieces together no matter how convoluted they were. He also knew how to ask the right questions to uncover the truth, something I observed closely and learned from.

Malloy took the address down and we sped to the scene, a possible suicide in one of the wealthier neighborhoods. We arrived in record time, a large two-story, with a wraparound porch and a spacious two-car garage. Several of the boys were already there, marking off the area. Malloy went in first. I followed, noticing a small statue of an angel in the front yard. It caught my eye because it resembled more a cemetery marker than a typical lawn decoration.

Sitting in the living room, slumped over, head in hands, was an African American male, mid-forties, fit and well dressed, button-up shirt, black pants. He was sobbing uncontrollably, his white shirt sleeves stained red. Malloy was already kneeling next to him, asking him questions.

I proceeded deeper into the house, passing a young officer with a notepad. I asked him what had happened.

He didn't mince words. "Wife is upstairs in the tub, wrists slit, blood everywhere. It's a nasty scene." He spoke without making eye contact.

I headed up the elaborate spiral wood staircase. There were crimson droplets on every step of what looked like very expensive oriental carpeting.

Just then, a voice called up to me. "Wait up, Trevor."

Coming up the stairs was Frank, the coroner. I had worked with him numerous times since I'd arrived at the station. He was from my neck of the woods and served two tours in Afghanistan. He was expecting his first child, a boy.

"Some place this cat's got," Frank said. "Some serious scratch, huh?" Frank kept his goody bag close to his side, like a toddler's security blanket. "Kid downstairs tells me it's an apparent suicide. Husband walked in on her. It's their anniversary. He was going to surprise her with a breakfast date. Guess he's the one who got the surprise, huh?"

Frank was not well known for his compassion. His nickname was Cold Cut because of two things, and only one of them had anything to do with his insatiable hunger for deli meats. "Guy's an oncologist," he continued as we approached the bathroom. "No wonder he's loaded."

We arrived at the scene of the crime. *The kid was right. What a mess.*

When we turned the corner into the room, you could immediately see her head, slumped down with long black hair. Frank entered and knelt by the tub, digging into his bag of tricks.

I slowly approached to take in the full scene. Her hands were in her lap. There was no water in the tub, just blood. She'd slit her wrists right below the palm, deep cuts. The blood in the wounds had already coagulated. The blade on the tub lip was covered in dried blood.

Frank methodically placed all his tools neatly next to his bag. He had to be one of the most anal people I'd ever met. I continued to take in the scene.

She was a beautiful woman, in her late thirties, early forties, wearing a yellow summer dress. She had on canary-colored sandals, and there was something in her left hand.

"Remember, don't touch anything," Frank said.

"Got it," I replied.

I bent over and discovered a small, beaded bracelet sticking out of the side of her fist. It looked like one of those baby bracelets. I looked at her face, the pain from her death frozen in her expression. "Looks like she bled out completely."

"We'll see," Frank replied, standing. "Okay, Detective, let me do my thing and I'll let you know my findings."

I shook my head and exited the room, meeting Malloy in the living room.

"Very sad," he began. "Guy came home to take the wife out for their anniversary and found her dead in the tub."

I looked over at the man, who was still sobbing.

"She's been there for a while. He thinks about an hour to an hour and a half. When he found her, he says he just fell to his knees, and leaned on the tub to check her pulse."

"Is that where the blood on his sleeves came from?" I asked.

"Seems so," Malloy confirmed. "Poor bastard. Lost his son and his wife in the same year."

Malloy's comment doesn't register right away. "What?" I asked, after processing his statement.

"Yeah, son died of cancer earlier this year. The husband wanted to try to do something special for his wife to bring back some normalcy to their lives. Looks like he was too late."

"The guy's a cancer doctor?" I asked.

"Yeah, runs the entire cancer wing," Malloy replied.

"Well, Frank is upstairs working with the deceased. You wanna head up there and check on him?"

"Nah, I know you guys are tight, but he creeps me the hell out. I'm going to call a medic to have them check on the doc, make sure he's physically alright." Malloy flipped his notepad closed and headed toward the front door, pulling out his cell. "I hope I can get a signal."

"Hey, was there any note?" I called out.

"No, just a text to the doc," Malloy said, without looking up from his phone. "Basic, really. It just said something like, 'I'm sorry, I just can't go on without him. I love you.'"

I approached the doctor. He was sitting up in the chair; the channels of his tears deeply stained his weary face. He looked up at me and sobbed, "She's the most beautiful woman in the world, isn't she?"

I stopped and just stared at him. *How do I answer that?*

Before I could speak one word, he continued, "More beautiful than when we first met."

He examined his sleeves and rolled them up. "This is all I have left of her now. She was my everything." His words felt like shards of glass tearing at my skin. "She gave me life."

I stopped in front of him.

"How does a man live when the best parts of him are torn away?"

He wasn't making a statement. He was truly searching me for an answer, and I had none. All I could think about was Sara and Grace. I broke the one commandment that every cop should never break. *Thou shalt not empathize.*

"Death hunts its prey without mercy, but I think it takes the most joy in the torment of those it leaves behind," he whispered.

I was frozen, feeling my eyes moisten. My heart started to beat faster and faster.

"How can I go on?"

His question blasted through me like a mortar round. We just stared at each other. There was no answer that could provide any comfort. Suddenly, I felt a hand on my shoulder.

"C'mon, the medic's here. Let them check out the doc," Malloy suggested quietly.

I rose to my feet. All speech had left me.

"Detective, do you have a family?" the doc asked ever so gently.

I struggled to answer and barely squeaked out, "Yes."

He paused, taking a deep, slow breath. "Never, ever forget, without them, you are just a man alone."

"You're not alone, Doc, you're not." It's all I could muster as any kind of condolence.

"We are all alone. No matter how hard we try to escape it, it always finds us," he quickly answered. He turned away from me and finished rolling up his sleeves.

"C'mon, pal." Malloy pulled me away as the medics brushed past us. I back out without taking my eyes off him. Never in my life had I seen such a state of desolation and utter loss. Even compared to Boone's death, this seemed to define all that was tragic.

We left the house, and the ride back to the station was in absolute silence.

"You alright?" Malloy asked as we pulled into the station's lot.

"Fine," I replied, fumbling for my cell. I hit redial, and the phone rang and rang before she answered. "Hey, babe, you want to have lunch?"

There was a pause. "I don't know, Alex. Gracie's being a real pill today."

"I could use that kind of medicine today," I replied.

She could always tell when I was troubled, when something was deeply on my mind. "Okay, I'll get her ready. You alright?" she asked gently.

I couldn't hide anything from her. Never could! "Just been a tough morning, and I need to remember what it's all for."

"Okay, we'll see you in a bit. I love you."

Those three words were never more important to me than at that moment. They were revival.

"Love you too. See you soon."

The conversation ended, and I stared into the sky. I don't remember what I was thinking, but I remember taking the rest of the day off, much to Malloy's chagrin. I left him with the lion's share of the paperwork.

We went to brunch, then the zoo, and home. Gracie had a ball, and I don't think I let go of Sara's hand the entire day. I just needed to feel her nearby. She knew something was up but never asked. We just enjoyed each other without questions.

Not long after, I started checking in on Doc Foster. It started as quick calls and visits to see if he was hanging in there. I'd heard he had a preacher friend who was really helping him out. Soon we became friends. We never spoke of the incident again. It was better that way.

A year later, he left the hospital and started his own clinic.

When I finally realized something was seriously wrong, he was the only one I could trust. He never told Sara. I made him promise, though he kept on me about it.

So many memories. I wake from the past and realize I'm back in the store. Who knows how long I've been walking around aimlessly. Jackson is standing at the counter, staring out the window. I try to reverse course, hoping he won't see me.

"I can smell a cop from a mile away," Jackson mutters with his back still toward me. "I knew you were a cop from the first moment you entered the clinic!"

"Is that so?"

"Yes, that's so. You don't remember me, do you?" he scoffs, still gazing out the window.

"Yes, Counselor, I do. Although it's been a long time."

"I thought you did. You know, you have quite an achievement you may be completely unaware of," he continues. "Do you know what that is?"

"No, why don't you enlighten me."

"You may have done more than you could've ever imagined."

"Are you speaking of the Gazelle Case?" I ask.

"Good memory, Detective Trevor, very good memory."

"It was my first trial."

"It was just one of many for me, all wins until that fateful case. I had the best record as a defense lawyer in the city. Hell, the entire state. I was being courted by every major law firm in the nation, a legend on the fast track. And then there was that damn Gazelle Trial."

He finally turns to face me. "Ellis Gazelle, accused of the murder of two of his best friends over drug money. No weapons found, friends had shady pasts, no witnesses. It was, as far as I was concerned, a home run. No jury in the world could find him guilty beyond a reasonable doubt."

He sat on the counter. "I already had the traditional celebratory bottle of bubbly chilling in my mini fridge at the office and a case of Cubans in the humidor ready to go."

"Sorry to have spoiled your little party there," I interject. "It must really suck for you when the truth trumps your snake oil."

"Pisses me off to no end," he retorts without hesitation. "Truth is subjective, Detective, and it's all in the way you tell the tale to the jury."

"For you, that warped reasoning may make sense, but for most, the truth is just that: the truth!"

"Yes, for the naïve. For years I swore by my way. That is of course until you came into my little playpen. You turned my entire world upside down in a little under ninety minutes. That was the exact length of your testimony, including cross examination." He shakes his head. "You were so very convincing to every one of those imbeciles. They bought every word you were peddling, hook, line, and sinker."

"That's what you missed, Counselor! I wasn't peddling anything. That's *your* M.O. I just told the truth."

Jackson pauses, then sighs. "Yes, you did, but that's never hurt me before." He grabs a pack of cigarettes from behind the counter and a lighter near the register. "Hurt me? Hell, it damn near destroyed me!"

He lit his cigarette. "That case garnered the national spotlight. Gazelle was the son of a senator and said senator made me a promise. If his boy walked, I would never have to worry for anything again." He blows out a huge billow of smoke. "I would have been set for life. Now that's my kind of truth."

He laughs, then hops down off the counter. "But it wasn't meant to be! Your testimony, added with the witness you found, turned my future inside out. How the hell did you pull that off? I mean, my team scoured the city, looked under every rock, and found zilch."

"It's called good police work."

"That, my friend, is an oxymoron!" A wretched and somewhat sorrowful smirk stretches across his gristle chin. "When Gazelle's very rich and powerful dad got through with me, I had zero chance in hell of ever being more than what I was. I promised him the world; he took mine away. All because of you, cop. And you're still playing the hero. Of all the people to survive with, it had to be the bane of my existence." He snarls, smoke drifting from his flaring nostrils, then points his cigarette at me. "I hate you in ways that would make the devil blush!"

"I recognized you after your little spat with Kayla in the clinic," I explain. "I usually never forget a face. I usually have instant and total recall. I guess in your case I wanted to forget."

"I wish I could have forgotten you!" He bit down on his cigarette, nearly cleaving it in two. "After Gazelle turned my reputation to shit, he assured me that every law firm in the United States would consider me as a legal leper. He somehow even managed to get me fired from my regular job." He took another drag, leaning on the counter. "Nobody wanted me. The media eviscerated me, and I was heading to rock bottom fast with anchors tied to my shoes."

He looked down at the floor. "I had nowhere to go, no one to count on, so I had to do the one thing I promised myself I would never do no matter what. I crawled back to evil incarnate, my father."

He pauses again and somehow pulls off a few more drags from the corpse of his cigarette, the wisps of smoke encompassing his head. As he ponders in silence, he puffs to the sequence of thoughts registering in his mind. "He was so happy to see me, so pleased that everything he'd prophesized about me had come to fruition. He always thought I was a loser. He used to say success and I were like oil and water, never mixing. He was almost giddy when I came to him with my tail between my legs, an utter failure."

He continues to stare at the ground, unfazed by his cigarette, all but ash now. "My dad finally got me a public defender's job in another city, advocating for the most atrocious of people." He laughs. "Right up my alley, huh?"

His tone and attitude abruptly change as he flicks his butt to the ground. "I just grinned and bore it. It was a second chance. Sure, it gave my old man all his power back over me, all the control. I was his little Pinocchio, a puppet with too many strings to count."

I find myself beginning to feel a little sympathy for this rat in a suit.

"My dad reveled in his little victory, me getting all the worse cases, defending the absolute dregs of humanity: pushers, pimps, perverts, the whole nine yards. Why I let that man manipulate me throughout all my life, I'll never understand. I guess no matter who you are, where you're from, or how old you are, every kid wants his father's stamp of approval. He played on that relentlessly with me," he says, his voice trembling with emotion. "And I let him. I gave in, like a pussy, every time. You think nearing thirty-five, I'd have used up the daddy syndrome excuses by now."

He wipes his face. "You'd think, right?" There's a small spark of humanity in his eyes, and a whole lot of pain. "Anyway, I took the cases, and I was nothing short of remarkable, as usual." He continues his bitter diatribe. "I destroyed every witness and expert. I used every tool in my bag of tricks, every con and ploy. It was something, really something."

He's fighting it back now, on the verge of a complete meltdown. "They were my greatest performances, and I was absolutely miserable." He coughs. "A few months later, I started peeing blood. I mean, I was having issues down there, but I chalked it up to stress or a possible STD. After I lost my job the first time, I drowned my sorrows in liquor and hookers." He laughs again. "Told you, rock bottom with anchor shoes."

Why is this asshole baring his soul to me?

"When I finally went to see Doc Foster, via a friend's recommendation, it was too late. The cancer was too advanced."

He lit another cigarette. "In fact, I was so sick by the time I started going to the clinic, I had lost about forty pounds and my entire appetite." He inhaled deeply and exhaled with an ever-expanding smile. "I couldn't even look at these things without puking."

He held up his third or fourth cigarette. I've lost count by now.

"You know, at first, I looked at my disease as a very good thing," he continues, undaunted. "It was a final escape from the clutches of my father. I mean, even with all his pull, he couldn't buy off or manipulate death, right? But as it got worse, and the pain medication began to be less and less effective, I found myself unable to cope, and fear and anxiety began to kick my ass. The only thing I had was my hair. I never lost it because I said no to the treatments. Small victory, but at least I'd look good in the casket."

He throws the cigarette down, grabbing a bottle of soda off the floor. Wiping it off, he twists the cap, his eyes almost glazed over. "It's such a fucking small world. This must be my own personal hell." He takes a long swig from his soda and belches. "You never escape your sins, Detective. They just wait for the most inopportune time to return."

He looks back at me and slides down to the floor. "I deserve this disease. My soul had already been devoured, and it was only a matter of time before my body followed. I needed a hell before hell, and still it would not pacify the ton of shit I've done wrong."

He tosses the pack of smokes across the room, and the soda soon follows, then he begins to bitterly weep. "I'm a wretch of a man. That's why I detest you, Trevor. You're everything—at one time—I aspired to be, and nothing that I am now! You're a real hero, and I'm an absolute shit pile."

How do you argue with fact?

"I'm a cowardly kiss ass, money and power whore, who has come to the end of his life only to find out that my very presence on this planet was unnecessary. No, scratch that. My existence made the world a worse place than it already was. Everything I've ever done has been for my own personal gain, nothing deeper. I blamed my father, rationalized that his controlling and manipulating crafted the narcissist I am today. It was one more lie I told myself. I wanted to be who I was, shamelessly, and now there's not a damn thing I can do to reverse it all."

I can't be sure if he's feeling sorry for himself or has had a real breakthrough.

He looks up again. "I'm sorry, Alex. None of us would have made it this far without you. I'm truly grateful. I know it's too little too late, but I needed to say it anyway. Thanks for saving my ass."

He looks back out the window, waiting for something. I had seen that stare before, that expression. It's hopelessness. He built his own cage and now he's looking for a way to hang himself in it. He begins to weep again, this time unable to contain it. He's lost all control. sobbing deeply, harshly.

As harsh as it is, I have no more time for him. I need to speak with the doc. We need to get to the station. Who knows what the hell else is out there, and we need to be ready. The sooner we do, the closer I'll be to home.

Please God, keep my family safe, and let them know I'm coming for them. Please don't be silent this time.

I have no words of comfort for Jackson. I don't think he cares. He's engulfed by his own guilt and shame. I leave him and return to the café. I need to find the doc.

CHAPTER 12

The Station

(Kayla)

Alex walks back into the café, seemingly lost in thought. Doc had brushed by me a few minutes ago, and he'd looked worn out. In fact, all the men are really showing the strain now, no matter how hard they try to hide it.

Meanwhile, Tara appears as though she's found a renewed strength. She transformed from the weepy damsel in distress into supermom. Maybe there's hope for her yet. Meanwhile, her son seems utterly numb to it all, acting as if nothing happened. Just another normal day.

Normal? Will that word ever mean anything again?

Alex and the doc converse in the corner. It looks rather intense. Matt pops back in, looking stunned. I haven't seen Jackson, but I smell cigarette smoke, so I guess he's taking a quick break.

I tried smoking, but it made me sick every time. Alcohol always worked much better at relieving stress. I wish I had a few shots right now. About a dozen might do the trick.

Alex leaves the doc, moving toward the middle of the room. Based on his urgency, it looks like he has something important to say. "Listen up, people. We are moving," he announces.

Is he fucking kidding? Where the hell are we going to go?

"We are no longer safe here," he continues. "My station is only a couple of miles north of here. We'll head there."

"Umm, Mr. Police Dude, how do you expect us to make it there without getting royally reamed by the stingrays from hell out there?" I challenge.

"We all still have some trace of those isopod swarmers on us. For those who don't, we have some left over. Those flying stingray things seem to be put off by it, so we'll use that as a defense."

"That's all you got?" I say in absolute disbelief at his half-ass idea.

"I have enough ammo to fend off another attack, and we'll use the Molotov cocktails to do the rest," he continues, undaunted by my pestering. "We have backpacks for everyone. Each of you will carry three liquor bombs on you."

"Even Jude?" Tara gasps in horror.

"Even Jude," Alex replies, without missing a beat.

"He's just a child!" she protests.

"We've already been through this," Alex says. "He's vulnerable, yes, but he's also proven his drive and determination."

"I won't have it!" Tara says angrily.

"If you want him to live, you will woman up and deal with it," Alex snaps back. His glare could cut through solid steel.

Tara shakes her head, but then Jude chimes in, "It's okay, Mom, I can handle it."

"Absolutely not. I will not allow my child to be endangered like that!"

"He's already in danger, lady. You keep babyin' him, and he'll be in a lot more," I snap, reaching maximum fill with her bullshit.

Jackson enters the room, as charming as ever. He sits down across from me, smugly leaning back in his chair. The smell of cigarettes reaches me in seconds. Normally a mere whiff makes me blow instant chunks, but not today. I wonder why?

"Eat me, Kayla!" Tara snaps back, her anger exposing every age line.

Shit, Mommy Dearest just grew a massive set!

"Enough," Alex says. "You two are acting like children. Tara, he needs to be able to protect himself. So far, everything we've encountered out there wants to kill us. We just watched innocent people get slaughtered, and we were completely helpless. These things don't discriminate. They kill at will."

"What if he hurts himself?" Tara's waterworks begin again, at full irrigation.

"If he doesn't learn to protect himself, he'll get worse than hurt," Alex says, stifling his own frustration. "Think about it, Tara, about all we've been through."

I would not have been as diplomatic. I'd have told her to shut it and deal.

"Can we get on with this?" Jackson arrogantly interjects. "You've made your point. If the chick wants her kid to die, it's America, let her let him die."

Tara jumps out of her chair, lunging for Jackson. Guess she's finally had her fill of him too.

Matt simultaneously jumps in, swiftly grabbing her as Jackson falls backwards in his chair. He hits the floor hard, head bouncing off the tile.

"Enough!" Alex scolds. "Do I have to say it again? I never asked any of you to come with me. I bailed your asses out numerous times when I should have been home by now. You all committed to follow my instructions. If that has changed, I'll be on my way, and you can fend for yourselves."

"I think what Alex is trying to say—" Doc attempts to diffuse, but is quickly thwarted by Alex's righteous indignation.

"No, Doc, I mean exactly what I'm saying. This is not a democracy. My family is all I care about, and they're alone out there facing God knows what while we stand here bickering like fools. This bullshit is keeping me from them. Now, you're either with me or welcome to your new home."

Everyone in the room is stunned into silence. Jackson stands, slamming his chair down. Tara stops struggling with Matt and calmly walks back to the table with Jude.

So much for momma bear's roar.

"What's it going to be, folks?"

Nobody answers.

"I accept your silence as affirmation, so here's how it's going to be. The police station is only two miles north. We can make it in less than thirty minutes. Should they come back, Matt, Doc, and I will use the bombs against those things. The rest of you will follow closely. We'll form a tight squad line and watch each other's backs. I'll lead. Matt will take the rear, and the doc and Jackson will cover the sides. Tara, Jude, and Kayla will stay in the middle, protected by the rest of us."

"I don't need anyone's protection," I snap.

"Yes, we've seen how well you've done for yourself thus far," Jackson snickers.

God, I so want to punch him until my hands and arms hurt.

"We move as one unit. Nobody breaks the line, under any circumstances. Understood?"

"Understood, Mein Furor!" Jackson gives him the infamous salute.

Alex does not look amused, but I don't think Jackson was really joking. "I'll get the cart from outside," Alex says. "Doc, douse anyone who hasn't been slimed by the swarmers so they stink, but good."

I rush over to him. "I don't need a babysitter," I snarl under my breath.

"I never said you did," Alex replies without losing a single step as he proceeds to the side exit door. "You're a fighter, Kayla, there's no doubt in my mind about that, but you're too reactive, and right now I can't afford to take that kind of chance with you."

"Reactive? Bullshit."

"Really? Wasn't it you who almost ripped Jackson's head off at the beginning of this little adventure, or was that some other bitter, bald girl in a puke-covered sweat suit?"

"You're not funny, not at all," I reply, though I can't help but grin.

"You're an amazing woman, Kayla. I want to see you live to see another day."

We stop as he looks into my eyes. It's like he can see straight through to my soul. What little I have left anyway.

"I promise we'll make it out of this!"

No one had ever called me amazing before. Come to think of it, nobody had ever referred to me as a woman. Usually, I get less kind descriptions of the feminine nature. But he's totally sincere, and I find it nearly overwhelming. We stand there silently for what seems like an eternity.

"C'mon, help me get the cocktails, and then go see the doc to kill that clean smell you have now. I'm not used to you smelling normal." He smiles.

We head out the side door, searching the sky. It's bizarrely quiet, but thankfully there are no sign of those things. He continues cautiously, gun drawn, then grabs the cart, pulling it quickly inside.

As he reenters the building, he lets out a loud sigh of relief. "That seemed like it lasted a lifetime!" He wheels the cart back toward the café. "Okay, girl, now go see the doc and then you can help me divvy up your concoctions."

His tone is not patronizing, or fatherly, but spoken as if we're equals. I still think he's crazy to think his family is still alive, but I truly believe that no one else can lead us out of this mess. I snort softly. "I'll see you in a bit, but don't get all comfortable thinking we're buddies or anything. I still think you're a psycho pig."

He smiles. "I wouldn't have thought anything less."

Matt comes our way with Jackson. I can smell them from here. Must have visited the doc already. I walk away, but only slightly, slipping into a corner where I can remain unseen and listen in.

"Make sure everyone has the stink," Alex says.

"Got it," Matt replies.

"You and Jackson will cover the rear. Matt, what happened to the shotgun you had?"

"I dropped it outside during the air attack," he reluctantly admits. "I don't know where."

"Great, now we're a gun down," Jackson blurts out.

"It wouldn't matter much anyway," Alex says. "It's probably out of ammo."

"True," Matt agrees, thankful for the pass.

"Each of you grab three cocktails and put them in your bag."

"I could use one of those for real right now," Jackson says.

"Three each," Alex continues, undaunted. "And make sure you grab a good lighter, one of those long grill kinds. I saw a few in the shop. In fact, grab one for everyone. Make sure they work. Having a defective lighter would be a very bad thing. If we fall under attack again, don't hesitate to use the cocktails. Just light 'em and throw 'em high, away from the group, so none land back in our laps. I'm hoping we nail a few and the rest might be scared off by the light, heat, and noise."

"And if they aren't?" Jackson says.

"Then this will be a very short trip."

"What about the kid?" Jackson asks flippantly.

"Equip him the same, and I'll give him a quick run through."

"You're asking for trouble. You know he'll make a mistake in the heat of panic and probably kill himself or one or all of us."

"Let me worry about that. He'll stay beside me. Kayla and Tara will stay together."

"Good luck prying him from Mommy Dearest," Jackson scoffs.

"I'll handle it," Alex says, sounding exhausted by Jackson's incessant nagging.

"Doc will hang in the middle with the ladies and Jude, and I'll take point. Jude is safest with me."

They all nodded, but I see the doubt thick in Jackson's eyes. Matt is cool, calm, and collected. I mean, really, does anything throw that guy off?

Doc enters the room and approaches the group, as do Tara and Jude. They meet, and Alex explains the plan again.

It only takes a few seconds for Tara to go back into full-on mama bear mode. "This is insane. I won't have it."

Doc attempts to calm her. "It's the only way, Tara."

"We have no choice," Matt throws in.

Tara ignores them all, her head shaking back and forth like Rain Man on meth. "It's not going to happen. He stays with me."

"Mom, I can do this!" Jude protests.

"Absolutely not, you're only a child!" Jude pleads with her again, but it falls on deaf ears. Tara firmly grips Jude's arm, pulling him to her. "We stay together and that's final. My son is not a soldier. He's just a boy, a sick little boy." She starts sobbing.

"I'm not a sick little boy, Mom, not anymore!" He pulls away. "I can do this."

Tara snatches him again, nearly pulling him off his feet. "You will be silent, young man. I'm still your mother. We'll stay here. We have food, water, and time. Eventually someone will come by."

"That's ludicrous, Tara," Doc says. "Think about what you're saying. That really would be a death sentence for you and your son."

"That's my choice, not yours, Rick."

"I can't believe this," Jackson murmurs, sighing. "The woman is a certifiable nutjob."

For the first time, I agree with the bastard.

Alex just walks away. He's done.

"Alex, where are you going?" Doc shouts to him.

He turns around. "That's it. She's not coming. I'm going to get the lighters, and then we move on." He turns away again, returning to the storefront.

Doc looks absolutely stunned. "He can't be serious!"

"I'm with Robocop," Jackson interjects. "This conversation's already dragged on longer than it should have. Good luck, kiddo." Jackson rubs Jude's head. "You're gonna need it. If those things don't kill you, the bubble mom will." He laughs, following Alex into the store.

Again, hate to admit it, but I agree with the douche bag.

"Tara, please," Doc pleads.

Tara shakes her head, dragging Jude away.

I can't take this anymore. I spring out of my corner, storming toward the wicked witch of west. She sees me coming and stops dead in her tracks. "Listen, bitch, I'm not gonna let you get this kid killed."

"Really, and what do you intend to do about it?"

"Kick your sorry overprotective ass from one end of this building to the other." I spin in front of her pretty little painted face.

"Really?"

"Yeah," I reply, grabbing Jude's arm. I swing him to me, aggressively freeing him from his mom's vice grip. "Your move, bitch!"

I can tell she's somewhere between fear and pure hate. Jude cowers behind me.

"Listen to me, little girl—"

Before she can get out the next syllable, I clock her across the jaw. She flies back, landing ass-down on the floor. Doc and Matt run to her aid. Jude remains behind me.

"Stay there, dude, I got this." I take a quick look behind me, seeing a small smile creep across his face.

The guys assist Tara to her feet, her lip bleeding heavily. She breaks free from Matt and the doc, lunging for me, and swiftly meets my fist in the center of her face. Jerking back, I sweep her legs, knocking her back to the floor. She hits again, ass first.

Good thing it is well cushioned.

"Kayla, what the hell are you doing?" Doc cries out.

"Stifle it, Doc. This is between us girls."

I step back, with Jude still behind me. He must be really pissed to watch his mom take a beating and not even flinch. But I've been there; abused, used, and no one to take a stand for me. My screams and tears fell on silent ears, pain unchallenged and unnoticed. I'd been raped, molested, tortured, and locked up so many times that I lost count. There was no knight in white shining armor to ride in and save me. No superhero to swoop down in the nick of time. No divine intervention. There was no one to step up ... not cops, counselors, psychologists, foster parents, or guardians.

Today is the day it stops!

Tara quickly regains her footing, taking a full swing. I nail her under the arm and then the gut. Two more hits to her sweet fat cheeks and she's back on the floor.

I don't fight like a girl. I fight dirty. That was how I learned, and I learned it fast. I had to. No hair pulling for me, but I will punch your appendix out. Before, I was never strong enough. Today, I am.

Doc and Matt run toward me.

"Back off, boys, or you'll get the same."

My words must carry some weight because they stop. Tara stumbles to her feet again. She can barely keep her balance.

Let me help you with that.

Three more rapid rabbit punches send her back down. I don't think she'll be getting up again. Madison Avenue meets the ghetto warrior. All my pent-up rage unleashed. I know she has to be hating life right now. I'm right, she stays down. Her nose is running blood like a broken faucet.

Jude breaks away. "Mom!" I guess he's finally seen enough. "Please, Kayla, stop," he screams.

A little late, kid, but I was done anyway.

Tara grabs hold of him. I don't know if she knows where she is. Matt and Doc are frozen.

Here comes Alex and Jackson. They must have heard the commotion. "What the hell?" Jackson blurts out.

Alex just glares at me.

"We just had a little talk, and Tara has agreed to come with us, without resistance. Isn't that right, Tara?"

Tara looks up, face bloodied and bruised. "Yes," she mumbles.

"Sometimes it takes a woman's touch," I explain to Alex, and walk away. "Now where the hell are those backpacks and lighters so we can continue this happy family field trip?"

"I've got them," Alex replies coldly.

Matt and the doc help Tara up again. She can barely stand.

Alex continues his visual lock on me. "We move out in five minutes. Clean her up and let's get ready." He walks over to me, never losing eye contact. "No more, Kayla. Save it for them." He points outside.

I nod. "No worries, just girl talk that got a little intense."

Surprisingly, he didn't find me funny.

"Jackson, get them ready," Alex says, without breaking eye contact with me. "The kid too. Kayla, you stay with Tara, and make sure you cover her ass."

"That's a lot to cover, sir," I retort, smiling ear to ear.

"I hope you're proud of yourself. You finally stooped to their level." His sharp gaze pierces me.

"Who?"

"Everyone who's ever did that to you," he replies.

His words cut me deep and hard. He stares for a moment more and then turns. "We stick to the plan. The station is three miles away. We make it there, we might stand a chance. Gather some food and water in the other packs. Doc, it's time."

I'm still paralyzed by Alex's comment. Tara looks at me; tears and blood filling her eyes. She stares for only a second, but it feels like an eternity.

Matt breaks the silence and helps her toward the door. "You're taking over in a couple of minutes," he calls to me.

Jude looks up at me. "I shouldn't have let you do that," he whispers. I see the guilt well up in his face. "She's my mom. She's seen so much, been through so much. She just can't let go of me," he says sorrowfully. "I was wrong. She loves me." He walks away, returning to his mom's side.

Thanks, kid, for nothing! Oh, by the way, you're welcome for just saving your life.

Alex returns, pushing a pack into me. Jackson hands out the rest.

"She's your responsibility. Where you go, she goes," Alex says sharply. "Her life is in your hands. Before I can argue, he silences me with one more hard stare.

"Okay, people, no fear, no hesitation. We move as one unit, and we watch out for each other. Lose focus for one second and you'll have none left. Jude, you're with me."

Jude slings his pack over his shoulder. He looks back at me. I've seen that look of disgust before. Usually, it's mine directed at others. I head over to Tara. Matt smears what's left of the bug juice on her, then hands a rag with it to Alex to apply to Jude.

I sneer as I look at Tara. "Okay, I guess you're with me."

"I don't know who I hate more right now, them or you," she replies, never looking at me. Her face is beginning to swell.

"Neither do I," I reply. "Let's make the best of it."

She reluctantly places her arm around me, leaning in. "At least I know you can handle yourself," she says, still looking away.

"Yeah, I guess so."

Alex takes the lead, barking, "Follow me, and don't break the line!"

All at once, I feel the anticipation of walking back outside. We all reek of bug slime. Not one of us has any idea what will be out there, and yet that's where we're headed. I can taste the fear. Tara's grip gets a little tighter. Apparently, I'm not the only one.

"Let's go," Alex says.

We move out, each step bringing me closer to the door, my heart feeling heavier. I watch each one leave until we reach the glass doors. I pause. Tara turns to me, cheek black and blue, eye inflated like a handball. I take a deep breath. She does too. I step outside. It feels like I'm stepping into a pool filled with sharks.

Everything is still that eerie blue. The sky is clear, still no sun or clouds. The air is still, neither cold nor warm.

Once fully outside, I feel naked, exposed, gradually assaulted by fear. We press on and follow the group. The tension is so thick it's nearly visible. We walk slowly down the street, stepping over body after body.

I won't look down. I can't!

We move away from the store and café. Everything is so painfully silent, yet eerily peaceful. For the first time in my life the idea of peace terrifies me. We walk on, the store shrinking in the distance. No one speaks, but I hear each one of them breathing, the only sound that exists for the moment.

The store is now a distant memory, each step feeling like an eternity. The sky is empty. But for how long?

Alex looks back. Our eyes meet and I feel a sudden rush of strength. Tara begins to walk on her own. Jude looks back at her and she blows him a kiss from her fattened lips.

We pass building after building, no movement, no sound. We're completely alone again. The world is dead; the blue surrounding us is the color of the cold corpse it had become. We're maggots just trying to survive, living off the remains.

What a wonderful thought!

What the hell are we surviving for? What hope can possibly exist in an open tomb? What are we working so hard to live for? Is it just to prolong the inevitable?

CHAPTER 13

Heroes and Martyrs

(Alex)

All I could think about is her.

I'm haunted by visions of Sara's face as she holds Gracie tightly, huddled in some small corner of the house. I'd spent Gracie's childhood telling her time and time again there were no such things as monsters. Every night I checked her room, under the bed, and in the closet to ensure all was well. I lost count of how many nights I followed the same routine to calm her fears. She trusted me with all her little heart. Now I know I lied to her, and to myself.

There are real monsters!

But these things struck without warning, appeared without notice. I had spent the last five years putting away the dregs of humanity, those who corrupted society and burdened us all with the waste of their existence. Fear was never an issue. My drive overshadowed every hesitation. I was a juggernaut from the gate.

In Afghanistan, I watched a father shoot his own son in the head after finding out he gave aid to a fallen solider. I saw daughters left in the streets for dead after being beaten in the name of an honor killing. So many times, I could have ended those maniacs' sorry lives. With a single bullet I could have made the world a better place. But I resisted, not because of protocol or fear of reprisal, but to prove who the mindless animals really were.

When we had several of our guys abuse prisoners, I held them to the same level of retribution as our enemy. You wanted to act like an animal, I would cage and muzzle you like one, no matter where you were from or what cause you subscribed to. The time I spent corralling those abominations prepared me for our own homegrown brand of mutants. I never crossed the line or broke the rules. I could have, but the only possession we truly own in this world is our integrity, and mine was never up for sale.

I've given my word to try to keep these people safe, but how can I in this utter chaos? How can anyone?

The longer they are with me, the greater chance of the unthinkable. The longer I'm with them, the farther away I am from reaching my family. They are an albatross around my neck, an anchor dragging along the sea floor. My family is waiting in horror without me.

Do they even know I'm still alive? How can they?

Please, God, be with them! I know I don't deserve your ear, but please, whatever you need to take from me, take, and keep them safe. Let me get there in time. Please!

This walk is endless. The station is getting closer, but time seems to have stopped. The world is cold and dead, a cemetery in the middle of winter. We're buried in fear and ignorance, entombed in hopelessness. The sky remains quiet, empty like an open grave.

I look back and see fear on their faces, in their eyes. The anticipation is relentless. Jude walks beside me, so close air barely passes between us. I'm afraid I'll trip over him. I don't know how he did it, found the courage to continue. He's a trooper, one brave kid. I know all too well, when someone faces death every day, they quickly become numb to it. Each day he opens his eyes is another twenty-four hours of borrowed time. Add to all of that, he's now forced to watch his mom suffer silently, knowing how scared she must be too.

What about this kid's dad? Is he absent?

I haven't heard him mention him once. Maybe he skipped out. Maybe he never met him. Who knows? This kid has more strength than most of the men I know.

Tara is a good mom, holding on to what little hope there is. Yes, she's overprotective, because time is not on her side. There's no guarantee of tomorrow for her, only today, this moment. Each second is precious. I can't imagine what she's going through.

If Gracie ever got sick like this, it would destroy me.

Sara has always been the stronger one. I admire the hell out of her for that. Everything she does, she does with such will and determination. I'm in awe of it. She amazes me daily.

God, I love her so much! Maybe I need her more than she needs me. Either way, I need to get to her.

We've walked a couple of miles, and all is well. No more bodies in the street, just empty cars and quiet buildings. The silence is deafening. Then I see it, off in the distance, but the shape is unmistakable.

Is it by itself? It's hovering, flying in slow, methodical circles. The group hasn't noticed yet.

Good.

I glance around, looking for shelter. There's a real estate office ahead of me, and that's it. We've hit an empty stretch of road. The exit to the interstate is to my left. We're about to walk over the highway.

Wait, is that another one? Shit, now there are two!

They're hovering like a couple of buzzards over a fresh kill. I can't see what's below them yet. The group is still unaware of their presence. I slowly unsnap my holster while flipping my backpack around to the front. I unzip the bag and forage out the lighter from my pocket. Placing the lighter in my mouth, I allow the pack to hang open over my shoulder.

Jude senses something and looks up at me. I flash him a quick wink.

Now there are three!

Jude sees them too. He opens his mouth to scream, but I cover it quickly, shaking my head. We continue walking without missing a step.

Now there are four. Have they seen us yet? No, not yet.

I hear Tara gasp and turn around. She's stopped dead in her tracks. She sees them too. Kayla stops with her. The whole line comes to a screeching halt, everyone almost tripping over each other.

I quickly take my hand from Jude's mouth and draw the revolver. Matt's eyes widen. Everything is moving in slow motion. Jackson drops to his knees, scrambling to open his pack. Doc moves toward Tara and Kayla. Kayla glances up at me, her eyes filled with terror. I look back up, and find the creatures gone.

Dammit, where the hell did they go?

I desperately search above, seeing nothing. Tara is frozen, her sight locked on something in front of us, not above. Doc is staring in the same direction, breathless.

Oh God, what now?

I move to them, still searching the sky, pulling Jude along with me. Jackson has a cocktail in one hand and the lighter in the other, ready to go. I motion to him to hold, but he probably has no idea what it means. Like flashing baseball signals during a soccer match.

Matt seems to have got it and grabs Jackson by the shoulder. I see his lips moving but can't hear him. Jackson is listening intently, though. He seems to be relaxing his stance. I make it to the doc and Tara. The sky is still empty.

Jude hugs his mom. "Mom, you okay?"

She appears speechless, slowly raising her trembling hand, pointing in front of us to the west.

Kayla gasps and covers her mouth.

Shit, what the hell is that?

About twenty yards ahead of us, foraging around some stopped vehicles, are three large gray behemoths that look like headless rhinos. Their skin is covered in thick, grayish-green scales. They have six elephant-like legs, ending with three long, sharp talons for feet the diameter of an SUV tire. Slowly swaying behind them are six-foot-long tails ending with large, spiked balls like scale-covered maces. No heads visible at all, just humongous torsos and rears. Where the skull should be are several antenna-like luminous protrusions that jut out from the front. As they slowly trudge around, these mutant antennae move erratically, touching everything in their path as they change color in a myriad of luminous hues.

They haven't noticed us. Yet.

One unexpectedly stops above a pile of human remains on the ground next to an open car door. It positions its center over the pile as its belly opens and spreads out. The creature descends upon the pile with a horrific slurping sound that echoes down the street. It lifts and closes its belly. I see something happening on the inside, some sort of movement.

Oh my God, is it chewing?

It shakes and then excretes a yellow substance from its hindquarters. As it impacts the ground, steam rises, a vile stench hitting us right away.

Well, that just topped the list of the worst things I've smelled today, which is impressive considering. The odor is a cross between rotten vinegar and burning tires. They continue to search around the cars, their antennae sweeping every inch with precision. I motion to the group to stand their ground, eyeing that real estate office again. If we move slowly and quietly enough, we might be able to make it.

I whisper to the doc, "Take the ladies to that building and head in. I'll cover you from here."

Doc nods and takes Tara by the hand. Jude sticks close to her side.

Kayla whispers to me, "That little pistol isn't going to have much effect on Jumbo over there."

I don't bother to answer.

Jackson moves toward me with Matt in tow.

"Go, Kayla, go with Doc," I whisper.

"You ain't gotta tell me twice," she whispers back. She slowly heads to meet them.

Jackson reaches me, still holding his cocktail. The herd still hasn't noticed us.

Cautiously, Matt approaches. "What are we doing?" he asks softly.

I reach into the bag and pull out a cocktail.

"I don't think these are going to have the effect we'd like," Jackson whispers.

The herd begins to move away from the cars, trudging northward.

"Oh no," Matt gasps, looking up.

I glance up quickly, only to view several of the winged menaces high up in the air, hovering over us.

"Shit!" Jackson sees them too. "We're so boned!"

"Behind us," Matt says.

There's a duo of the rhino-like creatures moving our way.

"The station is a mile north," I whisper.

"And...?" Jackson replies, straining to keep his voice quiet.

"If I can get there, I can get some substantial firepower."

"You'll never make it without getting noticed," Matt says.

The second two rhinos stop around another mass of derelict cars. The first group keeps moving. The flying menaces continue their slow hover. There are six, maybe seven now. I see Kayla, Doc, Tara, and Jude; they've stopped.

Why?

Then I see it, two more rhinos emerging from the side of the building, feeling their way around. The four slowly retreat back toward us, walking together in a tight huddle.

Shit!

"We've got to move forward, toward the police station," I whisper. "It's our only hope."

Jackson shakes his head with such force I think it's about to pop off.

"Why aren't they attacking?" Matt asks, continuing to stare up into the sky.

"It has to be the smell of the bug juice cologne we're wearing," Jackson replies.

"Or they're just biding time," I say.

Doc and his entourage finally reach us. The two rhinos by the building meet up with the other three behind us.

"They're getting closer," Tara gasps.

"We have to move," I instruct. "Now! Tara, Jude, and Kayla stay in the center. We'll move as one unit. We form a tight circle, like the Romans used to do. We move slowly and cautiously."

"What the hell do they have to do with anything?" Jackson scoffs.

I ignore him and continue. "If one comes too close, we nail it with a cocktail and bolt." Hopefully they're as slow as they are large.

We form a tight circle around the ladies and Jude, beginning to move ever so slowly north. The herd behind us has stopped. They sense something. The ones in front have moved out of our view.

"Why have they stopped?" Tara whispers.

"Just keep moving." I say. I feel her trembling next to me. "We can make it. Just stay together." I must keep them focused!

The rhinos' antennas all reach toward the sky. They must sense the flying menaces. Now there are about ten of them. My shirt is drenched in sweat, but I can't show them any anxiety. I must continue the fragile illusion that I've got things under control. We're making up ground, but it's too slow.

One of the rhinos stands upright on its hind legs like a grizzly. I see its undercarriage. It opens wide, revealing rows and rows of shark-like teeth. It swells up and then bellows loudly from its body. The sound shakes the ground and buildings.

Tara quickly covers her ears and tries not to scream.

It bellows again, louder this time, almost knocking us off our feet. The others stand up and follow suit. We're drowning in the vibrations. The other two from the front emerge and head our way, antennas moving wildly.

The horrific chorus continues, and I grab Matt's arm. "No matter what, keep them moving."

I again remove my pistol from the holster, releasing the safety. I see the station off in the distance. It's still a good bit away. All five rhinos are now on their hind legs, creating an aria from hell.

"It's for them," Kayla announces, her voice nearly muted by the oratory.

"What?" I call back.

"The bat things," she replies.

I shake my head, barely able to hear her.

"They must be trying to scare off the bat things."

She's right. The louder they get, the higher the flying menaces ascend. The rhinos still aren't aware of us. It's the perfect distraction.

"Move faster," I bark. "But stay together."

We glide past the other two rhinos with only about ten yards between us, passing a large group of abandoned cars. The station keeps getting closer, and our chances are steadily getting better. The demonic chorus continues, my ears feeling like they're about to bleed.

Then the awful sound is swiftly interrupted by an even more horrific piercing screech. I quickly look up to see a flying menace descending fast.

Looks like the rhino's scare tactic is an epic fail!

All ten swoop down, dropping rapidly in a death dive. I spin around and unload the revolver into the center of them. The group grinds to a halt. I hit several and they drop to the ground. The rest buzz us. One smacks Matt in the head. He too drops to the ground. Tara screams. I see Jackson toss two lit cocktails into the air.

"Everybody down," I scream.

The cocktails explode in the mist of the creatures, spewing flames and raining glass everywhere.

"Close your eyes, Jude," Doc yells.

We all hit the ground. I kneel over the group and realize I have no more ammo. Two more cocktails fly over my head.

Shit! The blast is too close and I feel the heat.

"I need more," Jackson calls out.

"Here's mine." Matt tosses him his pack.

I smell smoke. Shit, my pack's on fire! I throw it away from the group and it explodes, blinding me for a split second. The ground rumbles.

Oh my God, with all the focus on the air, we forgot about the rhinos. There's so much smoke that I can't see them. A flying creature slams to the ground next to me, spraying me with its fluids.

"Matt, where are you?" I scream.

The trembling gets stronger. I hear them coming. But how many? Then Matt trips over me. "Shit, Matt, where's your pack?"

"Jackson's got it," he replies, out of breath.

Another cocktail flies over my head, exploding only a few feet away.

"Dammit, Jackson, you're gonna kill us before you hit any of them," I shout back at him. But I can't see him.

"They're coming," Matt screams. He points to the east. I make out the large gray shapes of five beasts rushing toward us.

"Matt, get them the hell out of here, now!" I push him away, standing. "Everybody run!"

I see only Matt, and now the doc. I grab the doc, spinning him around.

"What the hell?" he screams.

I strip the pack off his back and run toward the charging monsters.

"What are you doing?"

"Get them to the station, now! You know where it is. Don't think, just do it!"

I run forward through the clearing smoke. The rhinos are only feet away, hurdling at full speed toward us. I can barely keep my footing as the ground bounces beneath my feet. It's like trying to balance on a sponge.

I stop.

"Throw it," Jackson screams.

"Go, Jackson, run to the station!"

"Throw it, you asshole!"

I light the pack.

"Throw it!"

Wait for it…

Wait for it…

Wait for it…

I throw the pack in front of the lead rhino, and it explodes. The concussive wave knocks me back, sending me onto my ass. The rhino stumbles, flipping over and rolling toward me at full speed, flames wrapped around its torso. I can't get to my feet in time, covering up as the rhino launches over me. I feel its rough, scaly skin brush against my arms as it passes overhead. It lands only a few feet away and continues to tumble.

The others stop. They appear to be either disoriented or frightened. Their antennas are flailing around wildly. The lead rhino rolls into a car, crushing it like an empty soda can. I get up quickly, reviewing my surroundings. I see the group sprinting northward toward the station. The sky is empty again, but the ground is littered with burning winged corpses. My ears ring ferociously. Jackson is nowhere to be found.

The other four rhinos remain confused, which gives me enough time to begin my run to the station. I only take a few steps when I realize the two rhinos are now cautiously approaching.

I'm pinned in! Do they notice me?

I'm completely unarmed, moving slowly toward the right side of the street as the creatures lumber in my direction. The others must have used the sidewalk to get past them.

I can only hope.

The smoke is steadily clearing, but there's still no sign of Jackson. I take one step at a time, moving away from the beasts. They still haven't noticed me. They reach the body of the fallen rhino. It's still smoldering, the smell indescribable. I cover my mouth and nose with my shirt as the other four rhinos slowly approach. They too are searching. They pass over the remains of the flying menace. I'm parallel to the other two, still moving silently.

The four reach the bodies, then they stop. Somehow, they must detect them. Within seconds they descend on them, ferociously devouring the remains. The sound of their feasting is horrific. I'm almost past the other two. The rest of our group is nowhere in sight.

God, I hope they made it. The sky is still clear. Their meal is almost over. I need to speed it up.

The two that examined their leader stand on their hind legs, opening their chests. They bellow louder than before. The bone rattling sound alerts the other four, who stop their dining and begin to gallop toward the sound.

Can they hear the sound, or do they sense the vibrations?

The six come together and rise, bellowing loudly. It shakes everything. I feel it in my soul. Could it be they are mourning the fallen?

I'm about twenty feet away. The chorus stops almost as soon as it starts, and there's absolute silence. Even their antennas are still.

What now?

Then, their antennas stick straight up in the air. The creatures appear frozen. What are they doing?

I continue but don't try to pick up my pace yet. I can see the station. If I get a full sprint going, I think I can make it. I may be able to outrun them. They're still frozen. It's now or never.

I sprint at full speed. The rhino's antenna all shift in my direction. Shit, they do sense movement. They go from statuesque to full charge within seconds. I pick up my speed, but the ground is literally moving out from under me. The asphalt is going to break apart. Windows in the buildings and cars shatter. The faster they run, the more difficult it is for me to remain on my feet. The station is getting closer. Even if I make it, will these things charge right through the walls?

Oh God, I'm leading them right to the rest of the group!

The unstable terrain finally trips me up and I stumble to the ground, falling face first, but I catch myself and flip over.

Looking up, I see a blur of gray heading straight for me, the ground vibrating so hard it makes it difficult to catch my breath.

Maybe after they get me, they'll move on.

Doc knows the station well. He's been there a hundred times. Everything they need is there: shelter, guns, food, and water.

I'm so sorry, Sara and Gracie. I never should've gone back. God, please be with them!

I don't know if the anticipation of being trampled, or the regret is worse. It doesn't matter. It'll all be over in a few more seconds. I hear an engine roar behind me, tires peeling.

What the hell?

I look back and see a large black pickup heading right for me. I roll to my left as it just barely misses me, leaving me covered in a thick plume of exhaust. The truck speeds toward the charging mass. I finally catch sight of the man inside. It's Jackson, grinning like a madman.

I struggle to my feet. What the hell is he doing? Committing suicide?

There's no use in screaming at him. Between the rumble of the stampede and the truck's racing engine, he'll never hear me. Mere moments before impact, Jackson leaps from the driver's side. He hits the ground at full impact with both legs extended. The truck runs over his legs, then spins Jackson down into a ditch, off the highway before continuing with a fury, striking the lead rhino head-on. The creature bursts like a water balloon, spewing its blood and remains everywhere.

The truck then slides sideways, taking out two more of the charging giants. It rolls over the top of them and lands on the three creatures in the rear before erupting into flames. Fuel sprays everywhere, igniting an uncontrollable blaze that engulfs everything. The truck launches about ten feet into the air with two of the beasts catapulted with it. Shrapnel and body parts rain down everywhere. I duck down and cover my head, feeling burning embers striking my neck and hands.

I hear the truck hit the ground and then two more thuds rattle the street and surrounding building. Looking up, I see one of the rhinos split in half, and the other is splattered all over the asphalt. The fire is intense. It's breached the distance between me and it. The truck is now a twisted metal wreck, barely recognizable. Smoke fills the street. It blows by me as if it's trying to escape from the flames.

"Jackson," I call out. "Jackson!"

There's no answer. I run toward the scene, witnessing a small blood trail to the right of me. I hear a faint moaning near some trees and sprint toward it as the smell of the roasting beasts fills the air, accompanied by a constant popping and sizzling sound. The moaning gets stronger as I reach the edge of the road.

"Jackson, can you hear me?"

He's lying spread out, legs broken and turned in the wrong direction.

"Well, that was a brilliant idea," he grumbles between moans.

I slide down toward him. His pants are drenched in blood. "Dude, that was some epic shit." I laugh as I bend down to check on him.

"Shut up," he growls, his face lying in a big puddle of what I hope is mud. "My legs are killing me!"

"Just be glad you can't see them from there."

"Not even a consideration right now," he replies, eyes closed, face covered in filth.

"Now how the hell am I going to get you out of here?"

"Just do it. I don't want to even think about it," he says, his voice broken and weak.

"Hang in there. I'll figure it out."

"Did I get them?"

"That would be an understatement! What the hell were you thinking?"

He laughs softly. "I tried to think of what you would do."

"And that's what you came up with?"

"Well, you're kind of a gung-ho asshole, so yes. Besides, the only two cars I could get to start were a Prius and the truck … and gas mileage really wasn't a factor in this case."

I laugh. Who would have thought, of all the people to pull my bacon out of the fire, it would be this guy?

"Please tell me I'm face down in just mud!"

I chuckle. "Yeah, it's just mud this time."

"Thank God. I swallowed about a gallon of it when I slid down here. Of course, after all we've seen, my gross sphincter is kinda numb."

I laugh again. "I have to roll you over … and it's gonna hurt like a whole new kind of hell."

"Why are you still talking? Just do it already," he growls.

"Jackson, it may cause more damage to your legs."

"I know, but I don't think there are any ambulances running right now."

His voice is steadily weakening. I know he's in real trouble despite the levity of our back and forth. His legs are completely mangled, bones totally shattered. No matter how much care I take, the slightest move is going to make the situation worse.

"What would've happened if that hadn't worked?" I ask, trying to distract him.

"Never thought it through that far ahead." He chokes out another laugh.

I quickly roll him over.

He screams in pain. "Damn, shit, mother—" He begins to cry before he can complete the stream of profanity. "Oh my God, that hurt so fucking bad!"

"Well, at least we know you can still feel your legs, so there's no spinal trauma."

"Really?" he gasps. "Of all the things to say to comfort me right now, and that's the best you got."

"Okay, now I gotta lift ya."

"Shit, let me catch my breath."

I give him a stick and tell him to bite down. He takes it, placing it in his mouth between his teeth. "What is the purpose of this?" he mumbles.

Before he can mutter another word, I scoop him up in my arms and power lift him straight up. His legs hang from my arms like sacks full of broken glass. Blood streams down my forearms.

Jackson screeches in pain. "Oh shit, oh shit, oh shit," he sobs. "I think I just swallowed the stick."

I carefully work my way out of the ditch and back up to the road. I do a quick visual search, east, then west, north, then south. Everything is strangely clear and quiet. I hope it lasts this time.

I make it to the street and start toward the station. Jackson is desperately trying to remain conscious. My arms are covered in his blood and dirt, his legs swinging freely like socks filled with pool balls.

"My dad hates me," Jackson muses. "I don't know why. All I ever did was anything and everything he wanted me too."

I said nothing.

He laughs weakly. "When I told him I had cancer, I could swear I saw a little twinkle of relief in his eyes. As if he was thinking, 'problem solved.' I really wanted to make a difference. I wanted to change the world. In the end, all I did was sell my soul."

I can see the loss in his eyes, as if he's mourning a best friend. I recognize it quickly. It's the same look I had for months after Boone's death. "I'm sorry, Alex, for being such an ass. I guess old habits die hard."

"Don't worry about it."

He's getting heavier. We've only travelled a short distance, but it feels like miles. The sky is still clear. The mangled corpses of the beasts that threatened us lay strewn across the highway behind me. The fires still burn, gray and black smoke the only contrast to the never-ending blue hue that surrounds and taunts us.

"What you did was amazing, Jackson. You saved my life," I say, breathing heavily.

He half-laughs. I see he's losing consciousness.

"Come on, guy, stay with me!"

I see the station growing larger. My legs are cramping, but I have to make it. I hope the rest of them made it. I've been so focused on Jackson that I didn't consider what happened to the rest of the group.

"I think they sense movement and heat," Jackson says, interrupting my introspection.

"Oh yeah," I gasp.

"I think when there's too much heat, like a fire, it frightens them." He's slurring every other word. "You know, like loud noises startle us."

I'm glad he's somewhat lucid. "Don't worry about that right now, Jackson. We're almost there. Save your strength." I'm hurting, but determination outweighs pain. We're almost there.

I see the doc peer out the glass front doors. Thank God, he made it.

He waves, then sprints to meet me. I pick up the pace, working through the fatigue and soreness. He meets me in only a few seconds. A sudden jolt of electricity runs through my body, piercing my mind. My thoughts race in a chaotic jumble. I feel like I'm about to black out.

Doc rushes toward me. "I'll take it from here." He reaches out for Jackson.

Thank God. He must see the pain on my face! Using the last bit of juice I have, I pass Jackson gently to the doc. I see the deep concern in his face. Jackson groans but does little else.

"Let's go," Doc says after we make the switch.

I limp behind him, my mind still racing, images passing before me that I'd never seen before. It intensifies.

I think I'm going to puke.

"Is everybody alright?" I ask, catching my breath.

"Yes," he replies. "We were praying you both would be too. We heard the explosion. It shook the whole building. What happened?"

"Action Jackson here happened, and you see the result. He saved my life."

I don't know how much longer I can stay upright. It feels like my head weighs a ton. When we make it to the station, I've never been so happy to see a place. Hopefully, we've finally found safety in all this chaos. I grab the door and hold it for the doc. He streams in with Jackson.

Old guy still has some fire.

We head inside the foyer, and I swear I can hear Gracie calling to me. "*Daddy, where are you? Please come home. I'm so scared.*" The thought is unbearable.

Please, God, just a little more time! Just a little more time!

We head down the hall past the front counter. I stop and lean against it, trying to catch my breath, and also fight off whatever is affecting me. It finally begins to subside. I stand back up and continue down the hall, feeling better and better.

What the hell?

There's a small lab in the back for basic first aid. Kind of like the nurse's office back in high school. We enter the room, and the doc gently lays Jackson on the middle of examining table. Jackson winces in pain, although he's barley responsive.

"We have to act quickly," Doc announces, the anxiety thick in his voice. He rushes to the cabinets on the wall, opening each one and searching frantically, collecting supplies. Jackson is barely hanging on. I grab his hand and squeeze. Another jolt passes through my body. I feel ill again, but even worse this time.

Doc scrambles to put supplies together. Jackson moans. By the looks of his legs, and the doc's nervous speed, I know how much trouble he's in.

How are any of us going to survive this?

I fight past whatever is happening to me, but now all I can think of is Gracie and Sara. As selfish as that sounds, I don't care. I must get to them. Time is an enemy as much as those monsters out there, and just as merciless. Doc pushes me out of the room so he can work. I stand there in the hall, my world silent. I watch the doc work on Jackson, but it's all a blur, no color, shapes, and sense.

The weird sensation passes again, and my head becomes clear, as did my purpose. Despite Jackson's condition and what's at stake, I make my decision, and nothing will distract me from it.

Just a few more hours. Just a few hours more!

Hang in there, Gracie.

CHAPTER 14
Training Day
(Kayla)

Why is he just standing there?

Alex is frozen, staring into the room. I approach, placing my hand on his shoulder. He doesn't move.

"Alex, you alright?"

I peer into the room and see the doc working frantically on Jackson. He notices us both staring, stops, shakes his head, then moves to shut the door. Now, Alex is staring at a closed door. I repeat my question, with still no answer.

"You saved his life. You know that, right?"

Silence.

"I hope he appreciates it."

"He saved mine," he corrects.

"What?" I gasp.

"He saved mine. The son of a bitch saved my life."

I'm speechless. He's dead serious.

"I don't know why, but he risked his life. Hell, by all rights, he should be roadkill!" He turns to me, stone-faced, shakes his head and walks away, nothing more said. As I watch him leave, Jude slips in behind me.

"Kayla?" He tugs on the back of my shirt.

"What, kid?" I watch Alex disappear down the hallway.

"I found another laptop and it works."

"Congrats for you, kid."

"The internet is still up."

Alex enters a room at the end of the hall.

"And I care why?"

"I think I found more survivors," he replies excitedly.

"And…?" My back is still turned to him.

"The chat rooms are filled with people, hundreds, maybe thousands of them."

I wake from my daze. "What?"

"I did a search and found about a dozen chat rooms with people who are trying to make it just like us."

I spin around and grab the laptop. "Let me see that!"

The kid's right. I see the scroll of chat rolling as we speak. "What are they saying?"

"Tons of stuff, about the monsters, how they think it all happened, everything," Jude gleefully answers.

"C'mon." I lead him into one of the interrogation rooms. I'm way too familiar with them. We sit at the table as Jude gives me a virtual tour.

"I haven't found anyone local yet, but there are some from America and a lot from other countries, like England and Spain."

"Can you understand what they're saying?"

"Some of the text is in English. The rest is in other languages." He points at the screen. "Here's a guy from Alaska who's held up in some kind of fallout shelter his dad built. He says his family was attacked by those bug things and they barely escaped. They watched their neighbors get attacked and eaten alive."

"Oh my God," is all I can mutter. I hear Tara calling for her son down the hall. "What else?"

"There are some who've seen other things much worse than what we have."

"Worse? How much worse? Shit—oh, sorry, kid."

He smiles. "Don't worry about it. I said the same thing."

Tara's voice is getting louder and closer. He points at the screen again. "This guy says he saw something that looked like a cross between a large dog or bear and a shark."

"No shit," I blurt out. "Sorry again!"

"No shit," he replies, grinning.

I glare at him. Tara is right outside the door. She peers in. "There you are. Why didn't you answer me?"

"I think your son has found something. I gotta get Alex."

"Oh, okay," Tara replies as I jump to my feet and blast by her.

"Keep up with it," I scream back to Jude.

"I will."

"Alex, Alex!" I call as I blaze down the hall.

Matt steps out of another room. "Kayla, what's going on?"

He startles me and I almost trip. "Where the hell did you come from?"

"I'm getting supplies for the doc, trying to find some more first aid stuff, but without much luck."

"Jude found more survivors!"

Matt appears stunned. "What, where?"

"On the computer. I mean, on the internet, there are bunches of them all over the world. He's in the last room to the right. Go check it out."

Matt nods and sprints down the hall. I continue my search for Alex, finding him sitting on a bench at the far end of the hallway, his head down.

"What's wrong with you, dude? You can't hear me screaming your name?" He doesn't respond as I stand in front of him. "What are you doing?"

"Thinking, Kayla. I just need a moment." He doesn't look up.

"Jude found something."

"What?"

"Survivors!"

"Where?" Alex finally looks up.

"Everywhere!"

"You're serious?"

"Yes! They're chatting with each other, describing more creatures."

"Where is he?"

"He's in the room at the beginning of the hall."

He stands. "Come with me." He speeds down another hall to the right.

I follow. "Where are we going?"

"Just follow!"

We move to a door that's marked stairwell, where he pulls out some keys and unlocks the door. We enter and descend the stairs.

Before I can ask, he says, "We're heading down to the evidence locker."

"But what about Jude and the stuff I just told you?"

He remains silent, his expression determined in our journey. We descend about two floors and encounter another door. Alex opens it, and we enter another hallway. The walls are gray concrete and stained.

"This was once an old bootlegger's tunnel. They discovered it back in the fifties," he says. "The station is built on top of it. The tunnel literally runs under the street and down the block. They think there may have been an underground distillery here at one time. The evidence locker is down here as well as the S.W.A.T armory. It's a perfect place to securely store their equipment."

The fluorescent lights hum as we continue to a gate. He unlocks the gate, and we proceed in. Surrounding the room are shelves and shelves of what appear to be confiscated stuff. Everything is either bagged or boxed and neatly stowed.

"Don't touch anything."

"Yes, sir!"

I wonder what this half-ass tour is all about, but I keep my mouth shut. For now, at least. We move past the evidence room to a steel door. He unlocks it and we enter. I'm floored. It's Rambo's wet dream. Peg board lines the walls with rows and rows of weapons. Handguns, shotguns, rifles, machine guns, gas masks, oh my. Below the peg board are locked cabinets occupying all four walls.

"Grab that cart." He points to a rolling cart near the door.

I do as he says and roll it over to him.

He methodically unlocks each cabinet, removing a myriad of items. "What size are you?"

"What?"

"Never mind, I got it." He pulls out several Teflon vests and throws them on the cart. He then grabs a metal box off the floor and fills it with ammo magazines and boxes, moving so fast he's a blur. Heading to a large cabinet on the back wall, tall and wide like an old-fashioned wardrobe, he opens it quickly. Hanging inside are some kind of black outfits. He removes them one by one. They appear to be heavy by the way he's transferring them. He moves to the wall and begins removing weapons.

"I assume there's a reason for all of this."

He doesn't answer. The cart is finally full, and we move back toward the door.

"Head upstairs and bring the rest of the group down," he commands. "Doc, too, if you can. At the other end of this hallway is an indoor firing range. Bring them there." Before I can answer, he grabs the cart and speeds down the hall.

I ascend the stairs, confused but determined to fulfill his request. When I arrive at the top, I notice the hallway is empty and quiet, so I move quickly down to the room where Jude was. I enter to see them all huddled around Jude and his laptop. The room where Doc and Jackson are is still closed.

"Matt, Tara, Alex needs us downstairs," I say.

"Kayla, have you seen this?" Matt asks, never lifting his head from the screen. They are all mesmerized.

"Yes, but Alex needs us, and now."

Matt looks up. "Alright, Kayla."

"It's simply horrific," Tara gasps. "The whole world has gone to hell."

"Mom!"

Tara rubs her forehead, the concern showing heavily on her face. "How are we ever going to make it?"

"We will, Mom, we will." Jude places his hand on her shoulder, offering comfort. She half-smiles at him, concern chased away by fear. "Kayla, we counted about 2,235 people online so far," Jude gleefully exclaims. "Some are as close as Virginia."

"That's great, kid. You stay here and keep up with it. We're going downstairs to see Alex."

"Why can't I come?"

"Because what you're doing is too important to quit. We need you to keep gathering that vital information."

"I may be a kid, but I'm not stupid, Kayla. Don't patronize me."

"Okay, wiseass, the grownups need to talk, then I'll come get you."

"Whatever!"

"Watch it, you little harlot. I'm staying with my son," Tara snaps.

"Tara, you need to grow the hell up and stop giving me shit. Little man will be fine."

Tara stands and growls, "Round two will not go in your favor, queenie."

In a blink, I'm in her face. "Is that right, Martha Stewart?"

"Count on it, bitch," Tara snarls, unflinching.

Matt quickly interrupts our standoff. "Ladies, enough already. Let's go." He grabs me by the arm. "I said let's go!"

I stand down for now, but there will be a later. I guarantee. Uppity bitch. She represents all the things I hate about people who think they're better than everyone else, like their shit just don't stink. Yet, she loves that kid and is willing to sacrifice everything for him. I want to kill her and admire her at the same time.

I haven't been here before. It's a strange sensation. I concede to Matt but pull my arm free, leaving the room with Matt and Tara in tow.

Tara kisses Jude on the forehead on the way out. "Baby, I'll be right back. If you need anything, Doc is in the room across the hall."

Jude kisses her back. "Okay, Mom, I love you."

She runs her fingers through his ever-growing hair, obviously struggling to hold back tears. It's a disgustingly painful sight. We all head down the hall as she wipes her eyes.

"Where are we going, Kayla?" Matt asks.

"Downstairs."

"I can see that, but why?"

"You aren't going to get the doc?" Tara asks.

"No, he has to take care of Jackson."

We head down the stairs at a pretty good clip and enter the basement. "This way," I say.

I lead them down the hall to Alex's location, hearing movement down the hall. We enter a large room, about the size of a two-car garage. The walls are all concrete. At the front of the room is a long metal rail about four feet high running the length of the room. It has a narrow, worn wood counter attached to the top of it.

No doubt now. It's a firing range.

Down at the end of the room are all kinds of targets, some hanging from the ceiling on wires and rods so they can move front to back. Alex is standing to the right, next to several tables, a myriad of items neatly spread out across their surfaces. He looks down and then turns to us.

"Okay, we're set up, so listen up. We have very little time and a lot to cover. This facility was once used to illegally manufacture and store booze during prohibition, mostly whiskey. Above the entire structure was a speakeasy. The tunnel was used to run under Main Street. A distillery existed at the opposite end of this hallway that was dismantled about twenty years ago, before this station was completed. When this was discovered, the city decided to completely gut and renovate it to be utilized for S.W.A.T training. Both their weapons and equipment are stored here, and they use this range for training.

"The public is unaware of this facility. This room can be used as a standard firing range, as you can tell, but it can also be used for breach training and set up in various configurations. The rail can be removed, and the area can be set up to resemble a room in an apartment, a crack house, or in any configuration needed for training. Breaching is the process in which S.W.A.T enters a room to clear it, rescue a hostage, or arrest the bad guys. It's the most intensive and dangerous process in their routine."

"The history lesson is cool and all, but is there a point to all this?" I say. "I mean, what does this have to do with us?"

"We're going to use this room to train you to fire a weapon properly and effectively. I need you to develop skills in a very short amount of time, to be able to remain calm, clear, focused, and safe. We have only hours to accomplish this, and then we move on."

"That is fucking impossible," I snap.

"She's right, Alex, it can't be done," Matt adds.

"I don't think any of us have ever even touched a gun, let alone fired one," Tara says.

Alex's face remains stoic and intense. "We can and we will. If we fail, we die. I need your complete focus, and you must do everything I say without variance. If you do, you'll learn quickly, and if you don't... Well, do you understand?"

There's absolute silence. I don't think anyone has any idea what to say.

"Good, by your silence, I accept that as agreement. On the tables, you'll see the resources you'll need to survive. Believe it or not, the S.W.A.T team we have here was one of the most elite and well equipped in the state, which is to our benefit. As you view what's on the tables, you'll notice there are several full body armored suits. This team was one of the few issued this type of protection. A combination of E-Sappy Plates and Kevlar, which will protect seventy percent of your body. They are heavy and hot, but they'll keep you alive. You'll get used to wearing them. I can even rig one up for Jude."

Tara's expression is blank, the woman obviously overwhelmed.

Hell, we all are!

"Hopefully, these suits will protect us from any attack those things out there can offer. At least we'll be better protected than without them." He lifts a gas mask off the table and holds it up. "Put simply, this gas mask will protect you from most noxious elements."

This is all so surreal. It can't be really happening. I look at Matt and Tara, seeing they're pale and blank. The group listens but are any of us absorbing this?

"That's your defense, now for the offensive. Each of you will be issued two weapons. This sidearm…" Alex holds up what looked like a 9mm handgun. "This is a Glock G17 RTF2 9mm. It holds seventeen rounds of ammunition. This is one of the most effective handguns in the world. It balances power with ease of use, defining maximum firepower with minimal recoil. These, again, were special issue to this team. Each of you will carry one of these and seven magazines of ammo. Four goes on your gun belt and three in the packs we'll be carrying." He motions to the objects on the table. "I've loaded each with hollow point bullets instead of full metal jackets."

"Huh?" I say. The others are just as dumbfounded.

"Full metal jackets have maximum piercing power but run the risk of moving through a target and possibly into one of us or any civilian we may encounter. We can't take that chance. The hollow point enters through a small hole and leaves a larger one upon exit, solid stopping power. I only hope they'll be effective against any of those things that have scales or natural armor, like the rhinos we encountered. If they don't, all my ammo will be full metal jacket, just in case. Matt will be taught to use it as well, in case something happens to me."

Matt loses so much color in his face, he's nearly transparent.

"Relax, Matt, you'll be fine. Tara, I have a .22 for Jude to use. It is a small caliber pistol."

"Are you kidding me? He'll either shoot us or himself!" Matt shouts.

"I'll train him."

Tara shakes her head vigorously.

"Trust me, Tara, he'll be protected. Wherever we go, Jude will stay in the middle. If we encounter anything else, he'll be wearing the armor and he'll stand close to one of us. These creatures appear to be animalistic, and like most predators, they'll seek out the weakest first. Jude will be the easiest target unless he learns to protect himself. Can you handle that?"

Tara remains silent. The seconds seem like hours. She finally looks up at Alex. "You just keep my boy safe. Promise me you'll do everything to ensure that."

"Absolutely, we all will."

Wow, that went in a totally different direction than I expected! Tara wells up again, but I see her fighting it back. Can it be the belle of the ball is finally growing a solid gold pair?

"You'll see three shotguns on the table." Alex motions to the weapons as he returns the pistol to the table. He holds up one. "These are called Eight Ball breaching shotguns, special issue. Their primary purpose is for opening locked doors when there's no key. But their power, in this case, can be useful against something large. Unfortunately, they are most effective at short range, so hopefully we'll never have to use them. Matt, Doc, and I will carry them. We have limited ammo, so every shot will have to count." He places it back on the table.

"Finally, the most important weapon you'll carry is the AR-15." Alex holds up what looks like the mother of all machine guns. "This weapon can be fired single fire, semi-automatic, or fully automatic. This is not the movies. If you use the automatic feature and fire erratically, spraying an area, it will only result in limited aim, loss of balance, and a better chance of injuring or killing one of us. You'll learn how to fire this weapon with optimal proficiency and accuracy. We shoot to kill and every shot counts. Fire it carelessly and we will deplete our ammo with little effectiveness. This back piece will stabilize the weapon when placed like this." He demonstrates. "If it's wedged properly, you'll achieve the accuracy you need, and the armor will cushion the recoil."

He's confident, but I don't know if his audience is as sure of themselves.

He puts the rifle down. "Now, also on the table are about a dozen flash bangs. These are explosive devices that discharge a loud noise and blinding flash. You've probably seen them used in the movies or on TV. It appears that the creatures out there may be sensitive to vibration, sound, and heat, so these may be the most effective weapon we have for both distraction and damage. If we need to escape another tight situation, these will be our lifesavers. Then you see eight hand grenades." He points to them. "These were confiscated in a raid last week from a local militia. Matt and I alone will be responsible for these. All you have to do is pull the pin, and once you release it, you have ten seconds until boom. These will tear a man in half, so basically death in the palm of your hand."

Matt looks speechless, mentally overloaded. "What the hell is that?!" he exclaims, pointing to an object in the corner.

Alex looks over at the end of the table on the floor. "That is a makeshift flamethrower we confiscated from the same group. It uses a small propane tank, and it works. Again, if these things react to heat, it may be highly effective."

"And who's going to carry that?" Matt gasps.

"Let me worry about that, Matt. You'll have enough on your plate. Additionally, each one of us will carry a week's worth of rations in their packs, and as much water as can be carried."

"You expect us to carry all this crap? How are we going to pull that off?" I question.

"We will because we have to," he quickly responds.

"Why can't we find a ride and drive out of here? It certainly would be a lot better protection," I retort.

"Because the roads are most likely stockpiled with abandoned cars and there probably won't be a clear route."

"What about all the traffic cameras?" Matt declares. "There must be about twenty or thirty of them. I know they came in handy during the last ice storm. You can see the road and traffic congestion."

"Jude has his laptop. Can't he tap into them?" I add.

"Matt, that's brilliant," Alex says. "There's a crime scene van behind the building. If we can find a clear route, we can use it."

"But won't those things be able to sense the van, feel it move, like you said?" Tara chimes in.

"Good point," Matt agrees. "It may turn us into one large moving target."

"We'll have the ladies and Jude ride inside and protect it. It'll also allow us to carry more food and water. It's worth considering. Matt, here are the instructions on how to put on the armor. You guys gear up. You need to learn how to do it on your own. We won't be able to dress each other if we need to get up and go fast. Okay, you've been officially debriefed. I'm going to get the doc."

He heads back upstairs.

Tara approaches the table. "How are we going to manage all this?"

"We will because we have no other choice," Matt gently replies.

"But it all seems so futile."

"That's the purpose of faith."

"How?" Tara asks, desperation thick in her voice.

"Faith exists when all hope is absent. It propels us through the darkness when there is no light at the end of the tunnel that we can see. Faith drives us when logic and everything around us says stop. It's now that we must have faith in each other, in Alex. If we hold onto each other, draw from our collective strength, we can survive."

"Do you really believe that?" Tara asks. "Even in all this?"

"With all that I am. We've found the strength to overcome all these terrifying, unimaginable obstacles so far, and in all this horror, there are small miracles emerging. You just ran your fingers through your son's hair, something I can only guess you haven't done for years. We thought we were alone and suddenly Jude discovers others are out there. And now, your boy may be able to assist us in finding a safe passage through the city. Did you ever think he would be capable of any of that? We're all finding our strength, finding that we are more than we ever thought we could be."

Her expression speaks volumes. It begs to Matt; *Hold me up and don't let me fall.* They embrace.

I'm going to be sick. I'm sorry, all that religious stuff always causes an immediate gag reflex for me. It's sad but true.

They separate, and Matt rubs her shoulders. Tara is again battling the tears, but I see the semblance of a slight smile form through the fear.

As Matt and Tara look over the uniforms, I quietly head back upstairs to check on Alex and the doc. Alex is already way ahead of me. I sprint up the stairs and try to catch up. In the hall, the doc steps out of the room to meet him. I duck into a nearby room to listen, barely able to hear their conversation.

"How's he doing, Rick?"

"I can't help him much more here."

"How bad is it?"

"One leg appears to have been shattered with multiple fractures and breaks. I'm trying to control the swelling with a combination of heat and cold, but I'm afraid there may be some internal bleeding. As for the other leg, it looks like he broke his tibia and ankle. He's in a lot of pain, and I don't have anything to manage it."

"We busted a kid who broke into a local pharmacy a couple of weeks ago. He grabbed a load of prescription pain killers. It's all been stored in the evidence locker; there may be something there to help."

"That may solve the pain issue, but without X-rays, I won't be able to determine the full extent of the damage. I'm flying blind here. I need to get him to a hospital with the proper equipment at my disposal. There's another concern. If there is internal bleeding, there could be major complications. I'm also concerned about blood clots forming in the legs. A single clot could cause a graver issue if it moves into his heart, lungs or, God forbid, brain. It could kill him."

Alex says nothing for several long seconds. "The hospital is the opposite way, at least by ten miles."

"I know, but if we don't find a way to get him there, he may die."

"There may not be a clear route, and we certainly can't carry him. It's too big of a risk. Even armed, it would put us at a huge disadvantage."

"Then I'm sorry to say the outlook is grim."

They pause.

Alex breaks the silence again. "Matt came up with an idea. He suggested we could check the traffic cameras online and piece together a possible path."

"Okay, and what if, like you say, there is none?"

"That presents a massive problem. It would take two people to carry him on a stretcher. That's two people who won't be able to protect themselves, or Jackson for that matter. We could duck in and out of buildings, but a trip that would normally take minutes by vehicle would take hours on foot. If we run into trouble, I don't know if we can escape intact. Not to mention we don't know what state the hospital is in. It could be overrun by God knows what."

"The other survivors we ran across came from the hospital?"

"Yes, and you gotta ask yourself, why did they leave?" You'd think that would be one of the safest places to be. It had food, medical supplies, etcetera."

"It's not looking too good, is it?" Doc says.

"Can he make it a few more hours?"

"What, why?"

"Just answer the question; can he make it for a few more hours?"

"All I can do is guess … it's fifty, fifty at best, and that's being overly optimistic."

"I'll get you the drugs to help manage his pain, and you keep a close eye on him. Just a few more hours, that's all I need."

"For what?"

"To train everyone how to handle a gun without getting themselves killed."

"And then what?"

"I go home to get my family and bring them back here."

"You're joking, right?"

"No, I've never been more serious. My house is about seven to ten miles away. I can make it. I'll use the traffic cams to construct a path, see if I can spot any nasties, and then head out."

"That's suicide, you can't go by yourself."

"Rick, it's not an option. I'm not asking you; I'm informing you."

"And if Jackson dies while your away?"

"It would be the same if he died within the next three seconds. It would be tragic, but it doesn't change my plan. I'm going to get my family."

"I can't believe what I'm hearing," Doc gasps.

"Rick, this has always been about my family. Nothing's changed. I brought you and this group to safety. We can wait it out here. We have food, weapons, water, and shelter, everything we need to hunker down. Now, I need to go save my wife and daughter. Where they are now, they don't have the provisions or resources to survive."

"You go out there and you won't last the trip. Who knows what else is out there. There's no way to prepare for it!"

"Then you and Matt will have to take charge."

"Do you even hear yourself?"

"Loud and clear, Rick. I don't think you're hearing me. This is non-negotiable. In a few short hours, I'm leaving to retrieve my family. As far as I'm concerned, I've gone well beyond the agreement I never volunteered for. This has always been about my family."

"Then at least let me or Matt go with you, safety in numbers and all."

"That's ridiculous. I need you to stay here. You're the only one who knows how to use a weapon safely, and your medical expertise is invaluable. You'll need Matt to help keep everyone focused."

"We can't lead them like you can."

"Yes, you can. You may have robbed these people of the better leader by putting me in charge."

"That's nonsense, absolute nonsense. We would have never made it this far without you."

"I'm going alone!"

"And what if you get there and...?"

"They're alive, Rick. Jude found a host of people who survived while searching online."

"And if they're not?"

I can feel the tension through the walls.

"Rick, nothing you say is going to change my mind."

"You didn't answer my question, Alex."

"There's no reason to answer it."

"I already know the answer, but I want you to face it."

"They're alive, Rick. I know they are."

"And if you're wrong, are you still coming back?"

"What? What kind of question is that?"

"A valid one. I know why you want to go alone."

"Really? Enlighten me."

"Alright, you want to go alone because you've already prepared yourself for the worse."

"You know what, I'm done talking."

"You can't walk away from this, from me. We've been through too much together."

"I'll get you the drugs, then I'm heading downstairs to start the training. Are you coming or not?"

"Don't forget, Alex, I was there, in the darkness, following the same path you might be on. You remember, don't you? You saw it in me and stepped in."

"One has nothing to do with the other." There's a definitive change in Alex's voice, harsher and biting.

"I didn't want to go on without them. I would've done anything to be with them," Doc says. "When I lost them both, it was like forgetting how to breathe. Life lost every ounce of purpose. I couldn't see tomorrow; I couldn't see past the next second."

"I haven't lost them, Doc, but I know I'm wasting precious time with this, time I don't have."

"How many times did I try to hide away," Doc continues. "To retreat to a place where I could be alone? Wanting it to overtake me so I'd have no choice but to end my suffering. That's the way I reasoned it. That's the way I made it make sense."

"Enough, Rick, enough," Alex says, his voice cracking.

"No Alex, you have to face this, just like I did. I spent my whole life being a survivor, overcoming racism as a child, a teen, and a young man. People telling me I could never be a successful husband, father, and doctor. I fought the system with every bit of who I was, not from time to time, but on a daily, minute-by-minute basis. I built my practice on a foundation of integrity and endurance.

"I forged my own way with honesty and sincerity. When others played the victim, I rose above my circumstance and plowed through all the doubt and fear. In reward for all that, when I should have been able to rest in my accomplishments and family, my son got sick. The disease took him so fast I didn't even have time to react. Then I lost my wife, the love of my life, dead in a bathtub full of her own blood. I loved my family with my entire soul. Trust me, I wanted to join them so badly, wanted to pull that trigger and be with them ... until this young cop decided to take an interest in me.

"A total stranger who had nothing invested and nothing to gain. He could see what I was planning. He became my lifeline and brought me back from the brink. Why? I still have no idea, but I thank God for him every day. Between you and Matt, you both saved my life, and restored my faith. Two things that seemed impossible to salvage."

Alex remains silent.

"I know what you're feeling, Alex, and I know what'll happen if you walk in the door and darkness is waiting. I know the love you have for your wife and child. I know you won't stop until you save them or face the unthinkable. I know, because you're me, and the tables are turned now. Let me return the favor you so selflessly offered me, to keep you from the darkness."

"My wife and child are alive, Doc. I'm going to find them and bring them back here, and then we'll all venture to the hospital with Jackson. I don't need saving, they do, and right now I'm wasting time arguing with you, time I don't have. I could leave now, but I'm choosing to prepare these people to protect themselves. You can either help me or get out of the freakin' way."

"You have no idea what those things are capable of."

"We're done here."

I hear footsteps and duck deeper into the room. Within a few seconds, Alex passes by. I slink back toward the door and watch him descend the stairs. Peeking around the corner, I see the doc standing there, rubbing his eyes. I step out into the hallway, and he looks up, just staring at me.

Jude breaks the silence. "Doctor Foster, come check this out."

The doc is still standing there, looking at me, through me.

"Doctor Foster," Jude yells again.

"I'm coming," Doc says, breaking his stare. He shakes his head and starts up the hall toward the room where Jude is. Jude has the door cracked but not open. He enters, and I turn around, trying to digest what I just heard.

Is Alex really leaving? Is the doc serious? Would Alex blow his own brains out if his family is dead? What would we do, then?

Fear takes hold again, everything finally sinking in. No matter how many guns or bullets we have, without Alex, we're as good as dead. Might as well be naked out in the street.

I finally walk down the hall back to the stairwell. I trudge down the stairs, my mind heavy with dark thoughts. At the bottom, I hear them talking, but their words make no sense.

My anger begins to take over. I look at Alex. Now it's my turn, and he better hold onto something!

CHAPTER 15

Revelations

(Alex)

She pulls my arm so hard that she almost dislocates my shoulder. I try to pull it back, but her grip is firm. She's a strong little minx, I'll give her that.

"What the hell were you thinking?" she growls slowly and quietly.

I refuse to face her. She pulls harder. I know she won't let go until I acknowledge her, but I'm as stubborn as she is. More so.

"Answer me!"

Tara and Matt haven't noticed her yet; they're too busy puzzling over their gear. They have their body armor on, almost right.

"Answer me!"

Another violent whisper. I knew it. She's not going to give up. My head is pounding. It's all beginning to get to me, but I can't let them see it. I growl back, "I'm busy, kid. Why aren't you suited up?" I still refuse to turn around, even though she's cutting off the circulation to my arm. "Kayla, I don't have any more time for this. Now suit up!"

My command falls on deaf ears.

"Fuck you. I know what you're gonna do. You're fucking crazy," she says, her voice gaining volume and fierceness.

Tara notices her attachment to me. "What's going on?"

"Nothing, I'll be right back." I spin around and grab Kayla by her arm. It's far too tight of a hold, but I don't care. My nerves and patience have peaked. In the blink of an eye, I yank her into a corner, out of sight, slamming her against the wall. She's unfazed. I knew she'd been here before, too many times. "Listen, I don't have time for your games!"

She stares relentlessly at me.

"Did you hear me?" My tone is venomous.

"Go ahead and slap me, call me a bitch, bend me over and fuck me! Go on, it's not like I haven't been here before!" It all spews out; she can't stop. The pain pours from her lips like water from an open faucet. Her glare pierces me, sharper than any bullet or knife's edge.

The years of anguish and sadness course from her veins into mine. Every slap, punch, and violation occupy my every nerve, violating her innocence, stealing her faith and peace, ravaging her senses with levels of violence that can only be measured in hell. I can't let go. Her torment latches on to my soul and tears at it with talons made of iron.

"Go ahead, take away every piece that's left and let me die here. Let it end once and for all." Tears fall like drops of blood. "I hate you. I hate all of you, every last one of you. I want to see you die and your rotting corpses stacked in front of me."

I finally pry my hands off her, feeling like I'd been tazed ten times over. I've never felt so lost, so helpless. This is so vastly different, so much darker and endless. She glares at me again, her face soaked in tears and anger. I feel how much she wants to hurt me, kill me. Kayla is gone and only hate remains.

"Then do it," I roar, pulling my gun. I spin it around and hold the butt toward her. "Take it, kill me, kill them all with a single bullet." *I don't know what I'm saying. Who am I?* "Take it, finish it now." I force the gun into her trembling hand.

Make no mistake, her uneasiness is not caused by fear, but pure hate-ridden desire. Her hand embraces the pistol. I stare at the squared barrel of my Glock. She points it at my head as a psychotic smile stretches across her face. I can already feel the bullet burrow through my skull, barreling into my brain and exiting with brute force.

"Do it! This is your one chance to exact the justice you've been robbed of all your life. Kill them all, Kayla. Kill them all."

Her hand steadies, her face the shadow of death, gleefully horrific.

"Do it, now!" I roar.

I hear the hammer pull back … click … click … click. The sound claws mercilessly up my spine. I wait. Wait to die.

"Please pull the trigger, Kayla. End this. I can't bear these burdens anymore. I want to die, just to breathe again."

The silence is deafening. It lasts for an eternity. Then a muffled sound rips through, broken and quiet at first, then ever so slowly it rises. The sound of bitter weeping.

But is it hers or mine?

The weeping grows stronger, followed by a dramatic thud.

As abruptly as it starts, the darkness dissipates, like fog rising after dawn. I hear another thud and intense weeping. My sight returns, murky at first, then ever clearing, until I see her kneeling, her head in her arms, the gun dangling from her hand. I bend down and gently take the gun from her.

"Why?" I ask.

She raises her head, face devoid of all color and life. Her voice is fragmented but she strains to answer. "Because they would have finally taken me, the last bits of me."

I'm lost in her eyes, filled with so much sorrow, too much to absorb or define.

"They can't have anymore. I won't let them have anymore," she whispers, but there's a rising newfound determination in her tone. She's not quiet because she's weak; she is reborn, finding her feet again. I carefully take her hand, slick with sweat and tears, and ever so softly bring her to her feet. She rises slowly but defiantly. I look at her arms. They are bruised with the dark imprints of my hands.

Dear God, what have I done?

She places her hands on my shoulders and pulls me into her, her voice sweet and bitter at the same time. "Would you have died for me?" she whispers, like a child desperately reaching out for a father's strength.

"Yes, if it meant you'd be freed," I respond.

I don't see her anymore. I see the face of Gracie, worn by time, scarred by pain. I have to look away. It's too much to bear.

"*Daddy, please help me!*" The words ricochet throughout my skull. Please, God, make this stop, whatever it is. I'm not strong enough to see her like that. It's worse than death, more horrifying than war.

"*Daddy, where are you?*"

I pull her to me and hold her tight, my arms embracing her with love instead of anger, support instead of hate. I want to heal her, take away every moment of pain, save her. I would freely give my very soul for the chance. Her tears saturate my shirt, her head buried deep in my neck.

"Please don't leave me. You're the only one I believe in." Her voice wraps around me like a lifeline, her heart pounding, begging me for assurance. "Please don't leave me."

I love her so, more than anything, more than myself. She's my universe. I can't remember living before she was gifted to me. We hold each other while time again ceases its reign. Peace washes over both of us, quiet in this endless storm. For a moment, the world has returned to normal again.

Without warning, she pulls away and looks at me. Gracie's face dissipates like ripples in water. Kayla has returned, but she's just as beautiful as my child. Her expression shows confusion.

I don't let her speak. I get it now. Together, somehow, we both travelled along each other's road, immersed in the deep oceans of our past. We saw the very heart that beats within us, the siren's call of our deepest pain and desire. We stared into the heart of darkness and survived it. How and why seemed pointless now.

"You would have let me kill you?" she gasps as reality rushes in.

"Yes," I reply without hesitation.

"Why?"

For the first time, I see innocence filling her tired, swollen eyes. Pulling her to me again, I caress her ever so gently. She rests her head against my shoulder and weeps, her body trembling. I don't have an answer for her, not one I can put into words.

"Please stay," she sobs.

"You know she needs me," I whisper.

"I know. I could hear her, feel her too," she replies.

"Then you know what I have to do."

"Yes, but I don't want you to."

"I have no choice."

She pulls away again and stares deeply into my soul. "You can't promise me you'll come back." There's such desperation in her face. I witness firsthand the depths of death and damage, loss and loneliness. Not until today had I stared into the face of absolute hopelessness.

"I'll come back."

"How do you know that? How can you even say that?" she struggles to ask in between her tears.

"I have no choice."

Our eyes lock. She must see something because the fear dissolves and the glimmer of a smile begins to creep across her tear-stained face. She leans in and kisses my cheek. It's awkward but heartfelt. It may have been the first time in a long time she was able to demonstrate emotions while feeling safe.

"Now, I've got to get these guys ready. Are you in? I mean, *really* in?"

"I always have been. It just took me a while to know that you were."

"Just get in there and get dressed."

"Yes, sir!" She flashes me a half-ass salute, then walks by me, touching my arm. It's a gentle but purposeful touch, quickly reminding me of the way I manhandled her.

Guilt wells up. "Are your arms okay?"

"Yes." She holds them up, contorting them around. The marks are gone, completely gone. "Why?"

I'm dumbstruck, bewildered. The confusion on my face must be evident.

"You alright?"

"Yes, go suit up." I vigorously rub my face, then follow Kayla. Tara and Matt have all their body armor on and seem oblivious to how long we've been gone. "Are you both deaf?" I call to them.

"What are you talking about?" Matt says.

"You heard nothing?"

"No, what were we supposed to hear?"

Kayla mischievously sneers at me as she heads to the table. She acts as a child who just stole a piece of candy. I must be losing my mind.

"You heard nothing?" I repeat.

Tara shakes her head.

"I really wish I knew what you were talking about," Matt says.

"You and Kayla were only gone for a couple of seconds," Tara chimes in. "What were you doing?"

A couple of seconds?!

"Making out," Kayla quips as she slips her vest over her head.

"That's sick," Tara responds.

"Not all of us are stale like you, babe," Kayla says, her voice muffled by the vest as she yanks it over her head.

Tara grunts and glares at me.

"What did you expect, Tara?"

I played along even though I'm totally lost. They can't see it; my poker face is strong.

Kayla finally gets the vest past her head. Her hair is everywhere. Was it that long before? She shakes her head and brushes the blonde bangs from her face. She giggles. "Haven't had that problem in a long time."

The whole thing is surreal. It's like nothing happened, yet the memory is burned into my identity. I feel the residue of everything I've seen and felt. Looking back toward the corner, I wonder if I'm losing my mind.

"Deal with it," Kayla says, as she grabs the rest of the armor off the table.

Now what? Is she able to read my mind too?

She's as giddy as a schoolgirl. Like the weight of the world has been lifted off her shoulders. Should I press and question, or let this girl who's stared into the abyss repeatedly and survived celebrate her newfound release? She's reverted from cynic to child, her chains broken, shackles loose.

What is happening to us?

Tara sighs. "What are you talking about now?"

"Is there a ladies room in this cave?" Kayla asks as she blows a few remaining strands from her face.

"Down the hall," Matt replies. "Alex, are you going to show us how to load this thing?"

Matt carefully removes the Glock from the table. Kayla passes by me with the biggest shit-eating grin on her face. She heads to the bathroom, skipping and goofy. Everything feels like it's been turned upside down.

The doc rushes down the stairs. "Alex, I need those items you promised."

At first, I just stare at him, lost, then I remember the conversation upstairs. "They're in the evidence locker. I'll get them." I head down the hall to the locker, my head still spinning. The locker is unlocked, gate wide open.

Shit! It was Perkin's shift this morning. His uniform is barely recognizable, covered in that goop. Despite the vomitus appearance, there's still no odor.

Perkins was a good guy, a little quiet and quirky, but who wouldn't be hanging out down here all day. He got blitzed at the last Christmas party and trashed his computer à la Office Space. It was hilarious and sad all at the same time. We all knew he hated his job. He once told me he wanted to be in the FBI, bragged about becoming the next Fox Mulder, droning on and on about it. He'd been to Nevada at least a hundred times. Roswell, New Mexico was his favorite vacation spot. He spent hours upon hours watching the night sky for visitors from above. Just crazy shit.

Well, maybe not so much now.

I head over to the pharmacy cabinet. It too is open, wide open.

What the hell?

The cabinet is a wreck, bottles and evidence bags everywhere. I look behind me and see one of the gun cabinets is also open. Bullets are everywhere, a hodgepodge of different calibers strewn across the floor. I can't tell if any of the guns are missing.

I draw my weapon again and cautiously search the remainder of the cage. There's a trail of ammunition leading to the back, and I carefully follow it. There are two large metal shelving units in front of me, obstructing my view. I hug the first case as I slink by it. Reaching the end, I cautiously skirt around the corner, seeing a pair of boots on the floor, souls toward me. Someone is lying there, not moving.

Or are they just waiting?

I approach silently, cocking the hammer back. Whoever it is, they're wearing a police uniform. I step over more ammo, pill bottles, and baggies filled with pot and coke.

Should I call out?

I covertly continue my approach. I see a hand, grayish blue and stained with dried blood. I swing around and discover a body with blood all over the floor. There's a gun in the other hand with more blood on the barrel. The wall behind is covered in brains and the blood, so is the table the body is leaning against. It's a male and his head is down. I don't have to look any further. It's Brinks.

Shit! I just talked to him yesterday. His new baby was born a week ago, his first, a boy, Tanner. He and his wife had only been married a couple of years. We used to swap stories about the Gulf. He served a tour. Good cop. Better husband. Loved his wife in a way you only see in the movies, like in one of those goopy chick flicks. We were the odd men out in the way we carried on about our gals. We took a lot of jabs for it, but it was worth it. The back of his head is missing. He used a .45 caliber.

I gently lift his head. Damn, he put it in his mouth.

Part of his tongue fell out, along with some teeth. I barely recognize him. He did major damage to his face. One of his eyes is hanging out. Must've been from the pressure of the blast. Not a pretty way to go.

There's a pile of pills in his lap. Why? Did he debate on which one would be quicker? There are more pill bottles on the table. I gently let his head down and stand up. The table is a mess, paperwork strewn all over, covered in blood and fragments of skull. There's a piece of paper with black marker written all over it. I lift it up and discover a cell phone below. It displays the last number called. A picture of his wife is on the screen.

Before I consider it any further, I hit redial. The phone rings, and then voicemail. I hear a sweat voice asking me to leave a message, then a beep and silence. My heart falls into my stomach. I wonder how many times he called. Frantically dialing and redialing, praying the next one she would answer.

I guess she never did.

I look at the piece of paper in my other hand, barely able to read it through the blood stains. All I can make out are two lines: "...*why me ... forgive me.*" It's a suicide note, but to whom? You would think the entire scene would sicken me, but that phone number haunts me more than anything else.

How long before he pulled that trigger? How many times did he call before he just gave up?

I redial again, shaking my head, and suddenly a soft voice answers. I freeze.

"John, is that you?" she cautiously beckons.

My heart's in my throat as I search desperately in my mind for her name.

"John, please tell me it's you." I can hear the tears well up in her throat.

"John, he's dead, the baby's dead." She begins to weep.

Wren, stupid, her name is Wren! Answer her! "Wren, it's Alex, Alex Trevor," I say, my voice trembling.

"Alex, thank God. Where's John?"

"Where are you?"

"What, why? I'm at home. Where's John?" With each question, she struggles through her abject fear and confusion.

"Are you alright?"

"What? No, please let me talk to John. Is he there?"

"He's not here, Wren. What happened to the baby? What happened to Tanner?"

Why did I ask?

She struggles between deep sobs. "He's dead, Alex. I found him in the crib this morning." Her grief overtakes her as she weeps bitterly into the phone. She tries to explain, but her words are intermittent and difficult to decipher. "It was the first time he slept through the night. The first night I slept for more than three hours. I took advantage of it and didn't check. I overslept, Alex, for the first time I overslept! When I finally went in his room…" Her weeping finally drowns her voice.

"Wren, talk to me, please."

"He's dead, Alex. I can't take it. I can't believe it. I can't go back in there." Panic fills the call.

"No one is asking you to. Please calm down."

"Where's John, Alex? Please tell me if he's there. Are you at the station?"

How can I tell her? "Yes, he's here. He's busy helping out survivors." I lie. I have no choice.

"Thank God! Wait, there are more survivors?" A fleeting gasp of hope escapes her lips.

"Yes."

"Not here. I checked all the houses hours ago. They're all dead. And there's nothing left but those awful mounds. They are everywhere. What happened, Alex?"

"I don't know, but I need to know where you are."

"At home now, but I'm afraid. There are noises coming from the basement."

"What kind of noises?"

"Scratching, and it's getting louder and louder."

"For how long?"

"It just started a few minutes ago. Why, do you know what it is?"

"Yes. Can you leave the house, Wren? Can you go to a neighbor's house?" I try desperately to constrain the anxiety welling up.

"No, there are things outside now."

"What kind of things?"

"Large plantlike things. They're everywhere; they're hard to describe." Her voice is violently shaking. "The scratching is getting louder, Alex!"

It's all developing too fast for me. I can't keep up with it. How can I help her? I can't even get to her.

"Alex, there's something down the hall. I can see it moving!" The terror in her voice is thick.

I feel my body tighten. Dear God, no, please no! "Wren, you have to get out of there now!"

"Where am I going to go?"

I hear the scratching on the phone now, that familiar chitterling sound that sends chills down my spine. Before I can say another word, she screams, a blood curdling sound.

"Wren!!!"

She drops the phone as the rush of the swarm echoes through the line. I hear her running and screaming; a door opens and shuts. I hear them trampling the phone as it cut off. In a fit of uncontrolled rage, I throw the phone, and it shatters against the wall.

Doc rushes in. "What the hell is going on?" He sees the body and horror all around it. "Oh, dear God."

I try to regain my composure, assaulted with frustration, anger, and helplessness.

"Alex, what happened?"

"He blew his fucking brains out because he thought his wife and kid were dead." So much for my composure.

"Oh my God." Doc bends down.

"Don't bother, Doc. He's a mess. Been dead for a while." I run my fingers through my hair. "His wife was alive. She was alive!"

"What? How do you know?"

"I just talked to her. She was alive, but her baby was dead, but they got to her and there wasn't a damn thing I could do!"

"Who, Alex? Who got to her?"

"Not 'who … what,' Doc. Those fucking swarmers. They attacked when I was on the phone with her."

"When?"

"Just before you rushed in. She was terrified, and I couldn't help her."

Matt bursts in. "What's going on? We heard yelling—Oh, dear Lord!" He just stares at the body. More footsteps speed down the hall. Matt stops Tara and Kayla from entering. They try to push through, but Matt is a wall.

"Tara, Kayla, please stay out. You can't see this!" Doc bellows.

"What is it, more of those monsters? Oh God!" Tara cries.

"No, just get out," I say.

Matt continues to block the two girls and steadily powers them outside the cage. I hear him explaining something to them, but I just don't care right now.

"Doc, she was alive, and now she's dead," I continue. "Do you understand what I'm saying? If Brinks had been there, she would have survived."

Doc was silent. I think it's finally sinking in now. "Has she answered the phone yet?" he asks.

The room falls silent. For the first time in my life, I could deck him. "No, Doc, she hasn't, but I haven't stopped trying." I walk straight up to him, face to face, breath to breath. "And I won't stop!" I pull my phone out of my pocket, and it rings, jumping to voicemail. Sara's angelic voice fills the room. I hold it up to him, inches from his nose, so he can take it all in. "Hear that, Doc? That's what keeps me breathing."

The message ends and I hold the phone to my ear. "I'm coming home soon, honey. Hold on. Love you both!"

"It's madness, Alex!"

"There is a fine line between faith and madness, Doc. I'm willing to cross whatever line I have to, as long as it brings me home." I head back to the table and grab some bottles, quickly reading the labels. "These are pain killers, mostly Percocet and Codeine. There's more in the cabinet over there. Help yourself."

"Alex, I'm sorry. I crossed the line."

I heard him, but forgiveness was not on the menu now. "What was said was said, Rick! Doesn't change anything."

"This guy, Brinks, is he the one you told me about before?"

I stop. "Yeah, his wife's name was Wren."

"I remember her. You asked me a lot of questions about her condition."

I turn around. "Yeah, while they were dating, they found out she had breast cancer. Brinks took a year off to care for her during her treatments."

"Why? Was she in remission?"

I pause again. "She was ... until after the baby was born."

Where is he going with this? Is this some sick way to make amends? I don't have time for conversation.

"She was sick again?" Doc presses.

"No, they just found something. Brinks wouldn't elaborate. He said they had to do more tests."

"What about Brinks How was his health?"

"I don't know, why?"

"The pills you just gave me have his name on them: John Brinks."

What? I sprinted to him, grabbing a bottle from his hand. "Why would John be taking Percocet?" That doesn't sound like John. He was as strait laced as they came.

"Are his parents alive?" Doc asked.

"Yeah—I mean, no. His mom was. His dad died of lung cancer three years ago."

"John smoke?"

"Yeah, about two packs a day. He was trying to quit."

"Looks like it may have caught up with him," Doc replies.

I pause again. He never told me anything. Then again, he never knew about my prostate cancer. No one did. Time for this little interrogation to end. "What's on your mind, Doc?"

"Your gun lesson is going to have to wait," Doc replies. "I need to check on Jackson and something else."

"Care to share?"

"Not yet," he responds, then breezes out of the cage before I can say another word. I follow, but he's up the stairs like a bolt. Matt's in the hall, still arguing with the ladies.

"What the hell is going on, Alex?" Kayla scolds.

"We found a corpse. He was a friend of mine, blew the back of his head off and all its contents on the wall. You're more than welcome to view the freak show, or we can start training. Choice is yours."

I walk past them to the firing range. I may have overreached; they are frozen. I grab a Glock off the table and load it with a mag, then turn back to them. "Anyone?" I hold up the gun.

"Really, Alex, really?" Kayla shakes her head. Her armor is on wrong, no big surprise there. Tara and Matt look like lost puppies.

Tara just stares, speechless, which is kind of refreshing.

How am I going to teach these guys anything?

"Let's do this," Matt says, walking toward me.

Kayla follows, still shaking her head.

I begin my training, demonstrating how to load the weapon and fire it safely. We practice on the targets. They are shaky at best. I shouldn't waste ammo, but I need to make sure they can hit something. Matt is catching on fast. Tara has managed to miss every shot. Kayla is fucking John Wick. Training is second nature for me. I'm going through all the motions, but my mind is somewhere else. It's with them, Sara and Gracie. All I hear is that damn scratching, and Wren's screams. They haunt me relentlessly.

I stand behind Tara, teaching her how to aim. I brace her arms and tell her to fire, supporting her with each pull of the trigger. She leans against me to help steady her aim. I feel her hair on my face. It stinks, but I deal with it. She's a beautiful woman, but the wear of Jude's disease has left its mark. She looks weathered, aged by the toll of his care, sapping every bit of her time and strength.

I bet she was a knockout when she was younger. Probably a cheerleader, prom queen, and there's no doubt she comes from money: spoiled, waited on hand and foot, fought over by jocks and yuppies alike. A lifetime of needs supplied by an endless line of simps. She probably never dreamed she would be tested like she was when Jude got sick.

Tara finally hits the target square, once, then twice. Her stance is stronger and her grip tighter. She's really feeling the weapon. Kayla has already gone through three targets, and Matt's aim is dead on. They are learning faster than anyone I've ever taught before. With confidence running high, we switch over to machine guns. I run through another quick demo, and they're off.

This time they pick it up even faster, both firing single shots and then rapid fire. They should be sweating up a storm, but they're cool and calm. The weight of the armor seems to have little effect. It's amazing to watch. Nothing seems to break their concentration, not even the white elephant in the other room, Brink's slowly rotting corpse.

Time flies by, the hour passing like minutes. Soon, Matt is using the breaching shotgun, firing it like a pro. They are learning at a rate I can't explain. Kayla is probably unleashing years of frustration and pent-up rage with every pull of that trigger, but she's controlled and calculating. Matt is developing into a real leader, calm, collected, and focused. Even Tara has the hang of it. One small victory bringing me closer to my family. They still don't know my plan. Well, all except Kayla and the doc. It's better this way.

In a ridiculously short time, they accomplish a newfound sense of self and self-preservation. As they continue to expend the allotted training ammo, I head back up the stairs to find the doc. I proceed down the hall to the room where Jackson is. The door is open, and Jackson is finally asleep. Doc has him covered up pretty good. I check on him, pulling the covers off his legs to check them out. Doc has one splinted and the other is swollen and red.

Jackson has lost a lot of color, and his breathing is labored. He doesn't move as I cover his legs back up. Doc has him doped up pretty good. Making my way to Jude's location, I hear talking. The doc is with him. I enter the room, and the two are huddled over the computer. Doc had tons of notes next to him. He's still frantically writing as Jude feeds him information. They don't notice me.

I lean in. "What's going on, gentlemen?"

They both jump out of their skin. "Dammit, Alex, don't do that," Doc gasps.

Jude starts laughing. "That was epic, dude. I almost peed my pants."

"It's not funny, Jude," Doc scolds.

"Yes it is." Jude laughs harder and harder.

"What you got, Doc?" I ask.

"Answers." The doc stands up.

"Answers to what?"

"Come with me. Jude, keep the search going, okay?"

Jude is laughing so hard that all he can do is nod. We exit the room and head into the lobby. All the shades have been pulled and the lights are off.

"This wasn't like this when we got here," I say.

"No, it wasn't, but now it has to be," Doc replies as he sits at the counter. He places the papers in front of him. "Are you ready for this?" He recognizes the puzzled expression on my face. "I may finally know what's going on and why we survived," he continues, "but it's not going to be easy to digest."

"Okay, what've you got?"

Doc hands me a sheet of printer paper. It has a picture on it. "Tell me what you see."

I look closely. At first, I can't make it out, but the more I search…

What the hell! I look up.

"And that's just the beginning," Doc replies.

CHAPTER 16

Answers?

Kayla

I got this!

I look around for Alex and notice he's left again. Where did he go now? I slip away from the others, checking the evidence room. Not here.

Ascending the stairs, I enter the hallway, where I hear someone frantically typing. Jude is still in the room where I'd left him, engrossed in his work on the laptop. There are papers everywhere, even on the walls. I hear Alex and the doc speaking softly in the lobby, so I move in closer, staying just out of sight. Alex is staring at a picture of some sort.

"That's a picture of a group of dogs being ambushed by an unknown creature," Doc begins. "It was taken by a young man using his cell phone. The attack allegedly lasted about five to six minutes, then the creature seemed to disappear. He took several pictures of the incident. The one you're holding in your hand is the best of the bunch.

"The young man posted the photos online and they became an immediate internet sensation among UFO and conspiracy nuts around the world. The snapshots gained such momentum that the scientific community began to take notice, even being allegedly examined by several biologists and veterinarians. However, they could not identify it, so it was rationalized to be a hoax.

"A week ago, that same picture was discovered by a marine biologist while he was idly searching the web. It piqued his interest, so he had several of his colleagues take a look. They verified that the pictures were in fact a hoax via a fairly in-depth blog."

He handed Alex a pile of papers.

"One of these experts stated that this sort of crustacean's size, an arachnid hybrid, was implausible as its exoskeleton would not allow it to grow to the dimensions proposed in the photos. He further discredited it all by noting that's its overall anatomy would make it a physical absurdity. They continued their analysis with a follow-up article, examining the alleged victims of the attack, the three medium-sized dogs. There were four pictures of both the animals that died, and the one that survived the assault. However, the young man later noted the third canine eventually died from its wounds. The terrier-like dogs appeared to be torn apart, as if they had been through an industrial fan or thresher, while the surviving dog had piercing wounds that were inflamed, indicating an allergic reaction due to a sting or bite."

He paused to take a breath. "The story was picked up by one of those conspiracy websites called Shadows of Presence. They sent three of their journalists—and I use the term loosely—to the site of the incident and scheduled an interview with the young man in some small rural town in Mexico. When they announced their trip, their site was deluged by reports of similar sightings and attacks from across the globe. Several of those posts emanated from the same small town they were slated to visit. One of those reports was about a farmer attacked by a similar creature. He was stung multiple times in the leg, which resulted in an amputation. Another post described an entire herd of slaughtered goats, originally attributed to the chupacabra. The final told the story of a young girl stung so many times that her corpse was unrecognizable. Her mother demanded the police investigate.

"All had been previously explained away by the local authorities. The farmer, a known town drunk, had recently complained multiple times of "flying spiders" plaguing him. Although he did lose his leg, the police explained that it was caused by the onset of gangrene resulting from an untreated injury, probably from an equipment accident. The goat attack was attributed to a pack of wild dogs that had been roaming the area for several days. Those animals were allegedly later captured and euthanized. Finally, the young girl was determined to be the victim of killer bees. She had unknowingly disturbed a colony while playing by a local tree. But before the investigative team could interview anyone, they disappeared. All their equipment and additional notes had suspiciously vanished with them. However, their last blog contained pictures of a carcass that resembled the creature in that picture. It was found in an abandoned pool, badly decomposed, and the blogger stated that the stench was unbearable. Here are a few more pictures." Doc hands Alex another stack.

Alex breezes through the photos. "Where was the team seen last?" he asks.

"It doesn't say, only that they called their editor and said they had discovered another witness. Their blog concluded with the statement that they were moving to another site of recent activity … and there's more."

Alex looks up from his examination. "More?"

"Jude did an intensive search. These are the results." He grabs another stack of papers from the desk. "Based off the website and blog, Jude used keywords to locate any other references. This is what he found. Pages and pages of information, all emanating from the last two months, describing in a myriad of ways similar sightings, encounters, and even deaths."

Doc begins to neatly and methodically lay the papers out across the counter, describing each one as he concisely places them in an order that only he truly understood. "Here are more pictures of UFOs shaped like flying spiders or stingrays. Photos of weird looking insects moving in the shadows. Here are more of alleged bite wounds and stings. The story of strange plants growing in corn fields that seem to move from one area to another, with jellyfish like protrusions ascending toward the heavens. Many of these strange beings float in and out of existence, disappearing and reappearing without rhyme or reason."

When he completes his dissertation and obsessive coordination, he looks up at Alex, his expression shifting from one of intrigue to undeniable concern. "These things were here before. There was a buildup to all of this." He stares at Alex silently, waiting for him to marvel at his discovery.

Alex moves to the counter and examines more of his documents. The silence only lasted for a few seconds, but the doc can't contain himself. "There's more!" he says.

"Slow down, Rick. I'm not as quick as you." Alex, like the investigator he is, carefully surveys the sheer glut of data spread before him.

"There are theories—" The doc can't stop himself, like a kid with a new toy.

"What theories?" Alex asks, still engrossed in the information, obviously attempting to make sense of it.

Good luck, dude ... I'm lost as fuck!

"Theories about these things?" Alex holds up one of the pictures.

"Yes, that, and more importantly, why they are here. And ... why we're still here."

Alex's expression is indescribably intense, like stone on fire. Doc motions him to sit down while he simultaneously takes a seat at one of the detective's desks.

"Are you ready for this? It requires an open mind."

"Right now, my mind is so open that my brain may fall out," Alex snaps.

"You have to put aside all that you think about our physical universe and be willing to accept things you may not truly understand," Doc begins. "Let's first discuss why or how we survived."

Good fucking starting point!

"We know that all those vile blobs and piles are the remains of people."

"Yes, it didn't take long to figure out," Alex concedes.

"Well then, the simplest way to put the question is why them and not us."

Alex nods in both affirmation and anticipation.

"That answer may be the most disturbing part of all of this. If what I'm gleaning is correct from all this information and my understanding of cellular make up and processes, we survived simply because we were going to die."

Alex's bottom jaw drops like it's about to fall off. Doc stops, creating the most uncomfortable pause in human history. He doesn't wait for Alex to speak.

"I believe what we witnessed is some sort of cellular degeneration occurring on a global and expedited scale."

Okay, I'm totally lost!

"Think of what cancer does to our cells. It degenerates them, destroys them, viciously, methodically, until our organic systems completely break down. Imagine that on a worldwide scale at a rapid-fire pace, so fast the whole process would take minutes, maybe seconds, instead of months and years. The human body both aging and then decaying at such a rapid rate that within a tiny span of time it's completely reduced to masses of simple cellular matter. I believe this is what occurred. And I can validate that because I witnessed this horrific process firsthand."

"What?" Alex says

Doc pauses and swallows deeply. "Diana, my newest nurse, started only a few months ago. Her nickname was Sunshine, because she was just so full of life and brightness. That's why I hired her, assigned to all my younger patients. She was always up and positive. Nothing seemed to break her stride or spirit. The staff and patients adored her.

"This morning, she was unusually cheerful, almost glowing. I found out she was pregnant with her first child. I was very happy for her, and without missing a beat, I pulled out a pink and blue wrapped box and gave it to her. It was a porcelain figurine, a simple figurine, of a woman holding a baby in her arms. Etched in gold inlay at the base were the words—A mother's child is hers for a lifetime; a child's lifetime is a gift from their mother.

"I remember she started to cry and said, 'God bless you, Doctor Foster. I only pray I can be half the parent that you are.' Her words both pierced and comforted me. As she started to walk out, she turned and smiled at me. I'll never forget the way she looked. As she walked out of the room, she became lost in a fog. I tried to readjust my vision, but it worsened and rapidly became so distorted that I couldn't recognize my surroundings. The dizziness set in so quickly that it knocked me to my knees. Then the pain came, like nothing I've ever felt before. Such a mixture of pressure and excruciating pain tearing inside me, at my very bones and muscle. I could feel myself slipping out of consciousness. It was my body's only defense.

"But just as the blackness started to envelop me, I was pulled back, awoken by a piercing screech. Everything became crystal clear, more so than ever. Even through the pain, I still found a way to drag myself to the doorway in the direction of the wails and cries. As I crossed through the doorway, I could see her on the floor, strapped in pain, screaming. I tried to call to her, but my voice was paralyzed. I could feel myself forming the words, but there was no sound.

"She twisted and turned on the floor, her arms wrapped tightly around her torso. She flipped over and I could see her face. Our eyes met, and she screamed '*Help me*' with her stare. I tried to reach out to her, but it was as if I had a phantom limb. I could feel my hand stretching out, but my arm lay numb and useless under my belly."

The doc stops a moment, shaking his head from the haunting memory. "As she reached out to me, that's when it happened. Her hand began to age. The skin grew thin, wrinkled, and distorted. Her once young and beautiful face sank in, and the skin began to cling to her bone like wet paper. I could see every crater and aspect of her skull. Her eyes fell into their sockets, and a dark bluish-black ooze seeped out. Her teeth collapsed into her mouth and her tongue ejected out inches in front of her. Her jaw broke and her face dissolved into the floor, leaving pink, red, white, and black mixed together into a ghoulish abstract saturating the carpet.

"Her skin became like murky water, first opaque, then becoming clear as it poured off her body. Her body was reducing itself to a gelatinous mass, now unrecognizable, bubbling and burping until it settled, forming a greenish-black pile encompassing her uniform. The image is forever burned into my mind and soul, an absolute horror before my eyes."

Oh my God, he saw all of that? Shit!

"I could hear more screams coming from my nurses and what I thought were my patients. The terrifying scene before me only superseded my own pain for a moment. When the second round struck, I felt as though I was being crushed under its weight. I could barely breathe and realized the same fate as Diana must now be happening to me. I closed my eyes, praying silently that it would be quick, and I would again pass out. I finally received my wish.

"When I awoke, it was over, and I was surrounded in my own vomit. I tried to lift up my body, but I was shaking and too weak. By the time I could muster the power to lift myself off the floor, I heard your voice. It was such a relief. Not just to be alive, but to know I wasn't alone. Later, I discovered the whole horrific experience lasted only a few minutes, but it felt like a lifetime."

Alex just sat there frozen as the doc continued his brutal story.

"I looked over to Diana's remains, hoping they wouldn't be there, and the whole episode was nothing more than a hallucination brought about by my ordeal. Some of the survivors online witnessed the same horrific event, their accounts paralleling mine. I've seen the pictures; some of the piles have more remains than others, bone fragments, even segments or entire organs left intact."

"Why didn't we die the same way?" Alex asks, and I can hear the horror in his voice.

"Thanks to Jude, who's been like a madman at the computer, searching for data, I may have an answer. I've never seen him like this, an energetic, enthusiastic preteen instead of the sickly boy whose enemy was time. He was barely strong enough to lift an arm, let alone let his fingers dance across the keyboard. He always loved computers, wanted to design games, the bigger the better, but it was all just a dream, a hopeless fantasy, although I never let him believe that. Now, he's a monster on that laptop, pulling information and compiling data for me like a pro."

"That's all well and good, Doc, but you still haven't answered my question. The reason we survived?"

"Yes, right. Well, my theory is this; the same disease that was killing us may have preserved us, even saved us. Whatever happened, it sped up cellular degeneration within healthy cells. However, for those of us suffering from cancer, with damaged and dying cells, the process may have worked in reverse. Not only preserving us, but quite possibly curing us.

"Look at the evidence. Kayla and Jude are just two examples. They've been renewed. They show amazing strength and incredible regrowth of their hair. Everything about them indicates not just a remission, but possibly total cellular reconstruction. I realize I can't prove anything, but it's all I've got."

"It doesn't make sense," Alex says. "Why would the process work in reverse for us? Why not just expedite the process the disease had already begun?"

"Does any of it make sense? It's just a theory based on the information I have."

"Maybe it just slowed our disease," Alex says. "Maybe we'll go through the same decay process, just slower."

"That's also a possibility. Either way, Alex, we survived."

They stand there for a moment and just stare at each other, then Alex says, "Wait a second. If what you're saying is true, how did you and Jude's mom survive? We were the cancer patients."

The doc took a deep breath. "Alex, Tara survived breast cancer; in fact, her battle with the disease made her a local hero. About a month ago, we found another mass. She hadn't told Jude yet. The tests came back as malignant. She was facing chemo again. Her visit with me today wasn't just about Jude. As far as me, it's Hodgkin's lymphoma, diagnosed only a few weeks ago, the same disease that took my son and my father. To know I may have played an involuntary part in my son's death has been too much to bear."

The expression of loss and pain on his face is hard to look at. I turn away for a moment.

Doc takes another deep breath. "That's all water under the bridge now. Either way, we survived, and we need to continue to."

The room goes silent. I can see how uncomfortable it's making the doc. Alex's demeanor begins to slowly metamorphize. I can't quite explain it, but he just looks different, lost in deep thought. He quickly pops up and exits the room, heading right for me.

Heart pounding, I scramble to find a place to hide.

"Where are you going, Alex?"

Alex doesn't answer, increasing his stride.

Doc shakes his head and begins to put his papers back together. I sprint down the hall as fast as I can and duck into the stairwell, hoping Alex doesn't see me. I glance around the corner to see his face is red and glowing.

What the hell?

He turns quickly, entering the room where Jackson is. I watch the door close as I hear Jackson say, "Who's there?"

I quickly slink over to the door. When he slams it shut, it pops open ever so slightly. I can't see very well, but I can hear everything.

CHAPTER 17

Real Monsters
Alex

Full of rage, I flip on the light switch and move over to the table to stand over Jackson. Something has taken hold of me, something I can't explain.

What?

My mind is flooded with images, memories that are not my own. I see Kayla again, but in a way I hadn't seen her before. Anger grows and peaks, burning through me.

That son of a bitch! The Gazelle trial wasn't the only reason I knew Jackson. But how? How did I know it was him? I'm like a man possessed. He won't get away with it this time. I won't let him hurt her again.

"Before I go, we have to settle something," I growl.

"Alex, is that you? What—what are you talking about?" He's visibly shaken by my sudden presence, fear in his eyes, spilling across his face. He tries to rise. "Alex—"

Before he can say another word, I force him back down. "I know who you are, Jackson. I know what you are."

Jackson sits up. "What the hell!" He tries to find some morsel of courage. It lasts only a moment, as the fear swiftly returns to his face. He sees the unbridled hatred in mine. His voice trembles when he says, "What the hell is wrong with you, man? I saved your fucking life!"

"I know what kind of man you are, Jackson," I growl. "For a moment, I had the extreme displeasure of glancing inside what little soul you have. At first, I saw what you wanted me to see, an injured child desperately craving affirmation from a father who won't give him any. I felt pity, understanding how that could decimate a person's sense of self-worth. But then I realized it's all bullshit. I saw deeper, much deeper, beyond your pain, to the true coward and monster you really are. You're the worst kind of monster, one who hides behind lies, using them to shield everyone from revealing how deep the evil is inside you."

"What the fuck are you talking about, Alex?"

"You did everything in the world to please your father, to make him proud, but there wasn't anything you could do that would ever be good enough. At least that's what you told anyone who would listen. It's what you told yourself at first to excuse the man you were evolving into."

I continue to circle Jackson like a shark circling a wounded seal. "Then you blamed your brother. He was always the All-Star, and whether it was his achievements in sports, or his consistently successful business ventures, everything always worked out for him. Your father idolized him, while he thought of you as a simple sperm stain, who by sheer luck had made its way through. An unexpected pregnancy, a mistake destined to never measure up."

His face grew paler with every sentence, speechless.

"You made it appear as if you were lost in the storm of your father's ridiculous expectations, and though it may have been true, you weren't formed by his constant condemnation or jealousy for your brother. You don't have any secrets anymore, Jackson. I've stripped them all away, revealing the vile truth of who you really are."

Jackson tries to speak, but I won't allow a single word. "You could have changed, but that's not what you wanted. In that sick, twisted, rotting soul of yours, you found a sense of pleasure, even ecstasy, in your ability to hurt others. It gave you a warped sense of being, a reason for your pathetic existence.

"Don't ask me how, but we connected, Jackson, from the moment I carried your sorry ass away from that wreck. I saw your entire deranged and horrible life. It's an experience I could have lived without. I couldn't explain it. It didn't make sense. I thought I was losing my mind. Your entire life flashed before my eyes, your every thought."

Jackson's eyes widen, his face so white it's nearly translucent. I pause and take a breath, waiting for him to respond, but he looks completely lost.

"You chose to defend the truly guilty, the vilest creatures in the world, but inside, you saw them as kindred spirits. Defending them was something more intimate, a connection that ran deep down to your rotten core."

Jackson tries to rise again, but I quickly push him back down. Leaning over him, I snarl, "These men did things that you only wished you could do. Things you fantasized about in the darkest parts of the night when you were alone."

I stand upright again, taking a few steps back. "Your whole disgraceful career has been defined by taking advantage of the most ludicrous technicalities, twisting and manipulating a broken system to your benefit. You're an absolute expert in the practice, as if blessed with a power delivered from hell itself."

I stand at the foot of the table, glaring. "When I grabbed you from the truck, the first images that hit me were of you and your brother. Flashes of the schools you went to together, expensive and private. Then onto Harvard, where your brother was recruited to one of the largest firms in the world. Your father was so proud. He adored your brother, almost worshipped him. The good son ... his real son."

Jackson gasps, grabbing for his chest, as if in pain.

"That's how your father defined you, not by your actions or accomplishments but by your pedigree, or lack thereof. The woman you called mother was not your own, yet she was forced to accept you. Not by a joyous choice, of course, but as part of a payoff and cover up, the result of one of your father's many indiscretions, another one-night stand with a stranger. Was it a servant, former babysitter, business associate? Or maybe, one of the many high-priced whores he visited on his numerous business trips."

The memories come fast and furious, each one more infuriating than the last. "You only found out after your mother's death. How did she die again? You were told she fell down the stairs. It wasn't the first time. Your father blamed it on her endless drinking. She was always wandering around your massive mansion while blitzed out of her mind. It was bound to happen eventually. Despite your father's insistence, you knew all along it was a lie, and yet you accepted it without resistance.

"Not your brother though, the alleged good one—that was the straw that broke the camel's back for him. He knew about the abuse for years and only halfheartedly confronted your father about it. But even he was helpless, bound by his own shallowness, too concerned about the family's reputation to act. I mean, there was an image to uphold, one that made him a lot of money, and there lay the heart of your family. He left long before she died, only briefly returning for her funeral, as you stood, unwavering, by your father's side. He didn't share the same adoration that your father had for him. As for you, he saw you as a spineless lackey. It was one big dysfunctional empire ruled by secrets and sin. Despite his betrayal, and your loyalty, your father still held your brother up on a pedestal and despised you. Then he left again, for good this time."

I'm no longer speaking; instead, I'm standing outside myself, watching someone else. Someone I no longer recognize.

"He didn't even come to his father's side on his death bed. But you did. Stayed until his dying breath. The bastard child remained, shedding tear after tear despite all he knew, despite all he'd seen. Hell was too good a place for your father, too good a place for the likes of both of you."

The room falls silent again. I pace back and forth, with little self-control left.

"You used that monster of a man and what he'd done as a mask to hide your own identity. You created a mist of lies to hide the forest of your insanity. No one knew the truth behind the dark desires of your own cold, dead heart. You idolized your father and desperately wanted to be him, to become the abomination he was, so you helped monsters escape their rightful punishment for the heinous acts of torture and death they caused. The only problem was, you weren't smart, rich, or strong enough to pull off those acts without getting caught. Not like him."

The truth drips from my lips like saliva. I watch it repeatedly crush him. "You want to know the one that disturbs me most, the one that really brought it home for me? It was the Cramerton trial. Do you remember that name, Jackson? Do remember that monster?"

Jackson's mouth drops wide open, his eyes wide, his expression tight. My hands begin to tremble as I bend over, putting us face to face. Jackson is paralyzed. We're so close, we share the oxygen between us.

"Cramerton was the king of all of your monsters, the ultimate prize." I stand up and take a few steps back. "He was the quintessential sexual predator, and no one was safe from his horrific desires. Women, men, children, both boys and girls, he was the ultimate serial rapist. He'd frightened his victims so profoundly and effectively that the only one the prosecution could get to testify was her. The one he tortured for weeks before she found the strength to resist him and escape. He was a master manipulator, a chameleon with a litany of aliases. With each crime, he just moved on. Even in this world of high-tech surveillance, identification systems, and a heightened state of awareness, this monster was able to pass through the tightest of scrutiny. When they finally caught up with him, he'd been posing as a teacher for years, earning the respect of his students, peers, and even the school board. He was a philanthropist, donating his time and what little money he made supporting local schools and community charities. He had them all completely fooled. He finally wormed his way into the foster care system and became a foster parent for three young teens. Of course, that had been his plan all along."

The images passing through my mind are too horrific to bear, but I can't stop. It won't let me. "Kids who'd already been jerked around by the system, with no sense of real family, now unknowingly in the home of this psychopath. They had no idea this monster had raped and killed up to twenty different individuals of various ages. They had no idea that the police had been pursuing this beast for months, to no avail. He'd become so confident in his abilities that he believed he was untouchable. How could he know it would only take one girl battling an incurable disease, physically and significantly weaker than him, to end his hellish agenda.

"He abused her incessantly for weeks, using the most heinous bondage and sexual torture tactics. He viciously raped her, brutalized her, sometimes for hours, and then beat her to a point of unconsciousness. He wanted to break her, decimate her spirit, reduce her to her lowest form to provide a climax to his pleasure. Despite all this, she found a way to escape him, then found the courage to stand against him in trial. Because of her courage and determination to survive, she didn't just save herself, she saved them all. Her courage spawned an epidemic among his victims, and one by one they began to cautiously come forward to convict this monstrosity."

Oh, dear God! What that thing did to her!

"But you, you had to find a way to keep this beautiful evil being from going to prison, because if you did, it would be the greatest victory in that hellish mind of yours. Your hatred for every single victim was so intense it kept you up at night. The only way to free this hell spawn was to prevent their testimonies, to feed their fears. You had to find a way to break her publicly. If you did, the remaining victims would cower. If you could eviscerate her on the stand in front of all, the others would be a piece of cake. Her failure was the key to your success."

How did she survive all of this?

"In the beginning you tried to paint a picture that she was a drug user, a prostitute, a sexually deviant junkie who liked it rough. Despite her horrendous ordeal, she looked healthy, almost vibrant, and it was only a few months after the hell she had been through. You brought evidence to prove she was addicted to OxyContin and other painkillers because of her disease. You even found a doctor who accused her of stealing a prescription pad from his office, then used it to go on a drug-fueled spree.

"So-called witnesses came forward, former boyfriends who testified that she was a nympho, a slut, who traded sex for drugs. You worked your dark magic yet again, and it appeared you had the jury swaying your way. Until she testified. She fought back tears every second as she described in horrific detail the agony he put her through. The entire courtroom froze in horror with each revelation as she relived moment by moment his disgusting and terrifying acts. She concluded with the tragic result of his abuse— that she would never be able to have a child. She performed brilliantly on the stand, and you could do nothing to stop her."

I didn't remember hearing or reading about any of this, but all the memories, horrific images, were as real as if I was there, right in the thick of it!

"In the end, he was found guilty and sentenced to death. She saw the fear in his eyes when they carted him away, all his power stripped away by his own prey. It was probably the first time in his evil life. I bet he's really popular in prison—passed around quite a bit, only this time he's on the receiving end. It was a major loss for you.

"After that case you began drinking heavily, then came the diagnosis, liver cancer. Now, you're a complete failure, not because of your father, brother, mother, or even your disease, but because you couldn't free that monster. You were defeated by that worthless, meaningless little girl."

Jackson grits his teeth, his face growing red.

"When you saw her in the lobby that first time, your hate was naturally rekindled, the reason for the total implosion of your life. Reality flooded in and you finally realized what an absolute piece of shit you were. She held a mirror up to your face and forced you to behold the wretch of a human being looking back. You took great pleasure in seeing her in this weak and frail state, but that wasn't enough. She needed to die. It's all you could think about, but you lacked both the courage and creativity to make it happen. You sat in that doctor's office, facing your own mortality, and all you could think about was how to extinguish her flame.

"What I find unbelievable is that in all this chaos, with your whole world turned upside down, is your hatred for her remains stronger than before. This entire time, while the rest of us are struggling to survive, your main thought is to find an opportunity to take her out.

"You didn't save my life, Jackson. Even that was a lie. You were trying to escape in that vehicle, but your panic and fear took control, and you made a mistake. You knew in your heart of hearts that there was a reckoning on the other side of death, and there was no defense from the consequences of your sins. A personal hell that awaits you, punishing you for all the deeds you committed and devious thoughts you've entertained. You never thought about it before. You had the booze, an anesthetic, dulling your senses and mind just enough to keep those gnawing ideas at bay. But now the veil has been torn away and only the truth remains, draped in black with hands eagerly waiting to strip you of your flesh and devour your soul."

I pause, the silence deafening.

How can I remember that so vividly? The hurt, fear, disgust, shame, and anger is as real in this moment as it was then.

Jackson sits up on the table, stripping the thin sheets from his legs. They are covered in bruises but no longer broken. No scars and scratches, cuts or swelling.

Surprised, I back up.

"Look, look at my legs," Jackson says. "Look at them! I should be a cripple for the rest of my life. I should be dead from either my injuries or the shock. I fucking jumped out of a moving vehicle, for God's sakes, mangled myself. And look at me now. I know if I jump off the table right now, it might hurt like hell, but I could walk. How is that fucking possible?"

I take two more steps back. I can't believe my eyes.

"I'll tell you how this is all possible," Jackson vehemently continues. "Because we are all changing. Whatever happened has infected us all. I don't know how you know everything about me, but it must be the same reason my legs have healed. We've been changed in a way that none of us can explain. As far as I'm concerned, this is hell, and this is our new eternity. Maybe in this hell, I'll be cursed to heal from my wounds only so it can happen again and again. Maybe it's that all my secrets will be revealed so I can be punished repeatedly with shame. Or maybe all my darkest desires and nightmares have come to life in some aberrant form to torment me. Everything you said was right, down to the last detail. You're right, I'm a monster, always have been. It's true, it's not because of my father or my brother; it's because I chose to be."

Jackson is bold in his confession, a warped and twisted fearlessness that defies explanation. "You're right that I've never had the courage to act on my dark impulses. Even though I want to exact pain and control, I've never had the courage to act. I did admire those clients you called deviants. They were perfection in my eyes, the utter epitomes of strength, aggression, focus, and manipulation. I enjoyed being a voyeur. It was safer, cleaner, to be told the story rather than be a player in it."

My rage begins to build again. Jackson must see it. Is this his verbal suicide note?

"And detective, you're right about my hate for that little ragged whore. She took everything from me! She took *him* from me! I guess you didn't hear that they killed him in prison; they castrated him and fed him his own balls until he choked to death. Ripped away his dignity, all his beauty, and reduced him to a pathetic victim begging hopelessly for his life. Do you think the public would shed a tear? Of course not. In their minds, it would simply be another monster put out of its misery, buried with all his sins! As for me, they cut my very heart out."

I can't begin to comprehend this kind of evil. How can anyone wrap their mind around it?

"Do you know how many times he fucked me before the trial? The warped and erotic games we played. I tasted his power time and time again. He abused me, forced me to do things I couldn't begin to imagine in my most perverse fantasies! He controlled and used me like a thing, an object, born and created for his pleasure. I didn't love him. I worshipped him, and every second of pain was my praise. He was everything I longed to be, and the closest I came to becoming that monster, and the strength I could never obtain for myself. She took him from me, and now she has to die!"

I want to kill him. I must kill him! The urge is taking me!

"That little tart escaped me, bested me, and naturally that only fueled my rage. By then I had exhausted all my cash, and well, you know the rest. My obsessions began to seep out. People saw a change in me, and it frightened them. My friends abandoned me, my family was gone, and I was devastated and alone. It's amazing how far the money will take you, then how quickly the ride stops when the cash flow grows anemic. The drugs and alcohol only progressed my disease further, but I didn't care. By then I welcomed death. You would think with my acute awareness of my deviance, I'd be afraid. No, not for a second! I knew what I was; made no excuses. There would be no death bed conversions."

I struggle to control myself. He's blind to it, thanks to his insane tirade.

"And then, when all seemed lost, I found her. You know I was recommended to the doc's clinic over a year ago, but I didn't go. I finally went for a consultation to see if he would accept me as a patient, and there she was, emaciated, weak, worn to the bone. It was beautiful. She didn't recognize me; the cancer's toll had changed us both. I was much thinner, aged, not the spry, young, powerfully handsome man she had seen in the courtroom.

But despite her decaying appearance, I recognized her. A plethora of ideas raced through my mind. Did I have the strength to finally release the beast and exact my revenge? Torture her until she begged for mercy and then gleefully hurt her more. I was almost giddy. But before I could even consider taking it any further, all this shit broke loose."

I won't last much longer. My skin feels like it's tearing free from muscle and bone.

"At first, I was lost in the chaos, just like the rest of you. But as time passed, I realized that this is the world I was meant to exist in, this hell that arrived without warning. A land filled with monsters. My world! Yes, I was trying to escape when the crash happened. I was also trying to run your sorry ass over. You were the only thing that could keep me from killing her. How did you miss that, Mr. Spock, with your mind meld?"

I feel the snap when the blind rage takes me. In one fluid, animalistic motion, I pounce and pull Jackson off the table, throwing him up against the wall. I can literally hear the wind rush out of his lungs as he slams against the concrete.

"I did see what you wanted, Jackson; everything that you wanted to do to her!" I press against him with all my force. He's helpless, trying to squirm free without any success. At this point, I don't care if anyone hears or sees. It must be done. *Now!*

"I'm going to do this world a great a service," I growl. "One monster is about to become extinct!" I slam Jackson back onto the gurney and the gurney buckles under the impact.

Suddenly, Matt busts in. "Alex, stop!"

Matt grabs my arm, trying desperately to keep it from coming down on top of Jackson. My other forearm is constricting Jackson's windpipe. He's struggling to breathe. My stance and grip are like stone, immovable.

Matt can barely hold my arm back. "Please, Alex, stop," he says, grunting from the exertion used to try to restrain me. "Alex! Please!"

Jackson turns to Matt, his eyes drowning in fear. He's turning blue, death apparently no longer an appetizing venture.

I scream with frustration and push Matt to the floor, then viciously punch the gurney next to Jackson's head, leaving a perfect imprint of my fist deep in the metal. Jackson gasps when I nail him in the stomach with all my force. He curls up like bacon that's been cooked too long, coiling into a fetal position.

Matt tries to get up, but I mercilessly kick him back down. I reach into a drawer, pulling out a fistful of handcuffs, then flip Jackson over and cuff his left arm to the gurney rail. I grab his other arm and cuff it to the opposite rail.

Matt is up on his feet, but I'm just too quick. I retrieve restraints from a drawer and wrap a set around Jackson's feet, crossing them over one another before I pull the strap tight. Any harder and I would've cleaved his feet clean off at the ankles. I find the metal ring at the bottom of the gurney and pull another strap through it, then run the strap over Jackson's legs through another ring on the opposite side of the table, locking it off. Jackson is now restrained.

Matt gets in my way and tries to stop me, but I easily push him off again. I take the last strap and run it through another metal ring, across Jackson's chest, pulling it tight, then lock it off on the other side. Jackson's now completely restrained.

I slap him hard. "Now let's see what the monster can do!"

I grab Matt's arm and pull him out of the room. Before my exit, I turn briefly to Jackson. "You think you know fear? You don't know me!" I slam the door shut and see Kayla standing there.

Shit! She'd heard and seen it all. I grab her too, pulling both Matt and Kayla down the hall to another room. It doesn't take much to overpower them both, not in the state I'm in. I release them and shut the door.

"What the hell are you doing Alex? Have you lost your mind?" Matt says.

"Jackson is under arrest!"

"What? Under arrest? What are you talking about?"

"He's under arrest, Matt!"

"For what? What could he possibly have done to deserve all that?"

"Conspiracy to commit murder, and that's all I have to say. Trust me on this."

"Trust you? How can I trust you with the way you're acting right now? You almost killed him."

"That's right, and it would've been justified." I step aggressively into Matt's face.

"What is wrong with you, Alex? Back off! I'm not your enemy."

"You listen, Matt. The man is insane, and he wants to kill Kayla. That's not going to happen, not on my watch."

"What? Why?" Matt says, stunned.

"Because he's pure evil, and I don't have the time to explain anymore."

"Okay, okay, just relax and step back," Matt pleads.

I finally take one step back, the tension in the room nearly suffocating.

"I can't believe it. Why would he want to kill Kayla?"

"Why? Because we all know each other so very well?" I scold. "How well do you know Jackson?"

Kayla remains silent, dumbfounded. Her face is pale, drained of all color.

"What proof do you have?" Matt asks.

"I'm the proof," Kayla finally says. "I heard the whole thing. To be specific, he wants to torture and then kill me!"

Matt turns to her. "Oh my God, Kayla."

"Yeah, wasn't good news to me, either," she quips.

Matt looks at both of us. "What do we do now?"

"For now, he's contained. We'll deal with him later."

"How?" Matt gasps. "What he has planned is indescribably horrific."

"Again, don't worry about that right now. We still need to get ready."

"Ready for what?" Matt asks.

"For anything and everything we may face from this point on. Help me get the group downstairs to the firing range."

"But—"

"Please Matt, we need to focus!"

"Okay, okay, it's just a lot to digest all at once."

"I get that. Don't tell the others for now. They don't need this on top of everything else. I'll lock the door in a few minutes."

"Yeah, that's an understatement," Matt agrees. He nods, then exits the room.

I walk up to Kayla. "You, okay?" I gently place my hand on her shoulder.

"How the hell am I supposed to be okay?" She knocks my hand off her shoulder. "The whole world is going to hell. I can't remember most of my life, and to add to all of that, Ted Bundy in there wants to make a girl suit out of me. How would you be doing, Cochise?

I firmly grab both her arms. "He will never hurt you! Never! I won't let that happen."

She breaks free again. "Yeah, who's going to protect me from *you*? You want to explain to me what happened downstairs, how you stole my memories? I know you can read minds, like you did me, and apparently Jackson. I don't remember any of this. You took my identity from me."

I step back, rubbing my forehead. "I know, and I don't know how or why. I didn't just see your memories, I felt your pain, the weight of your past. It filled me so much I could barely contain it. God only knows how you did for all those years."

"How?" She begins to weep.

"I don't know. I don't know why Jackson remembers and you don't."

"Dammit, everything is just such an unholy mess." She forces back her tears.

"I know, but we have to move past it."

"How the hell do you move past all of this?"

"You have to focus on what we have to do now."

"And what's that, Alex?"

"Find a way out of this. Find a way to live through it. I need to train you all the best I can so we can all get through this together." I slowly and cautiously move closer to her. "I now understand what you've been through. I felt every moment of it. It should have destroyed you, and yet you found the strength to survive it. I don't know how, but you found the guts and spirit to move past it. Now I need you to do the same thing here. Help me prepare these people not just to survive, but to live. Listen, I'm not one for great speeches, so all I can do is be straight with you."

"I'm listening."

I take a deep breath before I continue, trying to think. "We don't know how long this is going to last. We don't know what else we'll face out there. Have we seen the worst or is there more to come? What I do know is that those things out there don't care whether we're ready or not. For whatever reason, they just want us dead. After all we've been through, after all we've survived so far, I'm not going to lie down and die today. Whatever is happening to us, we're just going to have to deal with it for now. We can't let it distract us from our goal. You and I are now connected in a way that we can't even begin to understand or explain. That connection is strong and real, more real than anything else in my life, except for one thing."

Doubt fills her eyes.

"Kayla, you're not the only one I feel inside. Yours is not the only pain and fear that reverberates inside me. The connection I have with you is nothing compared to the one I have with my family. This thing, whatever it is, has made it even stronger. I can feel them as if they're beside me, hear them as if they're whispering in my ear. I know for certain they're alive and I have to get to them. The longer I'm kept away from them, the more chance there is that I'll never see them again. And that's something I can't live with. Do you understand what I'm saying?"

"I'll help you anyway I can. You have my word."

Did she really mean it? "Then go to the others. Help Matt get them downstairs."

I reach out for her hand, taking it ever so carefully, but she pulls away again. She can't give me that much, not now. There's still too much she doesn't understand.

Will she ever be able to trust anyone, especially now?

She leaves the room. Somehow, I have this eerie sensation that she may know everything I'm thinking. I can't escape her now, which is both comforting and terrifying.

God, will any of this ever make sense?

Matt has already gone downstairs. Kayla is on her way. I head to the door where Jackson is, hearing nothing. Maybe he's dead. If only I could be so lucky. I walk to the door and lock it. He's not going anywhere for now. Downstairs, I join the others, standing in the middle of the room.

"Alright folks, let's keep practicing!"

Everybody reluctantly nods, then continues their training. They were all doing well when I left before, but now Tara is struggling again. I move over to her and try to help. She resists at first as I try to manipulate her into a proper position, I don't know why. She's holding the gun as if it were a scorpion about to sting her.

"Don't be afraid. You can do this," I whisper to her as I steady her hand.

Tara begins to aim again. She fires, and the gun sails back, almost cracking her in the face. I quickly retrieve it as she tries to walk away. I grab her arm, and it's like I'm hit with a thousand volts. My whole body shutters as a flood of new images and emotions assault me. I let go and feel like I'm going to pass out.

Tara grabs me to help, but another flash takes me, the sensation excruciating.

"Don't touch me!" I snap.

Tara is visibly frightened. Everybody stops. The wind leaves my body. I desperately try to regain my composure. Matt runs to my aid, but I stop him. "No, I'm okay. Work with Tara, please." I turn, steady myself, then head to the table behind me. Leaning over, I feel like I'm going to throw up.

"You okay, Alex?" Jude tugs at my sleeve.

"Yeah, kid, just tired, that's all," I mumble. I try to straighten up. Matt is staring at me with concern.

Kayla approaches. "You alright, chief?"

I look up at her, and she gasps. "Your eyes ... your eyes are pure white," she screams. "Shit, Alex, what's going on?"

Jude hasn't noticed yet, and I gently push him away before he can. "What did you say?" I notice my voice has become rough, almost creepy.

"Your eyes, man, what's up with your eyes?" she whispers, trying not to alarm the others.

I quickly bow my head and rush toward the stairs, covering my face. "Kayla, keep them going. Don't stop," I growl as I hurriedly ascend the stairs.

"What's going on now?" I hear Matt say as I leave.

"Nothing. He just got sick for a second and needs some time," Kayla says, covering for me. "He said to keep going."

I rapidly ascend the stairs and run into a bathroom down the hall to look in the mirror. She's right, my eyes are pure white, but my sight remains unchanged. What is happening to me? I quickly turn the water on and scrub my eyes.

Like this is going to help in any way.

My mind is overflowing. I can see every thought Tara ever had, but her most recent ones chill me to the bone.

CHAPTER 18

Set Free?

Kayla

I move back to the range and show Tara how to fire the gun again, but I'm only going through the motions. My mind is still on what happened upstairs, so painful and confusing. What frightens me the most is that I can't remember any of what they'd talked about. I listened to Alex drag out all of Jackson's sins, but all I really wanted to do was run away, escape what I was witnessing, but I couldn't. I had to hear it all.

I kept asking myself, *Who is this chick that survived all of that abuse?* I mean, at the time, it all sounded so familiar, but I couldn't place it. Maybe I'd read about it or saw it on TV. Then they said my name. I frantically search my memories, but they're gone, stolen from me. What else did he steal? All I have are bits and pieces of things, foggy images, flashes of events, but there are also huge holes.

I knew I was addicted to drugs, but that was it, just knowing. I can remember waking up from time to time in a cold sweat, but not the pain of rejection for being an outcast. I can barely see the faces of all my so-called foster parents, faces that used to drive my hate. The hurt, the deep sadness is gone. No matter how hard I try to dredge it up, it's useless. I feel lost. The very pain that used to define me has been stripped away. The things that made up who I was, that gave me purpose, as sick and twisted as that sounds, have disappeared.

I feel empty!

Who am I now? Without the pain, the absolute rage, what's left? I'm a hollow shell, stripped of self. Without those tragedies,

I have nothing to tell me who I am, where to go, how to act. I'm like a newborn trapped in this worn out, road-weary body.

There's a strange new feeling, very foreign, starting to rise and fill me, as if my spirit suddenly took a deep breath. It's a new freedom, unearned, beginning to fill me.

Is this what peace feels like? I don't know. It's as alien to me as everything else we've been through.

I remember feeling something like this once before. I had just turned fourteen, and I found an archery set in the garage of a redneck foster family I lived with deep in the boonies. There wasn't much to do, so I took it and went out into the woods. I wasn't sick then, one of the few periods when I felt somewhat healthy, almost normal.

I know now it was a compound bow, old and beat up, not much different from me. The first few times I could barely pull it back, but I was relentless and eventually I found the strength. In time, I found more control, balance, and confidence. Finally, I pulled an arrow out of the moldy quiver. A host of baby spiders made their exodus as I removed it. I dusted them off my arm and placed an arrow into the arrow rest and the bowstring into the nock. I didn't know what I was really doing then, but I pulled that first arrow back and fired; it landed two feet in front of me, a piss poor first try, but I was undaunted.

I kept at it, broke most of the arrows, strained both my arms, cut myself up pretty good, but I was determined. After a few weeks, I could hit the center of a tree from fifteen feet away. Then it was thirty. My aim improved with each attempt. As time went on, it almost felt like the bow was a part of me, comfortable, just right. I set up targets, and by the end of the month, I couldn't miss no matter what I aimed at. With each arrow I released, it was like I'd found a new strength from within.

I would leave home at lunchtime and return at dusk. No one cared, no one even asked where I'd been. It didn't bother me. I'd found my sanctuary. I remember practicing for hours in a rainstorm one day; still never missed, even with everything drenched. It was good—for the first time in my life I could use that word about something in my life. But my solitude wouldn't last long.

My foster dad caught me one day after I'd been out practicing. Not because he was looking for me. He'd just had another brawl with the missus and took a long walk before he got himself into more trouble. It was amazing who qualified to be a foster parent. In my experience, if you had a pulse, and no bodies in the basement (at least that the state knew of), you could get your blessing from the government.

He must have watched me for a while before he alerted me to his presence, which is creepy in retrospect. When I finally realized he was there, he just stared at me, speechless, then finally asked me where I'd learned to shoot; I told him I'd been teaching myself. He asked me for another demonstration. I hit five separate targets without missing a beat. He began clapping and approached me, telling me I had natural talent.

The next thing I knew, I met with the archery coach at the high school, trying out for the team. I aced the trials. Coach told me I had the best scores in years. I could see on her face the surprise that a girl like me could possess such talent. She was reluctant, but my skill outweighed her prejudice, and I was on the team.

It all happened so fast. The next week I was competing flawlessly. I could see their amazement with each win. How could such a degenerate possess such a talent? For the first time I was part of something important, but I was never part of the team.

It wasn't a good fit. I practiced alone. The other girls, they were all rich bitches who thought I was a charity case more than their equal. The girls tried to haze me, but they quickly found out the hard way that was a bad idea. Thankfully, no charges were filed despite the sheer volume of lawyers these suburban princesses had at their beck and call.

I never had friends, never needed them, and didn't want their drama on top of mine. Despite my team's lack of support and my coach's hesitant endorsement, I excelled. I was their workhorse, rough, unsightly, a lowly animal, a trained trick pony, a necessary evil.

I was on my way to the state tournament when my idiot foster father got arrested again for slapping his latest wife around. I lost my placement and was forced to go to a halfway house outside of my school's district. They wouldn't even let me keep my bow because they considered it a weapon, and I was too high of a risk to have it.

I thought the coach would fight for me after all I'd accomplished for her, the team, and that lousy school, but that was yet another false hope. The other girls despised me because of who I was and where I came from. They thought it would be better for a substitute to take my place. I learned later it was the girl I'd beaten out for my place on the team. I guess her father made a sizeable donation for new equipment.

How can I remember that so vividly, the hurt and disappointment as real in this moment as it was then, and yet everything else is gone?

It doesn't make sense.

Could that be the only good memory I have, even though it too was tainted? Was it worth holding onto while everything else was being erased?

When Alex grabbed my arm, there was a flash, and I felt electricity flow through my whole body. I knew something had happened, but what? All I remember was this release, as if my soul stood up on its own and stretched, like a cat after a long nap. He took my memories from me. It's the only explanation. It's getting harder and harder to find any anger, sadness, regret, even shame. How is that possible?

I can feel myself changing, getting physically stronger, but now I also feel stronger in my soul. Had I been freed from the contamination of my past, finally becoming human? So confusing but also refreshing.

What about Jackson? How the hell did his legs heal so fast? And what is happening to Alex? What's happening to all of us? I want to go to ask Alex, but something tells me to wait. Part of me fears him, while the other fights relentlessly to get as close to him as I can. God, will any of this ever make sense?

I glance over at Tara, who has stopped firing and is now clutching Jude as if gravity is about to give out and he'll float away. I hate and admire her. There's no doubt she loves that kid more than life itself, and yet she's a complete mess as a person.

Matt fires several more times, his aim getting better.

Doc seems much more confident. He told me he used to hunt before he got married, so he's no virgin to firing a gun, not like the rest of us. He hits dead on almost every time, chest, head, and stomach. Impressive!

Frowning, I think back to when Alex was helping Tara. I mean, what the hell happened with that? Tara is visibly frightened, though thank God the kid doesn't see it. Matt pauses and stares at me, as if he's going to say something. Then he shakes his head and continues to assist Tara. I can tell she's pressing him about Alex, but he does his best to refocus her.

Jude walks over to me. Great, like I need this! It seems despite my memory loss, my attitude manages to remain unspoiled. "You okay, Kayla?"

"Yeah, kid, I'm fine. How are you doing with your training?"

"Mom won't let me."

"Oh, really? Well, come over here with me."

While Matt has Tara distracted, I take Jude over to the stall on the other side. How in the world am I supposed to teach a kid how to use a gun? I mean, what isn't wrong with this picture? I try my best to mimic what Alex did. I have Jude put on his ear protection, then I put on mine. I hand him the 9mm and watch him nervously hold it.

This is going to be a disaster. I know right away this kid is going to either shoot himself or one of us. "Hold on, kid!" I motion for him to stay in place and head back to the table. I scrounge around, trying to find something smaller.

Wait, there it is, a .22 caliber. That'll work. I check to see if it's loaded. It's not my first time with a gun either. Not the first-time handling, loading, or even firing one.

Shit, why would I remember that too? But wait, why and when did I learn to shoot? I remember archery, but not this. The rest is lost in the mists of my mind.

I load the thing and walk back to Jude. "Now, watch how much ammo you use. I think Alex set out just enough for practice. The rest we need to save." I give Jude the gun. "Now, kid, watch and learn."

I aim it for him and help him pull the trigger. The recoil affects him at first but after a few rounds with my help, he starts to smile.

"Okay, Rambo, don't get too excited."

I let him fire it himself. He fires off a full magazine, hitting pretty much nothing while squealing with glee. *Yeah, that's a little creepy.*

I go to reload it, but Jude beat me to the punch. He switches the safety on and jettisons the spent magazine. Like a rabbit on caffeine, he reloads the thing and reset it, then fires round after round.

Shit, he's getting pretty good.

He hit the white, closer and closer to the outline of the target. He loads and reloads like a pro, magazine after magazine, getting more and more accurate. Well, if he fires it a couple of dozen times, he might actually hit something important.

"Okay, tiger, slow down. You're almost out of practice rounds."

He nods and gleefully loads his last magazine. This time he nails the target time and time again.

Hold the phone; how is that possible?

He finishes off the magazine and places the gun on the pulpit. "I'm done." He nods, sweat dripping down his face.

"You got that right."

"Thanks, Kayla. You rock!"

Tara is still unaware of our little session. She's been too busy working with Matt. Somehow, I think he was secretly and deliberately distracting her.

Jude bolts by me and back up the stairs.

"Hey, wait, you little shit!"

It's too late. He's up, up, and away. Where the hell is he going?

I turn to Matt and Tara. Tara is blasting the target. Matt stands back and gives me a smile. I head over to watch.

"She's a pro!" Matt yells at me. "She's hitting everything she aims at."

Tara finishes and ejects the magazine. I look at her face, frowning. This is not the timid, pathetic Bellezilla I had seen before. She now has a look of sheer determination. In fact, there isn't a single sign of our little confrontation from earlier. Not a scratch or bruise.

She places the gun on the pulpit and removes her headset. "How did I do?"

"Amazing," Matt says. "They won't know what hit them."

"Bullets," I interrupt. "They'll know it's bullets that hit them, trust me."

"Where's Jude," Tara asks.

"Upstairs. I was going to get him."

"You do that," she commands.

No, you did not just go there with me, chicky. I want to say something, but her gaze is harsh and serious.

Tara moves by me. "Hey, Matt, let's fire this again." She points to the automatic rifles.

Holy Sigourney Weaver, Batman. Tara just found her ovaries.

"I'm going to go check on Alex, make sure he's alright," I announce.

Doc walks over to us. "Alex's been under a lot of stress. I haven't seen him take a breather, though none of us really have. Probably why he needs a minute. Give him some time."

"Yeah, okay, whatever." I head up the stairs. The three new commandos don their arsenal and return to the stalls. I move up the stairs to the sound of bullets firing, both repeating and single fire. *This is getting very scary!*

Down the hall, I can hear Alex talking to Jude. I approach and see them both staring at the laptop. Alex turns to me, and I sigh in relief. His eyes are normal again.

"You good?" I ask.

"No, but better than I was." He stands up and tells Jude to wait for him as he guides me out of the room. "You, okay? I didn't scare you, did I?"

"Yes, a lot! What the hell happened to you?"

"Nothing, I just got overwhelmed."

"That was a tad bit more than overwhelmed, don't you think?"

"Let it go, Kayla. I'm fine."

I can see he's becoming agitated. "You know, as much as it pains me to say this, we need you, chief. If something is malfunctioning, you need to let us know. I mean, I can forgive the whole Jackson thing, but the ghost eyes can't happen again. I almost shit myself."

"I don't know what happened, but it's over now."

"For how long? Really, Alex, what the hell is going on?"

"Kayla, let it go!"

"What is that, your new catch phrase?"

"Never mind. How are they doing down there?"

"They're all Kill Bill downstairs, no worries."

"Kayla, I am serious."

"So am I. They're fine, real pros by now. Relax, chief, they got it covered. They're learning fast—I mean spooky fast."

"What?"

"Well, let me see. Tara is all G.I. Jane. Your boy Jude is a junior killjoy, and preacher man and the doc are doing fine. You got quite the little army there, chief."

"Is that right? And what about you?"

"Don't worry, I can handle myself."

"I know you can. That's why I worry." He finally smiles.

"What are you and the kid so into? I mean, we have advanced him to gunplay, so hopefully we haven't introduced him to anything else not suitable for his age group."

Alex is not amused, but I laugh anyway.

"Jude is helping me with something."

"Care to fill me in?"

"No."

Doc comes up the stairs and heads our way. "How is our fearless leader?" he asks.

"Cute, Doc. I'm okay," Alex replies.

"I figured you just needed a moment to decompress." The doc pats Alex on the back.

"Exactly. Besides, Kayla does a good job of checking up on me," Alex scoffs.

Doc begins to exit the room. "Great, I'm going to check on Jackson,"

"Hold up, Doc. I need to talk to you. Come with me."

Alex and the doc duck into another room and shut the door.

Well, fine, I got the hint. I slip into the other room to find Jude typing away on his laptop. "What are you looking at, kid?"

Before he can answer, I see a host of traffic cam feeds on the screen. What the hell?!

CHAPTER 19

Choices

(Alex)

"**A**nd that's the whole story," I conclude. I can see the doc is having a difficult time digesting what I just said. Who can blame him?

"But how do you know all of this?" he asks. "Did he confess it to you?"

"Yes." I can tell he sensed hesitation in my response.

"But how did you get him to confess? What prompted it all in the first place?" The suspicion in his voice is thick.

"Maybe it was the guilt of it all." I begin to weave my web of deceit. "I think he finally snapped and just needed to vent, get it all off his chest. Whatever the reason, he became so unstable I was forced to restrain him. He presents a danger to the whole group, Doc, but especially Kayla."

I'm not even remotely good at lying. It's just not in my character, but in this case, I feel it's a necessary evil, desperate times and all. I can see in the doc's eyes that he's really struggling with it all.

"If he said what he said, you're absolutely right," Doc says cautiously. "But I sense I'm missing a few pieces to this story. You've always been straight up with me, Alex, so if there are any missing pieces, you must have a damn good reason for keeping them from me."

I don't know how to react to this last statement, so I say nothing.

Doc pauses, then sighs. "I hope to God it's for the right reasons, because in all this chaos and darkness, you're our only ray of hope."

"I don't think I've given you any cause to doubt it, especially considering the fact you know what my primary goal has always been."

He pauses again. "I do, Alex, every moment, I do. And in all truth, I don't know if I could've made the same decision you did if the tables had been turned."

Without warning, the room grows dark, filled with shadows. It's a void, a vacuum. Doc is gone; the room is gone. I'm surrounded by deafening silence. Then a light rushes in. I can see her face as clearly as if she's right in front of me. I see each tear stream down her precious little rosy cheeks. I see her mouth the words in between the tears. "*Daddy, come home*! *Where are you?*"

My wife is holding her tight. I can't differentiate between where she ends and my daughter begins. Her tears drench Gracie's golden-blonde hair. I feel their fear, and it tears at me mercilessly.

I should be there with them!

I need to get back to Jude. His plan will work. It has to.

A voice shatters the darkness, unrecognizable at first, but more and more defined with every second that passes.

"Alex, are you okay?"

Suddenly, I'm back in the room again, every detail crystal clear. Doc is standing in front of me, bathed in concern. I realize I've been standing there in a blind daze. "Yeah, I'm fine. Are we good?"

"I guess so," Doc replies, not looking too sure.

"I have to go speak with Jude," I say, still trying to regain control of my faculties. "Can you go check on the others downstairs? After all, you're the only one besides me who truly knows how to handle a gun."

"Absolutely, as soon as you tell me what you're planning. I think I already know but humor me anyway."

I rub my eyes and sigh. I knew I couldn't lie my way through this one. "It's time, Doc," I say. "I can't wait any longer."

I find a chair behind me and take a seat. Doc remains standing, hanging on my every word.

"I think Jude has found a way for me to get home," I begin. "Thanks to the local news station, he realized he has access to over thirty different traffic cams set up all over the city. He's found a way to monitor them and map me out the best possible route home, if there is such a thing. It's my one and best chance. It won't be every mile, there are blind spots, some big ones, but it's still an advantage. We'll use cell phones to text so I can move as stealthily as possible. He can notify me of what he sees every step of the way, and I can relay back to him what the areas look like in those blind spots. I'll take videos as well. I trust the kid. We'll make it work.

I'm trusting a pre-teen kid with my life, and my family's lives. Nothing makes sense anymore.

"Yes, he's one of the brightest kids I've ever met," Doc says. "A bright kid who misses his father very much. It doesn't surprise me why he wants to help you so badly to get back to your family. The fact is, he's never truly understood why his father left, and Tara never had the heart to explain it to him. She was afraid he would blame himself. But she was too late for that. Jude overheard most of their arguments. He heard every time his father used him as an excuse for a reason to leave. Tara tried to shield him from it as best she could, but she failed miserably. Ever since then, Jude clings to anyone who has even the remote resemblance of a father figure. In the beginning, it was me. Tara would schedule regular visits, not for examination or protocols, but just so Jude could spend time with me. I would find time, despite my hectic schedule, because it was the right thing to do. To tell the truth, I had my own selfish reasons. He filled a void for me too."

Doc's eyes grow shiny with tears. He pauses and then resets. "Anyway, he loves computers, as you can tell, so I bought him one for the office—just for when he came to visit. Any chance I could find, I would spend time teaching him new things, spreadsheets, Word documents, anything and everything that would hold his interest. He was always a quick learner, an excellent student. If not for that damn disease, he could have been a real prodigy. He didn't deserve to have a father who abandoned him, using his disease as an excuse."

Doc pauses again. I hear him fighting back the emotion. This one hit close to home for him. "The nurses showered him with affection and attention. He became the office mascot. During one of my visits with Jude, Tara finally broke down. I was able to get him out of the room before she had a total emotional collapse. Between the bitter sobbing, she confessed to me some of the details of her marriage. She told me that her husband and their marriage had merely been a gateway to the lifestyle she'd so desperately wanted. The perfect marriage of convenience. He had money, and, in her youth, she'd been the perfect trophy wife, a demeaning title that she took as a deep compliment. She admitted she didn't even know if they'd ever truly loved each other, but they were both content with the arrangement.

"But once Jude got sick, he told her it was too much responsibility, and he wanted a way out. I didn't know the man personally, only what she told me, and the few articles that I read about him. The media thought of him as a pillar of the community, a shining icon of philanthropy in its purest form. They described him as the stalwart, dedicated husband, standing by his wife and selflessly supporting her through numerous treatments, a difficult and long recovery, and impossible pregnancy. They listed all his powerful connections and financial contributions. He was, in their minds, a god among men.

"Somehow, he found a way to justify his divorce within the media elite and miraculously avoided any public blow back. She said she made sure everything was kept as quiet and civilized as possible, her way of protecting Jude. They made a nice behind-closed-doors settlement, at least according to their standards. It was a windfall for her. She was paid well for her silence. Of course, he had a backup plan if she refused the money. A long, drawn out, public, bitter custody battle if she didn't cooperate. He would dredge up every misstep of her past, make it appear as if she was a gold digger obsessed with her lifestyle, and the constant approval of her Stepford friends. He had the lawyers, the best money could buy, make it happen. Not a new story among the rich and shameless.

"She ended her breakdown with a very definitive assertion. That the only good thing to come out of her marriage was Jude. Despite what you may see on the surface, her perceived shallowness and materialism, or how deeply she hates her husband, I know she loves that boy more than life itself. I've seen it, and that's something you just can't fake. Even if you have become an expert at faking your entire life."

I can't tell the doc that I know exactly what he's talking about, and so much more. I saw deep inside Tara's soul, and everything she and her son had been through. When she touched me downstairs, every moment of her life rushed into mine. The pain was almost indescribable, a mixture of sudden, continuous, sharp piercing pain, extreme nausea, and crushing pressure all at the same time. I still can't figure out how I held it together and made it back up the stairs.

And what the hell was going on with my eyes?

I kept having flashes of her life at the table, up the stairs, until they finally ended in the hall, thank God. Random, unconnected bursts of memories, things that she had repressed deep into her psyche, released to me in a flood of images and noises. The doc doesn't know what she's contemplating, the escape she's formulated in her mind. She's lost all sense of hope and is just going through the motions until the time is right. If they come again, she plans to make sure Jude won't suffer. I couldn't react to it then, but by the grace of God, I won't let her find her chance, even though it's on me that she's now armed. I have to tell someone. If I don't, who'll be here to ensure it never happens?

"Alex, are you listening?"

"Yeah, I heard every word, Doc. Just processing it all."

"I told you all that so you would understand this," Doc continues.

"What now?"

"That despite his love and respect for me, it's you who Jude sees as a real hero. In his eyes, you're the father he's always dreamed of and wanted."

Stunned, I never picked that up from my connection with Tara. How did she keep that one hidden from me? Unless she doesn't see it. Unless it's as foreign to her as any hope we'll survive this.

"Jude sees you as a hero, as a superman who will not stop until we're all safe," Doc continues.

"Then why is he helping me leave to find my family?" I reply. "Why take the chance? That just doesn't make sense."

"Because he believes in you. More than anything in his life, he believes in you. He believes you can make it home, get to your family, and come back for us. He believes you will bring us out of all this."

Tara doesn't share that idea because she doesn't have any sense of hope. She firmly believes this is the end, and there's nothing that can free us from this evil. Just like Jackson, she believes this is some punishment for her sins, and somehow, she's dragged Jude and the rest of us into it.

It's warped but, after seeing what she saw about herself, it makes perfect sense. Self-worth isn't attainable for her, either by her own denial or the constant reminding of her husband. He had a very specific idea of who she was and was never shy in conveying it to her daily. If her husband couldn't convince her with his words, then he used more physical means. Demean her, abuse her, just to exact his own fleeting sense of masculinity.

How can a husband do that to his wife?

I don't know why it surprised me. I'd seen it time and time again in the numerous domestic violence cases I'd investigated. It reared its ugly head in various ways, but it was always for the same reasons. They all used the same tired excuses, and the victims almost always forgave. A vicious cycle that seemed unbreakable, whether by choice or because she was so thoroughly broken that the pieces would never fit together right again.

You can't change evil.

The doc draws my attention back to him. "Alex, you with me?"

"Yes. This'll give me the means to travel as safely as possible to retrieve my family and return. I'm hoping we can hold up here for a while until we figure out what's happened. Like I said before, we have shelter, resources, and weapons to make a stand, at least in the short term. What we gather may give us a solid escape route to something better. It's not much of a plan, but it's all we've got."

"If you leave, you won't survive."

This argument is getting old. "With Jude's help, I will. Now, I've put this off long enough. I'm leaving."

Doc pauses. "Fine, I've said my peace and won't argue with you anymore. It's not that I don't believe in you Alex, it's just … right now, I believe in the reality of what's happening to us more. Still, I won't be responsible for you not reaching your family. God knows, I would've done anything to save mine."

"I know, Doc, and I hear you, but if anyone has the training to make this work, it's me."

"I don't think any amount of training can prepare anyone for this. It's insanity. Still, what do I tell the others?"

"Just what I told you. Honesty is one of the only things we really have left." I can feel the hypocrisy fill my throat. If he only knew the truth of what's been happening to me, he really would think I was insane.

"Whatever you do, don't let Jackson out. I'll deal with him when I return."

Doubt covered the doc's weary face. I get up and walk over to him, grabbing hold of his arms. "I will return, Rick. Count on it."

"You can't make that promise," he says, his tone defeated.

"Yes, I can. Keep the others focused on training. Don't let them participate in monitoring me. Nothing good can come of it. Keep Jude away from the group. He needs to focus on my little journey, or it'll be a very short trip. That's going to be tough, especially when it comes to Tara. Can you handle it?"

Doc pauses again. I let go and back up. "I'll do my best," he replies reluctantly.

I had a secondary agenda for keeping Tara and Jude apart, but I can't show my hand to the doc yet. I think Matt will be better equipped to deal with her hidden instability. As a pastor, he's had to deal with suicidal thoughts before. At least I hope so. Either way, he's my only real hope to ensure Tara doesn't commit the unthinkable.

I hand the keys to Jackson's room to the doc. "Keep these with you. Check on him, but don't interact with him." I'll have to trust he'll do the right thing. I wouldn't have had to worry about it if I'd put that dog out of its misery. No, that would've made things worse, justified or not. "He's extremely dangerous. Please be careful."

"Okay," Doc responds, with a slight bit more enthusiasm. "I get it, don't worry. He'll be taken care of. With all the freakish things we've faced, he's small potatoes."

I nod, having no choice but to trust him, then move back to Jude's room. "Hey, kid," I say as I peek in. "Give me a couple more minutes and we'll have a final strategy session."

Jude doesn't look up from his laptop. "Cool! It'll give me time to sync up the rest of the computers in here."

I shake my head. My partner in the most crucial mission of my life is an eleven-year-old kid. It's utter madness.

"Oh, better watch out for Kayla," he says, still deep in what he's doing. "She's pissed."

Big surprise. "And why is that?"

"She asked me what's going on and I told her." He doesn't look up from the computer screen.

"Shit, Jude, why did you go and do that?"

"You didn't tell me not to." Jude pops up and blasts by me toward the front offices.

"Thanks a lot, partner," I call out as he disappears down the hall.

"Welcome," he calls back, his voice softening in the distance.

As I move down the hall, I see Kayla leave the room that the doc and I were just in. She's fuming, and our collision is unavoidable. She stops dead, and I know this is not going to be pretty.

"Where the fuck do you think you're going?"

"I don't have time for this, Kayla," I reply without losing a step as I make my way back to the stairwell.

She follows me with purpose. "You can't leave now. I don't care what half-ass idea you and the kid came up with."

"Back off, Kayla. I mean it." I descend the staircase with her close behind, stuck to me like Velcro. When we reach the bottom, I can hear Matt and Tara continue their target practice.

Kayla grabs both my shoulders and spins me around to face her. *Shit, she's gotten strong!*

"It's not going to work," she screams.

"You're just a child. How the hell do you know what will or won't work, Kayla? I need time to prepare, and you're getting in the way of that right now. We're done! This conversation is over. This is going to happen. Now live with it!"

She retreats slightly, the shock in her eyes unnerving and unmistakable. I can feel the heat radiating from my face. Apparently, so can she.

"Fine!" Her voice begins to tremble. "Fine!" She turns away from me. "You really are just like all the rest."

"What?"

She turns back, her eyes filled with tears. "I thought you were different, but you're not."

"Really?" I say sarcastically. "Am I? Do you even know anyone who puts their family first before everything else? Kayla, you're just not used to a man who's willing to sacrifice everything for the people he loves."

She pauses, visibly taken aback, her expression empty, then it screams of disappointment and fear. "So what are we?" she questions, still weeping.

Shit, I wasn't prepared for that one!

I stand there, speechless.

"What are we, Alex?" she repeats. "Don't we mean anything to you?"

Again, I have nothing to give her. I frantically search my mind, but I find nothing. Even if I had an answer, would it cause more damage than good?

"That's what I thought. Thanks for nothing, hero!" She slowly stomps back up the stairs.

I just stand there, dumbfounded, stunned by her honesty, and hurt. Again, if I had answered it, the truth would just cause her more pain. Nothing I say will comfort her. I watch her disappear up the stairs.

A hand touches my shoulder, and I quickly pull away, swinging around. It's Matt.

"Whoa, what's going on, Alex?" he says, startled by my reaction.

"Nothing, just don't come up on me like that."

"Okay, sorry. It's just that I saw Kayla leave, and she looked upset."

"When is Kayla not upset? It's her normal mood," I rudely reply. But I'm preoccupied with her question; it's like a thorn in my mind.

"True, but is she alright?" he asks, despite my obvious tone.

"Everything is fine!" I snap. Unfortunately, I seem to be getting pretty good at this lying game.

Matt ignores my attitude. "Listen, we're going to take a break," he continues, beginning to take off his gear. "Tara is doing great. I think both of us have a solid feel for it. Of course, this is just practice. I don't think any of us really understand what'll happen in a real fire fight."

"Nobody ever does, not until they're in one," I snap, "no matter how much they practice."

Matt pauses. I see he's trying to figure me out. "You still with us?" he asks.

Am I? Will my half-ass plan even work? Is my family all right, or am I signing my own death sentence?

"Alex!"

Fuck! I keep zoning out! "Yes."

Tara approaches us.

"You sure you're okay?" Matt murmurs.

"Everything's fine, Matt. But we do need to talk."

"How we doing, guys?" Tara interjects?

"Fine, according to Alex," Matt jokes.

"Okay," she says. "So what's next?"

"Why don't you take a break. There's a refrigerator in the break room upstairs. It's stocked with water and soda and some protein bars in the cabinets."

Tara looks at me and nods. "Okay, thanks. How did I do, Matt?" she asks, almost giddy.

"Awesome, you're a natural," Matt replies. "Have you ever fired a gun before?"

"No, never!"

"That's impressive," I say.

"Thank you, gentlemen." Tara laughs as she begins to ascend the stairs.

Wow, this new Tara is refreshing, and maybe a little nauseating. *Now I sound like Kayla.*

"I'll meet you up there," Matt calls up to her. He turns to me. "It's like a weight has been lifted off her. Like night and day."

I wait until she's no longer within earshot to say, "It's an act, Matt."

"What?"

Where do I begin?

CHAPTER 20

The Quiet Chaos Before the Storm
Kayla

I sit at the top of the stairs as Tara literally skips by me. I don't have time for her. I have to try one more time with Alex, whether I piss him off or not. I just don't care anymore.

I descend the staircase, hearing Alex talking. I stop and hide in the shadows, listening.

"Matt, I have to tell you something," Alex says, "but I don't even know how to explain it. It sounds completely crazy."

Matt doesn't respond. He stands there in silence, waiting for Alex to continue.

"Something has happened to me, something that's going to be extremely hard to put into words. With everything we've been through, I hope I've earned your trust, though this may challenge that. If you were to tell me this, I know I would question it."

What the hell is he talking about?

"You're right, Alex, I don't know you very well, only what Rick has told me, but he thinks very highly of you, and he's one of the sincerest men I've ever met, a real-life example of integrity in a very cynical world. He considers each patient a part of his extended family and feels every bit of their struggle and pain."

Alex leans against a wall, his arms crossed over his chest as he listens.

"Rick and I are very much alike in that way," Matt continues. "As a pastor, when you fail a soul who comes to you for guidance, sometimes as their very last chance for hope, no matter what you say or do, it can't bring them the peace they so desperately seek. It leaves you feeling useless inside, something you can never prepare yourself for. Not only do you feel like you've failed them, but worse, you feel like you failed God.

"I counseled Rick after he lost his wife and son. We spent a lot of time together; long before I knew about my own illness. I never let on, but with each meeting I felt more and more useless to him. Every scripture felt stale and clichéd. In the end, I tried to just be there for him, not as a pastor but as a friend. Even then, I felt like I'd failed him because nothing I said or did kept him from falling deeper and deeper into his own personal darkness. But then, just when I believed he'd slipped into the abyss, out of nowhere, there was a change. Secretly, I was jealous because I knew I'd had nothing to do with it. It took me a long time before I got up the nerve to ask him."

Alex remains silent. I knew something had happened to the doc, but I never found out what. He'd kept all those pictures in his office, so I thought his family was alive. Strange that I remember that, but so little else. I lean in closer as Matt continues his story.

"Then I found out about my disease. I was terminal by the time I reacted to my cancer. My wife left as soon as she found out I was sick. The church abandoned me almost a year to the day later. I was alone, lost in my own trials, and I forgot what hope even looked like. I had reached a low I didn't even know existed."

And he expects me to believe in God? As if everything I've been through isn't proof enough that God doesn't exist, even the preacher gets left out in the cold. I mean, would all that have happened if God truly existed? I don't think so.

Matt continues, "But then I realized a great truth. God is silent for a reason. He stays silent so we become so desperate to hear him that we clear away every other voice that would distract us, or any of our own preconceived answers. We become humble and surrender ourselves to the knowledge that it is only God who can rescue us. At this moment, after weeks of torturous quiet, God chose Rick as His ambassador. Rick clearly saw me losing hope, and that's when he told me his own story. Every detail of what you had done for him. It really is a very small world, smaller than we can ever imagine. We're all connected, like a giant living jigsaw puzzle, with different pieces making up a beautiful whole, and it's God who fits the pieces together.

"We never know the impact we have on people, like ripples in the water after a pebble is dropped in, spanning out indefinitely. At that point in time, you saved my life, too. I never thought I'd be given the chance to tell you that. I feel I know you very well, Alex, so what is it you want to tell me?"

Alex remains quiet for a moment, as if taking everything in that Matt just told him. "Tara wants to commit suicide, and she plans to take Jude out with her."

What?!

Matt is apparently stunned into silence, so Alex says, "She doesn't see any hope anymore. She can't find a realistic escape from what we're facing. She's decided she won't let her or Jude suffer and die by those things out there. When the moment is right, when the next wave of terror comes, she'll make her move, a bullet for each of them in some dark corner."

"How do you know this?" Matt finally asks.

Yeah, Alex, how do you know? Like, maybe the same way you took all my memories!

"It doesn't matter how I learned. For now, we have to act like we don't know. I'm keeping Jude busy with a project we're working on together. We can't allow Tara to be alone with Jude, and she can't know we're trying to keep them apart."

"She just went upstairs," Matt said. "She's probably alone with Jude now. If what you're saying is true, we need to get up there now. Maybe I can talk to her."

I can't wait any longer. I take a chance and peek around the corner. Matt is trying to get past Alex, but he stops him.

"I need to talk to her, Alex. If everything you say is true, I have to talk to her."

"You can't. If you do, it might expedite her plans. Besides, how are you going to explain to her how you knew? Jude is safe, and the doc is up there. She won't try anything now. She'll wait until she's convinced herself she has no other choice."

"I don't have to tell her. I can work around it, strike up a conversation about how she's doing, maybe get her to admit it to me."

"Stop and think for a moment, Matt. She's not going to admit to something like that to anyone. I promise you, she is determined to do this."

"I don't understand. How can you *know* any of that? Wait a second; did she admit it to you?"

"No, she did not. Again, I'm asking you to trust me."

"Alex, you gotta give me something."

"I can't, Matt. I just can't." His face extremely pale, Alex pauses, and I can see him take a long, deep breath. "Save them, Matt, so I can go save my family. I need someone here who can lead during the short time I'm gone."

The utter confusion on Matt's face is unmistakable when he asks, "Gone where?"

"Jude is going to use the real time video feeds on his laptop from the traffic cameras to guide me home."

"But those things are out there. How are you going to protect yourself from them?"

"I'll find a way. You'll just have to trust me. I can't give you any more than that."

"That's a tall order, Alex."

"Yes, but I have no choice. Will you help me?"

You could see Matt's mind working overtime. "Does Rick even know about Tara?"

"Yes, I've already covered it with him too, but he has his own little babysitting assignment, keeping Jackson on lockdown and everybody else away from him."

"This is insane, absolutely insane!" Matt hisses.

"I know, Matt, believe me, I know, but again, I have no choice. I can feel my family. Every moment that passes, I can feel them." Tears well up in eyes. "They're alive, I know it, more so now than ever before. I need to get to them, and there isn't much time left."

"How do you know they're alive?" When Alex doesn't answer, Matt aggressively rubs his forehead. "Okay, okay, we'll make this work. Somehow, some way, we'll make it work."

The doubt is thick in Matt's voice. I can't believe he's agreed to this. Matt has become a member of this madness.

"Let me suggest this," Matt says. "Let me go with you, or possibly Rick. There's safety in numbers. You'll stand a much better chance if you have help."

"Not this time. I can't risk those things targeting anyone who goes with me. One man alone might be able to slip past them. One man stands a better chance, and this way I won't have to worry about anyone but me."

"I know you're a soldier, but nothing can prepare you for what's out there. It's crazy to go out period, but especially alone. You're talking about Tara wanting to die, but this is a death wish too. There's no other way to define it."

"Not for me, but it will be for my family if I don't go rescue them."

What will he do if he finds them dead? How will he react if he catches a glimpse of their lifeless bodies, or what's left of them? I already know. So does Matt. For Alex to exist without them is to not exist at all. But I believe him when he says he can feel them. To him, they're alive.

"I have to go upstairs now to finish coordinating everything with Jude," Alex says.

Matt nods. Somehow, I know deep down he's still against what Alex is doing, but he's reconciled himself to accept it.

"Come with me. I need you to help me keep the others occupied, especially Kayla."

And the patronizing dick has returned!

"Does she know what's going on?"

"Unfortunately, yes."

Just when I'd started rooting for the guy, he plays the dick card.

"Bet she's not taking any of this well," Matt says. "She won't be easy to handle."

Make that two dick cards!

"You have no idea!"

They head toward me.

Shit!

I sprint back up the stairs and see Jude rush from the front office back into a room. I move past the break room, finding the doc and Tara sitting at the table, enjoying a soda. The keys to Jackson's room are on the table next to the doc's hand. Tara looks tired. The exhaustion is setting in quick for her. I know so much about her now.

Too much!

The only thing that we really own in life is our memories and pain. Our mind is the only sanctuary of real privacy. And though we are worlds apart in every way, I feel like Tara and I have this one thing in common. Someone tapped into our most private place, violated our most sacred sanctum, like a thief stealing our thoughts in the dark. But unlike me, she doesn't have a clue about it.

Matt and Alex appear from the stairwell.

Jude exits the room and bolts past me toward them. He grabs Alex's arm, but Alex jerks violently away, almost knocking Jude to the floor. Matt stops Jude's fall, staring at Alex strangely. I was shocked at first, but then it hit me. He doesn't want Jude to touch him. If he does, will he experience the same thing that I did, and the desperate housewife did? He can't tell Matt why he did what he just did. I mean, it happened to me, and I still can't believe it.

What a heavy weight to bear alone.

Alex tugs at his sleeve, a look of relief washing over him. Jude had missed and only grabbed the fabric.

Jude seems completely unaffected by the interaction, too juiced up, completely wired. "Alex, I have to show you something!"

Alex tries to hush him as he scans the hallway, his gaze locking right on me. Great.

Matt sighs, then slips by me, heading into the break room. "I need a drink."

Alex glares at me, motioning with his eyes for me to follow Matt into the break room. I give it a few seconds, then comply. Matt walks to the fridge and extracts a bottle of water. He collapses in a chair next to the doc and Tara, joining the conversation. They weren't paying any attention to me, so I slip back into the hallway and slide over to the room Jude had gone into.

Peeking around the corner, I find them both standing at a table. Jude has created what looks like a makeshift mission control. I peek in for a better look, risking getting caught, but it's well worth it. Their backs are to me, totally immersed in Jude's elaborate setup. I see seven monitors set up on a table, each with multiple video feeds showing different street views. Each monitor is carefully labeled with corresponding keyboards running into CPUs below the table.

There's a cell phone in the middle of the table and two more sitting next to it, charging. A stack of legal pads lay at the edge of the table with a pile of pens. One pad is next to the cell phone with several pages flipped over, filled with hastily scribbled notes, barely legible to me, but I'm sure he can discern every letter. Next to the table is a mini fridge that's been relocated from the break room.

A large map of the city has been unevenly tacked to the wall with colored pins placed along a path leading from one point to another. I can't make out the destinations. There are pictures taped to the wall all around the map, images that he must have captured on the internet and then printed. Some depicted fuzzy images of creatures that I immediately recognize, while others I've never seen before. The adjoining wall is filled with articles he had printed, blogs and newsfeeds that he had carefully arranged to apparently tell a story. There were nearly a hundred papering the wall. Different color strings connect articles one to another.

Boy, has this dude been busy!

He's built all this in the short amount of time we've been here. I can't accomplish more than three things on any given day. This kid is MacGyver on meth. It's simply amazing. I'm speechless.

"I scavenged everything I could," Jude explains. "We're all set up and good to go on this end." He hands Alex two cell phones. "One is for the trip to, and the other for the trip back." He sits down at his command center. "I can view all the cameras now. I'll follow you each step of the way." He points to the wall. "And I was able to map out almost ninety percent of the route."

"Amazing job, kid!"

Jude's smile widens. "Thanks! It was nothing once I got it all set up in my head."

Alex moves closer to the wall of articles. "You want to explain these to me?" He points to the elaborate web of colorful strings.

Jude gets up quickly and darts over to the wall. "I tried to piece together a picture of what's happened to us and what we may be up against."

"How long did this take you?" Alex looks awestruck.

So am I!

"This is every article, every reference, every bit of information I could put together to try to figure this out. You know, there was information about this before, but it looks like nobody took it seriously. There were reports of creatures like the ones we've seen for at least a month, mostly in South America and Mexico. I think I heard Doctor Rick tell you some of this before, about the drunk guy who said he saw sky spiders. I think he also told you about the group of bloggers who disappeared while investigating the story, right?"

Alex barely nods before Jude continues.

"Well, there's more. Those rhino things that almost killed you and Jackson were spotted in Brazil by an environmentalist group filming a reality show about deforestation. They saw a whole herd of them appear, then disappear. They even snapped a couple of shots."

He points to several grainy images. I try to stretch my eyes to see them, but it's pointless.

"Sorry about the definition. Your printers here suck. There's a lady in Columbia who had a stable full of goats eaten up by a cat-like creature with six legs, no ears or eyes, and a mouth that contained multiple spear-like tongues. She thought it was a chupacabra. Who knows, maybe people have been seeing these things for years, but they've been either ignored or lumped in with other myths."

I guess by that logic Big Foot and the Loch Ness Monster are real, too?

"Doc thinks they're from another dimension that somehow crossed with ours. Like aliens from a parallel world that have been slipping in and out of ours for ages. Maybe the dimensions finally crashed together, and when they did, these things permanently escaped. Makes sense, doesn't it?"

Alex says nothing. He appears to be trying to take it all in.

"Maybe when the crash happened, it killed almost everybody but us. Doc thinks we may have survived because of our disease."

Did he really just say that? Even worse, would the doc really say that?

"Either way, they're here now, and they're obviously not friendly."

Understatement of the millennium!

He moves frantically from article to article. "There's story after story from other survivors describing the same types of monsters we're seeing. Here are ten about those insect things." He points to them quickly.

I don't know how Alex is keeping up.

"Based on what I've read, they like the dark areas, but not if they're wet or moist." He bolts to the other side of the wall. "Here are five about those rhino things. Most say they won't attack unless they're threatened."

How can anyone possibly know this shit?

Jude relocates again, like the Energizer Bunny on crack. "Over here are a dozen or more about the flying menace, as I like to call them."

Alex follows him around the room, trying to keep up.

"It looks like one will scout out the area, and the others attack when it finds food. They apparently send out a signal when they screech. It calls in the reinforcements. And they are not alone in the sky."

He scoots to the other wall and pulls a picture, handing it to Alex.

"This is a big one that apparently eats the little ones. It looks like a huge manta ray to me. I saw one once on the Discovery Channel. The guy who took this looked out his window when the flying menaces attacked a group of people who were walking along his street. He said there were about two dozen of them.

They killed them all the same way they killed those hospital patients. Then, this big thing swooped down and gobbled them up, like a whale sucking down plankton. I saw that on the Discovery Channel, too. You know what I'm talking about, right?"

I'm barely able to keep up with his excited and energetic pace. I can only imagine what Alex is thinking. No wonder this kid's a genius—he's watching nature shows, when at his age I was all about MTV. I mean, how do these things fly anyway? It doesn't make sense. It's like they float in the air, as if they're weightless, defying gravity.

Birds can't fly like that, right?

As Alex stares at the picture, Jude continues. "The guy thinks they have air bladders or something that fill up and make them float like balloons, then glide like bats."

Well, that answers that, I guess!

"There's more!"

More?

"There are some things we haven't seen yet, like those cat-like creatures I told you about, and there's even a couple of blogs about things that look almost human, groups of them even."

What?!

Alex looks up, his expression as stunned as I am.

"No pictures though, just sightings. Here's that blog. It's four pages long." He hands it to Alex, who's still holding onto the other picture.

"This one was written three hours ago. He was blogging religiously every fifteen minutes or so, then he stopped about an hour ago. In fact, as far as I can tell, every one of these articles from bloggers were the last entries they made. When I first logged on, the internet was buzzing, people blogging and chatting nonstop. They were all desperate to find other survivors. But not too long after we got here, the chatter dropped off a lot. Only a few of them, like me, are still posting stuff. The one thing we all have in common is they are all afraid, afraid that they aren't going to survive much longer. Oh, and one more thing, a lot of them talk about how they are either struggling with or had just been diagnosed with cancer. Something else we all have in common."

Alex looks back at the mass of paper attached to the wall and pauses.

"Do you think it's possible about the cancer?" Jude asks.

"Kid, at this point, anything is possible," Alex replies, placing the paperwork on the table.

Jude looks up at Alex with fear in his eyes, reaching for Alex's arm. "So far, I haven't seen any of these things on the cameras."

"Well, that's a good thing, right?"

"No!" Jude shoots back. "Based on everything I've seen and read, I don't think they come out unless they know or sense a food source is around. They must hide until then. They can't see us because they don't have eyes, and I don't think they can smell us either."

How can he possibly know this?

Jude grows still. He looks like he's become completely lost in his own calculations. "I think they feel us."

"What do you mean?"

"I think they can sense our heat, feel us move, maybe even our heartbeats. At least that's what I was able to figure out from what I've been reading. Once you go out there, they will sense you—and they'll know you're there. You won't be able to run or hide," he continues, his tone robotic now as he stares off into nothing. "They won't stop until they hunt you down and kill you."

Jude looks up and I can see all the color has disappeared from his eyes, just like Alex's had earlier. "We're all going to die," he whispers.

Alex and Jude stand there frozen in the room, lifeless and statuesque. Neither moves. I can't even tell if they're breathing. Then I realize…

Oh my God, Jude is touching Alex's bare arm!

CHAPTER 21

Safe No More

Alex

I feel a jolt of energy race through my arms and try to release it, but it's too late. The transfer had already started, leaving me paralyzed. His pain rushes into my heart and I feel every second of his shame, guilt, abandonment, loneliness. There's no escape. His eyes glow white, as suddenly my own eyes wax dark, then a bright light fills the room. I'm frozen in time. The walls illuminate and images race across them, surrounding me.

I see his father waving goodbye as he leaves for work on that crisp fall day in October. I can feel the chill in the air, smell the fallen leaves. He and I know he won't be back. The man smiles, but it's empty and hollow, false. Then the room spins, and the images flash forward. We peer into Tara's room. She's crying, talking to someone on the phone. I hear her say it's all her fault. If she hadn't rushed, he would have never gotten sick. She sees us, sprints to the door, and slams it shut. We spin the opposite way. The video plays again, a blink from the past. But now we are part of it, not just watching. Tara sings over our beds. Dad walks in and tells her he cancelled it.

She screams, "What?"

"The arrangement for becoming foster parents," he says as he rubs her head. His touch is chilling. He explains that they called, but he said no. She springs up and they begin to argue. I can barely make out what they're saying. It's all moving so loud and fast. He says something about violating his trust. He blames her. All of this happened because of her selfishness. She ruined everything. She's crying again. She attempts to slap him, but he ducks, and she nearly falls on the bed.

"So that's how it's going to be, you bitch," he callously scolds. He grabs her arm, jerking her to her feet, then drags her out of the room. She fights back, but he's too strong. He slams the door and locks it.

Crying now, we run to the door and shake the knob. I can hear a loud commotion; something slams against the wall. I hear screams and then repeated slaps against bare skin. The floor shakes as someone hits the ground. It sounds like he's kicking her. We violently shook the door, calling out her name. The chaos stops, only to be followed by the sound of silent sobbing.

In a very weak voice, she quietly calls to us, "It's alright, go to bed." Her voice is strained from weeping. Then we are jolted again, speeding through time and space. I feel like I'm being torn apart. We come to a bone-shattering stop, sitting on the edge of an examining table. Rick sits in front of us, handing us a book about Abraham Lincoln. It's one of the many he's given us over the last year. After we read it, he'll quiz us and then give us another.

"Lincoln struggled as well," Rick gently explains. "But because of that, it made him stronger. It's made him deeply appreciate life and freedom. Most of all, it taught him how to become a great man."

We nod and eagerly flip through the pages. This one is a long one—they get longer each time.

Rick smiles. "I know there are a lot of pages, but truth isn't always simple, and there are never any short cuts to find it." He's so wise, our hero. How many nights have we wished that he'd been our father? I feel the love we have for him. It's what keeps us going. We're really sick this time. It's getting worse with each visit. We're aware he knows that, but he doesn't say it. He never will. He begins his examination, and the room fades to black.

I'm now standing in an empty room. Jude is no longer with me. I don't know when the separation occurred. His absence is deeply felt, like an organ cut out of me. I walk down a hall; the light is steadily brightening. I enter a room and there is a body in front of me. I can't make out who it is, but I feel a deep sense of loss, despair.

I step closer. It's a man. I can make out his clothing, but not his face. It's like I'm looking through a smoky haze. I wrinkle my nose as I approach at the wretched, foul stench in the air, like something is burning and rotting at the same time. Standing over the body, there's no face, just an open void that seems endless. My heart stops beating and I can barely breathe.

Then, it sits up. Blood pours from the void, down its chest, filling its lap. I can hear screams, soft at first, then building. They tear through my flesh, right down to my bones. The corpse rises and stands, facing me. I'm frozen. It reaches out for my hand, completely drenched in blood. I'm terrified. The screams don't stop, drowning out every other sound. It grabs my hand, blood flowing down my wrist into my sleeve. It feels like ants crawling, biting my skin.

As the void changes, it pulls me toward itself, morphing into a hideous giant mouth with rows and rows of sharp yellow teeth. Its neck grows, becoming snakelike. It rises above me. If I don't move, it will devour me, but I can't. I'm frozen. The head grows larger and larger, and the sound of teeth grinding overpowers the screams in the background. It's hell incarnate. I hear a voice in my head: "*You know who I am, Alex! You know what I want!*"

I can't speak as its shadow engulfs me. Its hand became a tentacle wrapping around my wrist, then my arm.

It growls, "*It's time, time to die!*"

Boone is beside me. The wound in his chest is gaping, smoke billowing from it. His eyes are black, and lips snow white. He grabs it by the arm and screams at me, "Is this what you want? Do you want it to consume you? Fight, you son of a bitch, fight!"

Sara is on my other side, her flesh ripped and rotting. I can see straight through her skin to her muscles and bone. Her hair is falling out, eyes vacant holes filled with blood and darkness. She grabs my arm, her touch burning my skin.

"It's not her!" Boone screams. "She's not here!"

Gracie is crying, but it quickly mutates into something ominous and chilling. I hear her coming toward me. I won't look. I refuse to! I know death has left its mark on her and I can't bear that image. Rage and hate engulf me.

Boone pulls at my arm. "Don't fear it. Take it head on! Don't let it own you!"

I look up at the horrendous mutation that now hovers above me. The mouth of hell waits to take its final bite. I break away from Sara's hold and snatch the beast by its neck, feeling the scales tighten in my grip. "Finish this, Alex, finish it!" Boone demands.

The monstrosity pulls free from Boone. With every ounce of strength I have, I thrust my hand into its chest. I dig around, grabbing its heart covered in thorns, which bury themselves deep in the palm of my hand. I pull hard and yank it out, still beating. It screams horrifically and jerks violently back. I squeeze its neck with all my rage, my fingers digging deep into its muscle. I then rip its head clean off, shoving its beating heart deep down its throat as its teeth sheer the flesh of my arm.

The monster falls back and drops to the ground, blood spraying from its chest like a fountain, bathing me entirely. It burns my skin like acid. In excruciating pain, my arm throbbing, I step back and look down at the monster. It's shredded, its form not making sense anymore.

I begin to faint, but Boone holds me up. "You're not done yet, partner. End it now," Boone commands. My flesh is dripping off, falling to the floor like wet tissue. Sara is gone. The only screams are coming from the beast writhing in front of me.

"You can't win, Alex. You know you can't win!" the abomination screams, now lying mutilated and defeated on the floor.

I crush its head under my boot, stomp and stomp, each impact more violent than the last, breaking both bone and teeth. My body is on fire. I feel it dissolving and fall to my knees, beginning to pound on the creature's chest with my one good hand. Its head is squashed, spread over the floor like a trampled melon. I crush its ribs and continue to pound until it's just tenderizing raw meat. I try to stand back up, but my legs break off like dry wood. I watch them dissolve in front of my eyes into pools of crimson-colored goo, then I fall backward and lay spread out, melting into the floor.

Boone stands over me, smiling widely. "If you're going to live, you have to die. You must be remade."

I feel my head dissolve, my face caved into itself. All my teeth fall out, mixing with the human paste. I'm becoming blind, deaf, and mute. The room goes dark and cold, absolute darkness. I'm there, but I'm nothing.

"Now you're ready to finish this," Boone says, his voice echoing through the emptiness.

I open my eyes, and Jude is staring at me.

"I don't want to die, Alex. I don't want to become like them!"

We're standing in a room surrounded by those piles of goo, the remnants of those who did not survive.

"Please don't let me die," he cries.

I pull him in close, hugging him tightly. "Not a chance, kid, not a chance."

"Can you make that promise?" Boone whispers.

"Do you blame me, my brother?" It's the burning, haunting question I never had the chance to ask before.

"Never. I saw you carry me. I saw you face death without blinking just for the mere chance I might be alive. That's who you are, and that's why I love you."

Then silence. I know he's gone, but we're not alone. Sara is standing over me, all her beauty restored. Seeing her is like being bathed in light.

"That's why I love you," she whispers as she fades like a vapor.

It's just me and Jude in the room again.

"I promise I will do everything I can to protect you," I say. "That's all I can offer you."

"Thank you, Daddy."

I can feel his tears drench my shirt. I won't correct him. I don't know if he even realizes what he said. Let him have this moment. I know all too well he needs and deserves it. Time stops as he weeps into my chest.

The room takes form again. We're back at the station, my eyes clear. Whatever just happened, it's over. I pull Jude to his feet. "You're going to be alright, kiddo."

He steps back, wiping his face. "You saw it all, didn't you?" He looks up at me, his face flush and wet.

"What do you mean?" I cautiously inquire.

"You saw my memories; I know you did. I was there with you!"

"Yeah, kid, I did."

"I won't tell anybody, I swear!"

I rub his head. "I know, kid, I know."

Jude wipes his eyes with his sleeve and sucks up his snot. "Even if I can track you, I don't think I'll be able to see those things coming until it's too late."

"I know, but it might give me just enough time to escape. You'll be my eyes and ears. You'll get me there safely. I believe in you, kid. Despite everything they may be able to do, how aggressive they are, how much they're able to sense, no matter how dangerous they may be, they have never, ever come up against a stubborn bastard like me. And we have a couple of nasty little things in our arsenal to make them think twice."

Jude smiles for a moment, but the reality of everything is just too close. His smile quickly fades. "You have to come back." He grabs me, hugging me tightly.

"I will, I will. You just have to trust me." No bravado or pep talk is going to work on him. He's lost too much already. He doesn't have the strength or desire to risk anyone else he loves. "Jude, you know I have to do this. Together, we'll make this work."

"I don't want to see you die on camera," he weeps.

"You won't!" There's no promise I can make that he'll believe.

He squeezes me one more time. "I know."

I kneel again. "We'll make this work!"

Jude smiles through his tears. "If this does work, you'll owe me big time."

"You got it!"

I look into the eyes of a child but see a very old soul who's seen and experienced much more than he ever should have. I see how he amazes the doc on a regular basis, but I think now, there's something more. Jackson is right; we're all changing, Jude too. He's working on a level that defies explanation. Instead of questioning it, I find myself deeply grateful. He's right, I can't do this without him. I've always had hope, and with what he has accomplished, he's turned that hope into a reality.

"Okay, I've got to talk to the doc one more time, and then we roll."

"I'll get it ready."

We fist bump, and I exit the room. I feel his hesitance, but I also sense his overwhelming determination. I leave the room on the way to the doc and run smack into Kayla. Pissed doesn't even begin to describe her mood.

"Do I really have to go one more round with you?" But she surprises me.

"Go find your family," she whispers, turning away.

"Kayla," I call out. I don't know why.

She ignores me, continuing down the hall, wrapped in silence, disappearing into the room with Jude.

Of all the people in her life, I could have been the one to make a difference. Instead, I'm the one who finally robs her of any hope. The cycle of disappointment and senselessness will not be broken. But I can't sacrifice my family for her, or for them. This is not my fight. I didn't sign up for this.

"Alex, you alright?" Matt says. "You look as pale as a ghost."

"Yeah, I am fine."

"You sure? You don't look fine."

"I'm fine, really, Matt, I'm fine."

"Well, I just passed Kayla. She's very upset."

"Again, when is Kayla not upset?"

"No, Alex, she's in a corner, weeping like a child! What happened out here?"

"Where is the doc?" I snap, attempting to ignore his questions.

Matt jerks back, startled by my tone. "He's checking on Jackson."

"What, why?"

"The guy has been totally silent. Doc wanted to make sure he was still with us."

"Does it even matter?"

"Alex, he's a doctor. It's kinda not in his makeup to forsake a life. Besides, he doesn't hold the same ire you do. Remember, only you and Kayla saw him allegedly freak out."

"Allegedly?'"

"Don't get all bent out of shape, Alex. It's just a statement. I believe completely what you and Kayla said happened, so does Rick. Rick wanted to make sure he hadn't escaped or injured himself."

"Trust me, he's not going anywhere in those restraints!"

"Yeah, well, Rick wanted to make sure."

"Where's Tara?"

"Still in the break room, finishing off some coffee she made. I'm a little concerned about the food situation. I checked all the cabinets and there's not much there."

"I know. We'll figure that all out when I get back. Just ration what we have for now."

"Got it." But I see the doubt in his eyes. He's still trying to figure out what to do if I don't come back. I can read him like a book.

"Keep her away from Jude until I get back, just like we discussed."

"I'll do my best, but it won't be easy."

"If anyone can do it, it's you."

"I hope you haven't put too much stock in my talents," Matt joked mildly.

"I haven't, Matt. I know you'll take care of all of them while I'm gone. You'll take care of them no matter what."

Matt nods. Somehow, we've really connected; there's something there that's easily recognizable.

"As far as Kayla is concerned—" I begin, before hearing movement on the roof. We both look up simultaneously.

"What is that?" Matt searches the ceiling.

Something or someone is up there. The noises become more pronounced. It sounds like several individuals are up top. They're trying to move quietly, but the metal roof amplifies every step. Matt and I freeze where we stand, following their movements.

I immediately pull my gun from the holster. Matt notices. "Go get Rick! Get him now!" I bark, still staring at the ceiling.

"What is it?"

"Either way, it's trouble. Go get Rick."

The movement is random. Whatever is up there is searching the roof.

Matt rushes toward the room where Jackson is.

Tara steps out of the break room at the same time. "Did you hear that too?"

"Go back in the room, Tara."

The noise is increasing, not random scurrying. It's purposeful, steps heavy, like men walking, but with larger strides. They're all over. I hear banging a few feet in front of me. There's an air vent that must lead to the AC unit.

Jude and Kayla come out of the room. "There's something above us!" Jude yells.

Kayla wipes her face, eyes beat red. "It's really loud in there."

"Stay here and don't move!" I shout.

I realize Tara is still in the hallway as well, shaking, her expression terrified. No sign of Matt or Rick.

The banging gets stronger. "Are the blinds down in the office?" I ask Jude.

"Yeah, Doc pulled them down when we got here."

"I want everyone downstairs! Now!"

"You don't have to ask me twice," Jude says, and grabs Kayla's hand, dragging her down the hall.

"Wait a second!" She pulls back.

"Kayla, go now!"

More banging. Debris begins to fall from the vent.

Shit!

Kayla breaks free from Jude and stops next to me.

Matt steps out. "There's movement outside!"

Tara runs to him. "What's moving outside?" she gasps.

"I need everyone downstairs now!" I bark. I move forward toward the lobby. The banging intensifies, followed by a loud crash.

"They're coming in, aren't they?" Tara screams.

I can hear Jude bolt down the stairs. Kayla begins to back away from me.

"Matt, take Kayla and Tara downstairs now!"

Matt rushes past me and grabs Kayla. She doesn't argue this time.

"Get their body armor on," I yell back as they descend the stairs. I move cautiously forward into the lobby.

Tara is frozen in front of the room where Rick and Jackson are.

"Doc, can you hear me?" I call out. I'm just a few steps away from Tara. I inch toward her. The roof is alive with activity, and dust begins to rain down from the ceiling tiles.

Rick pops out of the room. "They're outside," he says. "I can hear movement near the windows. Should I—"

"No, get downstairs, now! Take Tara with you!"

Rick steps out of the room, but Tara refuses to budge. He tries to pull her, but she's glued to the floor. An object sails through one of the front windows, impacting the back wall of the lobby. Glass sprays everywhere, with only large chunks held together in place by the thick, heavy blinds. Tara hits the floor.

"Go now, Rick, go!" I yell. I move into the lobby and quickly search it with my eyes. A second crash as something soars by me, barely missing. It hits the floor, sliding down the hall. Everything is beginning to move in slow motion. I look back, and Tara is gone. Rick is huddled down on the floor, his arms over his head.

I turn back around as another large object penetrates the window, striking the wall. Shrapnel drizzles on me, stinging my hands and face. I close my eyes to avoid being blinded.

Tara screams.

I open my eyes just as another projectile flew past. I dive behind the front counter as another came in. "Rick, get Tara and head downstairs. Suit up and grab a gun!" I roar, not knowing if he's even still there.

I pop up from behind the counter, aiming at the windows. Ceiling tiles begin to fall and break apart on the floor. I turn and hit my head on something sticking out of the wall. Rubbing the side of my face, I feel blood on my hand. "What the fuck?" I murmur as I look up.

There's some sort of spear embedded in the wall behind me. The tip is buried deep in the drywall, the pole made of wood, decorated with intricate, unrecognizable carvings. It has thin bands of what appear to be leather and fur wrapped around it. The third and final window shatters as two more projectiles fly in. I duck behind the counter as a sharp spearhead penetrates the wood just inches from my head. It looks like it's made of some sort of carved bone. I pop up again and shoot through the windows, emptying my entire magazine, firing at nothing. Several more projectiles sail into the room, striking walls and furniture all around me. They're smaller, but similar.

Can they be arrows? Yes, they're fucking arrows! Shit, enough of this!

I crawl behind the counter, slithering around the corner back into the hall. I hear screams, almost like howls coming from outside. I look down the hall. Rick is gone. I call out to him but there's no answer. God, I hope he made it down the stairs!

Windows begin to break in the other rooms. Shit, are they in the building now?

I slide past the room where Jackson was and peer up. The table is empty, straps hanging down. They were cut. He's gone! Shit!

The window is broken in the room, but there's no glass on the floor. He went out the fucking window. Smooth move, asshole.

I call out to Tara several times, but there's no answer. Did Jackson take her with him? Did she make it downstairs?

More glass breaks. I have to make a run for it. I load a new magazine and back myself down the hall. Something crashes through the lobby window. Glass showers over everything. I move faster. There's movement in the room Jude was in. I hear another crash, objects slamming against the floor. Jude's control room is being violently trashed. I scoot faster, checking behind me with each good push.

More noises—clicks, vocalizations of some sort, in the lobby. I'm almost at the top of the stairs. There's movement in the break room, objects being aggressively tossed about. I spin around, sprinting down the stairs, taking three steps at a time until I reach the bottom, then slam and bolt the door. All I can think about is Tara and Rick.

Did I leave them up there?!

I head into the basement and, much to my relief, there is Rick, struggling to put his chest armor on.

"Where's Tara?" I ask.

"She's with Matt and Jude," Doc grumbles as he pulls the heavy vest over his head. "What the hell is going on out there?"

"Hell unleashed, that's what."

"Is it more of those creatures, the winged creatures or those rhinos?"

"Only if they learned archery."

"What?"

I don't answer. Instead, I run to the firing range. Matt is struggling to fit the body armor on Jude, using a lot of duct tape. I can't see Kayla.

"Where's Kayla and Tara, Matt?"

"They're in the evidence cage, grabbing more equipment. Kayla said she found some food rations too." He grunts as he wraps more tape around Jude's vest and body.

I rush to the table and grab a rifle, quickly loading the magazine. I slip three more into my pocket, then bolt to the evidence locker.

"Are they in the building?" Matt calls out.

"Yes, and they'll be down the stairs in a matter of minutes, if not seconds."

"Will the door hold them off?"

"It should. The door is solid steel."

I don't know if I even believe that, but I have to keep them moving. I enter the locker and meet Kayla face to face. She's completely suited up, gas mask and all. I barely realize it's her, until I see Tara still dressing.

"Do I have to put this all on?" Tara whines, shaking profusely.

"Yes!"

I grab a suit off the wall and kick off my shoes. Kayla fills a large backpack with water bottles and rations. Her movements are frantic but focused. She doesn't speak to me.

"Tara, where's Jackson?" I ask, continuing to dress.

"I found him strapped down to a table. He wouldn't tell me who did it," she replies, her face pale. "He begged me to cut him loose, so I did. I found a knife in one of the drawers."

"You did *what*?!"

Kayla strips off her mask.

"I cut him loose!" Tara says. "Once he got free, he pushed me down and went into the hall, but then something big flew by us. He panicked and broke the window and jumped out. I thought his legs were broken?"

Kayla stood there in complete disbelief.

"We don't have time to worry about him now," I say in disgust. "Finish suiting up and get your gear, just like we discussed."

Rick enters the cage and grabs his suit. "I can hear them in the stairwell!"

Even with layers of concrete above, the sounds of destruction echo above us.

Matt rushes in. "Rick, throw me a suit. I got Jude set up the best I could."

Something is pounding on the door. I head into the firing range, where Tara is about to pick up a pistol off the table. The look on her face is indescribable, a horrific mixture of fear and loss.

"Tara, hold up. I need to check your weapon."

She turns to me, her eyes vacant, dead.

"Jude, head into the locker and let Matt get the rest of your gear."

Jude blasts by me. Tara wants to say something, but she's in shock, completely overwhelmed by everything that's happening around her. Her suit is on but unzipped. She's trembling so hard, her own hands work against her.

I move toward her slowly as the pounding intensifies. I place my arm on her shoulder. "I need you now, and I need you with me."

Her gaze is empty; she's not here at all. "Tara!" I shake her ever so gently. "Where are you?"

Still nothing.

Kayla comes up behind me in full armor, loading her rifle.

"Be careful. Make sure you always point your weapon down when you load it."

"Yeah, I got this!"

She finishes loading her weapon and magazines on the strap, allowing it to freely hang from her body. She moves me out of the way with her arm and faces Tara. Without warning, she slaps her across the face. Tara winces slightly. Kayla follows it with another slap. They're so quick I can't react. A third slap, and I grab Kayla's arm.

"Enough!"

Tara screams and punches Kayla right in the jaw. Kayla falls to the floor. I try to catch her but fail.

"You bitch, slap me again and I'll rip your fucking uterus out!" Tara screams.

I pull Kayla up, who rubs her jaw. "See, I woke her up for ya. Good punch, princess. There may be hope for you yet."

"Tara, you alright?" I ask.

"No! Before I was just freakin' out, now my freakin' face is sore too!" she screams. "Keep that crazy bitch away from me, or I'll shoot her myself!"

Kayla scoffs and waves her off with her hand.

"Get the rest of your gear on!" I snap.

"Like any of this is going to matter once whatever those things get in here," Tara snarls.

"They're not getting in. So, get your gear on. Matt can help you." I give her back the pistol I'd taken earlier.

Doc meets us, in full regale. "Matt's almost ready," he says.

"Can you do a weapon's check, Rick? Make sure everything is on right and tight, and all guns are loaded properly."

"Yes. What about the grenades and that makeshift flamethrower?" he nervously asks.

"Throw the grenades, flash bangs, and flares in packs. I'll carry them. I'll carry the flame thrower, too!"

"Okay." He heads to the table with Kayla in tow.

Tara walks by me and turns. "We're all going to die, and you know it!" She says no more and walks to the cage.

The pounding continues, but the door is holding. There's no other way in, at least that they know about. I move to the cage. Matt meets me. "She has a weapon. We need to watch her every second," I say.

"I will, I promise."

I can't believe how well organized they all are, especially with all this chaos. There's been too little time with them to take the credit for my training. There's something greater at work, something inside. They were certainly not soldiers, but I had never seen a team prep with such speed and fluidness, especially under this kind of pressure and fear, not even seasoned veterans who'd been cut from the harsh edge of combat and survival. Hope and courage arrived when you least expected it, in the darkest and most chaotic of places and situations. It was contained in the most unexpected packages. Nothing defined that more than now.

These people want to live. It has become an involuntary response, overriding all doubt and terror. But there is still safety here. Will all of this hold up once we have to escape again to the streets—out in the open, where all there is between you and death is wits and determination?

God, I hope they're ready!

There's no more time for testing or preparation. Death is standing outside that door, and we have no idea what the hell it looks like. I'm sure that whatever it is, it'll surpass all our worst fears and imaginations.

Again, I hear my wife and child cry out for me: "*Daddy, where are you?*" I feel her reaching for me. They are utterly alone in this horror. I know they're alive, isolated and filled with fear.

But for how much longer?

CHAPTER 22

Escape to Nothing

(Kayla)

The pounding on the door is louder now. The whole basement shakes. Alex stands there in a daze. What the hell is wrong with him now?

I run over to him, grabbing his arm. He turns his head and stares at me. I know it isn't me he sees. "Alex, wake up! We need you now!"

He blinks, and I see reality flicker back into his eyes.

"Are you ready, Kayla?" he yells.

"Are *you*?" There was a loud thud and the door shakes violently. "They're trying to push it open!"

"Everybody move!" Alex bellows, pointing down a long, dark corridor.

Where the hell did that come from? "Where does that lead?"

"Out!"

"Where the hell does out take us?" I ask.

He doesn't answer; instead, he pushes me out of the way. Ceiling tiles begin to fall from above. Whatever it is, it's doing everything it can to get in. *But can it?* I want to ask Alex, but I don't know what I fear more right now, this new threat or his reaction to my question.

Doc places a bunch of stuff into a couple of backpacks. Tara is frozen, as usual. Jude struggles to move in the makeshift armor Matt constructed for him. I go over to them.

"Head down the hall," Alex tells Matt. "Take them with you and wait for me."

"Okay," he quickly answers.

"Take all the weapons with you," Alex says.

Matt rushes over to Rick.

"Kayla, what are you doing?" Alex snaps.

"You mean besides freakin' out?"

Another large, loud thud echoes throughout the room, shaking the door violently. Dust rains down from the ceiling, a snowstorm of filth.

"Are they going to seriously break in? I mean, you said the door was solid steel."

"But the frame around it isn't! It's concrete!" Alex yells over the orchestra of chaos. "It's not designed for whatever the hell is out there!"

He leaves me then, walking over to a small room in the corner that I also didn't notice before. I realize I really need to work on my attention to detail. He enters the room as Matt and the others swiftly proceed down the corridor. A large chunk of ceiling falls to the floor, its remains sprawled across the room, leaving a thick dust cloud.

Holy shit, they're actually getting in! What is Alex doing?

I run over to the room. It's slightly bigger than a closet, filled with pipes running up and down the walls, from the floor across the ceiling, with a large metal trunk in the center.

"Kayla, what are you doing in here?" Alex growls without looking up, hunched over with a flashlight, turning some sort of spicket.

"Maybe a better question is, what the hell are you doing?"

"Making sure we can get away."

I have no idea what he's talking about. Another loud crash and more ceiling came crashing down. The debris-filled haze makes it hard to breathe. "How can they get in?"

He doesn't answer but continues to turn the red spicket until it locks. He manipulates a few levers, and I can hear a loud hiss. That's when I notice a small pipe that's been disconnected.

"Is that gas I smell?" Shit, he's going to kill us all!

He grabs me, pushing me out of the room, then kicks the door off the hinges. It doesn't take much. The outer door shakes again. I see it begin to move forward, freeing itself from its surroundings. The concrete is cracking, fragments flying across the room.

Alex grabs me again, pulling me down the hall. Another large portion of the ceiling came down, littering the entire firing range lobby, breaking the table that once held all our equipment. The door groans again under intense pressure from the other side as the concrete frame slowly disintegrates.

We sprint down the dark hall. It's dimly lit and cold. The door slams, and cement crumbles with each brutal strike. We reach the end of the corridor and meet the rest of the group. Tara is holding Jude tucked in a corner, rocking and shaking. She's squeezing him so tightly that I don't think the kid can breathe. Matt and Rick are shining a flashlight up toward the ceiling, frantically talking to each other. I can't make out what they're saying. Alex joins them, and I squeeze up alongside him.

Up above us is a large metal trap door covered in rust. There's a steel ladder bolted to the wall, leading up to it. Alex flies up the ladder like a bolt, while Matt and Rick watch intensely. Tara is repeating something as she rocks back and forth, though Jude has finally struggled free and is adjusting his armor again.

Tara has totally lost it!

I look back up to see Alex is fooling with the latch and lock. Those things ram the door again and again, the sound echoing through the concrete-walled hallway. There's a fog of dust and debris creeping toward us.

They're going to break in any minute—any second now! I just know it!

Metal breaks and their pieces scatter across the floor, ricocheting all around our feet.

"I've got the lock off," Alex calls down. He lowers the ladder. "This leads out to the back parking lot behind the station. We head up and out into the parking lot and then down the alley. Hopefully, there'll be enough cover to get us to a safer structure."

"But if they see us, won't they follow us?" I ask.

"I'll take care of that. Once I give you the direction and destination, you run and don't look back."

"That's the plan?" I ask sarcastically.

He ignores me. "There's a small bait and tackle shop at the end of the alley. It's an older concrete building with very few windows, and they have some groceries and supplies. We make for that."

I shake my head. "Again, *that's* the plan?"

Still, he ignores me.

"How are you going to distract them by yourself?" Matt asks, clearly freaking out as badly as me.

"Don't worry about that. Just head for the shop. I'll take care of the rest. You fire on anything that moves, anything that is not us. Matt, get Tara up and get her straight. We've got no more time."

The metal door comes down like thunder, shaking the ground like a quake. A large, dense, gray dust cloud conceals everything down the hall. Alex sprints up the ladder with his gun drawn. He pushes open the large metal hatch and peers out. I can only see him from the waist down. He spins around, and I'm assuming he's searching the area for any threats.

Footsteps. I hear footsteps echoing in front of us, but I can't see anything. Shit, they're in the basement!

Alex slides down. "It's clear, now go!"

Matt pulls Tara to her feet, standing her up. "We have to go now, sweetie. It's not safe here. We have to go." Tara is zombified, but Matt persists. "Tara, now!" he finally screams.

Jude grabs her hand. "Let's go, Mom!"

She barely responds.

Alex pushes Rick up the ladder. "Rick, take point!"

Matt moves Tara toward the ladder.

"Kayla, you're next. Move!" Alex yells.

I respond without pause. I have no interest in seeing what'll be coming down the hall any moment now. I rush up the ladder, where Rick is kneeling, rifle out, finger on the trigger, scanning his surroundings. I pull myself out of the hatch and swing my rifle to the front.

Am I really doing this? I flip the safety off as if it's second nature.

"Get behind me, Kayla," Rick orders.

I quickly comply.

"Cover the rear," he says.

I aim my rifle, looking for a target, praying not to find one. I see Tara's head pop up. *There's one.*

She's standing up, looking lost. Jude pops out behind her, pulling his mom toward Rick. He helps her kneel.

"I don't have a gun," Jude whispers.

Matt exits next and sprints to us. He swings his rifle around. "Rick, see anything?"

"No, thank God, not yet!"

Matt aims his rifle around, searching the area. "I don't see anything either!"

"The shop Alex was talking about is south, that way." Rick points down the alley.

"We can't go now. What about Alex?" Matt replies.

"We go now. That's what Alex said. I'll take the lead; you cover the sides, and Kayla can watch our backs."

Really, you're seriously going to trust me with this? How are we going to pull this off without killing each other? "We're really going to leave him?"

"Let's move, Kayla. We don't have any time," Rick orders.

We begin to move south, hugging the walls of buildings, trying to eliminate at least one area that we can't cover. Alex's head finally peeks out of the hatch. Then he pulls himself out. I hear a screech, almost a howl, and then a sound I can't explain, but one I know I never want to hear again. I look up at the roof of the station and can barely make out the outline of a man.

Wait, not a man. Something else. Another appears, and then another. What are they? Do they see us?

"Run, run!" Alex yells at us as he pulls a backpack and some kind of tank from the hatch. We pick up the pace, but I don't want to lose sight of him or whatever is on the roof.

"Rick, do you see them?" I call out.

"Yes, I see about six or seven of them!" he yells back. "Keep moving!"

One holds up a long pole and then throws it. It sails toward us, landing just a few feet away.

It's a spear, a fucking spear! What the hell!

Then another sails by, striking the wall. How are they throwing them that far? Then another flies by. They're getting closer, and their aim is steadily improving. "Rick!" I scream.

Matt and Tara also see them. I turn back to see Alex hovering over the hatch with something in his hand.

"Matt, what is Alex holding?"

Matt looks back. "I don't know for sure, but it looks like a flash bang."

"What the hell is that again?"

Another spear sails by, taking a large chunk out of the wall above us. Debris rains down on our heads. "Okay, are any of us going to shoot?" I scream.

"It'll draw attention to us," Tara says.

Glad you could finally join us, space cadet! "Uh, I think we already have their attention."

Something smaller flies by. "Shit, what was that?" I look up. Oh my God … they're firing arrows at us! There must be a dozen or more of them, tall, slender, but muscular, on top of the roof now. Some are kneeling, others standing. And, as unbelievable as it is for me to wrap my head around, they are archers. I look back to see Alex jump up from his position and toss the flash bang into the hole. He grabs his gear and sprints away.

That can't be good! Wait—gas line! Flash bang! Oh shit!

Alex runs toward us, then abruptly stops and kneels, swinging around, aiming at whatever is now on the roof. "Run like hell," he roars and opens fire.

He has a lot better accuracy than they do. I watch in slow motion as he picks them off the roof one at a time.

Holy shit!

The creatures on the roof scramble as bodies fall to the ground. Alex relentlessly but surgically fires each shot. "Keep moving!" he yells.

Just as the last syllable left his mouth, the station explodes, erupting into a huge fireball that completely engulfs the building. The blast shakes the ground, and we all fall toward the wall behind us. I feel the heat from the roaring fire on my face and hands, the sound deafening, my ears ringing violently. Smoke races into the alley, consuming everything in its path, a thick, black unforgiving cloud paralyzes my throat, tormenting my eyes. It blinds us from everything else, filling our lungs.

The explosion rolls like thunder, as if it's never going to end. Shrapnel and debris begin to shower down upon us from the sky. I huddle into a ball, praying nothing large or hot comes down. I can barely make out any sound between the ringing in my ears from the roar of the building imploding. My eyes are burning too, making it hard to see in any direction.

Another explosion rocks the ground. Is this ever going to end? Did he blow up the entire alley? Then something grabs me, jerking me to my feet.

"Get up and move!"

I can barely make him out, but it's Alex wearing his gas mask. Would've been nice to give us some notice so we could put ours on too!

"Get up," he growls, muffled by the mask. He pulls me down the alley.

I can't see anything in front of me. Another smaller explosion. I almost fall again, but he steadies me, keeping me from stumbling. We continue until we bump into Matt, who is huddled with Tara and Jude. Jude is completely covered by his mother. More debris falls on us. Embers descend like flaming snowflakes on my exposed neck. They bite my flesh, and I can smell burned hair.

"We have to move," Alex says. "It's all coming down."

Matt pulls Tara up. Jude hovers under his mom's hunched body.

"We gotta go!" Alex pushes us forward like cattle. We run into Rick, who's coughing violently.

"Rick, you okay?"

He nods as he tries to clear his throat. Alex continues to push us along. He's carrying that same tank and backpack. "It's only a few more yards."

We trudge forward, swimming through the smoke. Debris slams into the ground all around us. I see other buildings on fire, the sky covered in smoke. For the first time in a while, the haunting blue hue is interrupted with shades of new colors, even if they are just white, gray, and black. I can finally make out a silhouette of a building in front of us.

"Almost there," Alex says, as I struggle forward.

My ears are slowly clearing, allowing me to hear more howls, the screeches echoing in the distance. We reach the building and head toward the door, barely able to catch our breaths. Alex takes the lead, opening the door, ushering us in. We enter, stepping over several large mounds of ooze. Once we're all in, he shuts the door and throws down his gear. "Matt, help me." Alex motions Matt over to a large display case. "We need to lift this and put it in front of the door."

They move to it and try to lift it, but it's too heavy. Instead, they drag it toward the door. They're struggling, so I jump in to help. I slide in next to Matt and push the case toward Alex. I put all my force into it, and it begins to move, digging a nice inch-thick groove, scarring the hardwood floors.

"Keep pushing," Alex grunts as we get closer and closer to barricading the door. Finally, it's set in place. "Everybody to the back of the building!" Alex yells.

Rick is still choking as Matt grabs some bottled water from a cooler near the front counter. "Rick, drink this." He hands it to the doc, then takes another and gently pours it over his head. "Calm down, try to take deep, slow breaths."

Alex jumps onto the counter and reaches toward the large windows. There are a total of three windows. He pulls down a large shutter, then locks it.

"I have no idea why these were installed, maybe security, but thank God they were," he says. "I knew the owner of this place." He closes the second, and then the final window. "We should be safe, at least long enough to regroup."

Rick is sitting on the floor, still coughing.

"Matt, is he okay?" Alex asks. He jumps off the counter.

"He's getting there," Matt replies. "He swallowed a full blast of the smoke and whatever was in it."

Alex squats down, concern dripping from his pours, mixing with sweat. "Doc...?"

Rick stops him and gives a thumbs up. "Just give me a few minutes," he grumbles.

Alex pats him gently on the back. "Sorry, I had to do something drastic."

"You got us out of there," Doc says between coughs. "That's all that matters. We may be a little bruised and banged up, but we're alive."

Rick slowly rises to his feet.

"And that's all that matters!" Rick says. His voice is harsh and raspy, but I hear strength behind it. He stands and pats Alex on the shoulder, then makes his way to the back.

"What were they?" I ask.

"I never got a good look, and I'm not unhappy about that." Alex cracks a half smile.

Matt sighs. "Well, you blew up half a block to make sure they couldn't follow us."

Yeah, despite all of this, I thought that was pretty boss!

"The fire won't stop them," Alex says. "It was a hell of a chance to take. We're not out of the woods yet. Those things wanted us badly. It would be a horrible mistake to think we've seen the last of them. They broke down a steel door to get to us."

"I would agree! But were they human?" Matt asks.

"They sure as hell looked close."

An expression of concern washed across Alex's face. "Whatever they are, they're more dangerous than anything we've seen so far. And that's saying a hell of a lot."

Alex and Matt continued their conversation as I scan the room. Hanging on the right wall are several brand-new compound bows. My heart skips a beat. I mean, literally skips a beat. I quietly move over to the wall and hop over the glass counter, landing in another pile of goop.

Shit!

I look down, seeing a shirt and pants mixed in it. Wait a second—that's a vest with a nametag. It's soaked in the vile mess, but I clearly see a nametag. I can almost make out the name.

Bill, his name was Bill.

I look away quickly. If I think too long, I'll lose it. I refocus on the wall, glancing at each bow. They're beautiful. I find a black and electric blue setup and almost shriek with glee. Alex and Matt haven't noticed my absence. I flip the price tag over. It's over six hundred dollars.

Wow, way out of my price range. Wait, I can afford—hmm, maybe free?

I gently pull it off the wall. It feels great in my hands. Seven-inch brace height, thirty-two-inch axle to axle length. It must deliver at least three hundred to three hundred and thirty FPS. The lingo drips freely from my lips. In fact, so did a little drool. It has throttle cam tech and a vibration dampening, carbon rod string stop.

I may orgasm right here!

Octane strings, protective coating, could be custom tuned. This was the bow I'd dreamed of, one of the rare, good things in my dreams.

I pull back. It feels so natural. I look down into the glass case and find thirty-one-inch arrows. *Nice!*

At the back of the case, the keys dangle out of the lock. Probably poor ol' Bill's.

I unlock the case and remove a handful of arrows. I also find a high-end black leather quiver. I load an arrow up and pull back. With ease, I send the arrow soaring through the air into the adjoining wall. It sticks perfectly, nearly six inches into the wood grain paneling. Wow, I've never sunk one quite that deep before. I quickly check to see if anyone heard or saw it hit.

Nope!

Alex and Matt are still lost deep their conversation.

I load the rest of the arrows into the quiver, then add some more, losing count. I grab another plastic quiver and fill it too. Then I find an arm brace that looks like it'll fit me. It's like winning a shopping spree.

And I never win anything.

In the next case, I find some high-end protective eyewear-slash sun protection. *Might as well.* I grab the most expensive kind. I hop back over the counter and notice a large black machete in the last case with a bunch of hunting knives.

Got to have!

I stretch over the glass and slip the back open, extracting the weapon. Oh, yeah! I'm like a little Rambette here. I move down the aisles, seeing a row of rations, the dehydrated kind. I find a duffle bag down another aisle and fill it to overflowing with the food items, barely able to zip it shut.

What else? I mean, I'm on a roll. I move to the back wall and step into another pile.

I gotta stop doing that!

I look down. Why, I don't know. Maybe morbid curiosity. This one has a dress or skirt mixed in. Hopefully, that's not Mrs. Bill. I move away as quickly as I can and see Rick and Tara talking, but I don't see Jude. I approach them with my goodies.

"They are going to get in here, too," Tara cries.

God, she's still an absolute mess.

"You need to calm down, Tara," Rick says. "We need you now more than ever. Jude needs you now more than ever."

She's too lost in her terror; it completely owns her ass.

"It's over. It's all over. All of this has been absolutely pointless!"

Rick pulls her close, wrapping his arms around her. She weeps deeply into his shoulder. Ah, there he is. Jude is behind them, standing there dumbstruck, trying to decipher what to do next to help his unstable mother.

"We're all going to die," she says, her voice muffled.

Jude puts his arm on his mom's shoulder, a weird mixture of sympathy and disgust washing over his face. It's obvious he's struggling hard against both emotions.

"You need to find your strength, Tara. Your son needs your strength."

"I can't. I can't," Tara sobs. "This is punishment for what I did to him, for all of my selfishness!"

Jude steps back.

"I forced the pregnancy—I pushed it, even when they told me it was wrong."

Jude's face quickly changes to anger.

"That's why he left us," she babbles. "That's why Jude's sick. That's why I'm alone."

Jude's anger burns brighter, his face almost glowing red.

"It's all on me," Tara continues her tirade, unaware of her son's growing anger. "I deserve for those things to consume me!"

Jude slams the wall with his fist. "You selfish bitch!" he screams. "It's not always about you!"

Rick's eyes widen like paper plates. I wonder if they're as wide as mine. We're both shocked at the outburst.

"You're a ridiculous woman," Jude continues. "A silly, stupid coward!"

Rick tries to speak, but Jude interrupts. "It's all your fault," he berates. "And you never, ever learn. I don't feel sorry for you. Nobody does, because everyone knows what you are."

Rick springs up, nearly knocking Tara to the ground. "Jude, stop that right now!"

"No, someone has to take a stand," he yells. "Too many people have let it go!"

Tara collapses into a ball on the floor.

"Just look at her. She's weak. Weak because she wants to be weak. Weak because she refuses to be strong!"

"Enough, Jude!"

"No, it's not enough. It's never enough." Jude refuses to back down. "She has to know. She has to face it."

Rick moves toward Jude.

Tears of rage stream down the kid's face. I had cried them too, many times in my life.

"No, stay away!" Jude pulls back. "If she wants to die, let her. We'll all be better off."

Damn! It's true, but damn, that's harsh!

Rick grabs Jude's arm. "Stop, son, stop!"

Jude jerks away. "No, I'm not your son. I'm nobody's son," he snaps. "Right, Mom? Nobody's son!"

Rick attempts to snatch his arm again, but Jude slips away.

"Answer me, you bitch. Why did you have to ruin my life, like you ruined yours?"

Hearing all the commotion, I can see Alex and Matt heading this way.

Jude stands over her huddled mass. "You're nothing," he screams. "Everything you touch becomes nothing!"

Rick bolts over to him, trying to grab him again, but the kid squirrels away.

"If you want to die, just die, but at least be quiet about it. We're all tired of your endless shit!"

Damn!

Rick grabs Jude from behind and pulls him close.

"I hate you!" he says, crying. "I hate everything about you!"

Tara remains still, and silent, balled up on the cold tile.

Rick holds Jude tightly. "Enough, son, enough."

Matt and Alex reach us, confused and concerned.

"Stop, Jude, calm down," Rick says.

"I have no one," Jude gasps, sobbing. "No one." He collapses in Rick's arms, spent emotionally and physically.

"What the hell just happened?" Alex asks.

Jude slips to the floor and Rick follows. Tara remains unmoved.

"Doc, what is going on?" Alex presses.

Rick just shakes his head as Jude weeps bitterly, limp in his arms.

"Kayla, get Tara up off the floor," Alex says.

"Who, me?"

"Now!" he barks. "Get her up!"

I don't know why I comply; I just do. I grab Tara's shoulders and try to get her on her feet. She's dead weight.

Matt tries to lend a hand. "Tara, get up. Enough of this shit."

Between Matt and me, we get her off the floor. She tries to fight us, but we overpower her.

Jude is still weeping. Rick has his chin resting on top of his head. "It's okay, son," he says gently, rocking him. "I'm here. I'm here."

We finally get Tara to stand on her own. She's pale, like there's no color at all to her skin, a ghost.

Alex walks up to her. "Wake up. I'm tired of this nonsense. Get over it and help us or stay here and die. I don't care anymore. You're becoming a liability, and I won't allow you to risk us all because of your childishness."

She looks up at him, her face flushing, eyes almost crimson red.

"We done here?" Alex snarls.

She slowly nods. Jude and Rick remain on the floor. He's still crying but he's used up all his tears.

Matt releases Tara. "Alex—" he begins.

"Not now," Alex interrupts. "We don't have time for a ministry moment *or* a counseling session. We have time to live or die. She needs to make her choice, and deal with it."

Tara stares at Jude and Rick—a blank, empty stare. Jude refuses to look at his mother, and it's obvious she's painfully aware of it. Even I can feel her pain. She turns to me, her eyes empty, dead. "I had found my strength," she whispers.

"Huh?"

"I had found my strength," she quietly repeats. "But I gave it back."

I have no fucking idea what she's talking about!

"Alex showed it to me," she says quietly. "I could see and feel it, but I let it go. I gave in to my past and pain. I could have kept it and been strong for him, but it was so much easier to live with the pain."

What the hell is she talking about?

"And now I've lost him forever," she says sorrowfully. "Maybe I wanted to. Maybe I thought it was my final penance. I deserve to lose him." She's not feeling sorry for herself. This is soulful, and there's an essence of undeniable honesty.

"You will take care of him, won't you?" she pleads. "If anything happens, you will look after him? It's what's supposed to happen anyway. If I had fought harder for you…"

She locks her gaze on me, and I can see remorse and agony swimming in her eyes.

"I should have fought harder. But that was always a weakness of mine. I never was a fighter. He is, but he didn't receive that gift from me. After the cancer, after I survived, it's like I'd used up all the spirit I had left. Everything became so much more difficult."

Why is she telling me all of this?

"I had a child before Jude, a beautiful little girl, but I couldn't keep her. I wonder if she remembers me at all. Or maybe she just hates me so much, she forced herself to forget. I wouldn't blame her. Not for a moment. She's everything I wasn't. Confident, strong, a real survivor. Someone who didn't allow the pain of her past to weaken her, keep her from having a future, even if she had to walk through hell to get there? I knew more about her than I knew about me. None of it matters now. This is the price I will pay."

She's not making any sense!

"I'm truly an unholy mess of a girl." She turns away from me. "Kayla, I am truly, truly sorry for everything." She walks toward the back but stops. She knows Jude is back there with the guys, but her feet don't move forward. "I'm glad this happened. He needs to break free from me. He won't survive this any other way." She reaches down toward her holster.

What is she doing now?

"He won't need to get over me. He already has." Her hand strokes it as her eyes glaze over.

Oh hell, what is she thinking?

"I'm not a fighter. Others died from the same disease, better people, and better souls. It should have never been me. I took the chance away from someone who deserved to live."

Wait, she was sick too?

She unsnaps the holster. Everything begins to move in slow motion. "Maybe, just this once, I can be brave enough to do the right thing for him. Not me, for him."

Where the hell is Alex, Matt, and Rick?

She fondles the handle of the 9mm.

Why am I just standing here?

She looks at me again. I can see death haunting her eyes. She smiles eerily, coldly. "Take care of him. Kayla," she whispers. "If anyone can teach him to survive, it's you."

Holy shit! This is really happening!

She gently extracts the gun. Her arm lies limp by her side, the pistol firmly grasped in her hand. Her fingers tickle the trigger as she slowly slides the safety off. I want to scream, but I'm afraid if I do, if I try to lunge at her, she'll move quickly to end her life.

"Tara, please," I whisper. How quickly this situation changed for the worst? Only seconds ago, I despised her. Then I felt sorry for her. Now, I would do anything to stop her from doing what I know she is hell bent on doing.

She looks at me again; the same blank, dark stare. "I have to." She raises the gun and places it at her temple. "I'm so sorry." Tears began to flow. "So sorry for everything, for the mess I made of my life, of my children's lives."

"Don't, Tara. Please?" *Where the hell is Alex? Anybody!*

Her finger wraps around the trigger as she presses the muzzle hard against her temple. She's either going to shoot herself or impale her skull with it.

"You can't do this," I whisper. "Think of Jude."

"I am. Don't you think I am."

Oh my God, she's really going to do it, right here in front of me.

"Peace, at last." She smiles and closes her eyes.

It's now or never. I jump forward, but it's too late. She pulls the trigger. I tackle her and we fall to the floor. The gun scurries across the tile, down an aisle, and disappears. I land on top of her, expecting to be covered in her brains and blood. It all happened so fast. I didn't even hear the gunshot. I lift up and there's Tara, lying there, weeping.

She's alive! What the hell?

"I can't even do that right," she cries.

Alex appears out of the back. "What the hell's going on out here?"

"Where the hell have you been?" I scream. He helps me off Tara, standing me up.

"You wanna explain this?"

"Barbie here just tried to blow out what little brains she still has," I scold, out of breath.

"What?"

"Yeah, she just tried to kill herself. In fact, she did, but the gun never went off."

Alex grabs Tara's arms and pulls her up. She collapses in his arms and holds him tightly.

"Why?" she asks, weeping.

"I gave you empty magazines," he replies. "It's the only insurance I had that something like this wouldn't happen."

She buries her head in his chest.

"Kayla, find the gun." I try to argue, but he demands again, "Don't argue. Just find the damn gun!"

"I could've died out there. What if I'd needed to shoot?" Tara screams.

"You didn't. Get over it. We both know I had no choice."

Just then, Matt and Rick came in. A huge thud echoes through the room as something slams hard against the door.

"They're here," Tara gasps.

Breaking their embrace, Alex signals for Matt to come over. He takes Tara from him. Another large thud shakes the door.

"Will it hold?" I ask, eyes fixed on the doors.

"No," he says as he unholsters his gun. "You find her piece?"

"Yeah." I go to hand it to him.

He hands me a magazine. "Load it and give it to her."

"Are you fucking kidding?" I respond as I take the magazine. "No, I won't."

"Do it, Kayla. We don't have time for any senseless shit right now. We need everyone on point."

"And giving that chick a loaded weapon is 'on point?' This is crazy."

"Just do it!"

Matt and Rick unholster their weapons.

"Get the supplies together and get ready to move out," Alex orders.

"Go where?" I ask.

"Out!"

"Yeah, well, the whole 'out' thing didn't work out so well the first time!" When he just walks away, I think, *Fuck it*. I grab my shit. Rick grabs the rest. Matt is still holding Tara, gun drawn. I load Tara's gun and hand it to her, staring at Matt. "Good luck with that."

Tara holds the gun, her hand violently shaking. She's gonna shoot herself or Matt, I just know it. *Good call, Captain Crazy!*

"Go get Jude," Matt calls to Rick.

He nods and sprints to the back with a load of bags and equipment hoisted on his shoulder. Another hard slam and the display case glass shatters. The roof comes alive with movement everywhere.

"They're back up top again," I scream as I hoisted up all my crap. "You're not going to blow the shit out of this place, too, are you?"

Alex ignores me. "We're going out the back. Everyone slowly back up." He holsters his pistol and whips his rifle around.

Matt moves Tara to the back, both of their guns pointed at the entrance. Rick disappears into the back hall. I follow. Whatever is out there hits the door again, and the display case falls on its side, fractured glass sliding across the floor.

"They're coming in! Move!"

I speed down the hall. There are three doors on either side. Rick emerges from the last door on the left. He's got Jude."

"They're coming in," I scream.

There's a door at the end of the hall, a fire door. I hear Matt and Tara coming up behind me.

"Stay there," Alex directs. "Stay until I reach you!"

I see him pull out a grenade. The doors buckle as they get hit again. I can barely see it over Alex's shoulder. He's obstructing the hall. He pulls the pin.

"Everybody down! Cover your heads and ears!"

We instantly crouch down.

Holy Shit!

He lobs the grenade at the door and turns away. It explodes, the sound burning through my ears. The doors shatter and wood flies everywhere. Shrieks, howls, and smoke fill the hall.

"Now go," Alex yells. "Out the back! Rick, shoot anything that moves!"

Rick kicks open the fire door, and the alarm begins to scream.

"Go, go, go!" Alex yells.

Rick exits and pulls Jude with him. Matt follows, with Tara in tow. I'm right behind them, as close as I can physically get.

Alex begins to fire, spraying the room in front. Casings ricochet off the floor by his feet. I'm outside the door, still watching Alex.

"Look out," Rick screams as he opens fire.

Matt covers Jude with his body, as Tara stands there, panic in her eyes. I see something on the roof and swing my rifle around and fire. I spray the gutter, and the rifle flies from my hands, hitting the ground.

Alex exits and bumps into me. "Kayla, move!"

The thing on the roof howls, and Alex blasts it. Its head explodes as black liquid rains down on us.

What the hell is this now? Oh God, is it blood?

Alex pushes me and I slam into Tara. Tara falls to her knees, frozen in fear.

"Rick, move!" Alex screams.

"Where?" he calls back.

"Forward, blast everything in your way!"

Rick presses on, frantically scanning his surroundings. Matt grabs Jude and they too move forward. Tara is still on the ground, almost tripping Alex.

"This way," I hear a voice scream.

I know that voice. I look over and see Jackson standing there, waving to us. That son of a bitch survived!

Alex pulls Tara up. Something jumps from the roof and knocks me down. It stands over me, holding a large spear. Time stops. The creature is tall, slender, with bluish gray, scalelike skin. I can only compare it to the same color as a shark hide, with the texture of a reptile or snake. It looks human, but it's definitely not. It has an elongated head with straw-like hair that's black as night. It glares at me with large white eyes, no visible lids, riddled with bright green lines that look like roots spanning from its large black pupils. Its face has only a thin layer of flesh covering it, accentuating every inch of its bone structure.

Where its nose should have been is just an open cavity filled with tiny, weird, luminescent tendrils moving within it. They remind me of neon maggots trying to burrow into its skull. It bends its long, thin neck, which is covered with intricate markings etched deep into its skin. I can see sharp, triangular growths running from the top of its head down its neck, ranging in size from an inch to several inches. They are like small shark fins.

Its chest is covered with brown and black leather-like armor, interwoven with different types of fur and what looks like bent, scorched bone. It's so tight fitting that I can see the muscle definition behind it. The markings run down its arms, covering even its hands and horrifically shaped fingers. It has bone sticking out from its elbows and also around its wrists. I count four fingers, three long and one that appears to be some kind of thumb. They too have bone framing the outside of their strange skin. At the tip of each finger is sharp, talonlike nails stained and yellowed.

Its waist is covered by an elaborately decorated leather loin cloth. It's standing on long, thin, but muscular legs with curved bone protruding from its knees and around its ankles.

How does bone grow on the outside?

It's amazing what can go through the mind in a few short seconds.

Large feet, almost clawlike, extend with a long narrow sole and ball-like heel. It's as if it wears half its skeleton on the outside. The creature raises its spear, the large, sharp bone tip aimed right at my chest. It opens its mouth wide, exposing sharp, fanglike pearl-white teeth. It howls, the sound piercing my soul. I prepare to die.

Just as the spear is about to pierce my heart, its chest is riddled with bullets, and black ooze sprays all over me. The creature screams in pain as a final shot opens its skull. Blood, bone and what I can only assume is brains, shower me. Vomit fills the top part of my throat, burning my tongue, as the creature falls stiff to its side, landing a few feet away from me.

"Kayla, get the hell out of there," Alex screams as he takes out another one. "These things are everywhere!"

I hear more gunshots in the distance. Rick and the rest are way ahead of me. I have no idea where they're heading. Tara is lying on the ground. Was she dead?

Jackson calls out again, "Follow me, guys!"

He's leading the pack. A group of those things ran down the street toward us. I get to my feet and head toward Tara.

"That's right, guys, go that way," Jackson directs, his voice echoing down the alley. He heads back toward us. "Don't worry, guys, I'm coming!" He's sprinting now. His legs are strong, as if nothing had ever happened to them.

I got to Tara as several spears sail by us. Alex is a blur, firing at the oncoming hoard. I shake Tara. "What?" she screams. "Just leave me here to die!"

"If you don't get up, I'm going to shoot you right in your ass!" I yell. "Then I'll leave you!"

I see Jackson getting closer. He's smiling wickedly. He looks down and heads for something on the ground. It's my rifle. Boy, that travelled far!

Alex reloads. The alley is littered with bodies. I grab Tara's arm and pull her to her feet. "Get up, bitch. We're leaving!"

She doesn't fight me this time, but she doesn't help either. Why not just let these things have her if that's what she wants! Why am I trying so hard to save someone who doesn't want saved?

"Kayla, behind you," she shrieks.

I spin around into the hand of one of those creatures as it slaps me down. The sound of gunshots ricochet through my ears, and I feel liquid spray on my face. *Why am I always the one getting covered in this shit?*

I look back and see it was Tara who wasted my assailant with three shots to the chest at point blank range. She stands there frozen in disbelief.

I spring up to see Jackson barreling toward us. I touch my face, feeling a long painful gulley dug into my cheek. Pulling back my hand, I see it's laced with a mixture of blood, mine and that thing's. The pain hits me like a bolt of lightning.

"Kayla, are you alright?" Alex yells as he blasts another two coming off the roof.

Where the hell are all these things coming from?

Jackson swoops down, extracting my rifle off the payment. He aims it.

Is he aiming at me?

"Time to die, bitch," he screams, stopping, preparing his kill shot.

Oh, shit! Saved from one monster only be taken out by another.

Tara screams as she realizes what's going down. I push her down so she won't get hit.

What the hell am I thinking? She's the one who wants to die!

Jackson fires as a spear impales him, piercing his chest and nearly passing through his body. He gurgles in his own blood, falling to the ground. The rifle flies out of his hand and into the sky. I feel my right shoulder, a warm, burning pain, then I fall to the ground.

Tara grabs me and gets me back on my feet. She throws my arm over her shoulder and begins to drag me away. I hear more gunshots; they are everywhere, but I'm too woozy to make anything out. I hear Alex talking, saying something about being out of ammo.

We're moving again. I keep slipping in and out. I hear more gunshots and then Tara screams. We fall to the ground. Alex shouts something, but words no longer make any sense. I'm trying to stay awake, but it's getting harder and harder; everything is so fuzzy. The only thing I can make out is a pool of blood.

Is that coming from me? Is Tara okay? Did she just save my life?

I'm lying face down on the pavement. The shouting is getting more and more distant. In fact, any and all noise is. I'm losing it, my head pounding.

Am I dying? I must be. I can't hear anything. I can't see anything. So tired. So very tired.

I can't…

CHAPTER 23

The Tribe

(Alex)

Tara is kneeling above Kayla, weeping, blood surrounding them. I call out to the doc as I fire several more rounds. They are coming at us from every angle!

I fire three through one's chest and watch it drop backwards to the ground. Turning quickly, I see the doc heading back toward us with Matt in tow. Tara is screaming. I spin around and find two more creatures only feet away from them. I take the first one out with a headshot. I blow out the second one's knee and it falls forward to the ground, howling and screeching as I fire two more shots into its back.

Tara screams again, "Watch out, Alex!"

I spin around, and it lunges for me. I fire again, striking it in the face. It sails past me, slamming into the pavement. I fire three more times, finally killing it. I can't keep up. There are just too many coming too fast.

"To your left!" Doc yells.

I swing left and blast at four more. They aren't given a chance to loft their weapons at, those long, cumbersome spears they seemingly toss with ease. Doc hovers over Kayla, while Tara sits on the ground, weeping, her head buried deep into her arms. I refuse to think about why she might be weeping like that. I can't.

I hear gunshots behind me. Matt fires on more of them in the distance. "Conserve your ammo," I command. "Make every shot count!"

"I'm doing my best," he calls back.

I was expecting way too much of him, of all of them. They are not soldiers. Even soldiers wouldn't know what to do in this chaos.

"We have to find a way out," Matt screams.

There's nowhere to go!

"Watch out," Matt yells, just as I get sacked by one of the creatures.

We both fall to the ground hard, my rifle skidding across the pavement. I lay on my back, the creature on top of me. I grab its boney wrists when it brandishes some sort of large dagger, the blade as long as my forearm. As I twist his wrist to the side, it digs its knee into the side of my leg. The bone protruding from it burrows into my body armor, reaching my flesh. The pain is amazing, warm blood soaking my pant leg.

I tighten my grip as blood fills my palms. The bone surrounding its wrists is sharp, like giving a thorn bush an Indian burn. I see its face clearly as we struggle, its eyes glaring with hatred, the green lines spawning from its pupils almost glowing. Then they roll back, turning black as coal. There's no life to them, no sense of awareness. It has only a thin layer of skin covering its elongated skull, the flesh constricted on its face, accentuating every feature. It grimaces from my ever-tightening grip, revealing its ivory-white, sharklike teeth. Its thin black hair sticks to its face as we tussle.

It tries to dig the bone from its knee deeper into my leg. The only thing preventing full penetration is my body armor. It's like this creature's entire body is a weapon. Its left hand breaks free and it strikes me in the face, a solid punch. My cheek lights up with pain. I grab its neck, closing my fist like a clamp. It grabs my arm, trying to free itself, but I refuse to relinquish my grip. I slam its other hand against the ground repeatedly, trying to knock the weapon free. Its grip tightens, and I can feel the pressure through the flesh and muscle down to my bone. Such incredible strength.

I need to get to my sidearm, but it's impossible. As it begins to pry my hand free from its neck, I lift my free leg and knee it in the crotch. *I hope the hell it has balls!*

I strike one, two, three, four times with as much force as I can muster. It wails in pain, and we roll over, with me on top now. I slam its hand against the ground hard a final time, the knife finally breaking free. Throwing his hand off to the side, I begin to pummel its face. I hear more gunshots, rapid-fire this time. It sounds like it's all around us.

Matt and Doc! I have to get free to help them!

I continue my assault, its jaw breaking under the beating. Finally, I free my other leg. The pain claws up its length as the bone from its knee tears through my armor. I used the pain to fuel my anger and my attack.

Just as I release my sidearm from its holster, I get tackled by another creature. As we roll down the street, I feel a blade slice through my sleeve, and then my arm. I whip my gun around, firing it into its abdomen. Black ooze sprays everywhere. I raise my weapon and shoot it in the neck. It howls, then gurgles as blood fills its throat. Shooting it in the head, it goes limp in my arms. I cast the body off me, trying to rise, when I get tackled again.

I see the first creature lying still to my right. On my back again, a third assailant tries to drive the bone from its knee into my thigh below my groin. I fire into its face, shattering it. Bone and black sticky blood spray all over me. It smells metallic, almost like rust. I thrust it off me, trying to get up yet again, covered in blood—theirs and mine.

I look up just in time to see another creature barreling toward me, dagger drawn. I fire at it and miss. Firing again, I strike its leg, but it has little to no effect. Instead, it increases its speed. I fire again, grazing its shoulder. Just as I'm ready to fire again, I get sideswiped and pulled to the ground. We roll into a nearby wall as my handgun goes flying. The creature looks deep into my eyes and smiles.

The bastard is literally smiling.

It tries to thrust its dagger into my stomach, the armor stopping it again, but it burrows deep enough that I feel it. The jagged tip catches my flesh, tearing a small chunk away. It grabs me by the neck, and I do the same to its hand. Its grip is ironclad, its eyes rolling back to black. I grab its other hand before it can stab me again as my windpipe closes.

A burst of electricity rushes through my entire body, surpassing the battle and pain. Images rush through my mind so fast I can't make sense of them. I hear something speaking, but the words are alien. Everything fades to black as my head pulses.

I'm filled with rage and fear, loneliness and panic. The images converge on me, burying me, the sounds and pictures drowning me. Just as their weight feels like they are about to crush me, it suddenly stops and there's total silence. It's all gone, and with it the pain.

I stand up in the darkness, lost in a void. Taking a step, I find nothing beneath me, and yet I'm suspended above utter blackness. I take another step, feeling like I'm moving through glue, nothing but emptiness and silence all around me. Looking down, I see I'm clean. There's no blood, and all my wounds are gone.

Shit, I must be dead! I lower my head. The others won't make it without me. I failed them. I finally failed them.

The guilt cripples me. Tears roll down my cheeks into the void, falling endlessly. Gracie, Sara, Kayla, Matt, Tara, the doc, Jude: each name pierces my heart, sharper, harsher than any knife or bullet. I can't bear it. They mercilessly shred my soul. I would have fallen to my knees, but they refuse to buckle.

A voice echoes in the void as I wander aimlessly. Then another and another. Their voices are all around me, male, female, children, but I can't understand what they're saying. They mix with the white noise. Then, as quickly as they arrive, they leave, and I'm alone again.

A light appears, dim at first, then grows until it illuminates everything around me. It becomes so bright that it's nearly blinding. I shield my eyes as the glare becomes more intense. I can hear noises again and strain to see beyond the light. There's wind on my face, a dry, hot breeze.

Stepping forward, I feel terrain under my feet. There is grass and weeds, but they appear foreign, feeling wet and sticky, almost slimy. I continue forward, finding brightly colored flowers that look more biological than botanical. I sense danger from them, that their beauty may mask a more devious purpose. The field grows, sprawling out into the distance, then the light fades back to a blue hue, the same blue hue I'd become so familiar with. The plant colors radiate within it.

To my left is a field of monopod-like plants—tall, thin, reddish-green trunks supported by tentacle-like roots that skate across the ground. Large, hair-like incandescent tendrils reach out to the sky. They resemble jellyfish stingers. There is a flock of them moving together, as if in unison. The other plants part as they pass through, as if out of respect or fear. Smaller Venus Fly Trap-looking flowers intermingle among the tall, seaweed grass.

The ground is soft and spongy beneath my feet. I feel a slight bounce with each step. There are larger flowers, beautifully colored, as if drenched in a liquid rainbow—but their petals are sharp, almost spear-tipped. Everything appears hazardous, unfriendly, and beautifully dangerous. I walk through the field, with hills and mountains surrounding the landscape. There are large rocky formations that glisten even though there is no sunshine. In fact, the sky is blank, no clouds, sun or stars, just the murky blue hue that encompasses everything. Shadows slide under my feet.

How can there be shadows without sunlight?

I notice the blue brightens randomly, providing its own form of luminance, strange and yet familiar. I look up and recoil. Those creatures, the flying menaces, flock above me. There must be a dozen or more gliding in formation.

I go unnoticed, thank God!

There is a slight breeze, but not enough to support flight. They ride the air, gently flapping their wings. They again look like some sort of stingray, their long, pointed tails waving behind them like snakes slinking through water. I slowly realize I'm not dead. I'm having another vision.

A larger version approaches from the distance. Its size evolves exponentially as it approaches. Its body eventually fills the sky. The smaller ones scramble as the big one floats nearer. It swoops in above the horde, its belly open, revealing rows and rows of jagged teeth. Five tentacle-like tongues spring forth, snatching the smaller creatures in midair. The tentacles have a claw-like appendage at each end with three long, sharp fingers made of bone. They jettison from their tips, piercing their prey, then close and retract as the tentacles quickly wrap around the victims, drawing them back one at a time into that horrific mouth.

The feeding continues, with only a few barely escaping. The monstrosity moves on as the smaller creatures descend, only to be snagged in the tendrils of the monopod plants. The plants sting them repeatedly and the creatures go limp. I can't see what they're doing as the plants pull their prey in, but I'm sure it isn't pleasant. The behemoth moves on and the sky becomes quiet again.

In the distance, I hear a growl and see movement in the taller grass. Something is watching, stalking. I back up, but there's nowhere to go. I can barely see the shape of an animal slinking through the foliage. At the same time, I feel movement, something heavy coming slowly toward me. I spin around, finding those rhino creatures, but here they are strangely different. A whole heard of them steadily but cautiously approach.

There are four of them, and they appear to be grazing. I watch their massive skulls open as a network of tendrils extract grass from the field and draw it in. Their skulls close after they pull in masses of vegetation. I don't know if they are chewing or simply digesting it.

Hearing a second growl, I spin around to see a large, slender, feline creature slink by me. It's as long as I am tall and had what looks like eight legs. It walks on four with two smaller arms wrapped around the animal's abdomen, and two more extended, with talon-like claws that arch up above the creature's head.

It has no eyes, just a large conical structure protruding from the front of what I believe is its face. It looks like it's made of black bone. The sheen on its body reflects the bluish atmosphere surrounding us. There are no visible ears, its skull perfectly round, covered in a coarse black fur. It has no tail, moving silently, almost as if it's floating as it covertly stalks the herd of rhinos. I back up anxiously, awaiting the attack. The feline stops and appears to be listening, waiting for something. One of the rhinos takes a few steps forward. They still don't notice the predator that stands poised only a few feet away from me.

The creature leaps forward, jumping high into the air, landing on the larger creature's back, digging its front claws deep into its hide. The mammoth jerks forward and begins to barrel ahead, the others blindly following.

I jump out of the way to avoid being trampled in the stampede. The predator hacks at its prey, tearing at its tough flesh, exposing its infrastructure as blood sprays everywhere. It writhes in pain as it stumbles and rolls to the ground. The predator leaps off and lands perfectly on all four feet, the first strike lasting only seconds.

The smaller arms stabilize the predator. They have flat, hoof-like appendages at the end of them, but they're not hard like those of a horse or cow, but rather soft and pliable. It searches for his prey as the rhino tries to rise, severely wounded and bleeding profusely. I realize the predator is using its smaller appendages to sense vibrations in the ground. It pinpoints its thrashing prey in the grass. The remaining horde has left their wounded friend; they are far ahead, shrinking in the distance. Apparently, there's no love lost in this jungle.

The predator strikes again—this time opening its cone structure to expose a cylinder covered in small, thorn-like teeth.

It plunges it into the back of its prey. The object spins like a drill, tearing through flesh until its head is submerged. Bloody debris rains down all around the assault, a hideous scene. It continues to burrow until it disappears into the beast completely, erupting out the other side, covered in blood and matter. It shakes itself off, its prey now definitely dead.

It approaches the exposed chest and closes the cone, then its head falls forward, dangling freely, exposing a void behind it. It stops and a second head, large, black and eel-like, rises out of its interior. Its red eyes glow brightly as it opens its mouth, revealing rows and rows of snakelike teeth. It stretches out as long as the animal's body, rising above the mangled mess, then striking at its flesh. Pulling free a large chunk, it swallows it in one gulp. A half dozen similar predators emerge from the tall grass.

Holy shit, where did they come from?

They quickly join the feeding frenzy, tearing at the carcass, shredding it in a matter of minutes. I back away from the scene as the bloody buffet continues. It's clear I've moved for no reason. After all, it's only a vision. If I'd been here for real, I would've been part of their lunch. Growing bold, I walk over to the beasts to get a better look, but I'm robbed of my chance to observe further as darkness rushes in.

I was back in the void, surrounded by nothing. It's become evident I'm experiencing all the memories of one or more of the creatures I touched in battle. That may be why it took some time to discern it all. I've caught a glimpse of their world, my mind filled with information about what I'd just witnessed. Each morsel of data is as clear as if I'd known it my entire life.

The voices return, but now I can interpret them, expressions of fear and confusion, as they too don't understand or can't explain this strange new world. These things attacking us are not just monsters. They are fathers, sons, brothers, and mates. I hear their children crying, begging them for answers as to why their world has changed so quickly, so strangely. Females cling to their mates, lost in a place they don't belong. I begin to see that they are tribal, primitive, but not dumb creatures. They are intelligent, organized, industrious, and committed to each other—far more than we could ever begin to be.

They exist in a world fraught with danger, with a million ways in which to die. It's a treacherous existence, where every moment of survival is a gift. They literally face their own extinction every day in a land where everything that surrounds them wants to devour them. Yet this world, our world, is a far more frightening place. I can't comprehend how.

I now know their names, the names of each one I had killed. They can't be pronounced with any language we possess. Their world can't be analyzed or comprehended by the laws of ours. Our understanding of science is useless compared to how they exist, how their universe works. They are similar to us, but simultaneously opposite. It's impossible to discern.

My sight gradually grows darker, and the pain returns with a vengeance. I'm thrust back to my world, bruised and bleeding, sitting on the street. My assailant lies on top of me, the back of his head missing. I'm covered in drying blood. Matt runs up to me, speaking, screaming, but I'm deaf to it. He pulls me up, and I try to find my feet. He points to the doc and Kayla. She's back on her feet, wearing a makeshift bandage on her arm. Tara is up too. Matt shakes me. He can tell I'm not fully with him.

Sound begins to slowly return. Matt fires to my right. It feels like I've been gone for an eternity, but apparently, it's only been a few minutes.

"We have to go!" Matt screams. He puts my rifle back in my hands. "I don't know where your pistol is."

I shake my head, still sluggish.

"We have to run. There are too many!" he screams.

Where will we go? Grimacing from the pain, I tighten my grip on the rifle and step forward.

"There's a neighborhood that way." Matt points. "We're going for that!"

I nod, then shake my head, trying to get rid of the cobwebs. Matt fires again, taking out another creature. I'd been so worried they wouldn't be able to handle themselves without me, and yet Matt took the lead, just as I'd hoped. He must have killed my assailant—saved my life. I scan my surroundings, seeing the creatures coming from every direction, only a few hundred feet away.

"Let's go," I command. "Take point, Matt. Lead the way."

Matt agrees and calls out to the rest of the group, directing them toward his destination. I release and inspect my magazine. I don't need to reload, so I reinsert it. Kneeling, I fire in front of me, aiming at the ground, trying to disperse them. The revelations still echoing in my head are now challenging my use of force.

I may know them, but they don't know us.

We are considered a threat, and they will do anything in their power to eliminate us. Right or wrong, we are their enemy, and their only goal is to take us out. I have no choice but to kill. I won't sacrifice our safety.

I glance over my shoulder. Matt is leading them out of the alley. I look up, seeing the rooftops filling with the alien beings again. Some are kneeling with bows. We're too exposed here. We won't make it out of the alley. Scanning my surroundings, I notice a propane tank attached to one of the buildings. I only hope it's full.

Backing away, I hope I'm far enough away from the potential blast. They're coming closer—it'll only be a matter of seconds before they're on top of us again. I fire repeatedly at the tank. The barrage of bullets pierce the metal casing, sparking the gas inside, and the tank erupts. The shock wave knocks me off my feet into the wall behind me, the impact forcing the wind out of me. The fireball is more immense than I thought. It engulfs the side of the building.

The oncoming horde howls and screeches as they take cover. I try to catch my breath as I watch Matt and company go around the corner, escaping the alleyway. Stumbling to my feet, I retreat the same way. Smoke fills the area, blinding me. I'm forced to use the wall to find my way, choking on the combustion.

I can hear the calls of my attackers but can't see them. Smoke fills the sky. Another explosion knocks me to my knees. I recover quickly and stride away, hugging the wall, heat and smoke engulfing me. The howls begin to diminish.

Are they retreating?

I continue, the thick smoke burning my lungs. I don't know how much longer I have before I collapse. I must have lost my mask after the first assault. My eyes fill with water as I reach another dumpster. Leaning against the wall, struggling to breathe, all I can hear is the rumble of the blaze and the pop and crackle of things burning, the chaos all around me.

I'm not going to make it.

A hand grabs my collar and pulls me forward, dragging me. A second arm wraps around my armpit and shoulder, yanking me through the smoke. He grabs my rifle, and we limp out together, my savior and me.

I look up, seeing a blurred image of Matt smiling at me.

"I got you, buddy."

I continue to cough, trying to speak, and fail.

"The rest of the gang is over there," Matt continues as he points a few feet away. "Kayla is hurt, but she's up and about. The neighborhood is only about a quarter mile west. Can you make it?"

I nod, still coughing.

"You sure?"

"Yes," I grumble, my voice severely strained. I try to stand, but Matt has to help me.

"Doc, he's fine," Matt calls out. "Let's move!"

I limp along with Matt, requiring his help as I have no strength left.

"We gotta pick up speed," Matt says.

I nod again as we start to walk, though he's doing most of the work.

"What is it with you and explosions?" Matt jokes.

I smile, still hacking, my chest on fire and throbbing. As we reach the rest of the group, my eyes begin to clear, and I see concern etched deep into Kayla's face.

"Is he going to be alright?" she asks, worry dripping from her tone.

"I'm fine, keep moving," I grumble in between hacking.

"Well, it's good to know you're still an asshole!"

Ignoring her sarcasm, I look forward and see a field in front of us. Doc is heading straight for it, with Kayla and Tara behind him. I can't see Jude. My sight is better, but I'm still having difficulty with distance. I hear howling again behind us.

"Are they still on the roof?" I ask, my voice hoarse.

"Not yet," Matt says. "Your high-powered diversion worked."

The doc is at the edge of the field. "Was this here before?" he calls out.

"No, I've never seen it before," Matt replies.

What are they talking about?

"Is there a way around it?" The doc's voice is getting closer.

"Doesn't look like it," Matt says. "We're going to have to go through. We certainly can't double back."

I look back, the smoke a wall of black, but I'm expecting the tribe to break through it any minute. "What is it?" I strain to get out.

"Some sort of field of strange plants. They look like stalks, maybe corn of some kind."

"Alright, looks like we go through," Doc says.

"Wait, no!" I stop dead and pull Matt back. "Do not go through there," I mumble, my voice barely discernible.

"There's no other way."

"We have to find one," I continue. "Trust me, those aren't plants."

"It's too late—Doc and the rest have already gone in. Besides, those things are right behind us."

"Stop them, those things are deadly," I yell as loudly as I can.

"I can't; they're too far ahead." Matt pulls me forward. "We have to go!"

I reluctantly follow him. "Give me my rifle," I growl. He swings it over to me. "Doc!" I try to scream, but my voice just breaks apart.

"Doc!" Matt screams.

Howls fill the air, and I glance over my shoulder again. A group surfaces from the dense cloud, but they stumble over each other, struggling to catch their breaths. I free myself from Matt and spin around, firing mercilessly while they're at their weakest. I pick them off with ease despite my struggle to keep my balance.

Matt grabs me. "Alex, we have to go. We're completely outnumbered."

I empty what's left in my magazine, and the first wave exiting the smoke is annihilated. We hear Kayla scream, then Tara. I turn and run toward the field, ignoring my pain. Matt falls in behind as I rush toward the field, reloading as I approach.

It's thick with monopod-like plants. They're blocking my line of sight. The stalks are alive, their tops open as their tendrils fly freely in the air, reaching out to the sky. As I push through, they resist, blocking my way with their trunks. Their roots claw the ground, holding them steadfastly in place. I step on a set of roots and the plant reacts, recoiling its tendrils and closing its top. I remember my vision, remembered the facts imparted to me.

"Matt, step on the roots. Shoot at the roots," I call back as I begin to shoot at the bases of the stalks.

I continue to force my way through as the stalks begin to spread out, retreating from my assault at their tender, animated roots. One bends down in front, launching its tendrils at me. I stop dead, just out of their reach, and fire into the hole they are emanating from. The bullets tear through its head, severing it from its base. It falls to the ground. Behind me, the other plants congregate, closing the gap. It's only a matter of time before we're completely trapped.

I start blasting at the base of each stalk as they fall to the ground, stepping on them as I go. They try to sting me, but my armor and boots prevent any penetration. I hear Matt firing behind me, and I know he needs my help, but I continue forcing my way forward, reloading as I empty each magazine into the deadly foliage. I know how hard it is for these things to die. Even when they fall, they simply recoil to protect themselves. I know they'll quickly heal and rise again.

They attack in large groups, surrounding their prey, leaving them no way out. That's their ground strategy, and they execute it with fierce and terrible effectiveness. Their roots are their only vulnerable point, extremely sensitive to motion and temperature. They use their roots as both antenna and locomotion, the most effective predators in their world, feared by every form of life that co-exists with them.

The tribe won't follow us in here. They know all too well how the plants kill. They'll leave us to die with them. The plants sting until their prey is paralyzed, though left fully aware. Once the victim is down, they congregate as one unit and surround them. In small groups they hover above their prey, drenching them with a secretion that gradually dissolves flesh and bone. As the victim slowly decays, still alive, tubes emanate from the plants' bases and slither toward their catch. The tubes, like vacuums, suck and digest any liquefied material. Perfectly unified, absolutely horrifying. The victims can live for days as they slowly feed.

I can't think of a worse way to die.

"Shoot at the roots!" I yell at Tara. "Shoot at the base of the plant!"

She's shaking terribly but complies. I head toward the doc as a large clearing forms. I guess he heard me as he's already heeded my directions. Jude is locked onto his leg, frozen in fear.

"Where's Kayla?" I call out, joining him in his assault.

"She got surrounded over there," he replies and points. "They stung her in her face, and she became disoriented. We lost her among the stalks before I could grab her."

"They're going to move her to the center of the field to feed!"

"How do you know that?"

"Don't worry about that, just trust me."

"We can't get to her, Alex. We have to get out now!"

"We can't leave her!"

"We don't have a choice. If we stay, we all die!"

I want to argue, but he's right. We have to get out. "I'll clear the way. Have the rest follow me," I instruct.

Matt surfaces and joins Tara. Thank God he's alive!

I begin to blast my way out to the left, the stalks parting to avoid the painful barrage of bullets.

"This way, Matt. Don't let them close behind us or to the side."

"You got it."

I see the road. "I need more ammo!"

"Here, catch." Doc throws me a new magazine.

"I'm out too," Tara cries.

Jude grabs my leg.

"You can't hold me back, kid," I scold. "Make a break for the opening, now!"

Jude doesn't hesitate and makes a break for it at full stride.

"This way!" I stand firm, firing concise shots to keep the hole from closing.

Doc blasts by me, then Tara. "Are you coming?" she screams as she passes by.

"Just go. I'll be right behind you!"

Matt follows. "Where's Kayla?"

"Move, Matt, move!" I push him out, then follow. We sprint down the street and see the neighborhood ahead. "Keep running until I say stop!" I look back as the field closes in and begins to move slowly as one mass in the opposite direction. Nothing survives those fields. *Nothing!*

We head down the street, deep into the subdivision. "Keep going!" I yell. I keep my eye on the field, ensuring we're not being followed, even though I know for sure there's no way they can pursue. Those humanoids understand the deadliness of those things better than we ever will. They've lost entire clans in those fields. Hell, entire villages, male and female, adults and children. Those plants consume anything living without discrimination.

We continue to run down the street, the doc in the lead. "Can someone please tell me where we're going?" he calls back.

"Just keep moving," I reply. "Get as deep into the complex as possible." I catch up with Matt.

"Are they following us?" he asks.

"No, they won't make the same mistake we did."

"Is Kayla still in there?"

"Yes, but there's no way to get to her. We would've all died if we'd stayed any longer."

I left her! I can't believe I left her! I can't feel her anymore! Before, I could sense everything she was feeling. Now she's gone. I can't feel her fear *or* see her past. I can see Kayla's face in my mind but not like before. It's just a still image, lifeless, a snapshot instead of a filmstrip. I'm released from her pain as her memories quickly dissolve. She's not calling out to me like Gracie and Sara are. I can still feel my wife and child. That's how I know they're still alive.

We reach the end of the block. There's a wooded area that borders the cul-de-sac. "There," I call to the doc. "Head to the last house."

It's a large, beautiful, two-story brick house. Looks newly constructed. It seems so out of place in all this chaos. A haunting memory of the way things were … and will never be again.

"Okay!" he calls back. He speeds toward the driveway with Tara and Jude in tow.

I know this neighborhood. It's one of the wealthiest in town. Naturally, it had one of the highest burglary rates as well. Most of the homes have surveillance and alarm systems. That might provide us with some early warning. I hope they are registered gun owners as well. Unregistered would work just as well, considering.

Doc reaches the driveway and heads to the door. The house has a large garage, but it's shut tight. Doc opens the door and enters, instructing Tara and Jude to wait on the porch. As Matt and I reach the house, the air is finally still, everything peaceful—hauntingly so.

I enter the house as the doc comes down the stairs. "Top and bottom are clear," he says. "No sign of anyone remains."

"There are some on the porch. You stepped over them on your way in," I point out.

Matt enters with Tara and Jude, lifting his shoe as goo drips from the sole. We all stepped in it.

The keys to the house are lying next to a pile. It must have happened when they were locking or unlocking the door.

"Matt, check the garage," I say.

"I used to have a house like this. I think the garage entrance is attached to the kitchen."

Tara and Jude move into the living room and collapse onto one of the couches.

"Lock the door, and have Jude and Tara pull down all the shades," I say to Rick. "I'm going to find out if they have a surveillance system. And no lights. Tell everyone to be as quiet as possible."

I head up the stairs into the master bedroom. This is where they usually have them. I see three closets and search each one until I find a small room that houses the system and monitors. They're all active, but the cameras are on the inside. There's one in each room, even the bathrooms. They can be moved. I'll place them around the perimeter of the house.

Matt walks in. "Garage is clear. Found another pile in the front seat of their car. The whole thing reeks of CO2. The car must have been left running until it ran out of gas."

"Matt, see these screens..."

Matt walks up and looks around. "Yeah."

"Find the cameras and bring them up here. Once we collect them, we'll mount them around the outside of the house so we can hopefully see if anything comes our way."

"Okay, I'm on it!"

I stop him. "Thanks for saving my life—twice."

Matt nods but says nothing more. I stand there in silence as he leaves, my guilt almost too heavy to stand. If I hadn't had my little vision quest, I might've been able to save Kayla. Or we all could have died. Without the vision, I wouldn't have understood how the plants worked.

Doc pops into the room, and I barely notice him. "Hey, there's a basement too. I'm going to check it out," he says.

"No, stay with Tara and Jude. They need you. I'll check out the basement." I rise and head out the door.

Doc stops me. "You couldn't save her, Alex. None of us could. I know you're torturing yourself. Stop."

"Yes, I could have," I growl, avoiding eye contact. "It doesn't matter either way, she's gone." I descend the stairs and refuse to look back. Passing the living room, I see Tara and Jude weeping in each other's arms. I can't stop for them. If I stop, the weight will crush me. I head down the hall and see the door to the basement. Matt passes me with an armful of cameras.

I open the door and walk down the steps, flicking the switch on. I descend to the bottom, entering a weight room, professionally arranged. The former residents obviously spared no expense, high-end nautilus machines, mirrors on nearly every wall, a treadmill, and a top-of-the-line cycle, everything anyone would or could ever need.

I sit on the end of a weight bench; the tears will no longer be contained. It all came viciously crashing down and I weep bitterly.

CHAPTER 24

Resolution

(Kayla)

My face burns mercilessly. Just when the agony becomes intolerable, it abruptly ceases. Normally this would be a welcome relief, but as I look up at the sky, my body refuses to respond to any of my commands. I'm completely numb. Only my eyes move as the rest of my muscles surrender to whatever poison is now in my system. The only thing I feel is a mounting terror over what will happen next. They're all around me, and I don't know where I am. I can still breathe, but it's a tough, almost painful process.

They left me here!

I'm assaulted by silence. There are no sounds, not even from the stalks looming over me. At one time they were frantic with horrific life, but now they're almost statuesque, which makes my predicament even more frightening.

What are they waiting for?

These are not plants. That is just a deadly disguise. I strain my eyes, trying to see to either side. There's another body lying a few feet to my left, but I can't make out any real details—only that it's a man. When my eyes begin to water, I look to the other side and see a few more bodies, but their forms don't make sense.

I strain harder and immediately wish I hadn't.

I can't make out a lot of detail, but I can certainly tell there are things missing, things that should be there that aren't anymore. After only a few moments, I stop trying to figure it out. I can't tell if they're my friends. I hope to God not. Maybe they didn't leave me. Maybe they're still with me, just inches and feet away.

Shouldn't I be dead already? I'm paralyzed, completely paralyzed, but why? What's coming next?

I want to scream, but that isn't going to happen. Lying here, not knowing what will happen next, is terrifying. I continue to stare up into the sky, praying to see at least one cloud, a star, something. Instead, it's as empty as my fate. I'm being persecuted by this daunting blue hue that covers us all like a translucent blanket.

Is this where it all finally ends?

Wait a second! My memories! All my memories, they're back! How?

I remember everything, maybe even more clearly than before. It all came rushing back with a vengeance, racing in and filling my mind. It's all so clear, so sharp, cutting at my soul. I can't escape them or run away. I'm literally trapped within myself, a prison with walls made of every tragedy I've ever had to bear. But I'm not alone in this cage. There's someone here with me.

I had blocked him out before; shut him deep within the recesses of the darkest parts of my mind. When Alex touched me, he pulled him out, emancipated him from his tomb. But he'd also stolen all the horror and pain that the monster brought me, even his very image. But now, with all my mental faculties intact, he's returned. I can't lock him away this time; he's been freed to torment me once again. I see the monster's face as he hovers above me, feel his sweaty, oily skin slink across my belly. The sharp pain of each thrust as he forces his way in. I feel the blood and sweat drip down my leg as he viciously rapes me.

*

I turned my face away, but he violently jerked it back with his rough, dry hand. He wanted me to look into his eyes so he could see the helplessness robbing me of my dignity, strength, and hope. He stunk so bad, his body odor nauseating, but if I threw up, like I had the first time, he'd beat me until I blacked out. I couldn't scream—his enormous hand covered my mouth. I tasted the filth on his palm, burning my lips. He hadn't washed again, probably for weeks. As I slid across the floor, it aggravated the numerous sores on my back from the carpet burns. I knew they were bleeding again as the scabs were torn away. The intense pain couldn't distract me from his assault.

The room he kept me in had only one bed. He never used it for this. It always had to be on the floor. The walls were a dark gray, no windows, no light, his way of extinguishing any hope, making me feel like a trapped animal. He wanted to reduce me to that.

The floor was covered by a burlap-type carpet, and it was rough. It's why sores formed so quickly and hurt so terribly. They were all over my ass too. I couldn't sit anymore; it hurt too badly. I was always barefoot as well. It felt like sandpaper on the soles of my feet. After he raped me like this, he finished by turning me over and sticking it up my ass. The pain was indescribable. Some days I shit pure blood afterward.

The carpet was stained with my blood, leaving a twisted, terrifying map, patterns that painted a vulgar picture of each time he ravaged me. He had broken my nose, almost my jaw, and two fingers on my left hand the first, and last time, I struggled against him. He broke them one at a time until I surrendered. I wished I could have tolerated more, but the pain was too intense. He beat me for a week before he even began to rape me. He dislocated my shoulder the first time by slamming me against the floor. He may have taken it while I was out. I'll never know. He brutalized me repeatedly for the next few weeks. One more thing he stole from me—my sense of time.

At one point, he'd bruised me up so bad that I looked like I had the plague, black and blue welts covering everything. I hurt down there constantly. It felt completely raw, torn, damaged. He never let me bathe, only dumped a bucket of ice-cold water over me once in a while. He told me he liked it when I stunk. My hair was matted, and I always felt so dirty, totally disgusting. I had to scrape his dried cum off, peeling it like dead skin. He never used protection, so I was sure I would contract a horrific STD, although I never did. That was also when I realized I would never be able to have kids. If so, he would have impregnated me several times over.

The only piece of furniture other than the bed was a mirror on the wall. I would sneak a glance when I had a few moments of light. It was protected by thin, steel bars so I couldn't break the glass and use it as a weapon. Believe me, I tried, and nearly broke my hand. To this day, I still have issues with it. It never healed right. I know he wanted me to see myself after he was finished. It got him off. I hated that damn mirror. There's no doubt that got him off, too.

I knew there were other girls here. I heard one of them scream once, only once. She must have gotten free for a moment. During the trial, I found out he'd killed many of them. I could only assume that one of those girls was the one who'd screamed. In the courtroom, when it was all over, the other girls and I couldn't look each other in the eye. It was all too close. I don't think we would have kept our composure if we'd made eye contact. It was already tough enough knowing we would see him again.

The day I finally fought back was the day I decided I was ready to die. I'd had enough, and death seemed like the only relief. When he entered, I didn't acknowledge him, knowing it would incite him. I always had to call him master, bow, and open my mouth. That was our sick little routine. He loved to cum in my mouth. He shit in it once, too. I had forgotten that, pushed it deep inside. But now it's right there, mocking me, front and center. I couldn't hold anything back anymore. Every memory was brilliant, unrestrained, stark and brutal in its clarity.

All his sick and twisted rituals were designed to oppress me, treat me like an object, a possession. He called me over. His name for me was "third bitch." He numbered us to remove any sense of our humanity, identity. His way of wearing us down, making us believe the lies he was forcing us to hear. For us to decay into nothing more than a tool for his warped gratification, a living sex toy.

I would not budge, so he slammed his fist against the wall and ordered me to assume my position. I hadn't eaten for a while. So much so that even my own spit tasted good. He let us starve for what seemed like days on end. It was to further weaken us, to force us to beg for food. Another trigger to get him off. He wasn't a great housekeeper, which was obvious due to the number of roaches and bugs that were my only company.

I had to keep up my strength, so I was willing to eat anything. I think it was the moment they started tasting good, my mouth watering when they scurried across the floor, that I realized how much damage he'd done, not just to my body but to my psyche.

He stormed toward me. I said a little prayer. I don't know why. I wasn't a believer in anything, except my life had become one big shitball. So, religion was kind of a fairytale to me. The only time I spoke to God was to blame him for everything bad in my life. I had a lot of faith in that. The only kind I could truly call my own. Despite all that, I still prayed for strength, desperate times and such.

He reached the bed, and I sprang up. I could tell it surprised him, because he hesitated, something he only did to prolong his erection. I took a swing and missed. He slugged me in the gut, and I hit the floor. He cackled, thinking he had already gotten the best of me. After all, I was a feeble and fragile little girl to him, no threat and nothing to fear.

Not today!

As weak as I was, that only fueled my rage, and I aimed for the thing he treasured most. I hit him repeatedly with all my strength in the nuts. I used both fists clenched together, and swung like I was holding a baseball bat. I don't know how many times I hit him. It was enough to drop him like a bad habit onto his knees. Then I used the same technique to pound his head. I kept hitting him until I had nothing left. I think I put him out with the first headshot, but I didn't care. I wasn't interested in knocking him out. I wanted the bastard dead. I just didn't have enough juice left to finish the job.

I searched his body and found his keys, then unlocked the door and sprinted down the hall, hell-bent for daylight. I was in such an elated rush, I didn't shut or lock the door behind me. I realized I was in a basement, the smell of death and decay immediately assaulting my senses. I reached the stairs, ready to ascend, when I noticed I'd passed by a series of doors. Out of breath and still reeling from the pain in my guts, I stopped. I knew I didn't have time; he could wake up at any moment, but I couldn't leave them there to face his wrath if I escaped. I sprinted back down the hall and began unlocking doors, a total of seven, three on one side, four on the other, including my prison. My own little slice of hell.

I headed to the door that sat across from it, fumbling through the myriads of keys on the ring, frantically trying each one, fearing he would wake up and come for me. I finally found the key and opened the lock. What only took a minute or so had felt like hours. The door swung open, and the odor nearly knocked me off my feet. It was a sizeable room with a thick, blue plastic tarp that covered the floor.

There were roach motels everywhere, and fly strips hanging from the ceiling like morbid icicles covered with insect corpses. The walls were layered with black plastic with one lone light that shone brightly in the middle of the room, illuminating the macabre mess in its center. Naked bodies were stacked one on top of each other, rotting and festering like a death orgy. Men, women, even children, so intertwined from decay that I could barely make out one from the other. Puddles of blood and brown and black fluids surrounded the death pile. It was a scene from the pit of hell that screamed about the depths of this man's insanity—his concentrated evil.

I couldn't stand it anymore and I recoiled back in the hallway, vomiting what little I had on my stomach until the dry heaves nearly caused me to black out. It felt as if I was being ripped in two. I slammed the door shut and tried to regain my composure. I looked back into my dungeon to see its master still laying out cold on the floor in the fetal position, covered in blood.

I forced myself to the next room and again chaotically tried each key until I found the right one. I unlocked the door and saw her kneeling at the bed. I called to her, but she didn't answer. Her back was toward me. She was topless, only wearing deeply stained and soiled panties. The room reeked of feces and urine. I was afraid if I got to her, and he woke up, we would be trapped in there together, so I called to her again.

She remained motionless, bent over, as if she was praying. I had to chance it. I stepped inside and saw a pile of shit in the corner, almost a foot high and two feet in diameter. The bottom and middle layers were petrified white, but the top still looked fresh. Flies swarmed around it, a feast fit for a pestilent king.

I hurried over and grabbed her shoulder. Her skin was hard and cold, and I now saw that it was blue. She fell to the side. Her lips were chewed away, covered in maggots. Her eyes were gone, and the holes too were filled with a sea of larva. I wanted to scream but stifled my urge and quickly backed out of the room.

This would have been my fate. She must have died praying for relief, and death answered her instead. I rushed to the next room, fighting back tears of terror and the urge to puke. Same routine with the keys, but I was finding them faster now through the process of elimination. I opened the door and there was another female's body lying face down on the bed.

This was becoming pointless! Only death resided here.

I called out to her, but this one moved. Barely, but she moved. She slowly turned her head, her eyes blackened, lips chapped from dehydration. She saw me but was expecting someone else. I'd seen that look before. I owned it each time the doorknob turned. Fear would fill me as he stepped in the doorway, knowing what was going to happen next. It was a sickening feeling words can't begin to describe.

She whispered, "Help me," ever so gently.

I rushed in and carelessly pulled her out of bed. There was no time for gentleness. Death was only doors away. I pulled her up and carried her to the stairs.

Where the hell was I finding this strength? I sat her down at the foot of the steps. She leaned against the rail and whispered, "Thank you."

We were not out of the woods yet. I unlocked and opened the fourth door. My hands were becoming steadier, more confident. A woman screamed at the top of her lungs. She was fully dressed—jeans and a tee—handcuffed to her bed.

"Help me, please," she screamed.

I saw the walls were heavily insulated, not like my room or the others I had seen. She was a newbie. I ran to her and searched the key ring; it had to be here.

"I'll chew my arm off if I have to!"

"Shut up and be quiet," I snapped, "or we'll never get out of here."

I found it and unlocked her shackles. She jumped up and hugged me tight, almost strangling me. "Thank you, thank you, thank you," she whispered.

"We aren't safe yet," I replied and shuffled her out of the room.

"He took me yesterday," she explained through a trembling voice saturated with tears of joy. "He was wearing a cop's uniform and pulled me over. He had me get out of the car, grabbed me, and put some kind of rag over my face. I was out in a second, and I woke up in here."

He hadn't tainted her yet. I hated her. I don't know why. "I don't have time for your resume. Head for the stairs and take the other girl outside!"

"The other girl?" she asked.

"Just go! He's not dead, just out. He could wake up any minute and then we'll all be dead."

She finally agreed and headed out of the room. I exited too and watched her grab the other girl, who was now unconscious, lying face-down on the floor. She lifted her up and carried her up the stairs in her arms. We were all finding that inner strength, the one that drives us not just to survive, but to live.

I opened the fifth door. It was empty, clean, awaiting its newest arrival. I'll never forget how haunting the sight of it was. It was such a pristine scene in the middle of all this vileness. The ultimate deception, the decorated doorway hiding the entrance to an unimaginable hell.

I sprinted to the final door and heard groans beginning to echo in my room. I practically tore the knob off after unlocking it. There's a young girl standing in front of me, maybe twelve. She was silently sobbing. I went to her and knelt down.

"Don't worry. I'm here," I consoled.

She was wearing a tattered dress, worn and dirty. She'd obviously been here a while.

"Where's my brother, Kyle?" she wept.

Her question pierced my heart like a dull knife. "He's outside, waiting for you," I lied, knowing we had to get out fast.

"He took us both," she sobbed. "He told us mommy and daddy were dead, and he was sent to take care of us."

This man defined the very definition of pure evil!

I took her up in my arms and headed out of the room. I saw him crawling on the floor, exiting my personal chamber of horrors. I couldn't help myself. My fear turned to anger, my horror to rage.

"Burn in hell, you sick, twisted son of a bitch," I screamed so loudly that my throat burned.

He stared at me. All the confidence, condescendence and power had left his gaze, replaced by confusion and weakness. I gave him no more time, bursting up the stairs, down a hall, and through a door that was opened. I began to scream for help as we entered the street. My healthier companion joined me. Neighbors surfaced from their houses as we relentlessly scream *"Rape, rape!"* A few recoiled back inside.

Cowards! They all deserved to burn!

But then two or three ran to us. They were on their cell phones calling 911.

"He raped us. There are bodies in there, people he killed," I yelled.

I fell backwards with the kid in my arms, hitting the street hard, all my strength gone. The child still held tightly to me as I looked up at the sky, breathing in the free air. I felt something wet at the back of my head, but I didn't care. People gathered around us as I began to hear the ever-increasing strain of sirens approaching. It was the most beautiful sound in the world, and the last thing I would hear until I woke up in the hospital forty-six hours later.

I had made it! The kid made it! The chick made it!

The first girl I'd found died two days later from dehydration and malnutrition. I was just too late to save her. Kyle was found among the bodies; he had a broken neck. I found out the bastard had assaulted him for nine straight hours before snapping his spine.

I must have cried for a week. The doctors were concerned I would literally cry myself to death, but I refused any medication. I'd been a junkie when I went into that hell hole. That's how he got me. He sold me a tainted batch and took me after I passed out in the club.

I would never touch that shit again! Nothing would ever have that much control over me. No one ever would.

*

It almost feels as if it just happened and yet here I am, surrounded by things that have ultimate control over me. No amount of bravery or rage will save me this time. The inevitability of death surrounds me, taunts me, and I can do nothing to combat it.

I remember recognizing Jackson in the lobby today. If it still was today. He was the bastard that tried to save that maniac. I remember how he grilled me, tried to paint me as a whore who literally begged for what I got. A useless junkie, unimportant, just a simple burden on society, a deserved victim.

I am not a simple anything!

Why the judge let him go on and on, I'll never know, but in the end, I won. He lost. I had the power; he had nothing. When the verdict came down, it was the happiest day of my life, and life was still pretty shitty. That was until the day I read the bastard had been killed in prison, raped and murdered by his cellmate. I didn't care if it was wrong. It was the best news I'd ever read. I celebrated and never felt a moment of guilt about it. Hell had a new resident, and even hell was too good for him.

I felt the same way when that spear took Jackson out. Like a weight had been lifted off me. I'd heard of closure before, but I was always robbed of it. Not at that moment. Now they can be roommates in hell. Sometimes it takes monsters to kill monsters.

Alex had taken all those memories out of my head. He stole them from me when we touched that first time. Only a few very specific recollections remained. But now I can see it all clearly, feel every second of it again. He gave me freedom, peace, but I somehow knew it would only be temporary. Still, I'd hoped like hell it wouldn't be. I may not have remembered the specifics, but I knew that whatever I'd lost was better gone.

Why did it all return so quickly? Unless … unless we've been separated for good? Unless he's dead. That's why my memories are back. It has to be. All we did was prolong the inevitable.

I want to weep, but that ability is paralyzed too. It's strange, every memory so clear, except for one. I know Tara, but hard as I might try, I can't remember how, when, or why. I just know each time I see her, I'm filled with unbridled rage, incredible, insatiable hate.

Why? Who is she?

I mean, I know who she is now, but there's so much more to this story. I know it but can't find it.

Why do I even care? Who cares about my memories now? I'm going to die.

I won't be able to fight my way out of this mess. All I can do is wait and think. Fear begins to fade, but there's no peace, just numbness. It's an acceptance of fate I can't escape.

The plants begin to move. They move away from me and huddle around a body at my side, blocking my view. Then something strange starts to move across the ground, almost skirting through the sand and soil. It stops, silence follows. I strain to look over to the other side and see the mass of bodies still there. I smell the stench of death and something almost chemical, like a mix of rust and bleach. The silence is broken by a horrifying sound. At first it's hard to make out, but as it builds, it becomes clearer. It's sucking or slurping, getting louder, and in unison, becoming aggressive and relentless.

What are they doing?

The sounds become unbearable, but I have no choice but to listen. I see another group of plants move past me, slowly, methodically. They're floating over the ground as their roots slither ever so gently across the grass and dirt, carrying them forward. They head to the other side and congregate around the bodies. Same routine. It's the same sound, getting louder and louder.

Oh, my God! Are they ... are they ... feeding?!

My fear returns with a vengeance. I'd be shaking if I could move.

I can't die this way! Please, God, don't let me die this way!

I realize that it's the same prayer I prayed that night with the rapist, but I can't help but feel this time there will be no rescue. Tears stream down my face as the sound continues, violently gnawing at my ears, then my heart.

Please God, save me. How many times can I ask? My religion was based on the consequences of bad choices. It wasn't always my fault, but I had stacked up enough to overshadow any that were not.

Why would God listen to me?

If He was real, He knew me, knew all about me. He knew how fickle I'd been in my midnight confessions and promises of penance. I'd never come through on any of those last-minute commitments.

Then again, why should I?

My life hadn't exactly been ideal. And that wasn't my fault. My birth, my mom, those weren't my fault either. The foster system, the beatings, the rapes, they weren't my fault. I didn't want to live like that. I wasn't given a choice. I knew I would die some day, but not like this.

Haven't I suffered enough? Haven't I felt tragedy's cold, dark hand too many times? How much can one person take? The disease, the pain, the suffering, what did I do to deserve all of this? What sin did I commit before I exited the birth canal of that crack whore of a mother?

Why? Why? Why? It's all I can think.

The hellish sounds fill the air, overwhelming my thoughts. I can't see clearly as tears flood my eyes. All I know is fear now.

To die is one thing, but your soul dying first is quite another. I see stalks slowly moving in my direction. They are coming for me. I'm so very afraid, so very alone. This must be the hell before hell. They surround me; I can't count how many. I see their roots begin to dig into the ground. They're stabilizing themselves, anchoring into the dirt as they prepare for what's to come next.

My mind goes blank, the shadow of death darkening the air around me. The sounds continue. I feel the vibration from it beneath me, steady, unrelenting.

Wait! I can feel!

My face feels warm, throbbing in pain. My arms begin to twitch, as do my feet. Even the wound caused by the bullet that grazed my shoulder aches. The poison is wearing off, but it's too late. Even if I could rise, I'm outnumbered. I suddenly miss the numbness.

Now I'm going to feel everything they're about to do to me. To be eaten alive. This is my punishment; it has to be. All I can do is wait.

I don't know what's worse, the anticipation of death, or the revelation of the total sum of my life, and its worthlessness. Both are unbearable. Let it end already. I can only pray there will be some relief on the other side. But my last fear is that it'll only get worse from here. The depression is crushing.

They are on top of me, so thick around me that air can barely sneak between them. This is the end of me. It's been a long time coming … too long.

I wait for death.

CHAPTER 25

Rage

(Alex)

I stare into the mirror on the wall in front of me, but my reflection is absent. My eyes are glossed over by tears that now flow freely, drenching my face. I don't know what I'm looking for, what I'm hoping to see. The mirror is empty and cold, haunting, taunting me.

I see Sara gazing back at me. She's been crying, her eyes red, tears etching deep paths in the flesh of her cheeks. She reaches out to me, but I know it's just an illusion, my mind betraying me. I'm not sure why, but I stand and approach the vision. It's as if I'm being steered by something beyond my control.

She speaks but there's no sound, even though I know what she's trying to say to me. Her supple red lips curl around the words ever so gently. "*Help me, please help me.*" I feel each syllable crawl up my spine, then cross my chest and mercilessly burrow into my heart. I know her reflection isn't real, but her request is deafening. I look down and I'm holding Gracie in my arms. It's the day of her birth, but I'm not in the hospital. I'm still here, lost in all this chaos. She gazes up at me, so tiny, so fragile, and yet there's strength and wonder in her eyes.

She grabs my finger and squeezes it tight, holding it with purpose. Her trust flows through my arm and into my soul. Her stare is unbreakable, telling me how much she needs me. I've never loved anything or anyone more. I'm so careful with her. She's so precious, so helpless. I lift her to my lips and kiss her forehead ever so carefully, her skin so soft, so perfect. She's an amazing example of life at its most magnificent, a masterpiece of creation. I thought her birth was the greatest moment of my life, but every second with her trumps the last, a series of seconds reminding me of how blessed I am, how unworthy of her presence and love. My greatest commission is being her father, a duty I'm grateful for, and undeserving of. I smell her innocence, the newness of life.

I look to my left and see my wife lying in her hospital bed. Sara is asleep; she worked so hard, a fourteen-hour labor to bring Gracie into this world. She's an amazing woman. I don't know how she did it. I was useless in the process, as most men were in these circumstances. All I could do was rub her feet and tell her how much I loved her. She told me later that this was the best medicine. Somehow, my touch—my sincerity—gave her the strength to push through it. It was such a little thing, but for her it had great significance, just like the ball of wonder I held in my arms. I love them both so much. I don't deserve this kind of happiness, and yet I'm immersed in it.

Just as quickly as the moment came, Sara is gone, and the mirror is vacant once again. My arms are empty and yet I still feel them so deeply—their fear, pain, loneliness.

What am I waiting for? I know I can get to them.

The emotion becomes a weight, driving me to my knees. The sounds of rapidly exploding shells suddenly surround me. I'm kneeling in the sand, the air thick with smoke and ash. My arms are heavy and wet. I look down and Boone is limp in my arms. Smoke still billows from the hole in his chest, where he caught the full force of the blast. It tore through his Kevlar vest like paper. The wound is surrounded by cauterized blood, fabric, and flesh, the pungent smell stinging my nose and throat.

I'm there, and he's dead again. I pull him close to my chest and hold his head to my cheek. Tears stream without resistance, soaking my face and Boone's blood-stained hair. I rock back and forth, holding him tight, praying to God that I would wake up from this hell, that Boone and I would be sitting in his backyard, chugging a cold beer, like we had done for so many summers.

I kiss his forehead, tasting the soot and dirt that's caked on his skin. I want to call out his name, but my throat is paralyzed by unimaginable grief. *"Please God, don't take him from me,"* my mind repeats, but I know it's futile. His gaping wound mocks me again and again.

It's the one and only time I wanted to die, die with him. Boone was more than a friend; he was a brother. We'd been through too much, good times, bad times, for it to end so abruptly here. I never had the chance to tell him how much he meant to me. I never got to whisper a simple goodbye.

I startle awake when I feel a hand on my shoulder. I'm back in the basement, alone. I still feel the coldness of Boone's body on my fingertips and smell the burned blood of his wound. But I'm back now, still kneeling on the ground, still weeping as though it just happened. I look up at the ceiling and try to regain my composure. My arms are heavy, as if I'm holding someone else, but this time there's movement. I'm almost afraid to look down but compelled to do so. I gaze into Kayla's face. She's weeping too. I feel her, the warmth and softness of her arms against mine.

Her hair is lying across my hand and wrist, her eyes locked on mine, and a smile breaks free from her tears. Her hand slowly rises to my face. I'm frozen in her gaze. She's beautiful, unaffected by all that we've been through. There's newness to her appearance, as if I'm seeing a vision of who she truly is, free from the wounds and wear of tragedy and pain.

"Thank you for being my hero," she whispers. Her words are like knives digging into my flesh and heart. "You were the only one. The only one who saw my pain and didn't run from it. The only one willing to risk everything for me. The only one who truly loved me." She runs her fingers through my matted hair. "I'll never forget you." She leans up and softly kisses my forehead. "You saw me for who I am."

I'm speechless. Is this a dream—is this truly all in my mind? I feel her; she's as real as the ever-growing ache in my heart.

"I love you." Tears fill her eyes again, like pools of clear water, until they overflow. She begins to disappear, like a vapor caught in a breeze, dissolving like sand through a sieve. I reach for her hand but it's like trying to hold onto smoke or fog.

Is she a ghost saying her last goodbyes, a haunting visitation as she exits this earth? Why, why do the innocent suffer, and heroes get crushed, while evil remains stronger than ever? Why does chaos get a pass while the good are hewn down without so much as a care? Why are the lives of those who carry such significance so fragile?

I bow my head as the grief assaults me, pushing me to the cold, hard floor. I weep, a wretched weep that possesses my entire body. Faces flash before my closed eyes, those I'd let down. First my sweet Sara and Gracie, then Boone, and now Kayla.

I was supposed to protect her. I shared her torment, her past, knew her essence. I was closer to her than anyone in my life. We connected in a way that perplexed every facet of reason and logic. Now, she too is gone, lost forever, because of my failure.

I scratch the floor, burying my nails in the concrete until they bleed. My body tightens until it feels like the flesh will rip free from the bone. I can see her body, lost in that forest of death, waiting to be consumed. That's no way for anyone to die, to be dissolved both in body and memory. Only we will remember her. No one else will get the chance to see how remarkable, how wonderful, she truly was, or could have been, if circumstance had gone in her favor.

God, if you even care anymore, please give me one glimpse of hope to know my whole life wasn't an utter waste of time! Just one glimmer, just one taste!

My face rakes against the cold cement floor. I don't want to die, but I can't figure out what there is to live for anymore. I force myself up and trudge over to the wall that houses the small mirror, where it all started. I peer deeply into my own reflection and see a man beaten, destroyed by it all. My eyes are as red as crimson, surrounded by gray circles and deep bags beneath them.

I place my hands on the wall on either side of the mirror, the wall cold and damp, and begin to weep again.

I hear movement upstairs, steps, rummaging. Will I fail them too? I look back into the mirror and see her, Kayla, smiling back at me. Her hand reaches out of the glass and touches my face. It's cold at first but warms quickly. It's her.

"Save me," she whispers.

A chill runs up my spine.

"Save me, Alex."

Her reflection disappears and only mine remains. I'm knocked off my feet, pain resonating up my back as I hit the ground. I look up at the ceiling as her memories rush back in, every ounce of her pain, terror, and shame. In a brutal tidal wave, her life becomes mine again. Then the ceiling opens, and I stare up into a bluish sky. It's suddenly wiped away, and I see a horde of plants standing terrifyingly silent and still.

I see her clearly, lying weakly in the field among those horrific stalks, calling out to me. I feel her fear, her hopelessness.

As abruptly as the vision appeared, it's gone, and only the ceiling remains. I blink, and the moment is lost. I don't question the vision. I jump up, my grief replaced by rage. I smash the mirror with my bare fist, shattering it. Blood splatters against the wall. Taking control, I turn and defiantly ascend the stairs, having a purpose now, my only purpose.

She will be saved! SHE WILL BE SAVED!

Nothing will stop me!

I reach the top of the stairs, thrust open the door and sprint to the corner of the kitchen, where all our equipment is stored. I grab two AR15s and several magazines, then find a machete and its matching sheath. My pistol is missing, so I quickly rummage through and find another, loading it with a fresh magazine. I grab a second 9mm and load it as well. I quickly do a mental inventory. I'm still wearing my body armor, but where's that gas mask?

I fumble through the items in a controlled frenzy. Where's that redneck-engineered flame thrower?

I notice Kayla's archery supplies across the room. It further ignites my purpose. Doc walks into the room and stops dead in his tracks as I continue gathering my weapons.

"What's going on here?" he asks.

I remain silent. I have a crystal-clear picture of my mission and I won't allow anyone or anything to cloud or confuse it.

"Alex, are you alright? Why is your hand bleeding?" When I don't answer, he says, "Alex, please stop so I can look at that hand." He reaches for my arm.

I pull away and grab a duffle bag off the floor.

"Alex, what the hell is going on with you?"

I stop and take a deep breath. "I'm going after Kayla."

"What? Kayla? That's suicide!"

His words carry neither weight nor meaning to me. I began to take stock of everything I've laid out. "I need that gas mask," I murmur to myself. "Where the hell is it?"

"Alex, you can't do this. There's no way she survived. Kayla is gone. I know it's hard to deal with, but we lost her."

"Not today." I begin to holster my sidearms and fill my ammo belt.

"Alex, you're out of control. Please stop for a second and think about this. We need you here, especially now with those things out there. We don't know if they followed us, or when they'll attack again."

"You're safe for now. She's not." I sling the rifles over both my shoulders.

"How can you say that? You can't guarantee that."

Jude enters the room. Great, he probably heard all the commotion. I know how to keep him busy. "Jude, go find me any fire extinguishers in the house. I know I saw one in the basement. There may be another in the garage."

Jude nods and sprints out of the room. He trusts me so blindly.

"What the hell do you need those for?" Doc asks.

I strap the machete to my side and tie it off around my thigh.

Matt enters the room. "What's going on in here?"

Great, now I have two to deal with.

"Stop, just stop and explain this to me," Doc begs as he positions himself in my way.

"Doc, move, or I'll move you."

"No, not until you talk to me." We stare at each other, neither blinking.

"She's still alive. I know she is, and I'm going to bring her back."

"How can you possibly know that?"

"I don't have time for explanations, neither does Kayla." I brush past Matt. Rummaging through the duffle bag, I find several grenades and a couple of flash bangs. I grab a smaller bag and place them inside.

Jude returns. "Here's the one from the basement, but I couldn't find one in the kitchen."

"Check the garage," I say.

Matt stands there, dumbfounded by it all. "Seriously, what is going on here?"

"You heard me the first time." Ah, the gas mask is at the bottom of the bag. "I'm going after Kayla. She's still alive. This is not a discussion or a debate. It's happening and there's nothing you can do or say to change my mind."

"What about us? What about Jude and Tara? We matter too, don't we?"

I ignore him, even though he's not wrong. All I need now is that that flame thrower. It has to be here somewhere.

Jude speeds back into the room. "I found the other one." He places it next to the first one. "What are you gonna use them for?"

He's clueless to my quest. If he knew, he'd be as persistent as the others in trying to stop me. "Those plants can sense heat and movement," I say.

"How do you know that?" he asks, curious.

"I just do. They don't attack over one or the other. It must sense them both together, heat and movement, in the right configuration!"

"What?" Jude says.

"Look, they won't attack something that has a heat signature unless it's also moving. The same as they won't attack something moving that doesn't also have a heat signature. Jude, I want you to spray me with those extinguishers to mask any body heat that might escape the armor."

Jude picks up one of the extinguishers.

"Don't spray my face, boy, okay?" I adjust the straps to the gas mask and fit it tightly over my face.

Jude begins to spray me head to toe with the extinguisher. Doc and Matt jump back to avoid getting caught in the thick white mist. He empties the can, leaving me looking like a deranged, post-apocalyptic snowman.

"Get the other one," I call out, my voice somewhat muffled by the mask.

He nods and throws down the first canister. Doc and Matt cough as the room fills with its contents. That should shut them up for a few seconds. They both leave the room, knowing it's pointless to keep arguing with me. Good.

Jude sprints to the other extinguisher.

"Hit me again, kid!"

Jude covers his mouth and sprays me, covering all the exposed areas the first attempt failed to shield.

"You alright?" I ask.

He coughs, then smiles, giving me the thumbs up. He empties the second canister.

That should do it. "Back up, kid." I grab the two rifles off the table. Time to go. I'll have to forego the flamethrower.

Jude drops the second container. "Please come back," he says as tears fill his eyes.

"Count on it. I will, and so will Kayla."

The faster I move now, the easier it'll be to slip out before Jude truly understands what's going on. I don't have time for any more delays, or even goodbyes. I move quickly into the hallway.

Matt and the doc stand there, speechless. There's nothing more to say.

"Take care of them," I say, "no matter what." Not waiting for a reaction, I head out the door, slowly checking my surroundings, my AR15 poised for action. "Lock everything and turn off the lights. Stay away from the windows. Find a central location in the house and hunker down until I get back."

That might be the last command I'll ever give anyone. I cautiously move down the street, quickly checking every side street, then the sky above for movement. I slip down the street, hugging a building. The field is east. I scan again. It's all clear. I move swiftly toward the field, utilizing every ounce of training I've ever received. My steps are light but strong, everything eerily silent. I know why. Everything in their world fears those stalks. I saw inside that thing's mind. In a world of savagery and violence, the most tyrannical thing is a plant, an organism we take for granted. But in their environment, they're at the top of the food chain. They amass in small hordes at first, then others join them. Sometimes they engulf an entire area, miles wide. Nothing gets past them. Nothing survives once they are surrounded by them. Once trapped in the field, the only exit is a long, painful death.

But despite their ominous existence, they do have a weakness, just like everything else that lives here or anywhere else. Their brain, if you can call it that, is contained at the base of the stalk. It controls the root-like tendrils that provide the plant with movement, navigation, and communication with the others. A precise, hard strike to its base should take it out.

The acid they use to devour their prey is contained in the mid-section. Once it touches the skin, it dissolves it, and there's no reversing its effects or stopping it from taking the entire body. The acid spreads like a virus, eventually consuming the victim. A hellish death. But the acid is only activated when another ingredient at the top of the plant is mixed with it. Without this, it becomes as harmless as tree sap, otherwise it would burn through its host.

I learned all this from that one touch with the alien humanoid. If you cut the plant in half, it can't harm anyone. It's like two animals in one. The bottom is the locomotion, and the top is the hunter, and they can't live apart. It won't be easy, but they've never seen our weapons, our firepower, but they're about to be introduced. We'll see then who's at the top spot of the food chain.

I see the field in the distance, no sign of the tribe. That's what they are, a tribe, separated by clans that war constantly over territory and food sources. It's a life of constant conflict and danger. They're skilled warriors who live a lifestyle of violence and pain. It's all they know.

I continue to hug the buildings, searching my surroundings with every step. The field is getting closer. I see the alley we escaped from still burning, buildings smoldering. The deep, billowing black smoke is the only contrast in color against the sky.

Are we still in our world? Is this still our home? Or were we somehow moved to theirs?

The plants are motionless, but I know it's a deception. A trap. If I get any closer, they'll sense me, my movement. Hopefully, my body heat is hidden from them, but my cold white coating has already begun to decay. I left a trail of it behind me, melting on the pavement. Looking up, I see my advantage.

A building, three stories high, that's been abandoned for years. From the roof, I might be able to find her. I throw my rifle over my shoulder and sprint up the fire escape. Swinging my rifle behind me, I search the field for any clearing where she might be. At first, I can't see anything, just the stalks huddled close together. To my left, I spot a small patch with a stack of bodies in the center. Even from this distance, I see firsthand the horror of these creatures.

The skin has been burned off their bodies, exposing muscle and bone. They are writhing but making no sound. It's inhumane. There are three or four bodies. I can't make out the sexes. They're stacked one on top of the other in a terrifying pile. Below them is a vile puddle which I can only imagine is the dissolved remains. The ground is saturated with it. I see several plants move closer as larger tubular tendrils slither from beneath them, beginning to suck up some of the putrid mess. It's how they feed, in small groups, as their prey painfully, silently, dissolves. The bottom body collapses from the weight of the others, and the remaining bodies spill onto the ground. One rolls a few feet from the pile, leaving appendages behind it as it comes to a stop. I see its face, or what's left of it, mouthing something I'm unable to make out.

Several more plants congregate around it, sinking their tendrils deep into its flesh. I hear them draining fluids in unison, a horrific sound, indescribable, one I pray I never witness again.

Oh, God, Kayla. I can't let you die this way!

I frantically search the field again, praying I see her and that she's not suffering the same fate. All seems lost until I catch a glimpse of another open patch in the corner, near a parking lot behind some sort of garage.

Wait, that's Mike's shop. He works on all the patrol cars. I head over to the corner of the roof, the gas mask now obstructing my long-range view. I tear it off, letting it hang loosely from my neck, and peer into the distance. It's an opening, and there's a female lying by herself, with three other bodies not far away from her. None are moving. It must be her.

But how do I get to her?

If I go around via the parking lot, they'll close in on her. They move their victims by pushing them through the dirt using their stalk bodies. If I come in through the center, they'll attack me. My armor might protect me, but for how long? What if I begin to shoot them, aim for their bases, picking them off? How will they react? My newfound memories offer no solution. Those caught in the field were left for dead; there was no other recourse.

If I use explosives, I might harm Kayla, if she's still alive. She must be alive! I can feel her as if she's standing right next to me.

I have no choice. I'll have to flank them, enter by the lot, cut my way through, then try to exit the way I entered. Setting my rifle on single fire, so I don't accidentally hit Kayla, I find another fire escape and descend to the street. My steps are quick and sure. It's as if I'm walking on air. I reach the edge, only feet away from the field, and try to peer between the stalks. I can barely see her, about thirty feet from me, with those things all around her. My frozen cloak has almost disappeared. I'm now exposed, visible. I slide my mask back on to protect my face and neck from the tendrils.

Taking a deep breath, I know I'm alone in this, no backup. Once this begins, there's no turning back. My heart's racing, pounding so hard it's almost painful. I flip off the safety and take another deep breath. *This is it!*

I fire the first shot into the stalk's base. It stiffens, and I fire a second shot, then a third. I strike every target, my aim surgical. I fire again as I get closer and closer. The first plant falls like a dead tree and takes out a row of others, toppling them like dominoes. The shots echo between the buildings as I fire again and begin to clear the first row in front of me. I count each shot to track my ammo.

The plants begin to move, retreating backward. They must sense what's going on. Tendrils spread across the top of the field, covering it in a luminescent blanket, frantically, blindly, reacting to the melee. I ratchet up my strike, blasting away to continue to clear a path. I quickly check behind and above me, then continue firing, my aim still perfect.

I move into the field and clear a path. They continue to back up, confused by this new, strange, and deadly enemy. I can see Kayla clearly now. She's not moving. I fire again, ensuring they won't encircle me, closing off my exit. There are just too many. I empty the first magazine and quickly change it out in seconds, switching to semi-automatic to cover more ground.

I quickly throw a flash bang, hoping the noise and brightness might have an effect. It did, as the brilliant flash of light and sharp sound repels them farther back. I make my way closer and closer to her, praying with each step that all of this is not in vain. I empty another magazine, switch out, and continue my barrage. I've lost count of the fallen. My exit path is still clear. The sky is still empty. I'm just feet away from her, my heart in my throat. I continue to mow them down, the dead now blocking the living, leaving a low barrier they can't cross. I throw another flash bang. They have no defense against its powerful effect.

I'm only inches from Kayla, her body still lifeless. The forms of the other three bodies are all mutilated and warped. They're still alive, barely moving, a horrific sight. Who are they? Where did they come from? A male and two females. One of the females has no face, just her bare skull picked clean of all flesh and matter. But she too is still alive.

Dear God, how can this be? It's truly hell!

The other female is missing both her legs. Only twisted remnants of the appendages remained. The male is the worst, mangled, incomplete, and barely human anymore. He reaches out in my direction with his only arm, missing its hand.

Then I look down at Kayla, lying beneath me. "You came for me," she whispers through dry, cracked lips.

I touch her face, feeling nothing through my glove, but she's alive. Joy overwhelms me. "We're getting out of here," I whisper back. "Can you move at all?"

"No strength," she mumbles, barely remaining conscious.

"I need you to try. Grab onto my shoulder."

I continue to fire, creating a wall of stalk corpses to surround me. They're blocked from us. I hurl a grenade deep into the midst of them, as far from me as I can throw it. Now it's about damage.

It explodes, throwing debris high into the sky. I unload the third magazine, then bend down as Kayla reaches out for me. The stalks try to move closer, but they're still obstructed by the fallen.

The man reaches out again. For a moment I see Boone's face, but it quickly fades. "Please kill me," he gasps with what little breath he has left.

Kayla takes hold of my shoulder, and I begin to slowly lift her.

"Please," he gasps again.

I stand and brace Kayla against me, her back to the scene. I can see the pain emanating in the one eye remaining in his skull, parts of his face stripped down to the muscle. I raise my rifle.

"Yes, *please*," he says.

Before I can blink, I put a bullet into the center of his forehead. He falls limp in an instant. Kayla is oblivious. I pause and then shoot the other two as well. I have no remorse. It was their only relief.

The stalks are surrounding us, trying to maneuver over the fallen, but our exit path is still clear. I hoist Kayla over my shoulders, nearly dropping my rifle. I'd anticipated her being heavier. Steadying my rifle, I begin to jog toward our exit, picking up speed with every step, firing at anything that gets remotely close to us. I stabilize Kayla with my other arm, fighting to keep my balance as I sprint forward. Glancing up at the sky, I'm relieved to see it's still empty.

I allow my rifle to fall by my side, suspended by its strap, as I forage for two more grenades, pulling the pins with my teeth before I hurl them back as hard as I can. I rush faster toward the parking lot as I hear the grenades hit the ground far behind us. The explosions rock the ground, and I nearly stumble.

"You just love blowing shit up, don't you?" Kayla laughs weakly as we step onto the pavement.

I smile as we walk to the back of the garage between two derelict cars, a truck, and a sedan. I set her down for a moment to recharge, leaning against the garage door.

"Stay here," I say, seeing several gas containers against the back wall. She nods, and I grab the containers; two out of the four are full. I unscrew the caps and take a quick whiff. It's gas. I snatch the two and head back to the entrance of the field. They found a way to overcome the dead stalks. Let's see if these bastards can survive fire.

I throw the containers into the middle of the field. After they land, I steady my rifle and aim, shooting at each one, releasing the contents. Then I grab my last two flash bangs. This needs to be dead on.

I throw the first in front of the container as the field begins to close around it. I throw the second in the same manner. The first one explodes before it hits the ground. The initial bang is unimpressive, but it ignites the gas vapors, and the container erupts in flames. The second explodes only moments later.

Kayla's right, I do enjoy blowing shit up.

The fire rips through the field as well as those ferocious predators, turning the source of such horror and pain into nothing more than kindling. As smoke fills the air, I rush back to Kayla. "Time to go!"

She nods, the sound of the plants crackling and burning in the distance filling the air. I help her up, then freeze when she quietly screams.

I spin around and see them all around us. The tribe has returned, and in increased numbers. They are on the street surrounding the building, as well as the rooftops. There must be dozens of them. I sit Kayla down and raise my rifle, though I have a host of arrows pointed at us from each side and above. Even if I'm lucky enough to squeeze off a round, we'll be dead before it strikes its first victim.

A large male steps forward, covered in elaborate tattoos etched—no, almost burned—deep into his skin. He wears a leather chest piece surrounded by some kind of strange fur. His loin cloth is also covered in fur. It stretches down like a skirt over his long, bone-covered legs. His feet are bare, with four long talons instead of toes that look like they're digging into the asphalt. A thin black mohawk trails behind him, braided, dry and coarse. His enormous white eyes full of green and blue filaments change patterns as he glares angrily at me.

He snarls and I catch a brief glimpse of his bright white, sharklike teeth, a contrast against his bluish gray skin. Everything about him is intimidating, right down to the bow strapped to his back, the quiver filled with long arrows. A large dagger is strapped to his left leg, and around his neck is a necklace made of more bones and foreign items. He has to be at least seven feet tall, and I can't even guess how much he weighs.

I begin to see images again, recalling memories from a race that does not belong here. He's an elder, the chief warrior, leader of this tribe. I can't pronounce their language, but I understand it clearly in my mind. This is his clan. There must be nearly forty of them surrounding us. There had been more, but we reduced their numbers.

I sense their anger. It hangs thick in the air. A clan that once numbered over a hundred, families surviving their hostile world together, reduced to this. They hunt, plant, live and die as one, a relationship that far surpasses anything we call a family. They're as frightened as we are, maybe more so, in this chaotic new existence. They see us as a threat, more alien to them than they ever could be to us. In their minds, we invaded their world and not the reverse. They simply know their lives have been turned upside down, and we are responsible for it. No wonder there's so much hate in their hearts toward us. We're the occupying army that threatens their very existence.

I struggle to find the answer among this myriad of new memories. I feel Kayla's hand grab my leg. She's trembling.

The clan leader motions to the others, and they step back. He drops his quiver and bow. He lays them on the ground, then removes his large, curved dagger from its sheath. The clan begins to growl, low at first, but slowly, harmoniously, increasing.

Fuck, I know what this is. I know what happens next. It's the only way we can survive. The only way they'll let Kayla go. I remove my mask and step back, kneeling beside her. "When it begins, you have to get up and run as fast as you can," I whisper.

I know they won't pursue her. She's too weak to be a threat. They probably think she won't survive. Thank God, they don't know her like I do.

"When what begins?" She begins to quietly weep.

I stare into her eyes. "Run down the street to the neighborhood past the field. Follow the neighborhood to the end of the development. There's a cul-de-sac, house number 233. Go there. They won't follow."

"How do you know?"

"They want to watch the show, and they won't move an inch until it's over."

"I can't make it."

"You have to, because you'll die here if you don't."

The chief stomps his foot on the ground. A chill runs up my spine. The challenge has been laid down. Two more stomps and he'll strike whether I'm ready or not. He doesn't care if I understand his customs. I'm part of it now, like it or not.

"I can't even stand," Kayla says. "Too weak."

I know she's right. The only way out of this is to win, and that's an impossibility. The chief stomps again, and the growling crowd begins to chant. Kayla's eyes fill with fear as they begin to bang their spears and fists on the ground. The ones on the roof make just as much noise.

I rise and turn to face my opponent. His face is locked in a maniacal glare. One more stomp and it's on. If I shoot him, we die. If I shoot at them, we die. The only way out is to beat him. I drop my mask to the ground and raise my hand. It'll give me some time, but very little. I gently lay my rifle on the ground, then swing the other around slowly and lay it down too. I raise my hand again according to custom. He's responding, giving me a little more time. I remove the machete from its sheath and hold it up. He doesn't know about my side arms; they're still holstered. They may be my last resort if this goes badly.

And it will. I know far too well how strong these things are, at least the soldiers. I can only imagine what this guy has to offer. I look back at Kayla and smile. "Everything will be okay." I see my lie has fallen short in her eyes.

He stomps his foot again. The chants are so loud I can't hear myself think. He takes his stance, crouched, dagger held tightly in his fist.

Time is up. No more distractions, customs, pomp, or circumstance. I assume the same position. This will be a fight for both our lives A fight I can't possibly win.

CHAPTER 26

Worlds Collide

(Kayla)

What the hell is going on? Is he going to fight that thing?

The two face off only a few feet from each other, the tension thick in the air, nearly suffocating. We're surrounded with no hope of escape. We're out of one horrible frying pan straight into a more terrifying fire. They circle each in a warped dance of death.

Alex has a ferocious look on his face, but it pales in comparison to the monstrous snarl on his enemy's. The surrounding horde bangs the ends of their spears on the ground as they make deep, visceral growls in harmony; low at first, but gradually increasing in volume. They're cheering their champion on.

Some of them stare at me, but I'm too weak to stand. I won't let myself imagine what they're thinking. At this point, death may be the least of my concerns. The drumming and growling gets louder, continuing to build as Alex and that thing tighten their circle, getting closer and closer to each other. Just as the noise reaches a deafening peak, it stops, and there's an eerie silence. His enemy stomps defiantly one more time.

Alex appears frozen, as if he knows what's coming next. The creature springs forward toward him, his leg muscles so tightly defined you can see them constrict and relax with each brisk step. Time slows as he rushes Alex. Alex tries to protect himself, but the sheer force of the impact knocks him almost off his feet into a wall behind him. There's no way he can match this thing's strength. He grunts, the wind knocked out of him. The creature quickly picks him up and slams him against the wall. Alex's machete goes flying in the air, landing on the concrete, well out of his reach.

Alex repeatedly thrusts his elbows into its back, using all his force. It has little influence, and he's thrown across the lot like a rag doll, hitting the ground face up. He groans loudly, and I know the pain must be terrible. The thing stands stoically, displaying a satisfied grimace across its inhuman face, mocking Alex.

Alex tries to rise, but the monster sprints up to him and swiftly kicks him in the ribs, its taloned feet tearing at his vest and body armor. It kicks him repeatedly. If it weren't for Alex's body armor, it would have crushed his chest with the first blow.

Alex grabs its leg and goes for the knee. He punches it with great force and the creature howls in pain. Alex keeps punching until the creature drops down to its other knee, then he strikes its face relentlessly. The barrage is vicious, and the creature falls onto its back. The once silent crowd erupts into howls and screams. The sound slices through me, butchering my heart.

Before Alex can get back to his feet, the creature recovers and jumps back up with little effort. It kicks Alex in the head, sending blood spraying across the lot. Alex rolls three or four times across the concrete, leaving a bloody trail from the lacerations caused by its talons. He lifts himself up like a push up as the blood spills from his tattered face, soaking into the asphalt.

The creature ruthlessly kicks him in the stomach, lifting him off the ground. Alex drops back down, and blood fountains from his mouth. Then it violently grabs him by the back of his vest and throws him across the lot into a car door. The impact crushes the metal, leaving a dent the size of his body. I can see Alex desperately try to catch his breath, fighting through the pain.

The creature stands back and howls, raising his left hand high into the air. The crowd responds with a unified screech, an eerie affirmation that chills my soul. I reach out to Alex, but he's too far away.

Even if I could, what would it matter? The attempt only weakens me more. I don't even have the strength to muster tears at this point.

Alex struggles to get up, his face matted with dirt and blood. The creature doesn't allow him any rest. It grabs him, hoisting him with ease into the air, then slams him hard onto the hood of the car. The derelict vehicle slides off the cinder blocks that were under the rims, holding it up. The impact crushes the hood, bowing deep into the empty engine compartment.

The creature tears off Alex's damaged and tattered vest, tossing it into the air. The crowd gives an animalistic victory cheer as he rolls off the car and slams into the ground. Without hesitation, the creature violently stomps on his back. Alex is helpless as the creature picks his limp body up, holding him up in front of his face. It stares deeply into Alex's bloodshot eyes. I can't make out Alex's features anymore, distorted by blood and battle. The thing laughs, a hellish, menacing sound, holding him up for his fans to see. They react with even louder calls, filling the air.

As if he's weightless, it hoists Alex high over his head and carries him as he circles the lot, displaying his trophy before its multitude of minions. Blood from Alex's face and chest wounds stream down its arms. The armor had offered little protection against the sharp talons.

I know Alex is going to die. I'm going to die too. He risked everything for me, and now his family would be utterly alone. I really believed him when he told me they were alive. It was the unmistakable, undeniable conviction in his eyes that left me with no doubts. I never let him know because I didn't want him to leave us. I knew we couldn't survive without him. Now our selfishness—my selfishness—has led him to this. I took away our hope, and theirs: Rick, Matt, Tara and Jude. This man was their hero, the real deal, not some imagined icon or fantasy, and I led him to his death.

After his victory lap, the creature carelessly drops Alex's nearly lifeless form to the ground. Alex bounces like he's made of rubber. There's no reaction at all. I can't tell if he's still conscious. Maybe he's already dead. But then he coughs up some blood, nearly gurgling in it. The excruciating pain must have paralyzed him, his movements barely noticeable.

The creature circles him as the hideous clan cheers him on. It plays to the crowd, a demonstration of dominance and superiority as he hovers over Alex's torn and tattered body. It had dropped its dagger when Alex took out its knee, but now he gathers it up, holds it high in the air.

Oh God, this is the end!

It lifts Alex up by his left arm and drags him toward the closed garage door, then presses him up against the door by his throat. It raises its dagger high into the air. The gruesome audience howls, the sound shaking the very windows around me. It plunges the bone blade deep into Alex's right shoulder, pinning him to the garage.

Alex screams in agony, hanging there by a dagger that's been thrust between muscle and bone. He grabs it with his free hand, but it's been buried deep in his flesh and the metal of the garage door. Only the handle is visible, drenched in Alex's spurting blood. He cries out in agony again, unable to defend himself.

Why didn't it just kill him? Why continue to torture and taunt him? This is inhumane!

The creature steps back, deeply gratified. The crowd continues to celebrate in its own monstrous way. The creature glances around and eyes Alex's machete. It smiles like a Cheshire cat from hell.

Now I understand. It's clear it wants to finish the job with Alex's own blade. It must be a symbolic thing, some sort of rite, to do in their victims with their own weapon.

An ironic fatal bitch slap.

It scoops the weapon off the ground and holds it up. Defenseless, Alex squirms against the door as it arrogantly strolls up to him, savoring each final moment.

I feel some strength returning but what can I do? I'm still unable to stand or walk. All I can do is scream, but my small voice is muted by the roar of the crowd.

It stands before Alex, grinning widely, its jagged white teeth almost glowing as it looks over its victim one last time. Alex breathes heavily as he stares back at his assailant. Despite the ruthless, utterly barbaric beating, I can still see strength and courage in his eyes. Alex takes his hand off the bloodied handle, dropping it to his side. His face is covered in dark crimson. The horrific gash in his chest opens and closes with each labored breath. His expression is like stone. Despite Alex's remarkable resolve, his assailant remains unfazed by it.

Alex turns to me, his expression showing deep regret. I hear him say in my head, *"I'm sorry."* The connection we share is quickly fading away, that same connection I'd sensed so intensely when he saved me. My only hope.

A fool's hope! Now it's dissolving like sugar in hot water. He's really going to die. And so am I.

Alex turns back to his attacker, and his confidence returns as he glares deep into its eyes. His defiance is noticed, but it won't be enough to distract or detain it. The creature presses the blade against the center of Alex's chest. It holds it there for only a moment, but it seems like a year. Alex refuses to break his stare. It glances over at me now, nodding its head, verifying what is about to come. As it surveys the crowd, their cheering instantaneously lulls, morphing into a steady, muffled chant.

It turns back to Alex and pulls the blade back, still pointing it straight at its target. Alex remains stoic, unfazed by his impending doom. I think it notices that too, which I sense will make this kill even more satisfying for it.

It draws back, this time raising the blade above its head. It's going to drive it down deep into Alex's wounded chest. Time slows again, and my heart breaks like never before. Tears finally fill my eyes, dropping to the ground. In all the shit I'd been through and faced over the years, this agony is the most intense. All the regret, shame, loneliness, and hate reach its apex, drowning me as I struggle just to breathe.

I see the gate, smell and taste the darkness of death. The blade effortlessly slices through the air, slowly, silently descending to its mark. I'm completely alone, ready to watch the one person I truly love die a horrific death.

Oh my God, I do love him!

I collapse, emotion driving me to the ground. I don't want to watch any further and yet I can't take my eyes off it. I have to watch him die. I have no choice. As the audience goes wild, it plunges the blade toward Alex's chest. My heart stops. Just before the blade connects, Alex grabs its wrist, halting the momentum. The creature pauses, shocked.

So am I.

It tries to pull free, but Alex's grip is too tight. It attempts to strike him with his free hand, but Alex stops its fist with his palm. His hand closes on the creature's, trapping it. Blood sprays from Alex's shoulder wound as he tightens both of his holds. The creature pulls violently but can't break free. It howls in pain as it begins to drop to one knee. Its expression screams of pain. I hear something crunching and cracking as its head drops in agony.

Alex turns his hands, twisting the creature's wrists, forcing it to rise back to its feet, still grimacing in anguish. He headbutts the creature once, then twice, and finally a third time. It falls back, but Alex doesn't release his death grip. He kicks it repeatedly, mercilessly, in the abdomen, then releases it to fall backwards on the asphalt. The crowd falls instantly quiet.

How is this happening?

Black liquid—its own blood—now covers its face, intermingled with crimson streaks from Alex's. Alex roars and grabs the dagger's handle, slowly pulling it free from his shoulder. He throws it across the lot and steps from the door, a bloody silhouette remaining behind. He proceeds forward, slowly approaching the creature, his eyes black as night, no separation between the sclera, iris, or pupils. They look like balls of smooth charcoal, no longer human, void of a soul. He smiles maniacally as he continues to step forward.

The creature springs back to its feet, wiping the blood from its face. It stands firm, awaiting the next attack. It takes the initiative and lunges for Alex, only to be welcomed by a violent barrage of punches to its face and stomach. It has become an old school beatdown. Each strike lands perfectly on its mark. It absorbs the full impact of each blast, unable to counter. The creature falls back, but Alex isn't close to being finished. He punches its rib cage, then rains punch after punch to its face and head.

I don't understand how Alex was able to recover from the beating he took. His strength and the ferocity of his assault is unbelievable! It's animalistic, barbaric, and totally terrifying.

Unbalanced and disoriented, the creature frantically swings, but Alex grabs its arm and kicks it sharply in the side. He swings the creature around, slamming it into the same garage door he'd been pinned to. Alex bull rushes him, and the door almost caves under the brunt of the impact. He wastes no time picking it up and slamming it hard onto the ground. The crowd is frozen silent, lost in shock and awe. Alex mercilessly pulls it off the ground and again effortlessly swings it up, catapulting into the side of a nearby pickup truck. The windows shatter and the door bows upon impact.

My, how the tables have turned! I wonder why its minions aren't coming to its aid? They just stand there frozen, watching?

Without hesitation, Alex picks up the creature and throws it across the lot. It lands on a car windshield, spraying glass everywhere. The crowd finally begins to growl. Alex is a blur as he rushes to his foe, who is now barely conscious. He jerks it out of the car by its arm, then breaks it, as if it's no more than a dry twig. The creature screams in pain as Alex slams it to the ground, driving his knee into the creature's sternum. I hear an ominous crack as it convulses under the impact.

Alex looms over his victim, searching the lot with his black eyes. The crowd continues its low growl, though still not acting over the assault of one of their own. Only a few feet away is the creature's dagger, drenched in blood.

I don't understand how this battle has turned so quickly? What has Alex become? Why are the rest not attacking him?

Alex walks slowly over to the dagger and picks it up, caressing the handle as he glares at his fallen, convulsing foe. Kneeling over his foe, his eyes like dark opals, the crowd again falls silent. Oblivious to them, Alex looks down at his prey and smiles as he grasps the handle with both hands, raising it high in the air.

This will be a brutal end. Again, I want to turn away, but I can't take my eyes off the scene. Time slows. The creature's eyes widen as Alex plunges the dagger down, digging it deep into the concrete right next to its skull. The blade sinks into the hard pavement as if in soft mud. Alex pauses, still, statuesque. The crowd stops breathing.

He didn't kill it! Why?

His breathing heavy and hard, he bends down and growls, "Remember me!" I no longer recognize his voice. It's a sound of fear and hate mixed together in some hellish concoction. A set of dog tags dangles from his neck. Funny, I never noticed them before. He tears them free and drops them on the creature's bloodied chest. It doesn't respond, lying there motionless. Is it dead? As he slowly stands, Alex's eyes transform, returning to their original state, the maniacal smile dissipating.

Is he back? Where did he go? What just took his place here?

He looks around, then at his unconscious opponent. He appears as stunned as the rest of us. Dried blood frames his face, flaking from his skin with each expression. He continues to scan the crowd as he returns to me, picking up his machete on the way.

The crowd begins to growl again, slowly at first, but then intensifying. They're becoming increasingly animated now. I guess the show is over.

Alex approaches me, reaching out for my hand, assisting me to my feet. His expression alerts me that the danger isn't over. He braces me up and we turn.

"We're not getting out of here," he whispers.

My throat tightens, my stomach on fire.

"If you beat their chief warrior, they are supposed to let you go," he continues to whisper.

"That's good news, right?"

"In their world, that's how it works." We step ever so slightly forward. "But we're not in their world … or ours either anymore. They don't trust him, even blame him for what's happened. They can't understand it."

"Who can?" Wait, how does he know this shit? Does he somehow have the same connection with it that we have with each other?

"They're waiting for him to fail so a new leader can be chosen."

"That's all well and good, Alex, but what does it mean for us?" I whisper-hiss back.

The archers begin to raise their bows, as the rest beat the end of their spears against the ground.

"We die."

My heart is in my throat, my skin like ice against the heat of Alex's.

"Stay by my side." We're now at the wrong end of every arrow pointed at us. The banging and growling intensifies. "It'll all be over in a second." He turns to me and smiles.

What kind of shit is this? To survive everything else and go out like this. This goes way beyond cruel irony, a hellish joke. "You know this is fucked up, right?"

The archers pause, and I feel Alex's grip tighten around my waist. He locks eyes with me. There's so much to be said, but no more time to say it.

Fuck!

I bury my head in his neck and prepare to die. As if that's possible. I feel the icy hand of death run up my spine. Maybe there'll be time on the other side to tell him how much he means to me.

Alex throws me to the ground and covers me with his body as the loud chanting is interrupted by gunfire. I can't see anything. All I hear are rapid fire gunshots, howls, and screams.

"Stay down!" he roars. He frees his gun from its holster. "Hug the asphalt," he commands, then springs back up and spins around.

The ground trembles beneath me. What now, a fucking earthquake? I hear a truck horn echo through the alley, then more gunfire. Alex leaves me. When I look up, I see he's only a few feet away, picking off those things with deadly accuracy. More rifle fire follows. I try to scan my surroundings, but it's difficult from my position. A creature falls to the ground only a yard or so away. As it slams into the concrete, its head burst open, spraying me with black ooze. It's sticky and stinks.

Not this shit again!

Another falls, then another. I look to my left and see headlights tearing through the field. The stalks don't stand a chance as the tires of some sort of big rig grind them into pulp. It's a tanker truck, and it's barreling this way. Another creature falls to the pavement, the sound of its bones shattering echoing in the alley. Arrows pummel the ground all around me. Alex spins and fires at the creatures on the roof. The truck horn blares as it breaks free from the field, crushing everything under its tires.

Creatures scatter. Alex reloads as an arrow strikes him in the shoulder. He drops to his knee and grimaces, but quickly recovers and continues firing at the archers on the roof. A hail of bullets follow his. I peer over and barely make out Matt, kneeling and firing a blur of bullets above me. The loud squeal of tires fills the alley as the tanker cuts a hard right, its trailer swinging wide.

Oh my God, it's gonna flip over!

"Matt, throw me a rifle!" Alex screams.

Metal skids across the concrete. The arrow still protrudes from Alex's shoulder, buried deep, but he acts as if it's a mere inconvenience. He scoops up the weapon and with almost no effort aims and begins assaulting the remnant on the roof. I don't know where the others have gone. Alex's opponent still lies lifeless only a few feet away. Even more gunfire erupts, emanating from the cab of the truck. It's absolute chaos!

"Come get her!" Alex yells. "I've got you covered."

Unfortunately, I'm still too weak to walk. Matt rushes toward me as Alex continues his barrage. He crouches next to me. "Hey, kid, how's it going?"

Dumbest question ever!

"Alex, you're hit!"

"Yeah, no shit, Sherlock. Just get the girl. I'm fine," he snaps. Alex fires again, blood streaming from his wound. He should be dead just from the sheer amount of blood loss.

Matt turns back to me. "We're leaving. Hang on tight." He slides his arm under me, and I grab a hold of his shirt sleeve as tight as I can.

"Go, now!" Alex roars.

Matt pulls me up, but my legs won't cooperate, so he swoops me up in his arms and carries me across the lot. I look up at the roofline and see only a few stragglers remain. Most are fleeing. Arrows fly by, and my heart pounds. Alex picks off two more and the rest disappear behind the roofline. Bodies are strewn all around the lot, bleeding that same disgusting black ooze. The lot is covered in it.

"Head for the truck," Alex yells as he continues to fire.

We reach the truck, Matt breathing hard. He flings me into the cab, and I slide across the seats. Doc is on the other side, firing. What's left of the field is burning and in ruin. I hear liquid hitting the ground. Something is pouring out, the smell of gas heavy, almost suffocating.

"Doc," I scream. "I think it's leaking!"

Doc steps back and takes cover behind the cab door. "What, Kayla?"

"Can't you smell it?"

"Smell what?"

"Really! Are you fucking kidding me! Gas, Doc, gas! It must be leaking from the tanker! Look behind you!"

Doc finally looks back. "Oh, my God!"

I find enough strength to pull myself across the seat and look outside the door. Doc is standing in a puddle of it.

"This isn't going to work," he gasps. He steps out of the puddle and shakes the gas from his soaked pants leg. How the hell did he not notice that?

I realize there's a flamethrower on the passenger floorboard. Get that thing out of here," I scream as I look back into the burning field. Something must have punctured the tank as the doc tore through the stalks. Maybe an arrow hit it.

Who knows? Who cares! We need to get the hell out of here before the fire reaches us. Matt comes around from the back.

"Matt, stay there," Doc calls out. "There's gas everywhere."

Alex finally reaches the cab. "Why the fuck haven't you left yet?"

"The tanker is leaking," I snap.

"Fuck," Alex gasps.

I notice the arrow that hit his shoulder is gone; not even the shaft remains. "That had to hurt like hell," I say.

Alex pauses, looking at me quizzically, then realizes what I'm talking about. "You have no idea."

"What did you do, just yank it out?"

Before he answers, Doc interrupts. "There's another car; I saw it down the alley."

"What kind?" Alex asks.

"Some kind of Sedan. Does it matter, as long as it runs?"

"Can you reach it safely to check it out?"

"Yeah, cover me," Doc calls out as he bolts down the alley.

Alex follows, sliding out of my line of sight. I struggle to lift myself up to see past the windshield.

Matt comes back around. "Kayla, you okay?"

I can barely see over the dash, but I watch the doc speed down the alley and reach the car. Alex scans the area. It's fallen eerily silent out. The car is apparently unlocked, and Rick ducks into it for a moment. He pops out and gives Alex a thumbs up.

Alex heads toward the car. "Matt, cover us. Keep Kayla safe."

Matt is shaking and covered in sweat. He may not be a soldier like Alex, but he sure can kick a little ass.

My arms are beginning to tire, so I let myself collapse on the seat.

"We're getting out of here, don't worry," Matt says.

I wonder who he's trying to convince, himself or me?

Alex finally sprints back. "We need to clean something out of it, but it'll do."

I can only imagine what he means. Matt doesn't respond. He's staring up into the sky.

"Matt, did you hear me?"

Matt still doesn't answer. He's seriously starting to creep me out.

"Matt, what is it?" Alex yells.

Matt continues to stare blankly at the sky. Alex finally glances up. "Oh shit," he gasps.

"How many are there?" Matt whispers, his voice trembling.

"What?" I call out. "What do you see now?" I try to look up through the windshield, but my field of vision is totally obstructed.

"Get Kayla out of here now. Take her to the car," Alex commands, still staring intently into the sky.

Matt nods and breaks free from his trance. "C'mon, Kayla, we have to go." Matt reaches for my hand. I did my best to turn around. It takes everything I have left. I grab his hand, and he gently pulls me out of the cab.

"Go!" Alex commands, still gazing up.

"Is that why they haven't come back?" Matt asks Alex, as he takes me in his arms.

"No," he snaps. "But we certainly brought them here."

I look up and see a large mass filling the sky in the distance. It looks like a thin black cloud at first, but as it spreads, I know it's a flock of something.

Oh shit! Matt carries me to the car as I watch the mass get larger and closer. How the hell are we going to escape that?

"Doc, we're coming. Start it up," Matt calls out.

Doc opens the rear door as Matt sprints to the vehicle. He slides me into the back seat, trying to buckle me in. "We're going to make it!" I don't think he realizes he's yelling in my ear.

Doc jumps into the front seat and starts the car. "We'll head to the house."

Wait! What? What house?

Matt slips out and shuts the door. He speeds around to the passenger side of the car.

"What about Alex?" I ask.

Matt pauses at the door. Doc looks back for a moment. I follow and watch Alex jump into the cab of the tanker. He reemerges with the flame thrower.

Oh shit, what's he planning now?

Leaked gas surrounds the cab and trailer. He waves the doc on.

"He's kidding, right?" Matt says.

Doc steps out of the car.

Alex shakes his head and waves us on again.

"Get back to the house!" he roars from the alley. "Don't look back!"

I glance over at Rick, who stares into my eyes. He pauses for a moment, but his expression exposes his next move. "Get in, Matt. We have to go now."

He has got to be fucking kidding! There's no way! *No fucking way!*

"We can't," Matt shouts. "We're out of ammo. We have no way to defend ourselves."

"Everything is at the house. We have no choice, and no more time to waste."

"Go now! there's no time!" Alex screams.

I can see the conflict in Matt's eyes. "We can't leave him!"

Doc gets back in the car. "Matt, it's time to go!"

I look up at the sky. The mass is huge, hundreds of them.

Matt reluctantly gets in and checks his handgun. "I have one magazine left."

"It's not enough. We'll need it later."

"We're not doing this," I finally say.

Doc locks the doors. "He's giving us a fighting chance, Kayla." He won't look at me through the rearview mirror. "It's the only way."

"Fuck that!" I scream. "And fuck you!"

Doc puts the car in drive, finally looking back in the mirror. I see tears in his eyes. "It's the only way!"

Matt lowers his head and says nothing. I look back again, seeing Alex mess with the makeshift flamethrower. The mass is closing in. The field is indiscernible, just one large blaze devouring everything it can. It's only a matter of time before the fire reaches the lot and truck. It's a death race to see which will kill him first, the oncoming wall of flames or the flying menaces from above.

I unbuckle my belt and unlock the door. Before Rick can react, I'm outside the car. I don't know where the strength came from, but it compels me forward. I'm no longer in control of my actions. Doc swings his car door open, but I'm already sprinting down the alley. He calls me, but it has no effect.

Alex sees me coming and yells, "Kayla, get down!"

I stop and drop without hesitation. Not so much because he told me to, but more so because I'm completely exhausted. All the energy I used to escape the car just left me.

Alex slips the straps connected to the thin propane tank over his shoulders. The muzzle of the weapon hangs by his side as he looks up into the sky. He swings his rifle over his shoulder. It hangs next to the small, thin propane tank. He unholsters his pistol again and holds it next to his thigh. I hear him mumbling something but can't make out what. He stands defiantly in the middle of the lot, visible, completely exposed to the oncoming horde. He glances over at the truck and stares.

"Alex, what are you doing?" I scream.

He looks back at me, his eyes black as night again, smooth and shiny, like oversized marbles. He smiles—that menacing smile that sends chills throughout my body. He looks back into the sky. They are coming faster; their screeching filling the air, vibrating off the buildings. There are too many to count. If the sun was still present, they would have blocked it out entirely by their sheer numbers.

He aims his gun at the ground under the tanker. "You want me, come and get me," he growls.

Their screeches get louder, hurting my eardrums. Alex fires several shots at the ground and the sparks ignite the fumes around the tanker. In less than a second, there's a tremendous explosion that sends a huge fireball rocketing into the atmosphere. I roll under one of the derelict cars, away from the heat and scorching debris.

Alex lights the muzzle of the flamethrower. It hisses and then comes alive. The impact of the explosion has no effect on him. He doesn't even flinch. Smoke bellows from the fire, intermingling with the large gray cloud forming over the burning field. The flying menaces begin to scatter in the air, the blast and intense heat evidently overwhelming them.

Some descend and Alex lights them up with the thrower. At the same time, he raises his gun and begins to take them out one at a time with surgical accuracy. Unbelievably, he moves forward as more descend, only to be engulfed in the biting flames of his weapon. A second explosion rocks the alley as any remaining windows shatter, their glass raining down onto the street.

Alex drops his empty handgun, then encircles himself with fire. As the flying creatures try to flee, he swings his rifle around and begins blasting indiscriminately at them. More and more drop to the ground. The fallen are immediately torched by Alex as he continues his assault. Looking back, I can no longer see the tribe member who he'd fought with. Where did he go?

A third explosion destroys any remnant of the big rig as shrapnel and debris are dispersed everywhere. They rain down on the car and I pray it doesn't burst into flames. If it does, there will be no escape. Alex empties the rifle, drops it, and then slides his machete from its sheath. Fire surrounds us, the sky illuminated with bursts of yellow, orange, and bright red. More of the flying menaces try to flee as Alex sprays them with flame. The range of that thing is amazing.

The creatures are trapped in the smoke and slammed down hard onto the ground, like a bird that's driven itself into a clear windowpane with full force. Alex instantly burns them. Others he eviscerates with the machete, chopping large portions free from their bodies as they fly within reach. Thick black blood sprays freely, spraying him and forming large puddles on the ground. Lost in the smoke and flame, the creatures have no escape, becoming prey themselves. I try to cover my mouth as the buildings around us erupt in flames, but it's useless. My lungs fill with smoke and burn incessantly.

"You like the heat?" Alex roars. "Now choke on it, you bastards."

Something grabs my legs. I try to scream but the smoke stifles my voice. I cough violently as I'm dragged from beneath the car. I prepare to fight with what little strength I have left. As I swing, Matt grabs my arm.

"Whoa, nice shot!" He pulls me from the bottom of the vehicle and sweeps me back into his arms. "Had enough yet?"

I've never been happier to see him. "Let's go!"

He rushes me back to the car and throws me into the back seat. He jumps into the passenger side, yelling, "Go!"

Doc steps on the gas, and we speed down the alley. I push up enough to watch Alex continue his insane, relentless genocide. "We can't leave him," I scream.

"We're not going to," Doc yells back as we exit the alley. He turns the car sharply and we swing into a donut. I slide across the leather seat and slam against the other door. Doc revves the engine, and we race back down the alley. "I had to turn around. If you would've stayed in the damn car, we could've done it sooner," he scolds.

He races toward Alex and blows by him, drifting to the left, then spinning back around. I slide against the door to my left.

"Dammit!" I scream.

Doc jumps out of the car. "Alex, get your crazy ass in the car now!"

Alex is oblivious to our existence as he continues to burn everything the flamethrower reaches.

"Matt, go get him," Doc says.

Before he finishes the sentence, Matt is out of the car, rushing toward Alex.

Mistake!

Alex swings around and takes Matt right to the ground. "I'm not finished yet," he growls. Alex returns to his assault, until the tank begins to wheeze.

"It's out of propane," Matt screams, pushing to his knees.

"Just about!" Alex cuts the straps loose from his shoulders. He grasps one of the straps and hurls it up into the air.

It's a fucking amazing throw!

He snatches Matt's sidearm with lightning fast speed and fires at the tank until it explodes midair. The explosion engulfs more of the flying menaces. The blast sheers through the creatures, tearing them into indiscernible pieces. Their blood acts as fuel in the air as it ignites, leaving a trail of flames down to the street below. Alex fires again and takes out a few more. They are trying to flee, but he has no desire for mercy or survivors.

Matt tries to get up but is being pelted by debris from the disemboweled, sliced up creatures.

"Now you know," Alex screams. "Now you know who I am! Now you know what fear is! Now you know what death looks like here!"

I don't recognize his voice, and it scorches my very soul. He turns to the car, and the man before me is no longer the man I know. If he's even a man at all.

He looks like he has war paint on from all the crimson and black blood, like intricate tattoos etched into his face, chest, and arms, his eyes still smooth charcoal, haunting and vacant. He's scarred, bruised, and worn, but still exudes a horrific and intimidating strength. Death himself, with a wretched smile frozen on his face.

The alley is consumed by smoke, impenetrable, and yet he breathes with ease. His blood-soaked machete drips down onto the street as he holds it in his blackened hand. Alex isn't there. He's been replaced. What now exists is the product of all the pain, fear, hate, and anger that we've endured since this hell began. He walks toward us, and my flesh chills.

Matt stands behind him, speechless, the utter horror around us consumed by Alex's now ominous presence. I hear the doc swallow noisily as he stares out at him.

Alex pauses, completely still, almost statuesque. Is he even breathing? Matt slips past him, keeping his distance. Alex finally opens the passenger door. He slides his machete into its leg sheath, blood gathering at the top as it descends into the leather. He gets in, shuts his door, and sits perfectly still.

Matt enters cautiously from the other side and closes the door, hugging his side.

I'm more terrified than when I was paralyzed in the field.

"Drive," Alex growls, still staring dead ahead.

Doc complies without hesitation, and we speed down the alley, feeling a hard bump at every corpse we roll over. The sounds of bones crushing and flesh dragging is almost unbearable. As we escape what's left of the lot, I look back to watch it dissolve in the raging fire. The sky is empty of life though fully occupied by black, impenetrable smoke.

Alex continues to sit still, staring forward into nothing. We race down the streets, dodging any abandoned vehicles left on the road. I see the field from a different angle now. It's still burning. We're no longer lost and frightened prey. No, now we're the foe they never expected. We're the monsters they never imagined.

This is no longer a battle for survival. This is a war for life, the battle lines clearly, unmistakably drawn. They now know the cost of their challenge to our existence, the price to be paid for any attempt at our extinction. It's their turn to be afraid. Their turn to run and hide. Their turn to face their own mortality. This may no longer be our world, but we've just proven we won't let them make it theirs.

Alex turns around and glares at me with those black eyes, his smile gone, his expression blank, but the stare is cold, foreboding. The blood drains from my face as I wait anxiously for him to say something, anything, but he provides no such relief. We're all silent, desperately trying to understand any of this. He turns around, acting like he doesn't even know me.

Is the Alex I know even still there?

We arrive at a house and pull into the driveway. Doc breaks the uncomfortable silence without acknowledging any of us. "Let's get inside quick."

I can't stand to be in that car a second more and quickly exit, immediately falling to my knees. I keep forgetting how little strength I have left. Matt exits on the other side and rushes to my side, helping me up. Alex remains seated in the car, staring forward, as Matt helps me walk me to the front door.

"Are you coming?" I hear the Doc ask Alex.

"In a minute," Alex replies, his voice still unrecognizable.

Doc exits the car, avoiding eye contact with Alex. He assists Matt in helping me. "Let's go," he says softly. None of us say anything more.

I glance back as we approach the doorway, seeing a mushroom cloud of smoke hanging in the air in the distance. The world has fallen eerily silent again, like it has nothing to say either. Alex continues to sit in the car as we enter the house.

At least I hope that's still Alex.

Doc and Matt take me upstairs to a large bedroom. It looks like a freakin' penthouse. Matt sits me on the bed and says, "As soon as you feel up to it, why don't you take a shower." He helps me take off my vest and boots, then assists me in laying across the king-sized bed, covering me with silk sheets and a soft, luxurious comforter. I scan the room, finding dark cherry furniture, detailed and almost certainly expensive. Matt gently strokes my hair as my lids become heavy. I want to thank him, but I'm too exhausted to speak.

"Get some rest. I'll wake you in a few hours," he says.

My eyes surrender to sleep before he finishes his sentence, and I drift into darkness, awash in a fragile sense of peace. I can't argue with it. I simply submit to the silence.

CHAPTER 27

Connections

(Alex)

The water from the shower beats down on my face as the dried blood and dirt begins to dissolve, puddling around my feet. Funny, I don't remember how I got here. There's a brief, dark shadow over my memory, but the water is so refreshing that I find I don't care.

The basin quickly turns brownish red as the horror of the day rinses from my battered and bruised body. Finding a half-used bar of soap, I quickly lather up, trying to scrub the dirt and blood from my skin, and I'm soon standing ankle deep in filth. Closing my eyes, I run my head under the shower again, enjoying its soothing embrace. It feels good not to think. I'm finding it hard to remember which memories are mine and which belong to someone else. Separating them has become a chore, which is taking a terrible emotional toll on me.

I still see Sara and Gracie's faces, but they now share space with Kayla's tormentors, Tara's socialite friends, Jude's absent father. And now I have an alien landscape and their hideous occupants. They are a tormenting collection of broken takeaways forming a disjointed picture of identities and agendas. It's becoming painful to simply think anymore, even harder to keep my mental faculties from getting lost in the psychological fray.

I'm slowly losing who I was. Becoming who? That's the big question.

I slowly check myself for wounds, open gashes and lacerations, but I find none. Only scars, and there are a myriad of them, but not fresh. It's as if they've existed for a very long time, etched deep into my flesh. I'm healing at an exponential rate, and I have no idea as to how. It makes no sense.

After drying off, I slip on my pants, cringing a bit as dried blood and dirt flakes free from the fabric. My torn shirt is useless. I slip on my filthy socks and push my feet back into my boots, fighting to lace them through the caked on muck.

My hands are filthy again. It's as if I never took the fucking shower. After washing them, I walk out of the bathroom and glance down the hall, seeing a series of doors on either side. There are two on the left, three on the right. One of them must be a bedroom where I can find a fucking closet. I walk down the corridor past the dated wallpaper that lines the walls.

The first two don't offer me anything. One is a guest room and one an office. Nothing for me there. The third door leads to another bedroom, barely furnished compared to the others, just a bed and dresser with a mirror. The top is littered with toiletries, deodorant, cologne, and a few ugly ties, spare change, etcetera. In the closet, I find a black polo shirt. It's small but will have to do. At least the fabric is breathable and stretchy. The pants and dress shoes are definitely too small. I can tell just by eyeballing them. My boots will have to do for now. I grab the deodorant off the dresser and give my pits a much-needed refresh.

In the last room, I find Kayla sleeping on her side, her back toward me. The window curtains are drawn, the only light in the room a gentle yellow hue from a nightlight across the room.

This room is decorated to the hilt with what looks like European styled antiquities and furniture. A lot of money had been spent to furnish this home, for what it's worth now. I'm suddenly struck by that old saying—you can't take it with you. Never possessed such meaning or felt so harsh.

I move silently to the bed and take a seat in the hard wooden chair. It's as uncomfortable as it is ornately crafted. Watching Kayla sleep, I can't help but think, why was she chosen to exist this way? What possible sin could she have committed to condemn her to this life she's been forced to endure? My heart aches, like it's never ached before. She's sleeping so soundly, peacefully, probably more than she ever had in her entire life. I struggle to fight back the tears, but it's futile.

Her long blonde hair, now stained with blood and dirt, flows past the covers. She moves ever so slightly, and I quietly scoot my chair up to the edge of the bed. "I'm sorry, Kayla," I whisper. "I'm so very sorry. You deserve so much better from this life. You're such a beautiful young woman, worth so much more, intelligent, funny, and strong—the strongest person I've ever known."

If she only knew how deeply I meant that!

"Life gave you every reason to quit, but you never did. You didn't allow it to weaken you. Every time it knocked you down, you dusted yourself off, standing up even stronger than before. You've stared into the eyes of pure evil and refused to blink or even wince. You were never intimidated by them; instead, it made you even more determined not to let them win. I wish you could catch just a small glimpse into my heart and mind to see the picture I have of you. Then you would truly understand what a gift you are, how special you truly are."

I pause to take a deep breath, glancing over at a large picture hanging on the wall across from me. It's an elaborate painting of a lone lighthouse piercing the darkness in the midst of a violent tempest. It's beautifully crafted, breathtaking, the image unnervingly profound.

That's when I saw Kayla's reflection in the glass, her eyes drenched with tears. She's fighting to keep herself still as she silently sobs. "Please stop," she whispers ever so gently.

"I can't, Kayla. I owe you an apology."

"Please stop," she whispers again.

I place my hand on her shoulder. She's trembling. "I wish I would've had a chance to be your father. I would've been proud to be blessed with you. I would've given you the life you deserved." I said it before I realized I had. But I meant it with every fiber of my being. I feel her body tense.

Kayla abruptly turns over. "Stop," she says, her voice weak but defiant.

"Why? It's about time somebody told you how much you're truly worth. It needs to be said."

"Please," she says weakly. She grabs my hand and holds it tight, as if I'll somehow be stolen away at any moment.

I gently pull her hand toward me and kiss it ever so softly. "You are special, so very special, and I would've been proud to call you my daughter."

Her expression screams confusion, as if my words are completely alien to her. I can see the conflict in her weary eyes. She slowly sits up and stares directly into my eyes, her tears piercing my soul. Time ceases to hold meaning, and it's just the two of us trapped in a painful moment of silence.

She fights back tears and strains to speak. "You risked your life for me," she begins, her voice full of sorrow. "You risked everything for me. Why?"

"Didn't you just hear what I said?" My question is as futile as tears in a rainstorm. She's locked in a train of thought that nothing I say will derail.

"You risked your family for me," she continues between sobs. "Why?"

"Because it's about damn time somebody did." My mouth moves before my brain catches up. "Somebody had to stand in the gap for you!" My care for her defies logic. There's something visceral, a deep conviction. All else is diminished by it. I can see she's dumbfounded by it. "I love you, Kayla."

My words flowed from my lips as easily as my tears. She's captured my heart, my spirit. She isn't like my child; she is my child. Her adoption is undisputed, certified by our struggle, our fight for our very existence. I would have died for her today, without pause. If there's one gift I could have given her, it would've been that. She would not die alone.

She springs forward suddenly and hugs me, wrapping her arms tightly around me. She holds me as if her very life depends upon it, weeping so intensely that her body is convulsing. I feel the desperation begin to fade, and hope, even peace, rush in to take its place. She squeezes me harder, and I know she's never had anyone willing to do anything for her. Those actions were as alien to her as those creatures out there.

"Thank you," she finally whispers.

The weight of her appreciation is almost too heavy to bear. "I love you, Kayla. I'll always be here for you." I meant what I said. I still feel Sara and Gracie, even more strongly now, but there's room for more. I never thought there would be, but there is. I want to give Kayla so much, and now there's no time to do so. No time to repent for all the sins that life had committed against her.

"Please stay with me," she whispers in my ear. "At least until I fall asleep."

"I can do that," I whisper back.

When she pulls away, I see a new light in her eyes, one I suspect had never existed before. She lay in the bed, still tightly holding my hand. I scoot closer so she can lay there comfortably.

When she looks at me, I see Gracie in her eyes, pure innocence and absolute trust. For the first time in her life, she's found safety and a sense of home in all this chaos. She slowly closes her eyes, and I watch the years of pain and loneliness begin to wash away from her face. This is the girl who should have existed all along. Kayla, as she was always meant to be. I'm left in awe of her presence.

When her hand finally goes limp, I place it across her chest and cover her up. I didn't want to leave her side. I realize I have no idea what to do next. I force myself to quietly leave the room, leaving the door slightly ajar.

Doc meets me only feet from the door. How long has he been there? His expression warns me that this is not going to be an easy conversation. "We need to talk, you and me—about what happened out there, about what we all saw." His tone is stern.

"Not here," I say, pulling him into one of the adjoining rooms and closing the door behind us.

"You wanna tell me what the hell happened out there?" he starts, his tone still stern.

"Which part, Doc? There's a lot of turf to cover," I sarcastically snap back.

"I want to know who I'm talking to." The concern is thick in his voice. "Who came back with us?"

"It's me, Doc. I'm standing right in front of you," I respond, trying to stall.

"No, I know Alex Trevor. We've been through our own series of shit together, even before all this," he says. "And whoever was in the car with us in that lot was not Alex Trevor. He was able to do things that no one else could, or should, have been able to."

"I'm a soldier, Doc. You've just have never seen that side of me."

"That was no soldier, Alex. That was something more, so stop toying with me and tell me what's going on."

I paused, not sure how to begin. "Okay, you want the truth?"

"Yes, no matter what it is."

"I don't understand all of it myself. Ever since the incident that started this, whatever it is, I've been different. Something changed."

Doc slowly shakes his head but doesn't interrupt me.

"We've all been affected ... I mean, just look at Kayla and Jude. You can't tell they were ever sick by looking at them now, can you?"

Doc nods in agreement but still doesn't speak.

"She's beautiful, healthy and strong. Jude, too, is full of life—not the sickly boy I first saw, or that you've known for so long. Look at me. I took a beating today. I shouldn't be standing here, but I've never felt stronger, or more determined." I lift my shirt. "Look, not one fresh wound, only scars. Scars that look like they've been there for years. There's no logical explanation for it, but there it is."

Rick sighs. "I agree, Alex, it's beyond comprehension. None of it makes sense. I know I said it before, but I believe whatever happened affected us on a cellular level. I believe it was designed to either prepare us for this new world—this hybrid environment made up of large parts of our world and smaller parts of theirs— or it destroys us, like it did for so many."

"Designed? Designed by whom?"

"That I can't answer, and that frightens me most of all."

"Have you noticed any change in you?"

"Only that I feel stronger, healthier—almost renewed," Doc replies. "I no longer just want to survive; I want to live. That's a drive I haven't had in a very long time."

"Mine has been a bit more than just feeling stronger," I reluctantly interject.

Rick snorts. "That's an understatement."

I pause and take a deep breath. I can tell he's anxiously waiting for me to continue my explanation. "Somehow, I can connect with people in a way that defies reality," I blurt out, not finding any other way to buffer it.

"What do you mean?"

Frustrated, I shake my head. My frustration is not directed at him. I just don't know how to make him understand what I'm about to say. "If I touch someone, skin to skin, I connect with them. And by that, I mean I share their memories. Every damn one of them instantly transfers to me. And not just images, Doc, but all the emotions: pain, joy, tragedies, and triumphs, that are attached to them. It's as real to me as it is to them, and even more fresh."

Doc steps back, disbelief in his face.

"And not just people, but those things too, even the creatures," I continue, undaunted by his confused expression.

"What?"

"It started when we were attacked by those insect looking things, when we spread their blood over us to turn away the flying menaces. I didn't realize what was happening at the time, but as soon as I came in contact with their fluids, my mind was flooded by strange and horrifying images. At first it was just senseless data, chaotic and confusing, too difficult and disjointed to interpret. Just a jumble of vague visions and flashes, jolts of indefinable alien emotions. I thought I was losing my fucking mind. But then it happened again with Jackson, then Kayla, Tara, and Jude."

"All of them," he gasps.

"Yes, and that's when I realized what was happening, or as much as I could understand of it. And it's not just a one-time deal. Once the connection is made, in one way or another, I continue to feel and experience everything they do as it's happening. It's live and in living color, some feelings stronger than others. It just depends on the individual. That's how I knew Tara was a danger to herself and Jude. It's how I know how much more Jude misses his father than we realize, and how much of a burden he feels like for his mom. He's a truly amazing kid who has experienced way too much serious shit in the short time he's been on this earth. He loves you, Doc. You're his hero, and I don't think you understand how deeply he adores you."

Doc pales and takes a step back. He finds a chair and drops into it. I know it's an information overload for him, but I need to continue. If I don't, I'll never get it all out. He's one of the smartest men I know, but no amount of education or experience can prepare him for any of this.

Hell, it's happening to me, and I struggle to believe it.

"Sara always said I had a gift when it came to understanding and knowing people. I always thought it was just an acute gut instinct, but she called it a strong sense of empathy. I just blew it off. But now I realize, maybe it was always there, and what happened just amplified it."

"Maybe we're all connected," Doc interjects. "Maybe we always have been, but we've become so focused on ourselves, engrossed in our own trivial problems and agendas, that we couldn't hear or feel it anymore. I mean, the culture we've created thrives on individualism, supported by technology that allows us to hide in our own little bubbles. It reduces our personal interaction to lines of text, letters, numbers, and symbols to define our emotions and opinions, crudely crafted with little care for consequence, or even grammar or basic spelling, for that matter. We hide behind that tech with no concern about the impact of what we do or say in a blossoming virtual world buffered by our anonymity, like a digital anesthetic numbing our ability to relate."

My eyes widen, taken by surprise. "Go on," I say, seeing he has more to say.

"Maybe the sheer numbers that make up our population creates so much noise that there's no chance of truly hearing or seeing each other, but now, after this horrific event, with so many instantly gone, technology is suddenly stymied. The voices of the few left can be heard clearly now, no longer submerged by the overwhelming volume of competing expressions. You may just be sensitive enough to hear them now, or you may have all along, but there was just too much white noise to realize it."

"I don't know, Doc. How can any of us begin to understand, let alone explain, any of this? But it's because of this, I know without a doubt my family is still alive. I can feel them, and the feeling gets stronger and stronger with every passing moment I'm away from them. I can sense their hopelessness and fear increasing, their desperation mounting. I don't know how much longer they can survive without me, and that terrifies me beyond reason."

"I know," Doc replies solemnly.

I have to keep going. If I dwell too long on my last thought, my heart will collapse under the weight and reality of it.

"It's also how I know everything about those things out there, whatever the hell they are. I used the information to rescue Kayla. It's also how I know they now fear us … in the way they feel fear anyway. When I fought their elder, I saw everything, felt everything he did."

"You connected with him as well?" Doc said, awestruck.

"Yes, and I saw deep into his horrific world. It's filled with death. Every moment they survive is a literal miracle. Everything in it is designed to kill them. Rest, peace, and safety are all very alien concepts to them. Even as bad as their world is, ours has been even more frightening and dangerous to them because they can't understand it."

"Simply amazing," Doc murmurs, shaking his head.

"At first, they thought we had invaded their world, but now they're beginning to understand that we're just as lost as they are. It's fear that drives them, the same fear that drives us. He didn't attack me because he wanted to. He did so because he had no choice. He's struggling to keep his position, maintain his power and place as their leader. They blame him for what happened. As inconceivable as that may seem, they definitely believe it. There are several males vying to take control of the tribe.

"They are a nomadic people, wandering from place to place. With what they faced on a daily basis, it was suicide to stay in one place for too long. But instead of finding solace here, an escape from the horrors they face every day, those horrors followed them here—the same things that now hunt us. Killing and fighting are all they know. Protect their females, protect their children. The tribes war over territory daily. They massacre each other, a vicious, nonsensical cycle. Competing tribes offer no mercy or compassion for the survivors. They are left to fend for themselves in the wilderness, a certain death. It's better to die quickly in battle. It's a harsh life, a sad, tortured life, where birth seems like an absolute curse and the only escape is the death that waits for them at the edge of every breath."

"What are they going to do here?" Doc asks, shaking his head.

"I don't know. Their world has no day or night, no moon or sun, just this constant, depressing blue hue that now encompasses everything here too. They don't understand what the sun feels like on their faces, or the brisk and sudden chill of a winter night. They don't sleep because they can't. It would leave them vulnerable. They've never had a quiet rain refresh their flesh. The water in their world is far different from ours. It's more of a viscous gel than a free-flowing liquid. Its composition is similar in small ways but bizarrely different in others. Our water is toxic to them. There's something in it, maybe a lot of things, that acts like poison to them. They've already killed many of us, considering us a threat. They are monsters to us because that's how we appear to them. That chief fought me to maintain what little control he had over his tribe, not so very different from what we're trying to do. I took that away from him, so who knows what his future holds. That's why I let him live, despite everything. In that moment, I saw a father just trying to survive. I couldn't bring myself to take his life. Nothing makes sense anymore."

I take a deep breath and wait for the doc's response. He just stands there, his expression empty. Did I really expect anything more?

"So, what happened to you out there when all hell broke loose? You still haven't answered that," Doc finally asks.

I struggle to answer him. "I told you, we're all changing." I search for the words to explain the darkness I'd felt.

"Just say it, Alex."

"What you saw out there was me, but it wasn't me. I know that makes absolutely no sense."

"Your damn right," Doc scolds.

"Okay, it was me, but there was a part that's very alien. A dark part I never knew was there before."

"Can't you resist it?"

"I didn't want to. I let it out, freed it from its cage, because I wanted to, and it felt amazing. I was filled with unbridled rage and strength all at once. In that moment, I wanted to destroy those things, eviscerate them. And because of it, I could. It was raw power, pure freedom, and I was utterly intoxicated by it."

I saw the fear and confusion in his eyes, but I didn't know how to make this easier for him. "I felt my world and theirs collide within me, creating a deep transformation, even though I couldn't understand the semantics of it, but I didn't care."

"Is it still there, inside you?"

"Yes, but it seems to only come out when I'm desperate and all seems lost."

"Has it happened before?"

"Yes, but not that quickly, nor to that scale. Up till then, it was a slow, gradual process."

"When did it start?"

"From the very beginning. I just didn't understand what was happening at first, like the connections I felt. I couldn't identify it. It all came to a head in that lot, when I truly believed we were all going to die. But that wasn't the only trigger. I kept seeing Sara and Gracie, their faces fading into an abyss. I could feel them slipping away. In that moment, all the rage, fear, and frustration peaked, and whatever was happening within me was released in a single rush of power and purpose. I wanted it to take control so it could eliminate the threats. No excuses, no hesitations. I owned it, chose it, and I made it without reservation."

I feel my voice begin to tremble. "But now it's taking me, Doc. With each passing moment, it's taking another piece."

Doc stands and slowly approaches. He places a comforting hand on my shoulder.

"What's worse, there are times I want it to—I almost beg for it to, just so I can find the strength to make it through all of this. I feel if I don't give in, I won't have the power to save my family, or to save all of you. Without it, *we* won't survive."

I begin to sob, my resolve crumbling. Doc lifts my head and glares deep into me. "No, Alex, we're surviving because of you, because of who you are, and always have been. That's the truth. Whatever this is, it's not you. You may think you are finding strength from it, but I adamantly disagree. The strength you have, that you've shown from the first moments I met you, that's the strength that's pulling us through this, nothing more, nothing less. This thing can only change us if we let it. We're stronger than it. We've proven that time and time again."

"You really believe all that, Rick?"

"With everything that I am! You and I, we've been through too much not to."

"Then I have to tell you something that may finally shake that faith in me." I fight hard to regain my composure. This confession is going to take everything I have left. What little there is. I pull away from him and take a few steps to put distance between us.

"I killed Jackson."

Doc steps back from me, shock clearly defined in his expression.

"I threw the spear. My gun jammed, and he was about to shoot Kayla. It was the only thing I could do to stop him. I swear it. He was insane, Rick. I had no choice."

Doc backs up, sits down again, and then shakes his head. "Oh my God, Alex."

I can see how deeply he's been affected by my confession. The hero has fallen, the façade revealed. I'm not the ideal he perceived me to be. I'm reduced to an imperfect man, subject to the same weakness as anyone else, a flawed soul struggling to find meaning and purpose in this crazy world.

"He would have killed her, Rick. Trust me, I knew it all too well. I saw into the stark darkness of his soul."

Doc slowly stands. "I don't know how I'm supposed to respond to any of this?" He searches my eyes for the slightest hint of resolution.

"I don't know," I reply. I don't know what else to say. "Maybe I shouldn't have told you any of this. How could I expect you to understand it when even I don't?"

"I'm not sorry you did," Doc quickly retorts. "I asked for the truth, and you gave it to me. Thank you."

"Are you sure, Rick?" I'm a bit shocked by his answer and the calmness in his face after everything I'd revealed to him.

"Yes." Rick walks somberly by me and pats me on the shoulder. At the doorway, he stops and looks back. "You've always been the one who to face things that we couldn't begin to cope with. You're the reason why we're alive. You helped us, and you didn't have to. You risked everything for us. I can tell you honestly, if the tables had been turned, I don't think I could have. We owe you our lives, Alex, and I thank God you were in my office today."

I try to respond, but Doc stops me. "I said it before, and I'll say it again. I want to *live*, Alex, not just survive. We're in a whole new world, with new laws that we don't quite understand, that we may never understand. But we must still find a way to move forward. This'll be all but impossible without you."

I shake my head, surprised by his reaction.

"We'll help you find your family, Alex. It won't take much to get the others on board. It's the least we can do for you. I know you think it'll be easier to go it alone, but I think we can help you. We can help each other. We are connected, Alex. We always have been. Everything we've been through today has proven that. We need each other."

I'm left dumbfounded, speechless.

"We'll use the traffic cameras Jude discovered to set a path, just like you planned before. Maybe we can find a clear enough route that we can use a vehicle to get there. Maybe it'll keep us safer, maybe not. Although I firmly believe that those creatures out there now know we aren't going anywhere anytime soon, not without one hell of a fight."

Doc turns away and walks out of the room.

"Doc," I call out, sprinting toward the door.

He turns. "I'm going to check on Kayla." He smiles through the tears. "You need to get your plan together so we can get on the move as soon as she's healed and rested. Based on how we've all been affected, that shouldn't take too long. Believe it or not, Tara is cooking something for us to eat in the kitchen." He laughs. "I don't know how good of a cook she is, but you need to take a moment to eat and rest. If it's horrible, grin and bear it." He chuckles, struggling to make light of our situation.

CHAPTER 28

Consequences and Truth

(Alex)

As the doc heads for Kayla's room, I take the stairs down and turn toward the kitchen. I hear two people talking. In the living room, I see Jude asleep on the couch. All the blinds and curtains are shut, lights off. I approach the kitchen but stand outside the folding doors. Matt and Tara are speaking, their voices low, but I can hear them. I step closer, aware their conversation is meant to be private.

I peer in and see Tara quietly weeping at the table. Matt is sitting next to her, consoling her. I don't alert them to my presence. I'm not sure why.

"What's going on?" Matt asks. When she just sits there, weeping bitterly, he places his hand on her shoulder and carefully massages it. "Tara, talk to me. Let me help you."

She shakes her head and continues to cry. I see a few pots on the range, one with steam coming from it, but the burners appear to be off.

Matt places his arm around her, carefully pulling her closer to him. She lifts her head and nuzzles it deep into his chest, as if trying to hide within it. He holds her tighter, then removes his vest. His rifle is on the counter behind them. She sobs uncontrollably as Matt rocks her ever so slightly.

"Tara, it's going to be okay. It's all going to be okay."

"No, no, it isn't," Tara mumbles through his tear-stained shirt. "None of it is, or ever will be, okay. I'm paying for it all, paying for every sin, every bad choice I've ever made." She pulls away from Matt and rubs her fingers across her face, then through her hair. "I thought she was dead, gone forever, but he saved her. He risked everything for her. He did more for her than I ever could!"

"Who? Kayla? Are you talking about Kayla?"

Tara sits up and wipes her face with her sleeve. "Yes! But you don't understand. I should have, long ago. I had the means, but I never did." She jumps up, walking back to the stove, frantically moving pots around.

Matt follows her and gently grabs her shoulders. "Tara, stop," he says gently. "Just stop."

"I can't face this now," she sobs again. Tara pulls away again and moves to the end of the counter, leaning against it. "Don't you understand? I destroyed her life. It's all my fault."

Matt approaches her, but she pulls away again and heads back to the table. "How could it be your fault? I know you two didn't get along, but—"

"I was so young, so stupid, so completely messed up. I had no choice." When Matt approaches again, she holds up her hand and says, "No, stay away. I would've had an abortion, but I wanted to keep her." Tara chuckles uncontrollably. "Imagine that. I wanted to keep her. I thought being pregnant with her would change things, finally bring about something good in my sad and stupid life. But I was wrong. Big surprise, right? When have I ever done anything right, especially then. They lied to her about everything, and they were paid well to do it, more money than most people make in a year."

Matt looks completely befuddled.

He's not alone.

Tara continues her bizarre tirade. "I was a crackhead from the age of twelve, whoring my way through my teens. It was the only way to feed my habit. My mom died when I was only a child. She was a mega-whore. I knew that even then. I'm amazed to this day I wasn't born with AIDs, or worse, as much as she fucked around. Her drug of choice was heroin. I remember playing in that shit hole of an apartment of ours while she lay motionless on the bed, the needle still sticking out of her emaciated arm.

"A child shouldn't see that or be forced to remember it. I didn't have warm and fuzzies about school plays, Christmas mornings, and all that shit. My mental scrapbook contains images of my bitch of a mother strung out, naked, lying on her bed surrounded by her own filth. Do you know how long it took me to realize that a girl smelling like urine wasn't the norm, and that a house shouldn't reek of shit and vomit every day?"

She's shaking, barely able to stand on her own, but there's no stopping her. It all floods out with nothing to dam it.

"That was my life. I woke up to and went to bed to that every fucking day and night. So, what do I do? Do I break that vile cycle? Fuck no, I amp it up a couple of notches! I hated my mother, and the life of squalor and horror she forced us to exist in. I was there the day she choked on her own puke and died, but I didn't see it. Her lying sprawled out on the bathroom floor, laying in the shit that covered the tile. I didn't know at the time, no one did, until the stink got so bad one of my crackhead neighbors couldn't stand it anymore and came over. They found me playing with my ratty toys, half starved, and waiting for mommy to come out of the bathroom. When the police finally got there and found her, the way she was, they got sick, too. I never saw the body, but I'm sure it was a little slice of hell to see."

She begins to pace, her shaking getting worse. She dodges Matt every time he tries to approach her, her eyes vacant. She's lost in a memory, spewing every detail of her past. "They took me away and I lived either in foster care or on the street until I was nineteen. I lived for crack. It let me forget all the shit in my life, the only thing that kept me going, or gave my fucking existence any worth. I fucked so many guys, I lost count, sucked so many filthy, stinkin' cocks. I made my mom look like a nun."

She slams her hand on the counter. "And still, I never caught anything, not one STD. Ironic, isn't it? Fucking ironic. Then I got pregnant with her. Who the hell knew who the father was? And somewhere in my crack-addled brain, I figured I could keep her, raise her, change the past and break the cycle. Oh, I finally did get clean. I was clean the whole time I carried her."

She drops down in a chair, still trembling. "Then I found a clinic, a nice church family who took me in, even got a fucking job folding sweaters with the other mall rats. I was as determined as I was weak and foolish. She was born on a rainy night. They wouldn't let me have any drugs because of my past. They couldn't risk it. They were amazed I'd carried as long as I had, and they were also sure the baby would come out deformed or challenged. They were so fucking wrong, the patronizing bastards. It was the most agonizing experience of my life. When it was over, I held this little underweight soul in my hands—this helpless baby—and at that moment, I finally had true clarity. One of the few times in my life, I can count them on my fingers."

She couldn't be talking about Kayla, could she? I would have seen that. How could she keep that hidden from me?

"I had to give her up. It was the only way. It was one of the few selfless acts of my life. They took her right out of my arms, and I was left with nothing, again. I was clean but had no skills or talent, other than the one. I hit the streets right away, didn't even give myself time to heal, and started whoring. This time not to score the next high but just to survive. In a few weeks, I hooked up with a group of girls who were making it without a pimp. I started pulling in good money. We got a place together and were doing alright, for being pussies for hire anyway. One day, I met this lady through one of my friends, very refined and proper. She ran this upscale escort service, but rich guys don't like that terminology; it cheapens it. She saw potential in me and gave me a shot, despite my drug-riddled past. At first, I was passed around, didn't have any steadies, but the money was crazy, and I got to live in a fucking mansion. It was her own place. She'd inherited it after her third husband in a row died of mysterious causes. Her pussy must have been made of gold, because she could fuck her way out of anything. She had judges, cops, city officials, Washington big-wigs, and celebs all in her pocket.

"Then I met him. After just one date, he insisted that I be his regular. Like I said, I was very good at one thing. After a month, he paid her to ensure I was his and his alone. By that time, I had about fifteen to twenty regulars, so it was a large payoff. It only took a year for him to propose. This was by no means love in any way, shape, or form. This was a business arrangement. He needed a trophy wife and a place to park his dick, and I needed to be rich. Money had become my new drug, and I couldn't get enough of it. I learned that it really did make the world go around, and I had become so cynical and self-absorbed, I wanted to be one of the few that turned the gears.

"Then there was a second big payoff, this time to ensure that the madam forget about me, erased me from every fucking memory. I later found out that cash came with a threat. He would destroy her if she even thought about blackmailing him. At the time I didn't realize how much power he had, and how easily he could have done it. He could have destroyed the lives of thousands of perverts who held positions of high esteem in a matter of minutes."

She gets up again and paces the room, barely taking a breath before she continues. "He was always cunning that way, never without a backup plan or an advantage. He always had the upper hand, a true master of deceit, manipulation, and subtle cruelty. He was and still is today the perfect puppet master, controlling all the strings. I wish I had known that when he asked me to marry him. I know I paid for it after. The wedding was epic, the kind reserved for royalty. We bought a mansion, hell, a fucking plantation, smack-dab in the middle of the most affluent gated neighborhoods in the city. It was the capital of the Stepford community, white excess, ridiculous wealth, and plastic women as far as they eye could see. Our very own suburban kingdom, and we were the reigning king and queen. I became the center of this self-absorbed universe and quickly gained the role as leader of the desperate housewives. I built committees, formed charities, hosted the most obscenely elaborate parties, and became high priestess in their worship of materialism. I loved every minute of it, better than any rush drugs could provide."

She stops in front of the sink, her hands shaking. Matt keeps his distance this time. "Then, just when I thought I'd reached the high point of perfection and happiness, it all came crashing down. I'd survived all my years of addiction and whoring, escaped every conceivable venereal disease, only to be diagnosed with breast cancer. They found a lump during a routine checkup. As soon as the biopsy came back malignant, he wouldn't touch me anymore. Now I was damaged goods, right? Even though I was far more damaged when he found me. I could no longer live up to his expectations as a trophy wife, especially once the treatments started and took their toll. All the beauty he had paid so much for was in jeopardy.

"I mean, I knew he was sleeping around before, but I didn't care. I had it all—his wandering cock was a small price to pay so I could sit upon my throne. A man like that is never satisfied; he can never be forced to truly settle. He was always very discreet. He knew how to keep secrets. His whole life was made up of them. He may have made his rounds, but I was the one who shared his immaculate king-sized bed at night. I was the one draped with jewels and designer clothes, paraded out and hanging off his arm at all the high society functions. Whores know whores—they could do their best, but it would never be good enough compared to me. They were just mere snacks, appetizers, cheap finger foods, but I was the filet mignon, the fresh Maine lobster, the undisputed main course. But all of that was about to change.

"He couldn't just dump me. That would've made him look like a heartless monster—which he was, but he concealed it well. He had too many connections, was considered one of the world's great philanthropists, as rich in compassion as he was in cash. It was a masterfully crafted disguise, and no one questioned it. He was always the champion of the game, the absolute chess master, because he made all the rules. I found out the cost of that the hard way. In the end, he was even able to use my cancer for his benefit."

Tara pauses, grabbing for a chair and slowly sits again with the thousand-mile stare. Matt moves closer, but he doesn't attempt to touch her. He sits in the chair across from her, and she looks right through him.

She takes a deep breath, cracking some kind of weird, almost warped smile before she continues. "When I received the news, I was originally floored by it, but then I found this new sense of determination. Life had beaten me down since the day I was born, but I was not going to lose this time, even though the odds were stacked against me. So I fought it, but unlike others facing the same battle, I had the best resources money could buy to assist me. The best doctors, state-of-the-art treatments, and comfort that not many could ever afford. I beat the odds, won against my disease and went into remission."

Her smile widens, but the void of her stare remains the same. "I became so much more than just the queen of my realm, but a hero for a whole new community that stretched well beyond our ivy-covered walls. I was automatically thrust into the spotlight, becoming a shining example of perseverance, strength, and triumph. For the first time in my life, I was looked up to, not just because of who I married, but because of what I had done, on my own, or so I'd convinced myself. But even at the dawn of my newfound celebrity, something was still missing. I had no one to really share it with.

"My android friends had no real soul. Their friendship was based solely on what I owned and accomplished. My dear husband was as distant as the two poles are from one another. I wanted someone to share all of this with, someone who would love me, not for what I could give them, or what I represented, but just love me. My maternal instinct kicked in full speed. I thought about that little girl I had abandoned years ago and how wonderful it would be to share this all with her. To raise her in this place, with all this advantage, none of which I had growing up. Maybe now I could find her and finally give her the life she deserved, that we both deserved."

Her smile fades, but the gaze does not. "It was a mistake to even mention her to him. He blew up before I could get the first sentence out. He had worked so hard, paid so much, to erase my past, that he wasn't about to allow me to jeopardize that. He told me that he'd already looked her up, and she was doing fine, adopted by good parents a long time ago. That I would just interfere in her life, shake up her loving family for my own selfish gain. Foolishly, I believed him, more so because I wanted to. Later, I found out she never knew about me, that she believed the first foster home that took her in was her real parents, and that bitch abused her and later died of an overdose. She wasn't adopted, but tossed around just like I'd been, discarded just like me. She did things, godawful things, just like me. Worst of all, she almost died at the hands of some monster!

"I hadn't saved her from that legacy. All I did was ensure it would own her. She paid for every mistake I'd made, just like I'd paid for my mother's. I found out a lot about how he lied to me, not just about her, but about everything. In all honesty, it was my fault; I let him do it, believed the lies, because it facilitated the life I so desperately wanted. I was anesthetized by my greed. I gave up my search for her, abandoning her again to pursue having another child with him. He resisted at first, but I can be very convincing, a trick of my former trade. I sold him on the idea of an heir that he could mentor and develop in his own image. I could see the wheels spinning furiously in his eyes as I made my fervent paternal pitch. I could see the word 'son' literally light up like neon in his pupils. He finally gave in, and we began our journey."

She stands again and faces Matt. He still doesn't speak, only listens intently.

"But like everything else in my life, there had to be some insurmountable obstacle to overcome. The doctors told me pregnancy was impossible. Despite my remission, it was too large of a health risk. I went to ten different doctors, and they all said the same. No matter how much money I waved at them, or assurances made that they would not be legally responsible if anything went wrong. I didn't let him know. If I had, it would be over, so I tried that much harder.

"Sex became nothing more than a task, no enjoyment, but driven by my ever-maddening desire. Finally, after months and months, nearly a year, I got pregnant. Then I found an OBGYN who had a price tag, although it was considerable. It was a tough pregnancy, but I was determined to have this baby."

She heads back to the counter and begins to softly sob again.

"Still, I couldn't get her out of mind. So I hired a high-priced private detective to find her. Without my husband knowing, of course. After all, I'd learned how to keep secrets from the best. He thought I was preoccupied with designing the million-dollar nursery and planning the numerous exuberant baby showers. It took the P.I. over eight years to find the truth. Despite all my darling husband's efforts, connections, and finances, he couldn't bury it as deep as he'd wanted to. She ended up in an overcrowded, undermanaged foster system that placed her in the worst possible places imaginable. She was tossed home to home, became an addict, and whored herself out for money and drugs. It was like some horrific déjà vu. I truly had cursed her to the exact life I'd been trapped in. Not like, or similar, but exact, as if it was engrained deep within our DNA.

"The only highlight for her was a brief stint where she was on an archery team in high school. She went far and even won some awards, but then it stopped abruptly. Two years later she was held hostage by some beast—raped and tormented until she escaped. Then the final bit of bad news; she had developed Lupus, and later ovarian cancer. The Lupus had been there since she was a pre-teen, which is rare. They just kept misdiagnosing it, then did the bare minimum to treat it. The ovarian cysts were discovered just a couple of years ago. She'll never have children of her own. Maybe that was the only way to stop this vicious cycle."

She stops again, staring blankly at Matt, and then dramatically changes the subject.

"Jude was born underweight and very sickly, but he was the most beautiful thing I'd ever seen. When I held him in my arms, I was filled with overwhelming joy and guilt both at the same time. I would do anything, sacrifice anything, to love and protect him. Love that I'd been robbed of from the beginning. Jude was the first person I ever truly loved. I can't say as much for her. I worked hard to keep the shame bottled up, but the pressure and guilt became too strong to contain. I wanted her back in my life.

"So, I came up with an insane plan. We could foster her without her ever knowing who I was. I knew deep inside it was fruitless, but I had to try. I couldn't be apart from her any longer. I had made her endure too much for too long already. This was my only chance at penance, my only hope to restore to her some sense of being normal, having a real future. When I received the information about her, it overwhelmed me, and I erupted, spilling everything to him. But by then it was evident to us both that the marriage was ending. I was no longer the trophy he was proud to place upon his mantle, the years becoming more and more apparent.

"He had already found another, much younger, shinier trophy. But he couldn't just leave me. After all we'd been through, all that I represented, the hero mom who'd survived breast cancer. For the first time in his life, he was trapped. He had no escape plan. There was no number of connections and finances to erase me without an undeniably fatal consequence to the one thing he treasured the most, his monumental reputation. If they knew who he really was, the monster he was, he would have been an absolute outcast, a pariah. He couldn't let that happen.

"He saw me as weak without him, but then, realizing he no longer wanted me, he found himself locked in a prison he had constructed by his own sexist, elitist creation. There was no escape that wouldn't be messy. He saw Jude as weak too. His dreams of a prodigy taking the reins of his empire seemed instantly smashed when he saw his fragile form for the first time. This was not the strong, strapping infant that his sperm should have produced. His seed should have spawned a mighty oak, not a withering willow.

"As Jude grew, so did his disdain for both of us. He was constantly looking for a way out, but he couldn't find one, and I wasn't going anywhere." Tara returns to her chair. She places her hands on the table, forcing back more tears. "It was when I told him about her and what I had done that the beatings began. He said it was the ultimate betrayal. All it did was give him the ultimate excuse. It started with a slap, like most of these things do, then an apology and acceptance. Then it escalates. You make excuses for the visible signs—'I walked into a door,' 'the disease makes me bruise easily,' or that timeless classic, 'I fell down.' All the lame excuses our so-called friends and family accept to remain blissfully ignorant of the blatant truth. I mean, who wants to deal with all that drama, right? Who wants to get involved in all of that? No one wants to take sides, let alone have their good names attached to that type of lifestyle. It's not their life, so why get caught up in it? Somebody else will intervene, somebody more qualified. Doesn't that about cover the barrage of excuses people make? Especially in the fantasyland that I lived in. Matt, in your line of work, you've probably seen it from every angle."

Matt looks down, not replying.

"Jude saw the worst of it. I don't know if he remembers it. I hope to God he doesn't. The worst one nearly put me in the hospital. It took me two weeks to heal up enough where I could leave the house. It was after that he gave me the ultimatum. I leave, and he would ensure Jude and I would be well taken care of. A no mess, no fuss, mutual divorce. No courts, just papers, and a final grand payoff to ensure I'd never haunt his existence again.

"It would make it possible for both of us to keep our reputations intact. I would say I fell out of love with him and needed to find myself, and although he was heartbroken, he loved me enough to let me go. It was so well scripted, who wouldn't believe it? The settlement was large enough to allow Jude and me to live comfortably for a long time, even get Jude through private school and an Ivy League College. He even bought us a townhouse in another county. I don't think he thought Jude would make it; figured he would end up a real loser, just like his mother. In his eyes, he was simply the spawn of trash. He visited him at first, but with each passing year, he missed more and more.

"Of course there were the threats. If I even thought about making his life difficult, he made it abundantly clear what would happen. My past, which was supposedly erased, would come back like a tsunami. Everything I had ever done, every gory detail, would be splayed out for all to see. He would deny knowing any of it, and with his pull and power, no one would question him. He would play the victim, and with his reputation so deeply entrenched in everyone's mind, with all the good he had done, all the money he had spent, no one would doubt it. The evidence of who I was could not be denied. It would speak for itself. There would be no hiding from it. But for him, he had all the cover he needed. I was so dependent on him, naïve to what the cost of my submission would be, that I had no defense against his actions.

"After we split, there were some who blamed him, tried to paint him as the bad guy, but he expected it as part of the process. He was quickly able to spin it back to his favor, and without me speaking out, it was an easy task. I just quietly slipped away, moved into my new home with Jude and a massive bank account in tow. I had sold myself so many times before, how was this any different, except for the size of the payoff.

"We moved and were soon forgotten. I couldn't believe how fast. All my accomplishments—my victories—became the stuff of suburban legend and myth. He was dating six months later, and no one even winced. There were no more calls. All my foundations were transferred to his newly ascended replacements, and even the scholarships were renamed. Oh, how quickly the mighty have fallen when they are standing in quicksand. I faded from that existence as quickly as I was thrust into it.

"The only bright side of it was that I was now able to pursue her. But I was terrified I would look at her, and instead of seeing her through eyes of love, I would just be reminded of all my failures as a mother and a woman. She would quickly become a glaring example of all my shame, all the disgusting, reprehensible things I had done. A ghost of my past haunting me at every turn. That's exactly what happened when I saw her in the lobby; the very thing I feared instantly came true."

Wait! What?

She skips over that last statement and continues, unrelenting in her confession. "Despite all of that, I still needed to rescue her, but I didn't know how. I might not have been ready for her to come home, not until I got past my own issues, but there had to be a way to get her out of the system. So I concocted yet another brilliant idea. It took nearly everything from my bank account, but I was finally able to direct her to what I thought was a decent home.

"By this time, Jude's health had started failing. He struggled with poor health most of his life because of my push to get pregnant, even though my body wasn't ready, but this was something different. I'd ignored all the good advice and now he was paying for it. Yet someone else I cared about was also in pain. Instead of a life of vileness and tragedy, Jude was cursed with my disease, diagnosed with leukemia at eight, with very little hope for him. But unlike me, he was a fighter from birth. He refused to allow his illness to own him.

"He hated the hospitals and other specialists; they were so cold and pessimistic. They treated him like an object with an expiration date rather than a human being. I found Rick almost by accident. One of the only true friends I had recommended him to me. Him and Jude hit it off almost immediately. Overnight, Rick became everything his father wasn't. I could see there was more than just a doctor-patient relationship there, although I never knew the real story of his own family. I just naturally thought he was divorced, like me; I only found out the whole truth a few weeks ago. I fell in love with him, only a few months into it, though I never told him. He was everything I had hoped a man could be. I'd never met anyone like him, admired the hell out of him, and I think that's where it started. I couldn't wait to see him, even scheduled additional, unnecessary appointments for Jude just so I could be with him. I think he picked up on it a little, but never said anything. I couldn't take the chance to take it any further. Why would he want me anyway. If he knew the truth, he would have run off screaming, and who could blame him."

She pauses and there's a deafening moment of silence as Matt is obviously trying to figure out what to say, but before he can, she continues.

"You know, even my name is a lie. When my future husband found me, he changed my entire identity, even financed a new social and birth certificate. I became Tara Davis before I married him. I don't know where he came up with that. My name was Diamond Gold before that, a stripper name. Yes, I did that for a short while, too. I went by the street name Suzie before that. But I was born Famous Banning. My mom named me Famous— Famous Star Banning. She was a starlet for a short time in her youth, did some B-movies, then porn. That's where drug use apparently skyrocketed.

"I have no real identity, Matt. It's always been defined by someone else or hidden because of my past. I've become a shadow, shifting and shaping at a whim, with no stability or purpose other than to darken a path."

She quickly shifts gears back to another confession. "As much as I wanted to tell Rick how I felt about him, I couldn't bring myself to do it. Why would I believe for a moment that it would work out? I am so sick of sex, so tired of it. I can't find any pleasure from it anymore. What could I offer him, other than a worn-out soul who can't satisfy him without faking every second. Many men wouldn't care—as long as they got off, who gave a fuck? But he would, I know he would.

"I'm done, but for Jude, he had a chance. A chance to know a man who could truly be like a father to him. He loves him so much. And Rick has done so much for him. He's learned more from Rick than he ever could in school. Rick even taught him algebra, geometry, and calculus. Calculus, can you believe that shit? At age ten, he knew calculus. Jude is so very smart, and wise beyond his years. He's had to be, to crunch so much of life in so little time. Rick even took him fishing. I mean, before he got worse."

Tears form quickly this time. She slides closer to Matt and grabs his hand. "Rick said it was just a matter of time. None of the treatments were working. The cancer was just too aggressive, resistant to the chemo. But he'd never seen a child as resilient as Jude. He turned eleven a few weeks ago. He has no idea that Rick told me there was very little chance he would make it to twelve. The world would never know what a gift he truly was. My sin, all the shit I've done, corrupts everything I encounter, like a reverse Midas touch. I fucked up everything so bad here. I don't want to begin to imagine what waits for me when I close my eyes for the last time.

"I was trying to figure it all out when all this shit broke loose. And now that little boy in there looks healthier than he ever has, stronger than he's ever been. But, as usual, instead of a chance to experience some kind of relief, a moment of peace, we're stuck in the middle of this nightmare."

She takes a deep breath. "She's just as healthy. It was two years ago when I finally made the arrangements to have her transferred out of yet another hellhole. It cost me almost everything I had, but one of my rich friends owed me a big favor and was looking to get involved in fostering children. Her way of gaining the respect of her peers who had their own charity cases to prove how selfless they were. After a lot of coaxing, and most of what was left of my settlement, she agreed. She took her in and kept me posted.

"It worked for a while, but her rage, hate, and pain became too much for my shallow friend to bear. She'd wanted a cause, something she could parade before her peers to demonstrate her never-ending compassion. She never expected it might be actual work, that it would *get real*.

"Then she managed to piss off every doctor. None wanted to see her, and my friend grew tired of trying. I asked Rick if he would take over, told him that she was the daughter of a friend. I let him know right off the bat that she was a difficult case but well worth the effort. I paid him in advance, and he thought the money was coming from the foster family. My friend agreed, but only if she could drop her off and then pick her up after her shopping, or whatever inane activity she had going. I arranged it so we would never be there at the same time, no chance of contact. But today, the schedules somehow got crossed. Kayla was becoming increasingly ill, so she had to meet with Rick to see if there was any hope.”

Kayla! It is her! How can this be? Why didn't I know?

“Rick couldn't tell me how she was, patient confidentiality and all, and I certainly couldn't tell him she was mine, and my friend had stopped updating me. When I saw her there, she was so sick and pale, I was devastated. I couldn't stand it. Then all the shame and humiliation rushed at me at once and I could barely breathe.”

Matt sits there frozen, as if desperately trying to get a handle on her revelation. Tara doesn't miss a beat though—she continues her relentless confession, tightly gripping his hands and pulling them close to her.

“She glared at me with such hate in her eyes, as if she knew exactly who I was and what I'd done. But she hated me not because she knew who I was, but because of what I represented: rich, entitled, and self-absorbed. Just like her foster mom. God, if she had only known who I truly was, her hate would've been unbridled. I knew then she could never learn about me, that there would never be a happy reunion or a chance for penance. She could never forgive me, and I didn't blame her. I could never be her mother. I felt as though I'd died inside. That's why I've been so angry, so confrontational toward her. My maternal instinct is begging to free itself while my shame is holding it hostage. It's why I've clung so obsessively to my son, knowing he's all I have left, and though he was spared from the disease, he could be taken away from me at any moment by those monsters out there.

“I'm sorry. I'm so fucking sorry I failed her.” Tara breaks down again, slumping out of her chair to her knees. Her head falls to the floor, and she weeps so hard that her whole body convulses.

Matt immediately rushes to her side, holding her.

I stand there in utter disbelief, at a total loss trying to decipher everything I'd just heard. She was good at secrets, even at keeping them from herself. She buried it all so deep just to survive day to day that even our connection couldn't shake it free. She's so lost, so utterly empty, a soul void of hope created by her own warped sense of repentance, a carefully designed personal hell.

"You have to tell her," Matt says quietly.

She vigorously shakes her head.

"She deserves at least that," he gently pushes.

"She deserves to be free of me," Tara sobs. "You can't tell her. She's already been through so much. Nothing good can come out of it. She's better off thinking her mom died than learn the truth. It'll crush her soul. Please, she doesn't deserve any more pain from me. It's enough already, enough."

"But, Tara—" Matt begins, but she is quick to interrupt.

"Promise me, Matt, promise me you won't hurt her like that!" She looks up at him, tears gushing from her bloodshot eyes. "Promise me!"

"I won't say anything," Matt reluctantly agrees, but the conflict is still deeply evident in his expression.

She slowly stands, wiping her face with both of her sleeves. Matt remains on the floor, as she heads to the stove, leaning against it, sobbing again, trying to catch her breath. Matt gets up and turns to her. He gently spins her around and hugs her tightly. She holds onto him and continues to sob into his chest.

I step back, peering into the living room. Jude is dead to the world on the couch, barely moving. Poor kid! What a life to be born into.

My thoughts go to Gracie. I would do anything for that little girl, to keep her safe, provide for her. I can't imagine hurting her or even consider deceiving or manipulating her. My anger at Tara rises quickly. What kind of person puts their children through that kind of hell? I feel little compassion for her. She made her choices. But then she had to drag two unwilling souls into it.

Matt emerges from the kitchen, running his fingers back and forth through his hair. He moves forward, unaware of my presence as he trudges down the adjoining hallway. I silently pursue. I can hear Tara making herself busy in the kitchen. Matt's rifle is hanging from his shoulder. He looks tired, worn down, both emotionally and physically.

I follow as he makes it to the end of the hall, stopping in front of a large window. He cautiously peers past the closed blinds, standing there for a moment, searching. He turns around, noticing me right away, but I don't startle him. It's almost as if he expected me to be there. He says nothing at first, just looks me over.

I can see his mind working, still trying to make sense of it all. He couldn't offer any words to comfort her. How do you console such a disaster of a person without calling her out for what she is? You would have to completely avoid the truth.

"You need to tell her," I blurt out, breaking the silence.

"That's not my call, Alex."

"She deserves to know. She deserves the truth."

"She deserves to have peace," Matt replies, stoic and steady. "What good will it do to tell her now, after all she's been through. Do you really believe this is the appropriate time to drop that bombshell on her? Who would that serve, Alex? Who would benefit from that? Certainly not Kayla?"

I struggle for a comeback, but his reasoning has legitimacy.

"It might provide Tara with some temporary peace, but it will obliterate Kayla's chance of ever finding any. This is not the time or place. She's suffered enough, and you should know that more than anyone."

He's right—as wrong as it may seem. He's absolutely right. What good will it really do for anyone involved? Still, I feel the inert need to challenge him. "Can a preacher keep a secret? Is that what God would want?" I say sarcastically, then instantaneously regret it.

"No one keeps secrets from God, Alex. We may keep them from ourselves, or from others, but never God. I'm not keeping a secret from Kayla. She'll learn eventually, but it's not my place to tell her, and certainly not yours. This is a delicate journey, a minefield. If you rush into it carelessly, make just one misstep, the whole thing explodes in everyone's face. The damage from the aftermath may never be repaired. This is between Tara and Kayla, no one else. When the time is right, the truth will reveal itself."

Again, his logic is undeniable. Even as emotionally charged as I am, I can't argue with his reasoning. My anger remains though. It refuses to subside even when faced with the truth.

"With what you believe, how do you make sense of any of this? How do you put it together?" A small part of me is sincerely interested in his reply.

Matt pauses. It's apparent my question caught him off guard. He takes a deep breath and then looks at me. "Faith, Alex, plain and simple. Pure and unadulterated faith!"

His answer infuriates me. "Faith? Faith in what? That everything you've ever been taught, the stories that were regurgitated to you and me time and time again, were all fables and myths rather than fact and truth? I know them well, Matt. I went to church too, all through my teens. I had them all force fed to me. I probably know more scripture than you realize, and I know this is not how it's supposed to go. So what good is faith now? What good is any of it now? It was all just wasted time, just like I knew it was when growing up, putting away childish things and becoming a full-blown adult. Faith is just a childhood fantasy, like Santa Claus and the Easter Bunny, and just as useless."

Despite the initial shock of my first question, Matt seems completely unfazed by my sacrilegious tirade. "Are you finished?"

Now I'm taken back. I shrug.

"My faith doesn't come from knowing what's going to happen, Alex. It doesn't come from having all the answers. And it's not challenged when things or events happen that don't fit into the limited scope of my life. My faith is not shaken when my definitions of how the world works or should work are dismantled before me. It's not deluded or dissolved when questions begin to outweigh the answers. If it did, then what would be the purpose of having faith at all? I don't give up on my faith when all seems chaotic and indiscernible. No, that's when my faith becomes the most essential part of my existence."

"So, it's your crutch, Matt, is that what it is?"

"It's not just a crutch. It's the only strength I have to keep me standing at all. When all reason and personal power are gone, exhausted, it's the only energy my soul has to keep my heart from breaking or being blown apart."

I step back at his intensity, his presence filling the corridor, owning every inch of space. He pulls a small, well-worn bible from his pocket. Its leather cover is faded from the brutal wear of time, its binding dry and brittle. He barely keeps its contents together using a simple yellow rubber band.

"My faith is based in truth, not based on my interpretation of it, but what this says in black and white. This belonged to my father, and his father before that."

He holds up the bible. "My grandfather was a preacher. He loved God more than his own life and tried his best to raise his children to do the same. He taught them that even when they did not understand what was happening to them, or around them, that God still had a plan. He may not work on the answers or resolutions that make sense to them, but those that make perfect sense to Him.

"We want everything dumbed down for us nowadays, put in neat, easily describable, definable boxes. We want to remain like children who only play grown up, placated with rules and evidence that our immature minds can comprehend. Then when we realize life is as cruel as it is, and not the playtime we'd hoped or wanted it to be, we so easily resort to blaming God for making it too hard. Blame him for not providing the answers that make sense only to us.

We're more than willing to give ourselves the credit for every accomplishment and blame Him for every defeat, because it's easier that way. This is the way we remain blissfully ignorant and foolishly imagine that we have any control at all. We all possess faith, as eagerly as we like to deny it. We take ownership of some form of it, whatever version of it allows us the most comfort, free of conviction and constructed by our own selfishness and pride. But truth is truth, whether we chose to believe in it or not, it doesn't change the integrity or absoluteness of it."

Matt pauses and finds a chair sitting next to a cherry table in the hall. He sits, placing the bible on the table, his hand remaining on the cover. "My grandfather practiced his faith, every minute of the day, hoping he would instill it in his children, but they went astray anyway. When he passed, my father was willed this simple, raggedy bible. He tossed it in a drawer to be forgotten, a symbolic way of separating himself from it. He believed truth was definable by one's own perspective, and that God was, just like you said, a crutch, a fabricated concept to bring a false sense of peace to the weak and naive. He firmly believed that most events occurred due to pure coincidence, with no deeper meaning or purpose. He lived most of his young life lost in that fog, until one fateful day a series of simple events, seeming unrelated, proved to him that there is always a plan, especially when we are blissfully unaware of it.

"He was running late for his parttime job as a bagger at a local grocery store. Everything seemed to be going wrong the night before, which continued into the early morning. Nothing extraordinary, just a series of simple, inconvenient incidents, annoying hiccups easily forgotten once the day progressed. He ate something that night that disagreed with him, so he slept very little and spent most of it hunched over or sitting on the toilet. Exhausted and cramping, he tried to fall asleep and stay asleep for the remaining couple of hours he had left. When he finally drifted off, he fell so deeply asleep that he didn't hear his alarm clock until it had screamed at him for a half hour. As he sprang out of bed, he hit his shin on something, bruising it badly.

"He limped into the shower and fumbled through it, costing him more time. Still wet and hobbling, he tried to make himself a cup of coffee, but he used too much water, causing the filter to overflow, spilling wet granules all over the counter and floor. With no time to clean the mess, he speedily got dressed, brushed his teeth, and headed toward the front door to sprint to his car. That's when he realized he did not have his keys and, after fifteen minutes of searching, he finally found them engulfed by dust bunnies under his bed. He locked the door behind him and sped down the steps to the sidewalk to where his dilapidated car, a rust-colored, barely functioning Gremlin was parked. He was already over an hour late and was scared to death he would be fired, almost certain of it."

"What the hell does this have to do with anything?"

"Bear with me. Of course the car wouldn't start. It just sputtered and coughed at him. With his shin still aching, he decided to walk, no run, the five blocks to his job. As he did, he passed by the local pond, which had risen and swollen thanks to the weeks of rain they'd just had. The area was quiet, not a soul around. My dad's shift started at four a.m. Normally he went in the evening, but they had back-to-back shipments the previous night, and they needed extra help that morning. Three of the receiving crew were out that week for various reasons, the first time in years, and my father was their only back up. He made his way past the pond, with the dull pain in his shin following him. As he made it to its end, he heard a low voice calling out, then some splashing. He turned and scanned the area, but there was barely any light to see anything from that distance. He was going to ignore it and continue, but then he heard it again. He could have sworn he heard someone quietly call out, 'Help me.'

"It was weak, barely definable. He reluctantly approached the pond's edge, squinting to see if he could see the source. Then he heard it again, more clearly this time. 'Help me.' It was a woman's voice. He got closer and saw something bobbing out of the water for a quick moment and then submerging. The splashing is noticeable but not frantic. He moves down the edge to where he thinks the splashing came from. The water is now still, everything eerily quiet except for the occasional early birds chirping and the chitterling of insects."

I want to stop him, but he refuses to yield a second during his tale. I'm being filibustered.

"He stood there and searched the area, wondering why. Suddenly he realized how late he was again and began to turn away when he heard a large splash and a gurgling voice, crying out, 'Help me.' He spun around and found a young girl in the water, about to take her final plunge. Without a moment's thought, he jumped into the pond and swam toward her. That pond was normally shallow, maybe four to five feet in its deepest parts, but because of the recent rains, it had overreached its limit and risen to eight to ten feet deep in the center. He reached the girl—she was pale and exhausted—and grabbed her, pulling her to safety, his shin still reeling with pain. They reached the edge, and he dragged her to a grassy patch. She was barely breathing, and he was exhausted, but he began to administer CPR, a class he had not wanted to take. It was required as part of his job as a lifeguard last summer, the job he took in order to save enough to buy that old beat-up Gremlin.

"He worked on her for a few minutes until she vomited up what looked like a gallon of murky green water. As she opened her bloodshot eyes to look up at him gratefully, she forced a smile. Her hair was matted with mud and gunk from the filthy water, but to him, she was amazingly beautiful. He later found out she had been riding her bike early in the morning, earlier than usual, and a dog darted out in front of her. She swerved to miss it and hit a large rock that catapulted her into the pond, striking her head on the bottom, causing her to become disoriented. She swallowed too much water and began to drown. Struggling frantically and suffering from a concussion, she just wore herself out. If he had been one minute later, maybe not even that long, she would have died, and no one would have known for several hours, possibly the entire day.

"If he hadn't been late that day, exactly as late as he was, she would have been dead, and no one would have known. My dad never did make it in and was fired despite explaining the whole thing to his boss. As for the young girl he saved, they started dating. The very next day, for the first time in years, my dad dug out this bible, and he never put it down, not until the day he gave it to me when I graduated seminary. To this day it is still the greatest gift I've ever received."

Okay, thankfully that's over. His expression is so sincere, I feel awful for my irritation. I decide to throw him a bone just so he knows I've been listening. "Did they stay together, or did it end?"

"They were married for over forty-five years. Cynics would say it was just a series of coincidences, nothing more, nothing less. To believe in anything else was simple, blatant naivety, like a child believing in a fairy tale. They would say if God were real, why would she have fallen in at all? Why would He allow her to suffer? Why not have them meet up in some normal, uneventful, safe way? How many people did die that day, some horribly, and why was she spared? Does God play favorites? Is it all just an arrogant game and we're the unwilling, expendable pawns?"

Unfortunately for him, I would agree with the cynics, especially now.

"That's the thing about faith, Alex. It takes courage to say, 'I don't have all the answers,' and to believe there's a purpose to all things. What if God delivered us from all evil in a single bound, spared us from every form of tribulation? What then? Do you really think we wouldn't find some way to destroy ourselves, or injure those around us? Do you really believe we wouldn't create our own customized tragedy and suffering?"

He has a point. With all that I'd seen, the inhuman acts and vicious and violent crimes people committed with such ease, without any remorse, it's hard to debunk his logic.

"The men and women God has chosen to fulfill his plans are the most unlikely of individuals. They could never have accomplished what they did without faith. Samson was an egotistical whoremonger, Gideon a misguided nobody, David an adulterer and murderer, Rahab a well-known prostitute, and Moses a cowardly outcast. They were thrust into action, and it was their faith that made their success possible, success that had ramifications throughout history. Faith is never about the outcome. It's always about how we act and what we learn through the journey, and our willingness to carry on further. I don't trust in the interpretations or doctrines of man, but I fully believe in the truth of this word."

He holds up the tattered bible again. "Faith is finding hope when there's no evidence of it. Faith is creating hope when none can be found. Faith is not surviving; it's finding a way to live boldly no matter what the circumstance or difficulty."

He pauses. I think he's waiting for my response. Oddly, my ire with him is gone. Instead, I stand here finding myself deeply respecting him, seeing him in a way I had not taken the time to witness before.

"Once they found out about my cancer, I lost everything. Instead of supporting me in my darkest hour, my wife, my church, they both abandoned me. The same smiling people who sat attentively in pew after pew every Sunday decided my illness would hurt their church's potential. The same elders who showered me with compliments and accolades for all my service now doubted me at every turn. Instead, they immediately went out and found a younger, more renowned replacement, to shepherd them to the next level.

"When I first started, there were only a handful of regulars. The day they dismissed me, we exceeded a congregation of a thousand. In their minds my leadership ability was tied directly to my human strength. They were so scared my weakness would be contagious, spreading to the masses, and therefore their offerings and funding. I tragically discovered that every sermon I'd ever taught was a mere illusion, that despite their eager eyes and apparent attentiveness, they all fell on deaf ears. It was nothing more than a masquerade to disguise their real intentions. It wasn't to further God's kingdom, but more of a glorified country club. All that preparation to deliver the good news of

God's word was for me and no one else. It was never taken seriously by the very body I was so intent on serving, not for one moment. I couldn't believe how naïve I'd been.

"My wife stayed with me for as long as she could to keep up appearances, but she had left me in spirit long before that, absent from me even when we were lying in bed together. A few months later, she went back home. I found out a few weeks ago she's with someone new; the ink wasn't even dry on her divorce request. We'd been married for ten years. I foolishly thought we were happily married, yet another one of those grand deceptions.

"I was Job, forsaken by everyone I'd held in esteem, everyone I loved. I was tempted to doubt, to blame, deeply tempted, but it was only when I was stripped of everything I thought was vital, when faced with what I thought of as a hopeless situation, I realized what faith truly meant. I don't believe God did this to me, but I firmly believe He has always been with me to carry me through it. It opened a door for me, to minister on a simple basis, to assist those who God really needed me to be with without the distraction of church politics or putting on a religious show. To bring those who were suffering similarly the real-life experiences and credibility of my faith, so I could truly uplift and assist them in theirs. I was open to a new congregation, not contained and confined in a building, but everywhere God led me to go. I found hope when anyone else would have given up.

"So, again, Alex, my faith isn't just a crutch. It completely carries me. And I am not ashamed to admit that, not for one second. Even now, with everything that's happened, my faith hasn't been weakened. In fact, quite the opposite. I don't have the answers you want, why God would allow this to happen. All I have is my faith. We may never have those answers. This may have been the way it was always supposed to be. But I do know this, we've survived until now, and I firmly believe we can find a way in this new world."

I never knew his story. How could I until this moment? My respect for him just took an epic leap. I can't find the words to respond.

"I believe God brought us together because we need each other to survive this. He brought you to us and gave us the strength to carry on in a world becoming more and more alien and hostile. He made us a family, something that is even more alien to some of us based on our past and experiences. We need each other, Alex. Together, we'll find a way to live, to hope against hope. I know what you've sacrificed, we all do. What you've done for us is just short of miraculous. I can say with absolute certainty, we owe you our lives, every one of us. It's a debt we can never repay you, but there's one thing we can do. We can help you get to your family.

"I want to help you find and save them. I've talked it over with Rick, and he agrees. I know you think you'll have a better chance on your own, that you won't be able to keep us safe, but that's a moot point now. The threat is there no matter where we go, and we have a better chance facing it together. I know once Kayla is rested, she'll feel the same.

"Jude checked it out. We're only a few miles from your neighborhood, and he can use the laptop to continue to help us see ahead. Despite all the chaos and confusion, with no definable rhyme or reason, we've found a way closer to your home. It's as if we're being driven here. An impossible coincidence, don't you think?"

I'm speechless. I see the absolute sincerity in his eyes. A wave of deep appreciation and admiration washes over me. He approaches me and pats me on the back.

"We'll leave as soon as we can. I'll keep watch in the meantime. Why don't you get some rest?" Matt smiles and nods, then moves down the hall, leaving me to stew in my thoughts. I'm completely overwhelmed as I watch him walk away. I want to say something, anything, but there are no words that can define my emotions. Instead, I retreat toward the living room, and the recliner in the corner.

Jude left some granola bars on the end table next to a can of soda. I grab a bar and unwrap it, almost swallowing it whole. I force it down with a swig of the soda, not even tasting it, but my stomach thanks me. I fire down another one and finish off the soda as I collapse in the chair.

Exhaustion sets in, all my adrenaline spent ten times over. My eyelids get heavier and heavier as I slide the recliner back, I know any sense of safety is an illusion, but I have to rest.

I close my eyes and listen to Jude snore. I can hear Matt walking back down the hall. Thought fades away and sounds taper off. The images of everything that's happened, and those stolen memories from others, knock incessantly at the door of my mind, but for the first time, I'm able to keep them out. I drift off into a quiet, fragile peace.

Then, finally silence. Blessed silence.

CHAPTER 29

A New Dawn

(Kayla)

As my body begins to wake, light creeps in through my closed eyelids. I stretch my sore muscles and yawn loudly. My vision is blurred by what feels like inches of crud caked in the corners, itching incessantly as I rub them. Flakes of dirt and God knows what else break free when I shake my head, raining down onto the red satin sheets. I stretch again, drenched in sweat, and scowl at my own body odor.

Whew, I'm ripe!

The hardwood floor is cold and somewhat rough on the bottoms of my feet. Glancing over the room, it looks like a page torn from a *Better Homes and Gardens* magazine. I bet Martha Steward would totally get her rocks off here!

Stumbling across the room, I peel my pants off, sending more dirt and crap scattering across the shiny floor. It's disgusting. I need a shower.

My eyes water from the stench as I step into the shower. Scanning my body, I see swirls of blood, dirt, and shit I can't identify wrap around my legs and torso, decorating me like some horrific Easter egg. I find a bottle of body wash on a small porcelain shelf embedded in the wall. In seconds I'm covered in a soapy shell. I ferociously scrub every inch with a luffa I found hanging on a suction cup hook. I scrub my hair, not used to having to wash it. It's been absent for so long. I can't remember the last time I felt the strands run through my fingers like this. I rinse and repeat, wringing all the death and destruction of the day free.

Finally clean, I step out onto a plush purple bathmat, hoping to God I find a towel. I forgot to check before I got in the shower. Thankfully, I see a towel hanging from the rod near the sink. As I'm drying off, I glance at the mirror and see a stranger staring back at me with bright blue eyes. She has a beautiful face, with long golden hair that falls over her shoulders, leaving a few strands dancing across her cheeks.

I bow my head and begin to sob. Who is this person? That can't be me. Why did she choose to haunt me now?

We weep together, me and the beautiful stranger in the mirror. I step back and shake my head. This is who I was supposed to be. The woman Alex saw through all the shit. The woman he spoke about at my bedside. I see her clearly now, uninterrupted by my pain and past. She's free, unhindered by shame or defeat, full of hope and beauty, no longer veiled by anger and loss. I heard every word he said.

Tears puddle around my feet as she cries with me, but will she remain? Her eyes tell me yes, but my heart struggles to believe it. I don't want to leave her. I have so many questions to ask, but there's no time left. Reluctantly, I walk away from the mirror, but I can feel her follow me. I feel her step back into my soul, embracing my spirit. It's like I've been washed all over again, refreshed.

In the bedroom, I find a large dresser near the bed. Inside one of the drawers, I find underwear—frilly shit, and pink, of course, but it'll have to do. Her bras definitely won't fit. She was far more blessed than I am. I find a black tank and slide it over my head, my skin still slightly damp from the shower.

In another drawer, I find some T-shirts. I grab a red v-neck with a zebra pocket and slip it on. It's a little big, but again, I don't have the tits to fill it like she must have had. In the third drawer are yoga pants. Let's hope they fit.

I find a purple pair and slip them on. Perfect, though I'm definitely not going for a fashion statement here. Socks are in the top drawer. Draped over a chair in front of a massive vanity is a black leather jacket. *Oh, hell yeah!*

In the closet I find a pair of gray and white sneakers. They're a little loose, but they'll do. After lacing up the shoes, I head back to the bathroom, opening the medicine cabinet above the sink. Finding some deodorant, I hit the pits. Lord, knows they need it. I also find some expensive perfume and douse myself in it. Who knows when I'll get another round with a shower?

I grab the jacket, sliding my arms through one at a time. Now this feels damn good! It's a little loose, but who gives a flying shit. It's straight black, lightweight, and very G. I turn and look in the vanity mirror.

Oh my God, there she is again! And she looks amazing—so confident, so … so normal. It's as if my life has started over, reborn from this moment. Who I was before is gone. I'm facing a strange crossroads. One path has never been placed at my feet before. It leads to the unknown, each step created by the decisions I make now and nothing else. The other is a street I know all too well. It's paved with heartache, shame, pain, fear, and hate, a well-traveled road that offers no progress, circular in design, leading nowhere. It's the easier choice, despite the horror it represents, a journey I had been trapped in my whole life, like a caged animal travelling the same four corners of its cage, never leaving its confinement, and never knowing the difference. As much as it calls to me, mocking me that I'm not good enough, or strong enough, to break free, it's too late. I've seen her now. I know her. Her face silences the voices of my past. Her eyes lead me forward, my vision clear. I don't look back. I step on my new path, and with each step, I feel the old falling away, just like all that filth in the shower. I step out of the room and take a deep breath as she cheers me on.

To my right is a large room. Rick is asleep in a chair in some kind of study or office. I know he visited me earlier. I think it was right before I woke up, too out of it to acknowledge him. Looks like sleep finally got the best of him too.

I continue around the corner and enter the living room. Alex is asleep in his own chair. I can't see Matt, Jude or Tara, but I hear voices in the kitchen. It sounds like Tara and Jude. Someone is placing dishes on a table. I smell something cooking, and it smells pretty good! Mac and cheese, I think, hot dogs too.

I hear loud snoring and realize Matt is unconscious in a chair in the hallway, his rifle on the floor. He must've fallen asleep during his watch. Who can blame him. We're all so exhausted. I don't even know the difference between day or night anymore, or even how long we've been travelling.

I walk quietly into the living room, trying not to wake Matt. I slip in next to Alex and kneel by his side, reviewing everything he'd said, revisiting each emotion. He looks so different now. I place my hand on his and try to muster the courage to say what I want to say. Before I can, he opens his eyes and turns to me with a smile.

"Looks who's up," he whispers.

His voice is so wonderful, so comforting. You'd think I'd be all dried up by now, but I can feel a few stray tears dance down my cheeks. He notices immediately.

"No more tears, Kayla." He smiles as he gently wipes my cheeks.

I take his hand and scoot closer. "Thank you," I whisper. *Will he ever know how truly grateful I am?*

"We've already done this dance." He kisses my hand. "No need to rehash it."

I hug him tightly from the side. "We'll find your family, I promise," I whisper in his ear.

"I know," he whispers back.

I release him, and he slowly stands, pulling me to my feet. "Have you eaten yet?"

"No."

"Tara's got some grub in the kitchen. Go get some."

I stare into his eyes, seeing him so much more clearly now. I know him so well.

"Go on, I'll join you in a second." He releases my hand and stretches, smiling but saying no more. He walks past me and heads into the hall—I assume to find Matt or Rick.

I head to the kitchen and see Tara and Jude eating at the table. I startle her. I mean, I really scare her!

"Kayla, why are you up?" she gasps.

"Relax, Southern Comfort, I just wanted to grab something to eat." Just as I'd surmised, I see a pot full of mac and cheese on the stove and some cold hot dogs and buns sitting on the counter in front of the microwave. "Is it good, kid?"

Jude nods as he stuffs his mouth to a point of overflowing. He looks like a chipmunk with cheeks full of acorns.

"Chew, kid, chew!" I say, laughing.

Jude grunts as he continues to inhale his meal. I head to the stove. "Do you mind if I help myself, Tara?"

Tara doesn't reply. She just sits there and stares at me in silence, totally creeping me out.

"Okay…" I grab a bowl off the counter and begin to fill it with a spoon from the pot. "Looks good. Didn't think you had it in you to cook," I joke. "Thought your maids and shit did that."

She still doesn't answer. I sit at the table, seeing forks and napkins already laid out in the center. Jude is still gorging himself. "Kid is hungry, huh?" I joke again.

Still nothing. Whatever!

I begin to chow down. It's not bad, but it's pretty hard to go wrong with mac and cheese. "Could you throw a dog in the microwave for me?" I ask with my mouth full of food.

Tara nods and springs up.

What the hell is her issue?

Jude finishes off his bowl. "Mom, can I get some more, please?"

"Dude, slow down, pace yourself," I say, only half kidding.

Tara grabs his bowl. She throws a few dogs into the microwave and pops each button hard. The timer begins as she frantically clumps pasta into Jude's bowl. When it's full, she spins it around and gives it to him.

She anxiously waits by the microwave as it cooks, her fingers nervously tapping the counter.

"Tara, seriously, are you alright?"

She nods as she continues to stare at the appliance. Jude is still ramming food into his face, like he hasn't eaten in weeks.

"Jude, slow down," Tara snaps. "That was his favorite before he got sick," she explains, still turned away from me. "He's had to give up so much."

"Well, he sure as shit is making up for it now," I retort.

Jude giggles as he scarfs down another bite. "The hot dogs are pretty good, too," he mumbles over the food in his mouth, spitting debris everywhere.

I laugh. "Let me guess. He had to give them up too."

Tara doesn't respond. The timer beeps and she grabs the dogs out with her bare hands. She placed them into buns, almost dropping them, her hands shaking.

I take the plate from her. "How many has he had of these?"

"A few." She sits, looking like she's going to explode.

"Tara, what the hell is up with you?"

"Nothing. I'm fine, just trying to settle in," she replies, attempting to rise again.

"Bullshit," I retort, and grab her hand. She's really trembling.

"Kayla, please let go!"

"Listen," I begin, "I know we haven't always hit it off, but that doesn't mean I don't like you. Maybe you thought I didn't

… okay, maybe I didn't at first, but things are different now. You don't have to be like this around me."

Tara jerks her hand free and heads back to the stove.

I jump up. "What the fuck, Tara!"

"Stop, just stop. I don't want to fight anymore," she pleads, still refusing to face me.

"Neither do I, so tell me what the fuck is going on."

"Please don't curse anymore in front of Jude. He's already heard too much, seen too much, been through too much."

Jude chuckles. "Don't mind me. I don't give a rat's ass."

"Jude, don't you dare," Tara scolds.

I laugh as Jude put on the biggest shit-eating grin I've ever seen. That was pretty good, kid!

"Tara, don't change the subject. What's going on with you?"

Tara finally turns in my direction and just stares. Whatever is going on in there, it's tearing her up inside.

Jude looks up. He finally stops munching for a second. She looks at him, then at me. "I'm sorry," she says, breaking her silence.

"For what?"

"I'm just sorry, sorry for everything I've said, everything I've done, just everything." Tears begin to stream down her face.

"I'm sorry too. I shouldn't have been such a bitch to you from the start."

Tara looks completely shocked. I can immediately tell she wasn't expecting that. "You had every right to be!"

Okay, color me shocked now. "What?"

"You don't need to apologize for anything, Kayla. You had a right to be angry at me. Mad at the world, for that matter. I'm sorry for not seeing that right away, for not allowing it to buffer my harshness toward you." She's struggling not to cry.

"I don't need you to feel sorry for me, Tara."

"You're mistaken. I don't feel sorry for you, Kayla. I admire you."

What … the … ever … loving … FUCK!

"You faced things that would've completely devastated me, and you came out stronger for it."

"Listen, Tara, I don't know what you think you know about me, but—"

"See, this is why I can't talk to you. Even when I try to show you my heart, it goes so terribly wrong. Even when I try to make things right, only the worst comes out of it."

"Kayla, ease off on my mom," Jude snaps.

"Jude, stay out of this," Tara snaps back.

"No, he's right. I'm sorry. I shouldn't have snapped at you before giving you a chance to finish what you were saying."

Tara acts taken aback by my sudden humility. Hell, even I am!

"It's okay, Kayla, I understand. I would've reacted the same way if I were in your shoes. Some pompous ass tries to pat me on the head, talk down to me, or act like they understand what I've been through. It used to make my skin crawl, make me want to scream!"

"Oh, okay," I reply, gob smacked by the entire conversation.

"I've never been good at this," she continues, her eyes dripping with sincerity. "I always mess it up. I had to let you know that I was sorry, before we went any further."

"What do you mean by 'further?'"

"You know … in our journey … wherever we may go," she says, stumbling over her words.

I know she means something else, but I'm confused by her moment of contriteness.

She sighs. "I'm just sorry, deeply and truly sorry."

"Same here," I agree, trying to end the uncomfortable back and forth. "Can we move on now?"

"Can we?" Tara asks, as she turns away from me.

Alex and Matt rush into the room. "We've got activity outside," Alex says. "Break's over!"

"What?" Tara gasps.

"They're here. They're all over the place. Rick is getting his gear on. Tara, take Jude into the dining room and get his stuff on with Matt."

"Oh my God, not again!" Tara screams.

"No time for that now, Tara, get going," Alex orders.

Matt rushes toward them, grabbing Tara's arm. Jude springs up and sprints out of the kitchen into the dining room.

"Matt, wrap him up tight. We're going to have to move and move fast. When you're done, get him to bring up the cameras and find us a safe way out of here."

Matt agrees and bolts, with Tara in tow, out of the room.

"There really is no rest anywhere anymore, is there?" I gasp.

"No!" He's stoic again, solid as granite. He has no choice. I get that now, more than ever before. "Get dressed."

I nod and stride to where the equipment is in the dining room. "We're heading to your house, right?"

"What?" he snaps as he follows me in.

"There's no real safe place to go anyway, so we might as well go there."

"There may be."

Where? What could he mean? Doesn't matter, I tell myself. Stay focused. "Well, it'll have to wait until after we make that stop," I say.

All the body armor is neatly organized on the large table. Had to be Rick or Matt's handiwork. I find my shit and separate it quickly as the rest get suited up.

'Suited up,' listen to me!

I slip my vest over my head. It probably saved me from most of the stings from those fucking stalks. I pull my Kevlar pants on and grab my belt and holster. Removing my pistol, I check it, finding a full mag. I find three or four still on the belt. Then I grab a rifle. It's loaded and ready to go as well.

Wait, something's missing. Where is it?

I search the room and finally see my bow and quivers. I slink over and pick them up, slinging the leather quiver over my shoulder, then tightening and locking it into place. I place the other in a duffle on the table.

I watch Jude get dressed. No matter how hard they try, or what they do, the kid is the most vulnerable part of this equation. They're going to go after him first. It's only natural, just like any other predator trying to pick off the weakest of the herd. Whether that's the case or not, they'll have to go through me first. It's time I stood in the gap for someone else, just like Alex did for me. We may not be family, but I'll protect him like he is.

I rush over to Jude. "Tara, get ready. I'll take care of him!" She tries to argue, but I push her away. "You know how they say on an airline, if the cabin pressure drops, parents put their mask on first so you'll be able to put it on your child? So put your fucking mask on, and put it on right, or you won't be able to help him."

Tara reluctantly agrees. "You take good care of him, you hear me? Be a big sister to him."

Like I'd even know what that looks like. "Just go, I got this," I say. "Okay, kid, let's get you ready."

Jude gladly concedes as I duct tape his vest around him.

"Throw me an extra set of pants," I call to Matt.

He digs through a duffle bag and finds one, throwing it to me.

"They won't fit," Jude says.

"They will when I get done." I slip them over his legs and apply gluttonous amounts of gray tape around his waist until it fits. "I hope you took a piss already."

Jude laughs as I pull up his pant leg and match the Kevlar padding up as best I can, then tape it in place, tight enough to stay on without cutting off the little guy's circulation. I do the same to the other leg. He has no boots, so his sneakers will have to do. He laces them up, then I cover them with more tape so they won't come undone. The gas mask doesn't fit right either. I tear a piece of the dining room table's silk red tablecloth and create a makeshift bandana, tying it behind his head and draping it over his neck.

"When it gets bad, put this over your mouth and don't take it off unless I say to, okay?"

He nods. I don't know how much good it'll do, but it's better than nothing. He looks absolutely goofy, wrapped up like the kid from that Christmas movie, but at least he's safe. At least I hope so. I place the gun belt around his waist, taping it in place to secure it. I load a few mags in the holders, then grab the pistol off the counter.

Kneeling, I show him the gun. "You remember how to use this?"

"Yeah."

"Here's the safety. It's on now. If you pull it out, you have to flip it off to shoot."

"I know, I know," he nervously snaps.

"You need to make sure, Jude! You make a mistake and either you or one of us can get hurt—or worse, killed."

"I know! I will!"

This is not going to end well. I know it, but he can't. He has to believe he can do this. I can be a very good liar when I need to be. I had to be to survive. I can sell water to a drowning man or ice to an Eskimo. It's a gift, or a curse, or both. At least now it's being used for good. I slip the gun into the holster and secure it. "Matt, he's ready! So am I!"

Another lie.

I see Tara dressed in full armor. She's shaking. God, please don't let her be standing behind me if she has to shoot.

"How many are out there?" Doc asks Alex.

"All of them," Alex replies.

"Jude, come here and let's check out those cameras on the laptop," Matt says.

Jude flies over to him as Matt opens the laptop, and they begin their search.

"Find out if we can take a vehicle, and provide some cover to get there faster," Doc adds.

Alex exits the room, rifle in hand.

"How much ammo do we have, Rick?" I ask.

"Each rifle has two magazines left," he replies. "The pistols have three each, and that's it."

"What else?"

"I can't find the shotguns or their ammo. We must have left them at the station. Alex has four or five grenades, and I have about five flash bangs in the bag."

"Is that it?" Matt gasps.

"Yes, that's it!"

How the hell are we going to make it out the door alive, let alone to Alex's house?

Matt hovers over Jude and the laptop. I watch Jude point at the screen as they discuss what he's seeing. Tara leans against the wall, her eyes closed, lips moving. She's silently praying. Any other time I would've mocked her, but not today. I hope she mentions my name.

I notice Matt holding what looks like a small ratty book in his hand, curious about what it is.

Doc heads out into the hall, I assume to meet Alex. Matt and Jude are in a heated discussion that I still can't hear. I head out into the hall, where Doc and Alex are talking.

"What are they doing out there?" Doc asks, as he watches Alex peer through the window.

"I don't know. They appear to be just roaming the street. It's very strange. I think we can go out the back, stay in the yards, and make our way out of the neighborhood that way. If we stay low and quiet, we might be able to sneak past them. They seem to be congregating in one area about two or three houses ahead of this one."

"Are they going house to house?" Doc asks.

"It certainly looks like it. Get them to the kitchen now!"

Doc turns and sprints by me. I don't think he noticed me. I walk up to Alex. "Do you really think they're looking for us? Why?"

"I don't know, but they're certainly looking for something. A group just went into the house across the way."

He continues his surveillance. I turn and investigate the dining room. Tara heads toward the kitchen just as Doc emerges.

"Come on, Matt, we need to leave now!" Alex says. "Kayla, help me get them into the kitchen!"

I sprint into the room where Matt and Jude are still hunched over the laptop, its screen eerily illuminating their faces. "We're leaving, fellas, now!"

"Hold on one more minute," Matt says, still staring intently at the monitor. "Will it work?" he asks Jude.

"It should. It looks clear," Jude replies.

"What about driving it?" Matt asks.

"No, the main streets are packed, and there aren't enough back roads visible in the feed."

"Do you have enough charge in the battery to take the laptop with us?" Matt says. "And can you stay connected?"

"There's about eighteen hours on the battery. As far as the connection, we'll just have to see. The GPS application should keep us connected, and it runs off a 4G signal as well as Wi-Fi."

"Let's hope it stays online!" Matt takes the laptop.

"Don't forget, Matt, it's one of those you can turn the screen and make it into a tablet," Jude instructs.

Matt flips the screen around and retrieves his rifle. "Kayla, grab that duffle bag off the table and I'll grab the other on the floor."

"What's in them?"

"Food, bottled water, first aid kit, and some other essentials. I combined all the packs together." He flings it over his shoulder.

I grab the one near me. It's heavy, but I can manage it. Let's hope I'll be able to for the duration of the trip.

Alex meets us in the kitchen. "We go out the back. Stay silent. I'll take point, and Matt, you stay behind me with the laptop. Rick, you and Tara partner up, and Kayla—"

"I'll stay with the kid, don't worry," I say.

Jude looks up at me. He's counting on me, like no one else ever has. I won't fail him.

"Safety's off. Stay frosty," Alex commands. "No one fire unless I give the go ahead. Understand?"

Everyone nods. Shit, this is happening. Again!

Alex opens the door and does a quick check. Staying low, he carefully exits, still holding the door. "Okay, quietly," he instructs, moving forward.

Matt braces the door with a chair. Alex descends the three brick steps. We follow tightly, not more than two feet from each other. He hugs the back of the house as he travels across the yard. He peers around the corner and holds up his fist. Matt stops abruptly.

Okay, that must mean halt. Thanks for the debrief.

The pause is excruciating as we wait for what to do next. Alex finally signals for us to move forward, Matt moving slowly behind him. We pass through a well-manicured grassy lot between the two houses and swing around behind another home. As we pass, I see the alien guys standing in the middle of the street, their gazes locked in front of them. I do a quick count. There has to be a dozen or more just standing there gawking. Alex motions for us to pass him as he stays at the corner of the second house, watching. We line up behind him, facing the opposite way we were going.

What the hell?

"What is it?" Matt whispers, just loud enough for me to hear him.

"Something is wrong," Alex replies. "They're afraid."

"How do you know?"

"The chief is close enough I can feel his fear. Something is coming, something big!"

"Then let's get the hell out of here before whatever it is gets here!" I hiss.

CHAPTER 30

Behemoth

(Kayla)

"Why can't I see it?" Alex says, shutting his eyes tightly. "Why can't I see this one?"

"What are you talking about?" Matt asks.

"Whatever the chief fears, it's big, very, very big—but I can't see it. I have no memory of it."

"What?" Matt gasps.

Oh shit, did Alex connect with that thing like he did with me?

"Stay here," he instructs as he quickly but silently clears the corner, slinking up the side of the house.

"Wait, Alex," Matt quietly calls out.

"Stay put," he calls back. "I'll be right back."

I scoot past the troop, leaving Jude behind, and whisper to Matt, "Where the hell is he going?"

"I don't know. I didn't understand anything he was saying."

I peer past the corner and see Alex is at the edge of the house across from us, just barely out of their sight. I jet past Matt and head toward him.

"Kayla, wait!" Matt hisses.

He tries to stop me, but it's too late. I'm right behind Alex in less than a second. I look back at Matt, seeing him wave for me to return. I furiously shake my head.

"You wanna tell me what the fuck you're doing, Rambo?" I whisper.

"I knew you were there, Kayla. I knew you would be too stubborn to do what I clearly told you all to do," he whispers, obviously irritated.

"What the fuck are we doing here?"

They aren't moving anymore. They're still waiting for something.

"What are we doing?" Matt quietly interrupts.

My heart just about jumps through the roof of my skull, and I think I peed myself a little. Not cool, especially in a lacey thong. "What the hell, Matt," I growl.

"We need to go, now," he replies.

"Both of you shut the hell up," Alex calls back.

I slip in next to Alex, trying to catch a glimpse of what he's watching. I scoot a few inches to his side and stretch my neck out to catch a peek. Alex is oblivious to what I'm doing, too sharply focused on them. He's right; they're all frozen, staring endlessly forward into nothing.

This can't be good! There has to be at least twenty or thirty of them now. And not just warriors, but what looks like females and children too. They're motionless, waiting for something.

But what?

Then I see the chief, the one Alex fought with in the lot, right in front of it all. He's searching the area with his eyes. All evidence of his battle with Alex is gone, not a single wound visible. Just like Alex. What the hell is happening to him? To us?

The chief takes a few steps forward.

Shit, we're too far out from the house. He'll see us! I tug on Alex's arm, but he won't budge. He's as frozen as they are. The chief scans by us. I know he made full eye contact with me, stopping for only a moment, then continuing to survey the area.

Didn't he see me? How could he not? He looked right at me. Maybe he didn't care? "We need to leave! We need to leave right now!" I hiss.

The chief kneels, placing his hand on the street. He holds it there and closes his eyes.

"Do you feel that?" Alex asks. He frantically shifts his gaze left to right.

"Feel what?" I ask. The lump in my throat is too thick to swallow. "What do you hear, Alex?"

The chief lowers himself to the ground and places the side of his head against the asphalt.

"I can hear it," Alex gasps.

"Hear what?"

The tribe begins to stir as the chief holds up his hand. The group instantly stops all sound and movement.

"Matt, go back with the others and run," Alex commands without breaking his trance.

"What?" Matt gasps.

"Run, run as far away from here as possible. Head to my house and don't look back!" He begins to push Matt away. "You have to go now, before it kills them too!" He grabs me by the arm, moving me behind him. Shit, he's strong! "Kayla, go with him!"

Our voices are getting louder and louder, enough for them to hear. At this point, I don't think they care. They're oblivious to us. Whatever they're waiting for is a far bigger threat than we are.

"Now!" Alex roars.

Matt grabs my arm and begins to pull me along with him. Halfway there, I break free and sprint back to Alex's side.

"Kayla," Matt calls to me, trying not to scream.

"Go, I'm not leaving him!"

Alex turns to me, his eyes pitch black. "You have no idea what you've done," he growls.

"Please, Alex, come with me. Come away from this," I plead. 'It's happening to you again!" I feel the earth vibrate under my knee. I watch Matt make it back to our group and disappear behind the house. The rumbling intensifies.

"It's here," Alex snarls as he turns back toward the tribe. "And now there's no escape!" His voice has become dark and foreboding, almost alien. It's taken him again.

The earth begins to shake. I watch the tribe bend down, taking some sort of battle stance, weapons drawn. The archers do the same, arrows poised between their fingers.

Alex raises his rifle. "Get your weapon ready. You're in this now!"

I swing my rifle around. I can't figure out what's trembling more, my hands or the ground beneath my feet. I flip the safety off.

"Whatever happens, Kayla, find your courage, and don't let go of it," Alex commands, his voice nearly animalistic. "It'll be the only thing that'll keep you alive!"

The shaking intensifies until we're barely able to remain upright. Windows begin to shatter on the houses all around us. their structures moaning and vibrating.

The tribe members struggle to stay on their feet, but they manage far better than they should have. They hold steady, fully prepared for whatever the hell is coming next. They've been here before; there's no doubt of that.

The sound of things breaking in the houses around us is deafening. It feels like the ground is about to swallow us whole. Just as the wood is about to tear free from its foundations, it suddenly ceases. But there's no calm; the tribe is still poised for whatever is coming next. There's a final tremendous rumble as the houses break apart. I fall over on to my side and watch as the ground in front of the tribe opens, devouring the street.

They fall back as dust and debris fill the air. Both houses near the enormous forming sinkhole collapse in a matter of seconds. The tribe continues to quickly step back but remain vigilant in their stance. The street continues to disappear into the abyss, taking everything with it.

As quickly as it began, it stops. The sounds of the devastation continue as trees fall on roofs as well as the cars lining the street, crushing them under their weight. Glass and debris spray everywhere as a dust cloud rises from the gigantic pit. Alex stands over me with his rifle aimed right at the cloud.

"Stay down!" he growls. "Don't move!" His voice sounds a little more familiar, but his eyes are just as dark and lifeless.

In unison, the tribe begins to step back as a loud guttural roar erupts from the hole, shaking everything around us. I feel it in my bones. In an instant, something monstrous leaps from the crater and slams hard onto the asphalt. The impact drops another house to the ground, followed by an enormous dust cloud filling the air with thick, choking soot and silt. A second piercing roar rattles the ground.

"It's the behemoth," Alex gasps, his voice becoming alien again.

As the dust quickly settles, I see it rise, towering above everything. It's a gigantic, hideous worm, as tall as two houses stacked one on top of another. Brownish green, tightly woven scales cover its entire body. It turns its enormous beak-like head, covered with black spikes of all different sizes. Its skull rotates like a hellish drill, spinning freely. Large, fibrous tendrils writhe from his body. There are millions of them, sprouting from every inch of this abomination, translucent and thick, nearly identical to those of the stalks. They slink and shift like snakes with no apparent purpose. A large tail drags on the ground behind it, its huge round tip covered in bony spikes, each one larger than a man. The tendrils reach out into the air, putting on a freakish show as iridescent light flashes through them.

What the hell is it doing?

"It's finding them, "Alex whispers. "It feels them, senses each movement, noise, even their very pulse!"

The tribe remains perfectly still. The brilliant lightshow escalates until it becomes nearly blinding. Streaks of lighting jets through each tube, starting from its body and ending right before it reaches the tendril's tip.

Alex aims right at the creature. "Don't move until I tell you to. Stay as close to the ground as you can. It can't see you there. It won't be able to tell you from the surface."

"How can you possibly know that?"

The lights begin to fade, and the tendrils go dark. They slither toward each other, wrapping together in definitive groups. As they do, they form appendages, their tips reaching out, crossing together into talons and claws. As each one gathers, they change color and become as black as night. In a matter of seconds there are eight of them on each side. It's a horrific metamorphosis to watch. The creature bolsters itself up on them. A flowing fluorescent brownish green illuminates from within it. Its enormous tail rises into the sky, casting an ominous shadow upon the tribe and everything else.

The beak opens and folds like praying hands coming apart, forming a frightening mane around what could only be described as its neck. A large bulbous object emerges from it, dripping in yellow and white fluids that splash down onto the street, creating thin ponds around its feet. The bulb blossoms like a flower, exposing rows and rows of sharp teeth protruding from each terrifying petal.

In the center is a second mouth, like a canine's muzzle stripped of all flesh, just a thin layer of muscle covering bone. It roars again, and the soundwave rushes through the neighborhood, reducing any remaining glass to minuscule fragments. My ears pulse under the pressure, and I close my eyes, feeling like I'm being compressed to the ground.

A large tongue juts from the hideous beast's mouth and lashes toward the tribe. Before they can react, it breaks into a myriad of smaller tendrils with jagged tips that spear several tribe members. It brutally pierces their flesh and bone, quickly retracting them into its hellish mouth, devouring them in seconds. Alex is right, there's no escaping this thing.

It lashes out again, grabbing more, indiscriminately targeting them with surgical accuracy. The tribe fights back, hurtling spear after spear. Arrows fill the sky and descend on its back. They bounce off as if they're made of foam or rubber. The spears make even less of a difference.

The chief howls, leading a small party toward the beast. It lashes out with its tongue again, wiping out most of the front line in a single sweep. The chief barely avoids being ensnared and presses forward with the handful of warriors that are left. They creep past its legs, then sprint under the creature, stabbing at its underbelly with their spears. The creature reacts and begins to move forward. The relentless infantry follows, continuing their assault.

"It has to be its only weak spot," Alex confirms. "But they'll never do enough damage."

The tail rapidly descends backwards and then quickly rotates. It snaps down and thrusts under the creature, mercilessly clearing out its attackers in one quick and devastating motion. It impales several of them as it thrashes back and forth, forcing the remaining few to retreat.

This thing is prepared for anything.

"You're right, they don't have the weapons to stop it," Alex snarls.

Wait, did I just say that out loud? No, I didn't! Can he hear me? Can he hear what I'm thinking now?

"Yes, I can," he responds, as a chill dances up my spine.

The archers continue uselessly firing at it, rapidly exhausting their supply of arrows. The children step in, using makeshift slingshots, which are equally ineffective. Both the men and women are fighting side by side in this futile effort, facing their undeniable end together. It's tragic and inspiring at the same time. They refuse to flee, aware it'll only be their undoing.

"They're all going to die," I scream. "We need to get the hell out of here!"

The chief emerges from the chaos and howls. More warriors run toward him, spears and daggers in hand. Most are swallowed up before they even reach him, their screams deafening. The sounds of flesh tearing and bones breaking are absolutely horrifying. I don't know how much more I can take.

"Courage, Kayla," Alex growls. "Now it's time to even the score!"

What the hell is he talking about?

In an instant, he springs up and rushes toward the scene. For some stupid reason, I get up and mindlessly follow right behind him.

The behemoth wipes out another group with its tail, dragging several across the asphalt, their grated flesh leaving a bloody trail. The chief tries to muster another force, but chaos has taken control. The beast's belly is infested with a multitude of spears buried deep within its flesh, green and black ooze seeping freely onto the street, mixing with the black blood and remains of its victims. Their shafts scrape the road and break loose, ripping chunks from its abdomen, but still have little effect on thwarting it.

The archers advance, drawing large bonelike blades from fur-covered scabbards. It's all they have left. They're sprinting to their doom, and they seem hell bent on doing so. The children scramble to find more stones, their parents either absent or already dead. Alex stops only ten to twenty feet away from the monster, well within reach of its horrific tongue. He kneels again, aiming his rifle. He fires at its head with surgical accuracy.

The sound of gunfire fills the air, obliterating the screams and howls of the tribe. The bullets mercilessly tear away at the mammoth mouth of the beast, and it recoils. A few tribe members rush Alex with their weapons poised to strike. I quickly fire at their feet to warn them off. Alex, unfazed, continues his barrage, now aiming for the thing's front legs. He saws through one of them with a hail of bullets, and its blood spews out like a fountain. It lists to the left as Alex does the same to the other leg.

I feel the wind leave me as I'm violently slammed down hard to the ground. I lose my grip on my rifle and it bounces off the street. I'm aggressively flipped over, then she sits on my stomach, holding me down. A female warrior, her dagger's tip dancing across the skin of my throat. The creature roars again and shakes the surroundings. She looks up, and I use the distraction to my advantage and kick her off me. She rolls a few times as I spring up. With my rifle gone, I draw my pistol and dashed over to her. She's on her back. I press the weight of my knee deep into her chest as she tries to raise her dagger. I drive the muzzle of the gun right into her forehead.

"Bitch, knock the shit off," I scream as I tickle the trigger.

She lowers her hand immediately, but I add more pressure to her chest. If I push any harder, I'll shove the gun's muzzle right through her skull. She stares at me as I catch another female rushing toward me out of the corner of my eye. I quickly pull the gun up and shoot at her feet, stopping her cold. The first one brings the dagger back up, but I pistol whip her across the face, knocking her out cold. I instantly recover and fire another warning shot at my second assailant. She stops, then runs the other way. I slowly stand, thinking I'd scared her off, but then I realize Matt is standing behind me with his rifle pointed in her direction.

"You alright?" he asks.

"Yeah, thanks," I reply gratefully.

"Why didn't you just kill her?"

Good fucking question!

I don't answer. Instead, I sprint toward Alex, who's reloading as the beast continues to recoil with both front legs horrendously amputated. Matt follows close behind. We watch the chief assemble another smaller group, and within seconds they attack the monster again. Its tail swings up, ready to strike, but Alex answers with another hail of bullets, blasting away at its midsection. As tough as its scales may be, they are obviously no match for the power of the repeated pummeling. The bullets tear through it, piercing its skin.

"Matt, cover me," I scream as I locate my rifle.

Doc runs toward our position. I sprint to my gun and scoop it up, raising to fire.

Nothing! The trigger won't budge. I try to pop the magazine, but it too is frozen in place. It must have been damaged by the toss. I throw it down and swing my bow around. Let's see if I still have it in me.

I kneel and quickly emancipate an arrow from the quiver. With fluid efficiency, I set it and pull back. I wait for a shot at its head. The tail comes down, shattering the asphalt below. It's riddled with bullet holes and stained with its own blood.

The chief and his group continue to stab at it with their spears, doing significant damage now that the tail has been disabled. Alex reloads again and fires at the remaining legs. The creature opens its mouth again, ready to strike with its tongue. As it does, I notice a smaller round orb inside, right above its monstrous jaws. It's about the size of a large beach ball, translucent, filled with a viscous yellow liquid. Floating in it is something that looks alive, like a large black spider, but with tentacles instead of legs.

The tongue lashes out, just missing Alex as he quickly leaps to the side to avoid it. It erupts again into its many hellish appendages and grabs more of the tribe, instantly retracting them back into its beak. It crunches down on them, pulverizing their bodies into bloody messes as they helplessly scream and howl. I notice immediately that the thing in the orb moves as it occurs, almost as if it's controlling the direction of that strange tongue. I take a hard stance and aim for it. There's no wind to hamper me, nothing to obstruct my vision.

I pull back and steady myself, firing my arrow, watching it speed to its mark like a rocket. It strikes right above my target. Without pause, I load another arrow, reaffirming my aim. Matt is blasting at the thing's legs with Alex. Another tears loose and falls to the ground. A stream of blood follows it down. The beast recoils again, desperately trying to stay upright. More tendrils spring forth from its body, wriggling frantically at first, but then intertwining. They wrap together in groups, like husks of wires.

Fuck, it's trying to create new legs!

"Fire at its midsection," I scream to Alex and Matt. I'm hoping if this thing feels pain, it might bow up, opening its mouth wider, providing a better shot at whatever that thing is controlling the tongue.

Matt nods and unleashes a fury of bullets at its stomach.

They begin blasting at the bottom of the torso as Doc joins in on the melee. The tribe flees, all of their spears exhausted. The creature takes a massive step back and rises, towering over the street. As it does, our team blasts at it relentlessly. The chief and what's left of his tribe retreat toward me. I still don't have a shot.

"Grenade," Alex calls out.

Doc flips the duffle bag off his shoulder. He digs in and throws something to Alex. The beast slams down onto the ground, the force knocking us all off our feet. The houses that still line the street begin to violently sway, more collapsing in its wake. I can't see Alex or the rest through the dust and debris.

The monster's head emerges from the massive cloud and reopens, letting out a terrifying roar. The soundwave blasts past us, sending shrapnel and debris over our heads. I close my eyes and cover up the best I can, being pelted from every direction. The creature roars again, leaving my ears feeling like they're going to burst. I'm helpless, lost in all the dust and chaos.

Something roughly grabs my arm and yanks me backwards, dragging me across the street. I fight, but whoever or whatever is pulling me is too strong. I finally wrestle free after travelling a good distance and try to get up, but I'm disoriented. Helped to my feet, I find myself staring right into the chief's eyes. Time stops and so does my heart. We stare at each other for what seems like an eternity, then he hands me my bow. I didn't realize I'd let it go.

"Thank you," I say automatically.

He breaks his trance and looks past my shoulder. He has no weapons on him that I can see. For some unknown and absolutely ridiculous reason, I hand him my pistol. "You're gonna need this."

What the fuck am I doing?

I place it in his hand. He looks at me, puzzled.

"Just point and pull the damn trigger." I slowly demonstrate. "But not at me, or us, at it." I speak loud and slowly, as if that's going to help. Why do we always do that?

I turn to see if I can find Alex through all the dust. The monster is chewing on something, blood oozing from its boney beak. There's a lake of slime and gunk below it. I'm no longer able to differentiate what belongs to it and what belongs to its many victims.

"Gotta go." I pat the chief on the shoulder and run toward the monster. I'm probably lucky he didn't shoot me in the back. I barely see the orb again. I need to get another shot at it. It has to be the brain, or at least something like it, although I don't have any facts to back up my theory. I stop and scramble for another arrow, pulling one, but the shaft is broken and splintered. I grab another; it's in the same useless condition.

Please, God, cut me a break here!

I extract a third; still no luck. The creature is back on its feet, searching the ground. It's completely replaced any of its injured appendages with shiny, brand new mutated ones. There's no killing this thing!

"Fire in the hole," I hear a voice bellow through the chaos.

Matt and Doc speed toward me. "Kayla, get down," Matt screams as he hits the ground, covering his head.

Doc does the same. I duck and cover as an explosion erupts beneath the behemoth. It rattles what's left around us. Fire dances on the street and around the monster. I feel the incessant heat surround my head and arms. "Was that Alex?" I scream.

"Who else?" Matt screams back.

I look up and the creature is back up again, blood and fluids gushing from a huge hole underneath it, but I still can't see Alex. "Where is he?" I yell.

I get to my feet as Matt and Doc rise in unison.

"Doc, I'm out. How about you?" Matt says.

Doc throws Matt a magazine. "I have one more and that's it."

Matt catches it and quickly reloads. I realize the chief has been standing with us the entire time. Matt and Doc now realize it too. He stands there with a menacing expression. A few more of the tribe come up to us, and we're suddenly surrounded. Very few have weapons. Even the pistol I gave the chief is missing.

Okay, what do we do now?

The chief points at Matt's rifle. Matt looks down and back up. "That's a rifle," I explain slowly, over enunciating each word. Again, why? Like it helps in the least fucking bit!

The chief snarls and points at the creature.

"What? I don't understand?" Matt asks anxiously.

He points at it again as the rest draw their daggers, those who have them. They form a line facing the creature. The chief points to the rifle and ground behind the newly formed line. Matt looks at Doc, confused. The chief points to the ground again, more aggressively.

"I think he wants us to get behind them," I interject. "I think he wants us to back them up as they move forward." Like I know what the hell I'm talking about.

"No, they'll follow us." Alex appears out of nowhere. He gets face to face with the chief, playing an incoherent game of charades with him, motioning that we will advance, and he will fall behind. At least I think that's what he's doing. Alex points to the guns, then to the creature. He motions at their daggers and shakes his head no. The chief struggles to understand him.

We don't have time for all this shit!

"Doc, lead them forward," Alex barks, his voice sounding somewhat normal again. "Blast at the hole! Use the flash bangs to disorient it! I've got the grenades. Kayla, go to the edge of what's left of that house. Take my rifle and aim for the inside of its head. Aim for that bubble looking thing above the beak."

He saw it, too!

"What the hell are you going to do?" I ask.

"What I do best ... blow shit up." He grins wildly. "Go, they'll follow!" He turns and runs to the right along the sidewalk.

"Okay, let's do this," Matt commands.

I sprint to my position as Doc and Matt lead the remnant of the tribe forward. There's no way they're going to survive with what they have. I get up and run back to them, rushing to the chief, handing him my rifle. "Same thing! Just point and shoot." I gave him another quick demo.

Boy, impending death makes strange bed fellows.

He nods at me this time, like he understands. Will I ever truly understand the ramifications of what I've just done? I see how nervous Doc and Matt look, but do we have a fucking choice? I don't think so!

I quickly return to my spot as Doc, Matt, and the chief march shoulder to shoulder ahead. The remaining tribe follows behind. This is going to be a fucking blood bath!

I flip my quiver around and empty it onto the sidewalk where I'm kneeling. Three arrows, three fucking arrows left! I load up and try to aim. The creature has been busy searching for more prey. The remaining tribe is now hiding among the rubble, some inside what few houses are left standing. Somehow, I know, no matter how well they hide, it'll find them, stopping at nothing to consume them. This is an apex predator of epic proportions, the undisputed top of theirs or any other food chain.

I steady myself, but I still have no shot. The three start blasting single fire at the creature, desperately trying to aim at its wound. The chief fires once and drops the rifle but quickly picks it back up. He fires again, missing wildly.

Well, this is all going fucking well! Where the hell is Alex now? I can't see him anymore.

The creature advances toward them, thrashing its mighty tail through the rubble of the houses, casting debris everywhere. Survivors try to scramble away as they're exposed, like roaches scattering and scrambling away from the light. It's no use. They're quickly, mercilessly, retrieved and devoured. I still can't see the orb. Its thickly scaled mane blocks my line of sight. Matt, Doc and the chief continue to fire at it, doing very little damage now. Doc throws several flash bangs in its direction, but they also have little or no effect. It's like throwing firecrackers at a tank. It trudges toward them, undaunted.

"I'm out," Matt screams as he draws his pistol and fires.

I still have no shot—not one that will make a difference, anyway. My chances of hitting it are as likely as all of us surviving this. But there's no escape anymore. We have to face these things, this new world, bravely, with every ounce of strength and spirit we have left. There's very little chance we'll survive, but I'll be damned if I just lie down and die.

Alex climbs through the debris of a two-story, half-collapsed house. He swiftly scales the roof as the creature gets closer. It's back in the middle of the street again. A mass of refugees flee past us, trying to escape their almost certain doom.

"I'm out too," Doc screams!

"What do we do now?!" Matt calls back.

The chief is still firing, his aim improving, for what little good it's doing. I notice a large, gaping wound under the beast is beginning to close up. Thousands of thin tendrils fill the void, intertwining together again, forming a solid body.

Are you fucking serious?!

The creature is getting closer. In a matter of seconds its wound will be fully healed. It blasts through more of the rubble with its monstrous tail, scattering deadly debris hundreds of feet into the air.

"Take cover," Matt screams, as we all desperately scramble for shelter from the falling debris.

I grab my arrows and duck under a car as the shrapnel showers down, smashing windows and crashing down on the street. We've lost; this battle is over. As the debris shower ends, I slide out from under the car, the beast only twenty feet away. Its tongue slinks out of its mouth again as it prepares for another meal. One of the children runs in front of the beast, trapped in its path.

Where the hell did he come from?

It's a toddler, all alone. Matt sprints toward him. The creature turns. It knows they're there. The tongue shoots toward him as Matt grabs the child, and they tumble down the road just out of its reach. He springs to his feet and lifts the child over his shoulder, dashing for safety. A female runs toward them. Just as they're about to meet, one of the spikes from the creature's tongue bursts through Matt's chest. He tosses the child into the mom's arms as the creature pulls him in.

Oh, God, no! NO!

He's consumed in an instant; echoes of pulverizing bones reverberate in the chaos. One of his legs slides out of its beak, flopping to the ground as a small book falls free, landing in a puddle of blood.

No! You motherfucker!

Alex flies past its mouth and hurls a grenade into it as he sails past. He slams onto the ground hard, rolling into a nearby lawn, lying there motionless. The grenade explodes, shattering the beast's beak and sending the shards deep into the soft parts of its gigantic mouth. Its blood sprays all around, soaking everything in front of it, drenching the street. It rises, then falls as it shakes its massive head back and forth.

There's the orb again! Damn, it's still there! Even after all that!

I leap on top of the car, doused with huge drops of blood mixed with my tears. I wipe my face and raise my bow, fighting the grief trying to consume me. The creature violently swings its head back and forth as the remnant of its beak falls free, crashing to the ground by its feet. I then see the point of what appears to be a second beak peeking out from deep within its mouth.

Are you serious? It has a fucking back-up to that too.

CHAPTER 31

The Lost Road

(Kayla)

The orb is fully exposed now as it dangles from a short blue tube at the top of the mouth.

Fuck this!

I steady myself again and aim, pulling back with all my strength. My mind repeats the vision of Matt's death, rage overwhelming my sorrow. Time to fucking die, you horrific piece of shit!

I fire and the arrow sails fiercely through the air. I quickly reload for my second shot. As I do, the arrow pierces right above the orb. Shit, I missed!

The orb recoils and pulls itself up like it's trying to retract inside to protect itself.

Not this time!

I fire again. The arrow cuts through the air, finally striking the orb. I follow it with the final arrow. It too finds its mark. The arrows sear through the sack, spilling the yellow liquid all at once. Whatever's inside follows the deluge as it pours out onto the street. The creature jerks back and then stumbles forward, crushing the orb under one of its talons, the orb grinding and cracking under the weight.

Grow that back, you hideous son of a bitch!

The creature falls forward and slams to the ground hard. It rolls to its side as the rest of its massive body follows. The tongue spills out in front of it, motionless. It lets out a huge grunt as it exhales.

What a fucking stink! The stench of its breath surrounds us, choking us. I frantically try to cover my mouth.

Is it finally fucking dead?

The remaining tribe members emerge from their hiding. The female with her rescued child stands there, lost in their embrace. Oh, my God, is she crying? They cry?

Tears stream down her face as she pulls her child close to her. The chief and Doc are joined by the others. I hop off the car as the chief slowly approaches the beast and bends down over its tongue. He whips out his dagger and quickly cuts a piece free, holding it up and howling. All at once the rest do the same, a deep, loud animalistic cheer. It gets louder and louder as they jump up and down in celebration.

We actually did it! Shit, we actually did it!

Wait, where's Alex? I scramble back to the last place I saw him. He's not there! Oh, God, no! Not Alex too! I fall to my knees, tears quickly filling my eyes. Their celebration mocks my pain. I raise my head, rubbing my face as the tears stream down, then I feel a hand gently touch my shoulder.

"Oh God, Doc," I weep. "They're both dead. Why?"

His hand slips under my arm and lifts me to my feet. He turns me around as I bury my head against his chest, my eyes tightly shut to try to dam the tears. He strokes my hair and kisses the top of my head. There's nothing he can do to ease my pain. My body literally aches as I sob.

"It's okay, Kayla. I'm still here."

I open my eyes and slowly look up, seeing Alex smile back at me. His eyes are wet, tears diluting the blood on his face. He can't be real. I'm losing my mind.

"No, you are not," he reassures.

I hug him with all my strength. "You're alive!"

"A little banged up, but still standing."

I pull away again just to make sure this isn't some illusion, a trick played on me by my grief. I smile at him and chuckle. "You are one stubborn son of a bitch."

"Who loves to blow shit up!"

We laugh together. It's a fleeting moment that hides our deep pain.

Matt is dead. He's gone forever, and nothing will bring him back.

Alex massages my arms and then gently pulls away. He turns and walks toward the fallen monster, splashing through the blood and muck until he sees something immersed in it. Bending down, he retrieves that small book. Wiping the slime off, he smiles. As I approach him, I see he's holding Matt's dilapidated bible.

"How the hell did that survive?" I gasp.

Alex sighs. "Because it was meant to." He stands there, staring out into space. "What kind of man risks his life for his enemy?"

I step back. Who is he asking?

"The kind of man who has a faith that defies all logic," he answers himself.

I stand in front of him until he finally looks back at me, grief etched deep in his face, clouding his eyes. He shakes the bible. "He wasn't afraid because he knew what was at the end." He places the bible in his pocket. "I've seen it before, that kind of faith, and I hope to someday understand it."

He turns and walks toward Doc and the chief. The chief meets him halfway. They stand before each other, then Alex takes his hand and shakes it. The chief looks confused at first, and then something washes over him, and his eyes sharpen.

"It's ours to share now, this strange new world," Alex begins. "Your family and ours."

The chief cocks his head to one side. Does he understand him?

The chief pulls something from a fur-lined pouch and places it in Alex's hand. It's a red beaded necklace, with polished bone fragments placed in between each wooden bead. The coloring is faded. It looks very old.

"Remember me," he growls.

Alex freezes, his expression awed. The chief turns away from him and howls at what's left of his tribe. They chant back as they gather around him. He turns back to Alex and holds up the rifle. Alex nods. The chief drops it to the ground as he leads his people down the street, passing by the monster's body.

"So, what, we're all good now?" I ask.

"I wouldn't count on it." Alex sighs as he watches them walk away. "Common enemies make fragile allies, at least for a time."

Tara and Jude finally emerge from their hiding spot and join us.

"You two alright?" I ask.

"Where's Matt?" she cries as Jude holds her hand tightly. I can see in her eyes she already knows the answer.

"Gone," Alex says soberly.

She weeps. "Why are we doing this? There's no hope!"

"So we'll make our own—just like he believed we could," Alex says.

As the last of the tribe strolls by the body, the female with the young child looks back at me and smiles. She nods and waves. The child does the same. They are us, just as lost as we are, just as primitive. I wave back. "He was willing to die to save a stranger, Tara, someone who isn't even human. What are you willing to do?" I turn to her, and she just stares at me. She'll never get it.

That's too bad.

Some people can't break the cycle that controls their life. I'll make sure it doesn't apply to Jude. The kid has grown on me. Yeah, he's like one of those annoying little brothers, but maybe that's not such a bad thing. It'd be nice to care for someone other than me for a change.

Jude releases his mom's hand. "Alex, can we pray for him?" he asks as he chokes back the sorrow.

"Yeah, kid, go ahead."

We huddle together and hold hands. It's like an instinct, no one has to ask. Even with death all around us, the threat still very real, here we are, standing in the middle of the street, defying fear to take a moment to grieve. Jude leads us in a quick but deeply moving prayer, thanking God for saving us, and asking him to care for Matt. As I stand there and listen, I can't help but feel conflicted.

If God is real, then why allow all of this? Where is he? Why is he absent from us?

I scratch the back of my neck, sliding my fingers past the strands of my hair, taking a deep breath. I'm alive. I shouldn't be but I am. Maybe that's enough.

I don't have the answers and that haunts me. But what if I did, would it make the pain and loss any easier to bear? What if the answers were far more frightening than the questions? Jude concludes the prayer and begins to weep. Matt knew the answers, I truly believe that. He didn't just talk about it, he lived it. But did the answers die with him?

"Let's go," Alex says. "Jude, is the laptop still intact?" He may sound cold, almost callous, but he has to be. It's the only way he can get us through this. I have no doubt Alex feels the grief as deeply as the rest of us, maybe more. But unlike us, he can't afford the luxury of showing it. He has to carry the weight, all of our weight, in silence.

Jude sniffles. "I've still got it. Matt left it with me."

"Then lead the way, son."

"What about all those things?"

"I'm tired of hiding. It doesn't do us any good anyway."

We walk down the street. I can't help but look up and around with almost every step. We are naked and exposed, with very little left to defend ourselves now. Has Alex given up? Have we all given up and just disguised it as courage?

"Wait, Alex!" Jude screams.

Oh God, what now?

"Did you feel that?"

Feel what, what's he talking about? Something wet drizzles on my face. Oh shit! What could possibly be falling from the sky?

Alex looks up as rain splashes on his forehead and cheeks. A light shower falls on us, cool and familiar. Drops hit the street and leap up. Is it just water though? Yes, it's water!

Alex looks around, his eyes wide. I look up and see it too. Clouds! White billowy clouds!

I can't believe my eyes. On the street, I notice my shadow growing. I spin around to see the sun rising over the ruins of the neighborhood as the gentle rain continues. The warmth of the day begins to kiss my face. We watch it rise higher and higher into the sky as the summer-like shower continues. The sky comes alive, not with horrific creatures, but with color and light.

It's the dawn! It's back!

The blue hue quickly dissolves in the sunlight, and the world looks very ordinary, so beautifully ordinary. In awe, we stand there frozen, wonderfully lost in the moment. All is still and eerily silent. Only the pattering of the rain is evident, almost haunting.

"Let's move," Alex says. "We've all seen the sun and rain before."

Is he fucking kidding me? No, I guess not. He leads on, with Jude by his side.

Tara stares up into the sky. "Are we finally saved?"

"No, we're getting wet," I reply, and take her by the arm. "C'mon, let's go."

She smiles and follows me. Doc brings up the rear, his pistol out. "Here, watch over her," I say, placing her hand in his.

Doc smiles and nods as I speed up to catch Alex. Jude walks in front, carefully monitoring the cameras as we continue our journey to Alex's house. "Two more miles and we'll be there," Jude calls back.

The rain continues.

"Do you think it's over?" I whisper, once I catch up to Alex.

"No, but I think we're safe for now."

"How do you know that?"

He just glares at me.

"Oh, right, the whole mind meld thing."

He isn't amused and doesn't immediately answer.

"Am I to assume your silence is your answer?"

"No, I've just run out of answers."

"Well, that's comforting."

He laughs and cracks a brief smile.

"Is it over?" I repeat.

"No," he says, not hesitating with his answer. "But things have changed, and I think this time it may be in our favor."

The rain begins to slow.

"Did I ever show you this?" Alex removes a gold chain from his pocket. I know he's desperate to change the subject. He hands it to me, a simple locket.

I wonder if this is what he pulled out of that velvet box?

"My daughter gave this to me for my last birthday. She got it at some department store with my wife. Sara told her it was too girly, but Gracie insisted. She wanted to give me something that reminded me that she was my daughter, as if that was necessary. You know how kids think. She wanted her heart to always be close to mine." He pauses, obviously choking up.

I gently open the locket. "There are no pictures in here."

"I know. I never got around to getting them made. I kept putting it off, and when I finally got around to remembering to do it, I got my prognosis, and I had to deal with that."

"Did you ever tell them about the cancer?"

"No, not yet. Well, I was … I was going to try after my appointment today." He stumbles over the words.

"How long did you know?" I ask, even though I know he's not comfortable with my intrusion.

"A couple of months or so. I just couldn't find the words or strength to tell them. I never found the time to get it done, the locket, I mean."

"Yeah, we always think we have more time than we truly do." I abandon the conversation, knowing I may have pushed too far too fast. "It's a pretty locket, though."

"I know. I tried to tell her I didn't need anything to remind me that she was my daughter, that her heart was always with me, just like mine was with her. But you know, the more I thought about it, the more I realized how important it was." He took a deep breath. "It's amazing really, how something so cold and inanimate can hold such value, and so much emotion. If only to remind us of the good things in life, when we're faced with all the bad. It's been something I could hold onto when I felt like my whole world was crashing down around me. It became my hope, as silly as that sounds, hope in the face of pain and fear."

"No, that makes perfect sense." I hand it back to him. "We all need that, wherever we can get it."

"When I get home, I'm going to give it to her, have her wear it, so she'll always know my heart is near hers."

I smile. "Somehow I think she already knows that."

"When we get there, we'll gather supplies. I have a few extra guns stored away, ammo too. I have no doubt you and Gracie will hit it off right away." He laughs.

"I don't think I'm the right kind of influence you want for your daughter."

"I can't think of a better one." I see the sincerity reflecting deep in his eyes. He looks into mine and smiles.

"Anyway, they were having a classic car show at Gracie's school yesterday. It's right over the hill from our house. A bunch of cool cars from all over the city, and some military vehicles: jeeps, cargo transports, Hummers and such. I was supposed to go there after my appointment. If they're still there, we can use the vehicles to get us to where we're going. We can take it slow, dodge in and out of the abandoned cars, and go off road if we need to."

"And just where are we going?" I ask.

"The beach," he quickly replies.

"Really? That's a good bit away, several hours from here," I say, confused by his choice of destination.

"I know, but I think we can make it there. Plus, it's the middle of the week and spring break is weeks away, so it should be pretty much a ghost town."

"Why the beach? Why not the mountains, or the city?"

"I think we'll be safe there. I'm not sure why. The closer we are to water; I believe the safer we'll be."

Conversation stops after that. I want to press him further, but it's as if our conversation just dries up. I can't explain why. Maybe he doesn't have any more answers to give me, none I'll accept anyway. We walk together in silence. Jude, Doc and Tara keep up the rear.

They continue to talk behind us. Surprisingly, I even hear giggles. I turn to look back, finding them smiling, oblivious to everything but each other. They deserve some peace, as deceiving or temporary as it may be. We don't see a single sign of life the whole way. It's as if we're the sole beings on some strange planet.

The rain has almost stopped by the time we reach his driveway. It's a cute little blue house with vinyl siding in need of a good washing. There's a broken wood swing in the front yard. I can tell he isn't much of a landscaper; his lawn hasn't been mowed for a while. We pause for a moment at the beginning of the drive. There's no car there.

Maybe they left before it all happened? Maybe they went looking for him? What will Alex do then?

He walks up the drive, then to wooden steps that need a good sweeping. At the door, he takes a deep, long breath, slowly unlocking it, and enters. I hear him calling their names.

I stand by the mailbox with Doc. I know he wants to say something to me, but he can't find the words. He's not alone.

Tara and Jude stand on the lawn, anxiously waiting as well. It feels like he's in there for an eternity, the waiting unbearably painful. He's moving around in the house, and I'm fighting not to follow and go in. Doc looks at his watch. It's been almost fifteen minutes.

One more minute and I'm going in.

Alex finally emerges wearing a large backpack, with a shotgun in his right hand, and an extra holster draped over his shoulder. His head is down as he approaches. Doc steps away from me and walks toward Tara and Jude.

Alex stops right in front of me. My heart is pounding, feeling like it's going to burst from my chest at any moment. He looks up at me, his eyes bloodshot, grief scorched deep in his flesh. I'd never seen it so defined before, so unadulterated. I can actually feel it emanating from his body.

He sets down the shotgun and opens his hand, removing the chain from his palm. It's left a deep imprint. He gently places the locket over my head, past my hair, then places his left hand over the gold heart. His tears are heavy as they fall to the ground, as thick as drops of blood.

"I'm so sorry," I finally muster the courage to say.

He says nothing, just gently taps the locket and stares into my eyes. He bends down and picks up the shotgun. "My family is here." He places his hand on the locket. "This is where my heart is." He walks away in silence, heading toward a nearby hill.

"Okay, people, let's go over the hill," I say, as he silently walks on. "C'mon, step it up. We're done here."

I can't believe the words coming out of my mouth—the boldness. Even more incredible, they listen to my commands. Tara and Jude quietly weep as they proceed ahead. Doc follows with his head down. Alex disappears over the hill, and we slowly follow.

As I reach the top, I find Alex standing next to a cargo transport; at least I think that's what it is. The others slowly trudge down the hill, but I remain. The connection I have with Alex overwhelms me. It's become so powerful it nearly knocks me off my feet. I can feel all the love he has for his family.

It's incredible! Indescribable!

I can also feel his love for me. I see every thought he's had about me. I touch the locket and a surge of emotion rushes through me.

He looks back and our eyes lock. I hear him. He needs me to be his hope, to remind him of why we need to carry on, how to live past this. I call to him from the deepest parts of my spirit. *I'll be your light in this darkness. I'll be the hope you need.* I descend the hill to him. My past stays behind me; there's no more room for it. My pain, shame, loss, were no longer welcome residents. I have no more time for them.

I know who I am, who I need to be. I'm needed, loved, wanted. In all this chaos, I've found all the things I so desperately prayed for. They're mine and no one can steal them from me.

I make it to the bottom of the hill. He's waiting for me. And for once in my life, it all makes sense—clear, unhindered sense.

I'm no longer lost. I no longer need to search for hope.

I am hope!

ABOUT THE AUTHOR

Ronald Rossmann is a talented author and filmmaker known for his ability to craft gripping and immersive stories. In addition to his work in the film industry, Rossmann has written several compelling books that showcase his passion for storytelling. His works explore themes of suspense, action, and psychological depth, drawing readers into vivid worlds filled with complex characters and high-stakes drama. With a keen eye for detail and a talent for building tension, Rossmann's books reflect his cinematic storytelling style, making them a thrilling experience for readers. Whether on screen or on the page, he continues to push creative boundaries and deliver unforgettable narratives.

For more updates on Ronald J. Rossmann Jr.'s projects, novels, and upcoming film releases, follow:

Facebook: www.facebook.com/beyourownheroproductions
YouTube: www.youtube.com/@beyourownheroproductionsllc
TikTok: @beyourownheroproductions
Instagram: @beyourownheroproductionsllc
Twitter/X: @byohpofficial

Notable Directorial Projects:

"The Devil's Daughter: A Harley Quinn Story" (2021)
An award-winning fan film exploring the complex psyche of Harley Quinn, amassing over 40,000 views and earning widespread acclaim.

"Dusk Series" (2017)
A gripping blend of mystery, action, and supernatural elements, showcasing Ronald's ability to weave intricate and immersive stories.

"You're It!" (2024)
A thrilling slasher/horror feature film shot in Hickory and Alexander County, NC, reinforcing Ronald's expertise in suspenseful storytelling.

Convention Commercials—His studio has produced a range of parody commercials for major comic conventions, blending humor, nostalgia, and pop culture in innovative ways.

"Stro's SINister SINema" (2023)"—A tribute to classic horror hosts, featuring original comedy skits and nostalgic horror themes.

The award-winning **Rescue**, a chilling short horror film from his Book of Fate anthology, follows in the eerie tradition of The Twilight Zone and The Outer Limits.

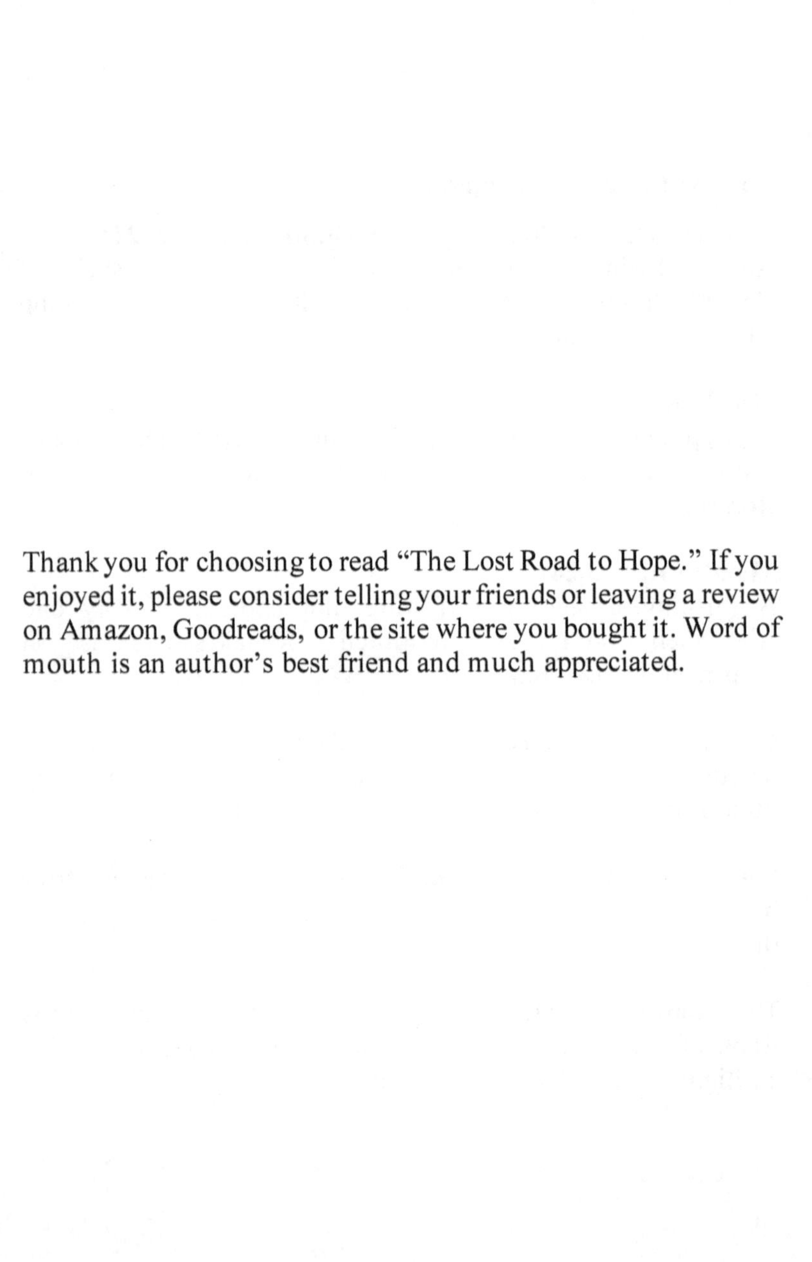

Thank you for choosing to read "The Lost Road to Hope." If you enjoyed it, please consider telling your friends or leaving a review on Amazon, Goodreads, or the site where you bought it. Word of mouth is an author's best friend and much appreciated.

www.ingramcontent.com/pod-product-compliance
Lightning Source LLC
Chambersburg PA
CBHW051551100726
47898CB00001B/48